P9-CRP-198

MOUNT DRAGON

A NOVEL

**Douglas Preston
& Lincoln Child**

TOR®

A TOM DOHERTY ASSOCIATES BOOK
NEW YORK

This is a work of fiction. All the characters and events portrayed in this book are either products of the authors' imagination or are used fictitiously.

MOUNT DRAGON

Copyright © 1996 by Douglas Preston and Lincoln Child

Cover art by Shelley Eshkar
Maps by Mark Stein Studios

A Tor Book
Published by Tom Doherty Associates, LLC
175 Fifth Avenue
New York, NY 10010

www.tor.com

The authors welcome e-mail sent to them from their Web site:
www.prestonchild.com

Tor® is a registered trademark of Tom Doherty Associates, LLC.

ISBN-13: 978-0-7653-5996-4
ISBN-10: 0-7653-5996-0
Library of Congress Catalog Card Number: 95-41323

First Edition: February 1996
First Mass Market Edition: February 1997
Second Mass Market Edition: December 2007

Printed in the United States of America

0 9 8 7 6 5 4 3 2 1

To Jerome Preston, Senior
—D. P.

To Luchie; my parents; and Nina Soller
—L. C.

ACKNOWLEDGMENTS

First, we want to thank our agents, Harvey Klinger and CAA's Matthew Snyder. Gentlemen, we lift our tumblers of single-malt Highland scotch in your honors: this project would never have been started were it not for the help and encouragement you've given us.

We'd also like to thank the following people at Tor/Forge: Tom Doherty, whose vision and support have remained equally unflagging; Bob Gleason, for believing in us from the beginning; Linda Quinton, for her refreshingly candid marketing advice; and Natalia Aponte, Karen Lovell, and Stephen de las Heras, for their sundry acts of authorial succor.

From a technical aspect, we wish to thank Lee Suckno M.D.; Bry Benjamin, M.D.; Frank Calabrese, Ph.D.; and Tom Benjamin, M.D.

Lincoln Child would like to thank Denis Kelly: pal, erst while boss, long-suffering sounding board. Thanks to Juliette, soul of patience and understanding. Thanks also to Chris England for his explication of certain arcane slang. Wotcher, Chris!

A pre-war Gibson Granada, along with a generous fistful of chocolate-chip cookies, to Tony Trischka: banjo diety, confidante, and all-around "good hang."

Douglas Preston would like to thank his wife, Christine,

who crossed the Jornada del Muerto desert with him no less than four times, as well as Selene, who was helpful in so many ways. Aletheia was a great sport, camping in the Jornada with us when she was only three weeks old. Thanks to my brother Dick, author of *The Hot Zone*, for his help. Thanks also to *Smithsonian* and *New Mexico* magazines, who helped finance our exploration of the ancient Spanish trail across the Jornada known as the Camino Real de Tierra Adentro.

Walter Nelson, Roeliff Annon, and Silvio Mazzarese accompanied us on horseback around the Jornada and were delightful riding companions. We also acknowledge with thanks the following people, who kindly allowed us to ride across their ranches: Ben and Jane Cain of the Bar Cross Ranch; Evelyn Fite of the Fite Ranch; Shane Shannon, former manager of the Armandaris Ranch; Tom Waddell, current foreman of the Armandaris; Ted Turner and Jane Fonda, owners of the Armandaris; and Harry F. Thompson Jr. of the Thompson Ranches. Gabrielle Palmer was very helpful, as always, with historical information.

Special thanks go to Jim Eckles of the White Sands Missile Range for a memorable tour of the 3,200-square-mile range. We would like to apologize for the liberties we have taken in describing White Sands, which is without a doubt one of the best run (and environmentally aware) Army testing facilities in the country. Obviously, no such place as Mount Dragon exists on WSMR property.

Finally, our thanks to all the rest who have helped us with *Mount Dragon* in particular and our novels in general: Jim Cush, Larry Bern, Mark Gallagher, Chris Yango, David Thomson, Bay and Ann Rabinowitz, Bruce Swanson, Ed Semple, Alain Montour, Bob Wincott; the sysops of CompuServe's Literary Forum; and others too numerous to mention. Your enthusiasm helped make this book possible.

Our symbols shout at the universe,
They fly off, like hunters' arrows
Into the night sky.
Or knapped spearpoints into flesh.

They race like fires across plains,
Driving buffalo.
                    —Franklin Burt

One window upon Apocalypse is more than enough.
                    —Susan Wright/Robert L. Sinsheimer,
                    Bulletin of Atomic Scientists

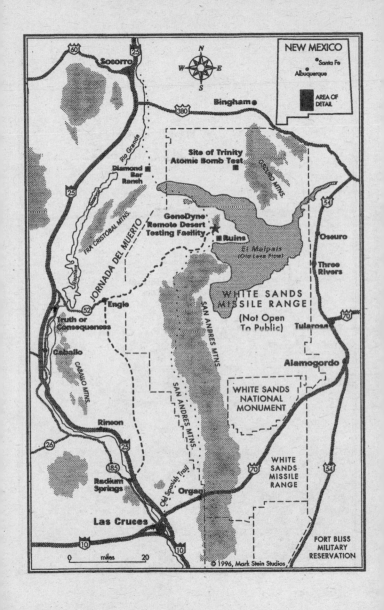

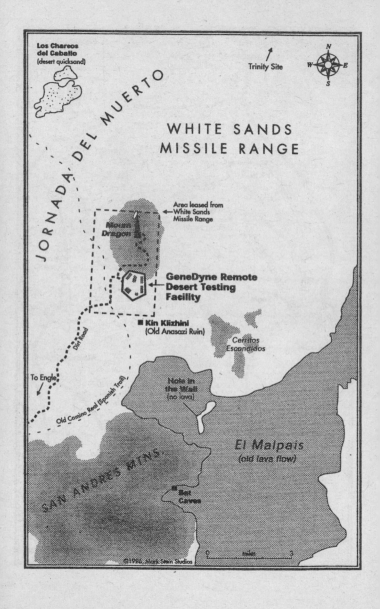

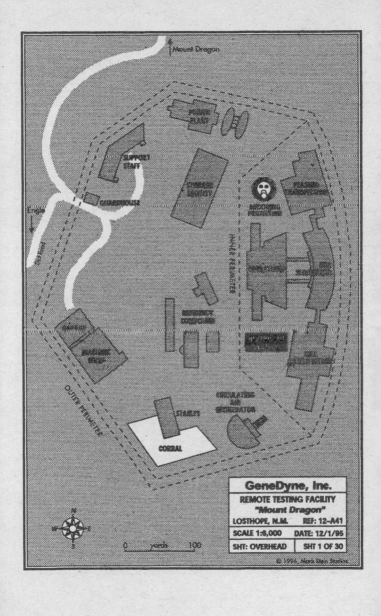

↑ Mount Dragon

POWER PLANT

SUPPORT STAFF

GUARDHOUSE

Engine

Dirt Road

STORAGE FACILITY

MACHINING PRODUCTION

FISSION TRANSMISSION

INNER PERIMETER

RESIDENCE COMPOUND

MACHINE SHOP

OUTER PERIMETER

CIRCULATING AIR INCINERATOR

STABLES

CORRAL

N
W   E
S

0   yards   100

GeneDyne, Inc.

REMOTE TESTING FACILITY
"Mount Dragon"

LOSTHOPE, N.M.	REF: 12–A41
SCALE 1:6,000	DATE: 12/1/95
SHT: OVERHEAD	SHT 1 OF 30

© 1996, Mark Stein Studios

INTRODUCTION

The sounds drifted over the long green lawn, so faint they could have been the crying of ravens in the nearby wood, or the distant braying of a mule on the farm across the brown river. The peace of the spring morning was almost undisturbed. One had to listen carefully to the sounds to make certain they were screams.

The massive bulk of Featherwood Park's administrative building lay half-hidden beneath ancient cottonwood trees. At the front entrance, a private ambulance pulled away slowly from the porte cochere, pebbles scurrying on the gravel drive. Somewhere a pneumatic door hissed shut.

A small, unmarked white door was sunk into the side of the building for use by the professional staff. As Lloyd Fossey approached, his hand came forward automatically, reaching for the combination pad. He had been struggling to keep the sounds of Dvořák's E-minor piano trio alive in his head, but now he frowned and gave up. Here in the shadow of the building, the screams were much louder.

The nurse's station was all ringing phones and scattered paper. "Morning, Dr. Fossey," said the nurse.

"Good morning," he replied, pleased when she managed to give him a bright smile amid the confusion. "Grand Central here today."

"Two came in early, bang, one after the other," she said, working forms with one hand and passing him charts with the other. "Now there's this one. Guess you already know about him."

"Couldn't help overhearing." Fossey flipped open a chart, searched his lapel pocket for a pen, hesitated. "Is our noisy friend mine?"

"Dr. Garriot's got him," the nurse replied. She looked up. "The first one was yours."

A door opened somewhere, and suddenly there was the screaming again, much louder now, various urgent voices acting as counterpoint. Then the door shut again and only office noises remained.

"I'd like to see the admit," Fossey said, returning the charts and reaching for the metal binder. He scanned the vitals quickly, noting sex, age, at the same time trying to mentally reconstruct the strains of the Dvořák andante. His eye stopped when it reached the words *Involuntary Unit*.

"Did you see the first one come in?" he asked quietly.

The nurse shook her head. "You should talk to Will. He took the patient downstairs about an hour ago."

There was only one window in the Involuntary Unit at Featherwood Park. This window looked out from the guard's station onto the stairway leading down from the Ward Two basement. As he pressed the buzzer, Dr. Fossey saw Will Hartung's pale, shaggy head appear on the far side of the Plexiglas pane. Will disappeared, and the door mechanically unlocked itself with a sound like a gunshot.

"How ya doing, Doc," he said, sliding behind his desk and setting aside a copy of Shakespeare's sonnets.

"Mr. W.H., all happiness," Fossey replied, glancing at the book.

"Very funny, Dr. Fossey. Your talents are wasted on the medical profession." Will handed him the log, sniffing loudly. At the far end of the counter, the new orderly was filling out med sheets.

"Tell me about the early arrival," Fossey said, signing the log and passing it back, tucking the metal binder under his arm as he did so.

Will shrugged. "Retiring type. Not much for conversation." He shrugged again. "Not surprising, given his recent diet of Haldol."

Fossey frowned and opened the binder again, this time scanning the admitting history. "My God. A hundred milligrams in a twelve-hour period."

"Guess they love their meds at Albuquerque General," Will said.

"Well, I'll write orders after the initial evaluation," Fossey said. "Meanwhile, no Haldol. I can't do an eval on an eggplant."

"He's in six," Will said. "I'll take you down."

A sign over the inner door read WARNING: ELOPEMENT RISK in large red letters. The new orderly let them through, sucking air between his big front teeth.

"You know my feelings about placing arrivals in Involuntary before an admitting diagnosis is made," Fossey said as they started down the bleak hallway. "It can color a patient's entire perspective on the facility, set us back before we've even started."

"Not my policy, Doc, sorry," Will replied, stopping beside a scarred black door. "Albuquerque was pretty specific on that point." He unlocked the door, pulled the heavy bolt back. "Want me inside?" he asked, hesitating.

Fossey shook his head. "I'll call if he gets agitated."

The patient lay faceup on the oversized transport stretcher, arms at his sides, legs straight to the ankles. From his doorway perspective, Fossey was unable to make out any facial features save a prominent nose and the knobbed arch of a chin, stubbled from a couple of days' growth. The doctor closed the door quietly and stepped forward, never quite used to the way the floor padding rose obligingly around his shoes. He kept his eyes on the prone figure. Beneath the thick canvas straps that crossed the stretcher, bandolier-like, the chest rose slowly, rhythmically. At the end, another strap stretched tightly across the leather ankle cuffs.

Fossey braced himself, cleared his throat, waited for a reaction.

He took a step forward, then another, mentally calculating. Fourteen hours since the release from Albuquerque General. Couldn't be the Haldol keeping him quiet.

He cleared his throat again. "Good morning, Mister—" he began, then looked down at his binder, searching for the name.

"Dr. Franklin Burt," came the quiet voice from the stretcher. "Forgive me for not rising to shake your hand, but as you can see . . ." The sentence was left incomplete.

Fossey, startled, moved up to look at the patient's face. Dr. Franklin Burt. He knew that name.

He glanced down at the chart again, flipping the top page. There it was: Dr. Franklin Burt, molecular biologist, M.D./ Ph.D. Johns Hopkins Medical School. Senior Scientist, GeneDyne Remote Desert Testing Facility. Somebody had placed marginal question marks next to the occupation.

"Dr. Burt?" Fossey said incredulously, looking again at the man's face.

The gray eyes focused in surprise. "Do I know you?"

The face *was* the same—a bit older, of course, more tanned

than he remembered it, but still remarkably free of the gradual accretion of cares and worries that gravitate to the fronts of foreheads, the corners of eyes. There was a gauze bandage on one temple and the eyes were badly bloodshot.

Fossey was shaken. He'd heard this man lecture. In a way, the course of his own career had been shaped by admiration for this charismatic, witty professor. How could he possibly be here, in four-point leather restraint, surrounded by mattressed walls?

"It's Lloyd Fossey, Doctor," Fossey said. "I heard you speak at Yale med school. We spoke for a while afterwards. About synthetic hormones . . . ?"

Fossey found his mind reaching out to the man on the stretcher, willing Burt to remember.

A moment passed. Burt sighed, nodded his head slightly. "Yes. Forgive me. I do remember. You challenged me on the link between synthetic erythropoietin and metastization."

Something inside Fossey relaxed. "I'm flattered you remember," he said.

Burt seemed to hesitate, as if considering. "I'm glad to see you practicing," he said at last, his lips twitching as if faintly amused by the awkward situation.

Now more than anything Fossey wanted to look at the binder in his hand. He wanted to read and reread the medical clearance and the consults, to find some explanation. But he felt Burt's eyes on him and knew the older man was following the course of his thoughts.

Of their own accord his eyes glanced down, scanning the typed columns on the chart. He looked up instantly, but not before he'd made out the words *fulminant psychosis . . . extremely delusional . . . rapid neuroleptization.*

Dr. Burt was looking at him mildly. Feeling a strange embarrassment, Fossey reached out a hand and found a pulse under the wrist straps.

Burt blinked, moistened dry lips. He drew in a long breath

of basement air. "I was driving north from Albuquerque," he said. "You know where I'm affiliated now."

Fossey nodded. When Burt had gone into private industry and stopped publishing, there had been the usual talk about "brain-drain" into the corporate sector.

"We're doing experiments with influencing chimp behavior patterns. It's a small setup, you know, we do a lot of our own running and fetching. I'd picked up lab equipment and some proprietary compounds from the GeneDyne site in Albuquerque. Including a test agent we'd developed, a synthetic derivative of phencyclidine, suspended in a gaseous medium."

Fossey nodded again. PCP in a gaseous state. Angel dust you could breathe like laughing gas. Strange use of research money.

Burt watched Fossey's eyes, smiled a little, or maybe winced, Fossey wasn't sure. "We were measuring inspiration rate through lung tissue versus capillary absorption. In any case, I was driving back. I was tired and not paying attention. I ran off the road into a stony wash just past Los Lunas. Nothing serious. Except the beaker broke in the accident."

Fossey grunted. That would do it, all right. He knew what even garden-variety angel dust could do to an otherwise normal person. In high doses, it simulated aggressive lunatic behavior. He'd seen it firsthand. It would also explain the bloodshot eyes.

There was a silence. Pupils normal, no dilation, Fossey noted. Good color. Some resting tachycardia, but Fossey knew that if *he* was strapped to a stretcher in a rubber room his heart might beat a little fast, too. There were absolutely no presentations of psychosis, mania, anything.

"I don't remember a lot of details afterwards," Burt said, a look of deep exhaustion passing across his face for the first time. "I had no credentials, of course, just a driver's license. Amiko, my wife, is in Venice with her sister. I have no other family. They kept me heavily medicated. I guess I wasn't too coherent."

Fossey wasn't surprised. An unknown man, battered from the accident, wigged out, perhaps violent, raving about being an important molecular biologist. What overworked emergency room would believe it? Easier to just arrange a psych transfer. Fossey pursed his lips, shook his head. *Idiots.*

"Thank God I ran into you, Lloyd," Burt said. "It's been a nightmare, I can't *begin* to tell you. Where am I, anyway?"

"Featherwood Park, Dr. Burt," he replied.

"I thought as much." Burt nodded. "I'm sure you'll straighten all this out. You can call GeneDyne now, if you like. I'm overdue and they're no doubt worrying about me."

"We'll do that shortly, Dr. Burt, I promise," Fossey said.

"Thank you, Lloyd," Burt said, with a slight wince. No mistaking it this time.

"Anything wrong?" Fossey asked immediately.

"It's my shoulders," Burt said. "Nothing, really. They're a bit sore from being pinioned against this stretcher."

Fossey hesitated only an instant. The PCP had worn off, as had most of the Haldol. More importantly, Burt's gray eyes continued to regard him calmly. There was none of that inner jitteriness you saw with faked sanity. "Let me get those chest restraints off you, get you sitting up," he said.

Burt smiled with relief. "Many thanks. I didn't want to ask myself, you understand. I know how the protocol works."

"Sorry I couldn't do it immediately, Dr. Burt," Fossey said, bending over the chest strap and tugging at the cinch. He'd clear up this travesty with a few phone calls. Then he'd have a couple of choice words with the ER doc at Albuquerque General. The strap was tight, and he considered calling in Will to help, but decided against it. Will was a stickler for the rules.

"That's much better," Burt said, sitting up gingerly and hugging himself, working his shoulder muscles free of kinks.

"You can't imagine what it's like, lying for hours, immobilized. I had to do it once before, for ten hours, after angioplasty a couple of years back. True hell." He moved his legs in their restraints.

"We'll need to run a few tests before we can release you, Doctor," Fossey said. "I'll get the admitting psychiatrist down here right away. Unless you'd like to rest first."

"No thanks," Burt said, raising one hand from the stretcher to rub the back of his neck. "Now is fine. Sometime when we're all back East, you'll have to come to dinner, meet Amiko." His hand moved forward, crept up his cheek.

Standing by the stretcher, making a notation on the chart, Fossey heard a sharp little intake of breath, like the rasp of a match on sandpaper. He turned to see Burt plucking the gauze bandage from his temple.

"You must have cut your head in the accident," Fossey said, closing the binder briskly. "We'll get a fresh dressing for you in minute."

"Poor alpha," Burt murmured, staring intently at the bloody bandage.

"I'm sorry?" Fossey asked. He moved forward to examine the wound.

Franklin Burt shot upward with an explosive movement, ramming his head into Fossey's chin before falling back heavily to the stretcher. Fossey's front teeth met in his tongue and he staggered backward, mouth flooding with liquid warmth.

"*Poor alpha!*" Burt screamed, tearing at his ankle restraints. "*POOR ALPHA!*"

Fossey fell to the floor and scrambled backward calling for Will, his bubbling cry redundant beneath the pressure wave of screams. Will burst in as Burt lunged again, sending himself and the stretcher crashing to the floor. He thrashed about, teeth snapping, trying to kick free of the restraints on the tumbled stretcher.

Everything was happening so quickly around him, but Fossey was slowing down. He saw Will and the orderly fighting with Burt, trying to right the stretcher, Burt gnawing at his own wrists now, a tug of the head like a dog worrying a rabbit and a sudden jet of blood spattering the orderly's glasses like tobacco spit. Now they were pinning Burt's arms to the stretcher, leaning hard on the writhing form, struggling to lash the thick straps, Will fumbling for his panic beeper. But the screaming continued unabated, as Fossey knew it would.

PART ONE

Guy Carson, stuck at yet another traffic light, glanced at the clock on his dashboard. He was already late for work, second time this week. Ahead, U.S. Route 1 ran like a bad dream through Edison, New Jersey. The light turned green, but by the time he had edged up it was red again.

"Son of a *bitch*," he muttered, slamming the dashboard with the fat part of his palm. He watched as the rain splattered across the windshield, listened to the slap and whine of the wipers. The serried ranks of brake lights rippled back toward him as the traffic slowed yet again. He knew he'd never get used to this congestion any more than he'd get used to all the damn rain.

Creeping painfully over a rise, Carson could see, a mere half mile down the highway, the crisp white facade of the GeneDyne Edison complex, a postmodern masterpiece rising above green lawns and artificial ponds. Somewhere inside, Fred Peck lay in wait.

Carson turned on the radio, and the throbbing sound of the Gangsta Muthas filled the air. As he fiddled with the dial, Michael Jackson's shrill voice separated itself from the static. Carson punched it off in disgust. Some things were even worse than the thought of Peck. Why couldn't they have a decent country station in this hole?

The lab was bustling when he arrived, Peck nowhere in sight. Carson drew the lab coat over his lanky frame and sat down at his terminal, knowing his log-on time would automatically go into his personnel file. If by some miracle Peck was out sick, he'd be sure to notice when he came in. Unless he had died, of course. Now, that was something to think about. The man did look like a walking heart attack.

"Ah, Mr. Carson," came the mocking voice behind him. "How kind of you to grace us with your presence this morning." Carson closed his eyes and took a deep breath, then turned around.

The soft form of his supervisor was haloed by the fluorescent light. Peck's brown tie still bore testament to that morning's scrambled eggs, and his generous jowls were mottled with razor burn. Carson exhaled through his nose, fighting a losing battle with the heavy aroma of Old Spice.

It had been a shock on Carson's first day at GeneDyne, one of the world's premier biotechnology companies, to find a man like Fred Peck there waiting for him. In the eighteen months since, Peck had gone out of his way to keep Carson busy with menial lab work. Carson guessed it had something to do with Peck's lowly M.S. from Syracuse University and his own Ph.D. from MIT. Or maybe Peck just didn't like Southwestern hicks.

"Sorry I'm late," he said with what he hoped would pass for sincerity. "Got caught in traffic."

"Traffic," said Peck, as if the word was new to him.

"Yes," said Carson, "they've been rerouting—"

"*Reroutin'*," Peck repeated, imitating Carson's Western twang.

"—detouring, I mean, the traffic from the Jersey Turnpike—"

"Ah, the *Turnpike*," Peck said.

Carson fell silent.

Peck cleared his throat. "Traffic in New Jersey at rush hour. What an unexpected shock it must have been for you, Carson." He crossed his arms. "You almost missed your meeting."

"Meeting?" Carson said. "What meeting? I didn't know—"

"Of course you didn't know. *I* just heard about it myself. That's one of the many reasons you have to be here on time, Carson."

"Yes, Mr. Peck," Carson said, getting up and following Peck past a maze of identical cubicles. Mr. Fred Peckerwood. Sir Frederick Peckerfat. He was itching to deck the oily bastard. But that wasn't the way they did business around here. If Peck had been a ranch boss, the man would've been on his ass in the dirt long ago.

Peck opened a door marked VIDEOCONFERENCING ROOM II and waved Carson inside. It was only as Carson looked around the large, empty table within that he realized he was still wearing his filthy lab coat.

"Take a seat," Peck said.

"Where is everybody?" Carson asked.

"It's just you," Peck replied. He started to back out the door.

"You're not staying?" Carson felt a rising uncertainty, wondering if he'd missed an important piece of e-mail, if he should have prepared something. "What's this about, anyway?"

"I have no idea," Peck replied. "Carson, when you're finished here, come straight down to my office. We need to talk about your attitude."

The door shut with the solid click of oak engaging steel.

Carson gingerly took a seat at the cherrywood table and looked around. It was a beautiful room, finished in hand-rubbed blond wood. A wall of windows looked out over the meadows and ponds of the GeneDyne complex. Beyond lay endless urban waste. Carson tried to compose himself for whatever ordeal was coming. Probably Peck had sent in enough negative ratings on him to merit a stern lecture from personnel, or worse.

In a way, he supposed, Peck was right: his attitude could certainly be improved. He had to rid himself of the stubborn bad-ass outlook that did in his father. Carson would never forget that day on the ranch when his father sucker-punched a banker. That incident had been the start of the foreclosure proceedings. His father had been his own worst enemy, and Carson was determined not to repeat his mistakes. There were a lot of Pecks in the world.

But it was a goddamn shame, the way the last year and a half of his life had been flushed virtually down the toilet. When he was first offered the job at GeneDyne, it had seemed the pivotal moment of his life, the one thing he'd left home and worked so hard for. And still, more than anything, GeneDyne stood out as one place where he could really make a difference, maybe do something important. But each day that he woke up in hateful Jersey—to the cramped, unfamiliar apartment, the gray industrial sky, and Peck—it seemed less and less likely.

The lights of the conference room dimmed and went out. Window shades were automatically drawn, and a large panel slid back from the wall, revealing a bank of keyboards and a large video-projection screen.

The screen flickered on, and a face swam into focus. Carson froze. There they were: the jug ears, the sandy hair, the un-repentant cowlick, the thick glasses, the trademark black T-shirt, the sleepy, cynical expression. All the features that together made up the face of Brentwood Scopes, founder of

GeneDyne. The *Time* issue with the cover article on Scopes still lay next to Carson's living-room couch. The CEO who ruled his company from cyberspace. Lionized on Wall Street, worshipped by his employees, feared by his rivals. What was this, some kind of motivational film for hard cases?

"Hi," said the image of Scopes. "How're you doing, Guy?"

For a moment Carson was speechless. *Jesus*, he thought, *this isn't a film at all.* "Uh, hello, Mr. Scopes. Sir. Fine. Sorry, I'm not really dressed—"

"Please call me Brent. And face the screen when you talk. I can see you better that way."

"Yes, sir."

"Not sir. Brent."

"Right. Thanks, Brent." Just calling the supreme leader of GeneDyne by his first name was painfully difficult.

"I like to think of my employees as colleagues," Scopes said. "After all, when you joined the company, you became a principal in the business, like everyone else. You own stock in this company, which means we all rise and fall together."

"Yes, Brent." In the background, behind the image of Scopes, Carson could make out the dim outlines of what looked like a massive, many-sided vault.

Scopes smiled, as if unashamedly pleased at the sound of his name, and as he smiled it seemed to Carson that he looked almost like a teenager, despite being thirty-nine. He watched Scopes's image with a growing sense of unreality. Why would Scopes, the boy genius, the man who built a four-billion-dollar company out of a few kernels of ancient corn, want to talk to him? *Shit, I must have screwed up worse than I thought.*

Scopes glanced down for a moment, and Carson could hear the tapping of keys. "I've been looking into your background, Guy," he said. "Very impressive. I can see why we hired you." More tapping. "Although I can't quite understand why you're working as, let's see, a Lab Technician Three."

Scopes looked up again. "Guy, you'll forgive me if I get

right to the point. There's an important post in this company that's currently vacant. I think you're the person for it."

"What is it?" Carson blurted, instantly regretting his own excitement.

Scopes smiled again. "I wish I could give you specifics, but it's a highly confidential project. I'm sure you'll understand if I only describe the assignment in general terms."

"Yes, sir."

"Do I look like a 'sir' to you, Guy? It wasn't so long ago that I was just the nerdy kid being picked on in the schoolyard. What I *can* tell you is that this assignment involves the most important product GeneDyne has ever produced. One that will be of incalculable value to the human race."

Scopes saw the look on Carson's face and grinned. "It's great," he said, "when you can help people and get rich at the same time." He brought his face closer to the camera. "What we're offering you is a six-month reassignment to the GeneDyne Remote Desert Testing Facility. The Mount Dragon laboratory. You'll be working with a small, dedicated team, the best microbiologists in the company."

Carson felt a surge of excitement. Just the words *Mount Dragon* were like a magic talisman throughout all of GeneDyne: a scientific Shangri-la.

A pizza box was laid at Scopes's elbow by someone offscreen. He glanced at it, opened it up, shut the lid. "Ah! Anchovies. You know what Churchill said about anchovies: 'A delicacy favored by English lords and Italian whores.' "

There was a short silence. "So I'd be going to New Mexico?" Carson asked.

"That's correct. Your part of the country, right?"

"I grew up in the Bootheel. At a place called Cottonwood Tanks."

"I knew it had a picturesque name. You probably won't find Mount Dragon as harsh as some of our other people have. The isolation and the desert setting can make it a difficult place to work. But you might actually enjoy it. There are horse stables there. I suppose you must be a fairly good rider, having grown up on a ranch."

"I know a bit about horses," Carson said. Scopes had sure as hell done his research.

"Not that you'll have much time for riding, of course. They'll run you ragged, no point in saying otherwise. But you'll be well compensated for it. A year's salary for the six-month tour, plus a fifty-thousand-dollar bonus upon successful completion. And, of course, you'll have my personal gratitude."

Carson struggled with what he was hearing. The bonus alone equaled his current salary.

"You probably know my management methods are a little unorthodox," Scopes continued. "I'll be straight with you, Guy. There's a downside to this. If you fail to complete your part of the project in the necessary time frame, you'll be excessed." He grinned, displaying oversized front teeth. "But I have every confidence in you. I wouldn't put you in this position if I didn't think you could do it."

Carson had to ask. "I can't help wondering why you chose me out of such a vast pool of talent."

"Even that I can't tell you. When you get briefed at Mount Dragon, everything will become clear, I promise."

"When would I begin?"

"Today. The company needs this product, Guy, and there's simply no time left. You can be on our plane before lunch. I'll have someone take care of your apartment, car, all the annoying details. Do you have a girlfriend?"

"No," said Carson.

"That makes things easier." Scopes smoothed down his cowlick, without success.

"What about my supervisor, Fred Peck? I was supposed to—"

"There's no time. Just grab your PowerBook and go. The

driver will take you home to pack a few things and call who-ever. I'll send what's-his-name—Peck?—a note explaining things."

"Brent, I want you to know—"

Scopes held up a hand. "Please. Expressions of gratitude make me uncomfortable. 'Hope has a good memory, gratitude a bad one.' Give my offer ten minutes' serious thought, Guy, and don't go anywhere."

The screen winked out on Scopes opening the pizza box again.

As the lights came on, Carson's feeling of unreality was replaced by a surge of elation. He had no idea why Scopes had reached down among the five thousand GeneDyne Ph.D.s and picked him, busy with his repetitive titrations and quality-control checks. But for the moment he didn't care. He thought of Peck hearing thirdhand that Scopes had personally assigned him to Mount Dragon. He thought of the look on the fat face, the wattles quivering in consternation.

There was a low rumbling noise as the curtains drew back from the windows, exposing the dreary vista beyond, cloaked in curtains of rain. In the gray distance, Carson could make out the power lines and smokestacks and chemical effluvia that were central New Jersey. Somewhere farther west lay a desert, with eternal sky and distant blue mountains and the pungent smell of greasewood, where you could ride all day and night and never see another human being. Somewhere in that desert stood Mount Dragon, and within it, his own secret chance to do something important.

Ten minutes later, when the curtains closed and the video screen came once again to life, Carson had his answer ready.

Carson stepped onto the slanting porch, dropped his bags by the door, and sat down in a weather-beaten rocker. The chair creaked as the old wood absorbed his weight unwillingly. He leaned back, stretching out the kinks, and looked out over the vast Jornada del Muerto desert.

The sun was rising in front of him, a boiling furnace of hydrogen erupting over the faint blue outline of the San Andres Mountains. He could feel the pressure of solar radiation on his cheek as the morning light invaded the porch. It was still cool—sixty, sixty-five—but in less than an hour, Carson knew, the temperature would be over one hundred degrees. The deep ultraviolet sky was gradually turning blue; soon it would be white with heat.

He gazed down the dirt road that ran in front of the house. Engle was a typical New Mexico desert town, no longer dying but already dead. There were a scattering of adobe buildings with pitched tin roofs; an abandoned school and post office; a row of dead poplars long stripped of leaves by the wind. The only traffic past the house was dust devils. In one sense, Engle was atypical: the entire town had been bought by GeneDyne, and it was now used solely as the jumping-off place for Mount Dragon.

Carson turned his head toward the horizon. Far to the northeast, across ninety miles of dusty sun-baked sand and rock only a native could call a road, lay the complex officially labeled the GeneDyne Remote Desert Testing Facility, but known to all by the name of the ancient volcanic hill that rose above it: Mount Dragon. It was GeneDyne's state-of-the-art laboratory for genetic engineering and the manipulation of dangerous microbial life.

He breathed deeply. It was the smell he'd missed most, the fragrance of dust and witch mesquite, the sharp clean odor of aridity. Already, New Jersey seemed unreal, something from the distant past. He felt as if he'd been released from prison, a green, crowded, sodden prison. Though the banks had taken the last of his father's land, this still felt like his country. Yet it was a strange homecoming: returning not to work cattle, but to work on an unspecified project at the outer reaches of science.

A spot appeared at the hazy limits where the horizon met the sky. Within sixty seconds, the spot had resolved itself into a distant plume of dust. Carson watched the spot for several minutes before standing up. Then he went back into the ramshackle house, dumped out the remains of his cold coffee, and rinsed the cup.

As he looked around for any unpacked items, he heard the sound of a vehicle pulling up outside. Stepping onto the porch, he saw the squat white outlines of a Hummer, the civilian version of the Humvee. A wash of dust passed over him as the vehicle ground to a halt. The smoked windows remained closed as the powerful diesel idled.

A figure stepped out: plump, black-haired and balding, dressed in a polo shirt and white shorts. His mild, open face was deeply tanned by the sun, but the stubby legs looked white against the incongruously heavy boots. The man bustled over, busy and cheerful, and held out a plump hand.

"You're my driver?" Carson asked, surprised by the softness of the handshake. He shouldered his duffel bag.

"In a manner of speaking, Guy," the man replied. "The name's Singer."

"Dr. Singer!" Carson said. "I didn't expect to get a ride from the director himself."

"Call me John, please," Singer said brightly, taking the duffel from Carson and opening the Hummer's storage bay. "Everybody's on a first-name basis here at Mount Dragon. Except for Nye, of course. Sleep all right?"

"Best night's rest in eighteen months," Carson grinned.

"Sorry we couldn't have come out to get you sooner," Singer replied, slinging the duffel, "but it's against the rules to travel outside the compound after dark. And no aircraft inside the Range, except for emergencies." He eyed a case lying at Carson's feet. "Is that a five-string?"

"It is." Carson hefted it, came down the steps.

"What's your style: three-finger? Clawhammer? Melodic?"

Carson stopped in the act of stowing the banjo and looked at Singer, who laughed delightedly in response. "This is going to be more fun than I thought," he said. "Hop in."

A wave of frigid air greeted Carson as he settled himself in the Hummer, surprised at the depth of the seats. Singer was almost an arm's length away. "I feel like I'm riding in a tank," Carson said.

"Best thing we've found for desert terrain. Takes a vertical cliff face to stop it. You see this indicator? It's a tire gauge. The vehicle has a central tire-inflation system, powered by a compressor. Pressing a button inflates or deflates the tires, depending on terrain. And all the Mount Dragon Hummers are equipped with 'run flat' tires. They can travel for thirty miles even after being punctured."

They pulled away from the cluster of houses and bumped across a cattleguard. Carson could see barbed wire stretching endlessly in both directions from the cattleguard, signs placed at hundred-foot intervals, reading: WARNING: THERE IS A U.S. GOVERNMENT MILITARY INSTALLATION TO THE EAST. ENTRY STRICTLY PROHIBITED. WSMR-WEA.

"We're entering the White Sands Missile Range," Singer said. "We lease the land Mount Dragon's on from the Department of Defense, you know. A holdover from our military contract days."

Singer aimed the vehicle for the horizon and accelerated over the rocky trail, a great rocket plume of dust corkscrewing behind the rear tires.

"I'm honored you came to get me personally," Carson said.

"Don't be. I like to get out of the place when I can. I'm just the director, remember. Everybody else is doing the important work." He looked over at Carson. "Besides, I'm glad of this chance to talk with you. I'm probably one of five people in the world who read and understood your dissertation. 'Designer Coats: Tertiary and Quaternary Protein Structure Transformations of a Viral Shell.' Brilliant."

"Thank you," Carson said. This was no small praise coming from the former Morton Professor of Biology at CalTech.

"Of course I only read it yesterday," Singer said with a wink. "Scopes sent it, along with the rest of your file." He leaned back, right hand draped over the wheel. The ride grew increasingly jarring as the Hummer accelerated to sixty, slewing through a stretch of sand. Carson felt his own right foot pressing an imaginary brake pedal to the floorboards. The man drove like Carson's father.

"What can you tell me about the project?" Carson said.

"What exactly do you want to know?" Singer said, turning toward Carson, eyes straying from the road.

"Well, I dropped everything and came out here on an hour's notice," Carson said. "I guess you could say I'm curious."

Singer smiled. "There'll be plenty of time when we reach Mount Dragon." His eyes drifted back to the road just as they whipped past a yucca, close enough to whack the driver's mirror. Singer jerked the Hummer back on course.

"This must be like a homecoming for you," he said.

Carson nodded, taking the hint. "My family's been here a long time."

"Longer than most, I understand."

"That's right. Kit Carson was my ancestor. He'd been a drover along the Spanish Trail as a teenager. My great-grandfather acquired an old land grant in Hidalgo County."

"And you grew tired of the ranching life?" Singer asked.

Carson shook his head. "My father was a terrible businessman. If he'd just stuck to straight ranching he would have been all right, but he was full of grand schemes. One of them involved crossbreeding cattle. That's how I got interested in genetics. It failed, like all the rest, and the bank took the ranch."

He fell silent, watching the endless desert unfold around him. The sun climbed higher in the sky, the light turning from yellow to white. In the distance, a pair of pronghorn antelope were running just below the horizon. They were barely visible, a streak of gray against gray. Singer, oblivious, hummed "Soldier's Joy" cheerfully to himself.

In time, the dark summit of a hill began to creep over the horizon in front of them, a volcanic cinder cone topped by a smooth crater. Along the rim of the crater stood a cluster of radio towers and microwave horns. As they approached, Carson could see a complex of angular buildings spread out below the hill, white and spare, gleaming in the morning sun like a cluster of salt crystals.

"There it is," Singer said proudly, slowing. "Mount Dragon. Your home for the next six months."

Soon a distant chain-link fence came into view, topped by thick rolls of concertina wire. A guard tower rose above the complex, motionless against the sky, wavering slightly in the heat.

"There's nobody in it at the moment," Singer said with a chuckle. "Oh, there's a security staff, all right. You'll meet them soon enough. And they're very efficient when they want to be. But our real security's the desert."

As they approached, the buildings slowly took form. Carson had expected an ugly set of cement buildings and Quonset huts; instead, the complex seemed almost beautiful, white and cool and clean against the sky.

Singer slowed further, drove around a concrete crash barrier and stopped at an enclosed guardhouse. A man—civilian clothes, no uniform of any kind—opened the door and came strolling over. Carson noticed that he walked with a stiff leg.

Singer lowered the window, and the man placed two muscled forearms on the doorframe and poked his crew-cut head inside. He grinned, his jaw muscles working on a piece of gum. Two brilliant green eyes were set deeply into a tanned, almost leathery face.

"Howdy, John," he said, his eyes slowly moving around the interior and finally coming to rest on Carson. "Who've we got here?"

"It's our new scientist. Guy Carson. Guy, this is Mike Marr, security."

The man nodded, eyes sliding around the car again. He handed Singer back his ID.

"Documents?" he spoke in Carson's direction, almost dreamily. Carson passed over the documents he had been told to bring: his passport, birth certificate, and Gene-Dyne ID.

Marr flicked through them nonchalantly. "Wallet, please?"

"You want my driver's license?" Carson frowned.

"The whole wallet, if you don't mind." Marr grinned very briefly, and Carson saw that the man wasn't chewing gum after all, but a large red rubber band. He handed over his wallet with irritation.

"They'll be taking your bags, as well," Singer said. "Don't worry, you'll get everything back before dinner. Except your passport, of course. That will be returned at the end of your six-month tour."

Marr heaved himself off the window and walked back into his air-conditioned blockhouse with Carson's belongings. He had a strange walk, hitching his right leg along as if it were in danger of becoming dislocated. A few moments later, he raised the bar and waved them through. Carson could see him through the thick blue-tinted glass, fanning out the contents of his wallet.

"There are no secrets here, I'm afraid, except the ones you keep inside your head," Singer said with a smile, easing the Hummer forward. "And watch out for those, as well."

"Why is all this necessary?" asked Carson.

Singer shrugged. "The price of working in a high-security environment. Industrial espionage, scurrilous publicity, and so forth. It's what you've been used to at GeneDyne Edison, really, just magnified tenfold."

Singer pulled into the motor pool and killed the engine. As Carson stepped out, a blast of desert air rolled over him and he inhaled deeply. It felt wonderful. Looking up, he could see the bulk of Mount Dragon rising a quarter mile beyond the compound. A newly graded gravel road switchbacked up its side, ending at the microwave towers.

"First," said Singer, "the grand tour. Then we'll head back to my office for a cold drink and a chat." He moved forward.

"This project . . . ?" Carson began.

Singer stopped, turned.

"Scopes wasn't exaggerating?" Carson asked. "It's really that important?"

Singer squinted, looked off into the empty desert. "Beyond your wildest dreams," he said.

Percival Lecture Hall at Harvard University was filled to capacity. Two hundred students sat in the descending rows of chairs, some bent over notebooks, others looking attentively forward. Dr. Charles Levine paced before the class, a small wiry figure with a fringe of hair surrounding his prematurely balding dome. There were chalk marks on his sleeves and his brogues still had salt stains from the previous winter. Nothing in his appearance, however, reduced the intensity that radiated from his quick movements and expression. As he lectured, he gestured with a stub of chalk at complex biochemical formulae and nucleotide sequences scattered across the huge sliding chalkboards, indecipherable as cuneiform.

In the rear of the hall sat a small group of people armed with microcassette recorders and handheld video cameras. They were not dressed like students, and press cards were prominently displayed on lapels and belts. But media presence was routine; lectures by Levine, professor of genetics and head of the Foundation for Genetic Policy, often became controversial without notice. And *Genetic Policy*, the foundation's journal, had made sure this lecture was given plenty of advance notice.

Levine stopped his pacing and moved to the podium. "That wraps up our discussion on Tuitt's constant, as it applies to disease mortality in western Europe," he said. "But I have more to discuss with you today." He cleared this throat.

"May I have the screen, please?" The lights dimmed and a white rectangle descended from the ceiling, obscuring the chalkboards.

"In sixty seconds, I am going to display a photograph on this screen," Levine said. "I am not authorized to show you this photograph. In fact, by doing so, I'll be technically guilty of breaking several laws under the Official Secrets Act. By staying, you'll be doing the same. I'm used to this kind of thing. If you've ever read *Genetic Policy*, you'll know what I mean. This is information that *must* be made public, no matter what the cost. But it goes beyond the scope of today's lecture, and I can't ask you to stay. Anyone who wishes to go may do so now."

In the dimly lit room, there were whispers, the turning of notebook pages. But nobody stood up.

Levine looked around, pleased. Then he nodded to the projectionist. A black-and-white image filled the screen.

Levine looked up at the image, the top of his head shining in the light of the projector like a monk's tonsure. Then he turned to face his audience.

"This is a picture taken on July 1, 1985, by the image-gathering satellite TB-17 from a sun-synchronous orbit of about one hundred and seventy miles," he began. "Technically, it has not yet been declassified. But it deserves to be." He smiled. Nervous laughter briefly filled the hall.

"You're looking at the town of Novo-Druzhina, in western Siberia. As you can see by the length of the shadows, this was taken in the early morning, the preferred time for image analysis. Note the position of the two parked cars, here, and the ripening fields of wheat."

A new slide appeared.

"Thanks to the surveillance technique of comparative coverage, this slide shows the exact same location three months later. Notice anything strange?"

There was a silence.

"The cars are parked in exactly the same spot. And the field of grain is apparently very ripe, ready to be harvested."

Another slide appeared.

"Here's the same place in April of the following year. Note the two cars are still there. The field has obviously gone fallow, the grain unharvested. It was images like these that suddenly made this area *very* interesting to certain photogrammetrists in the CIA."

He paused, looking out over the classroom.

"The United States military learned that all of Restricted Area Fourteen—a half-dozen towns, in an eighty-square-mile area surrounding Novo-Druzhina—were affected in a similar way. All human activity had ceased. So they took a closer look."

Another slide appeared.

"This is a magnification of the first slide, digitally enhanced, glint-suppressed, and compensated for spectral drift. If you look closely along the dirt street in front of the church, you will see a blurry image resembling a log. That is a human corpse, as any Pentagon photo-jock could tell you. Now here is the same scene, six months later."

Everything appeared to be the same, except that the log now looked white.

"The corpse is now skeletonized. When the military examined large numbers of these enhanced images, they found countless such skeletons lying unburied in the streets and the fields. At first, they were mystified. Theories of mass insanity, another Jonestown, were advanced. Because—"

A new slide appeared.

"—as you can see, everything else is still alive. Horses are still grazing in the fields. And there in the upper left-hand corner is a pack of dogs, apparently feral. This next slide shows cattle. The only dead things are human beings. Yet whatever it was that killed them was so dangerous, so instantaneous, or so widespread, that they remain where they fell, unburied."

He paused.

"The question is, *what was it?*"

The hall was silent.

"Lowell Cafeteria cooking?" someone ventured.

Levine joined in the general laughter. Then he nodded, and another aerial slide appeared, showing an extensive complex, gutted and ruined.

"Would that it were, my friend. In time, the CIA learned that the cause was a pathogen of some sort, created in the laboratory pictured here. You can see from the craters that the site has been bombed.

"Exact details were not known outside Russia until earlier this week, when a disenchanted Russian colonel defected to Switzerland, bringing with him a fat parcel of Soviet Army files. The same contact who provided me with these images alerted me to this colonel's presence in Switzerland. I was the first to examine his files. The events I am about to relate to you have never before been made public.

"What you must understand first is that this was a primitive experiment. There was little thought to political, economic, even military use. Remember, ten years ago the Russians were lagging behind in genetic research and struggling to catch up. In the secret facility outside Novo-Druzhina, they were experimenting with viral engineering. They were using a common virus, herpes simplex Ia+, the virus that produces cold sores. It's a relatively simple virus, well understood, easy to work with. They began meddling with its genetic makeup, inserting human genes into its viral DNA.

"We still don't know quite how they did it. But suddenly they had a horrific new pathogen on their hands, a scourge they were ill equipped to deal with. All they knew at the time was that it seemed unusually long-lived, and that it infected through aerosol contact.

"On May 23, 1985, there was a small safety breach at the Soviet laboratory. Apparently, a worker inside the transfection lab fell, damaging his biocontainment suit. As you know from Chernobyl, Soviet safety standards can be execrable. The worker told nobody about the incident, and later went home to his family in the worker's complex.

"For three weeks the virus incubated in his peritoneum, duplicating and spreading. On June 14, this worker felt ill and went to bed with a high fever. Within a few hours, he was complaining of a strange pressure in his gut. He passed a large amount of foul-smelling gas. Growing nervous, his wife sent for the doctor.

"Before the doctor could arrive, however, the man had— you will excuse the graphic description—voided most of his intestines out through his anus. They had suppurated inside his body, becoming pastelike. He had literally defecated his insides out. Needless to say, by the time the doctor arrived, the man was dead."

Levine paused again, looking around the room as if for raised hands. There were none.

"Since this incident has remained a secret from the scientific community, the virus has no official name. It is known only as Strain 232. We now know that a person exposed to it becomes contagious four days after exposure, although it takes several weeks for symptoms to appear. The mortality rate of Strain 232 is close to a hundred percent. By the time the worker had died, he had exposed dozens, if not hundreds, of people. We could call him vector zero. Within seventy-two hours of his death, dozens of people were complaining of the same gastrointestinal pressure, and soon suffered the same gruesome fate.

"The only thing that prevented a worldwide pandemic was the location of the outbreak. In 1985, movement in and out of Restricted Area Fourteen was highly controlled. Nevertheless, as word spread, a general panic ensued. People in the area began loading their belongings into cars, trucks, even horsecarts. Many tried fleeing on bicycle, or even on foot, abandoning everything in their desperation to get away.

"From the papers the colonel brought with him out of Russia, we can piece together the response of the Soviet Army. A special team in biohazard suits set up a series of roadblocks, preventing anyone from leaving the affected area. This was relatively easy, since Area Fourteen was already fenced and checkpointed. As the epidemic roared through the neighboring villages, whole families died in the streets, in the fields, in the market squares. By the time a person felt the first alarming symptoms, a painful death was only three hours away. The panic was so great that at the checkpoints, the soldiers were ordered to shoot and kill anyone—*anyone*—as soon as they came within range. Old men, children, pregnant women were gunned down. Air-dropped antipersonnel mines were scattered in wide swaths across woods and fields. What these measures didn't catch, the razor wire and tank traps did.

"Then the laboratory was carpet-bombed. Not, of course, to destroy the virus—bombs would have no effect on it. But rather to obliterate the traces, to hide what really happened from the West.

"Within eight weeks, every human being within the quarantined area was dead. The villages were deserted, the pigs and dogs gorging on corpses, the cows wandering unmilked, a horrible stench hanging over the deserted buildings."

Levine took a sip of water, then resumed.

"This is a shocking story, the biological equivalent of a nuclear holocaust. But I'm afraid the last chapter has yet to be written. Towns that have been irradiated with atomic bombs can be shunned. But the legacy of Novo-Druzhina is harder to avoid. Viruses are opportunistic, and they don't like to stay put. Although all the human hosts are dead, there is a possibility that Strain 232 lives on somewhere in this devastated area. Viruses sometimes find secondary reservoirs where they wait, patiently, for the next opportunity to infect. Strain 232 might be extinct. Or a viable pocket of it may still be there. Tomorrow, some hapless rabbit with muddy paws might wriggle through a hole in the perimeter fence. A farmer might shoot that rabbit and take it to market. And then the world as we know it could very well end."

He paused.

"And *that*," he shouted suddenly, "*is the promise of genetic engineering!*"

He stopped, letting the silence grow in the hall. Finally he dabbed his brow and spoke again, more quietly. "We won't be needing the projector anymore."

The projector image disappeared, leaving the hall in darkness.

"My friends," Levine continued, "we have reached a critical turning point in our stewardship of this planet, and we're so blind we can't even see it. We've walked the earth for five thousand centuries. But in the last fifty years, we've learned enough to really hurt ourselves. First with nuclear weapons, and now—infinitely more dangerously—with the reengineering of nature."

He shook his head. "There is an old proverb: 'Nature is a hanging judge.' The Novo-Druzhina incident nearly hanged the human race. And yet, as I speak, other companies across the globe are tinkering with viruses, exchanging genetic material between viruses, bacteria, plants, and animals indiscriminately, without any thought to the ultimate consequences.

"Of course, today's cutting-edge labs in Europe and America are a far cry from 1985 Siberia. Should that reassure us? Quite the opposite.

"The scientists in Novo-Druzhina were doing simple manipulations of a simple virus. They accidentally created a catastrophe. Today—barely a stone's throw from this hall—much more complicated experiments are being done with infinitely more exotic, infinitely more dangerous viruses.

"Edwin Kilbourne, the virologist, once postulated a pathogen he called the Maximally Malignant Virus. The MMV would have, he theorized, the environmental stability of polio, the antigenic mutability of influenza, the unrestricted host range of rabies, the latency of herpes.

"Such an idea, almost laughable then, is deadly serious now. Such a pathogen could be, and maybe *is being*, created in a laboratory somewhere on this planet. It would be far more devastating than a nuclear war. Why? A nuclear war is self-limiting. But with the spread of an MMV, *every infected person becomes a brand-new walking bomb.* And today's transmission routes are so widespread, so quickly achieved by international travelers, it only takes a few carriers for a virus to go global."

Levine stepped around the podium to face the audience. "Regimes come and go. Political boundaries change. Empires grow and fall. But *these* agents of destruction, once unleashed, last forever. I ask you: should we allow unregulated and uncontrolled experiments in genetic engineering to continue in laboratories around the world? *That* is the real question raised by Strain 232."

He nodded, and the lights came back up. "There will be a full report of the Novo-Druzhina incident in the next issue of *Genetic Policy*," he said, turning to gather his papers.

The spell broken, the students stood up and began collecting their things, moving in a rustling tide toward the exits. The reporters at the back of the hall had already left to file their stories.

A young man appeared at the top of the hall, pushing his way through the milling crowd. Slowly, he made his way down the central steps toward the podium.

Levine glanced up, then looked carefully left and right. "I thought you were told never to approach me in public," he said.

The youth came forward, held Levine's elbow, and whispered urgently in his ear. Levine stopped loading papers into his briefcase.

"Carson?" he asked. "You mean that bright cowboy fellow who was always interrupting my lectures to argue?"

The man nodded his head.

Levine fell silent, his hand on the briefcase. Then he snapped it shut.

"My God," he said simply.

Carson looked out across the motor pool toward a sweeping cluster of white buildings which rose abruptly from the desert sands: curves, planes and domes thrusting from the ground. The stark placement of the buildings in the desert terrain, along with a total absence of landscaping, gave the laboratory a Zen-like feeling of purity and emptiness. Glassed-in walkways connected many of the buildings, forming crisscrossing patterns.

Singer led Carson along one of the covered walkways. "Brent is a great believer in architecture as a means of inspiring the human spirit," he said. "I'll never forget when that architect, what's-his-name—Guareschi—came from New York to 'experience' the site."

Singer chuckled softly.

"He arrived in tasseled loafers and a suit, with this silly straw hat. But the guy was game, I'll give him that. He actually camped out for four days before he got heatstroke and hightailed it back to Manhattan."

"It's beautiful," Carson said.

"It is. Despite his bad experience, the man did manage to capture the spareness of the desert. He insisted there be no landscaping. For one thing, we didn't have the water. But he also wanted the complex to look as if it was part of the desert, and not imposed on it. Obviously, he never forgot the heat. I think that's why everything's white: the machine shop, the storage barracks—even the power plant." He nodded toward a long building with gracefully curving rooflines.

"That's the power plant?" Carson asked in disbelief. "It looks more like an art museum. This place must have cost a fortune."

"Several fortunes," Singer said. "But back in '85, when construction began, money wasn't much of an issue." He ushered Carson toward the residency compound, a series of low curvilinear structures gathered together like pieces of a jigsaw puzzle. "We'd obtained a nine-hundred-million-dollar contract through DATRADA."

"Who?"

"Defense Advanced Technology, Research and Development Administration."

"Never heard of it," said Carson.

"It was a secret Defense Department agency. Disbanded after the Reagan years. We all had to sign a lot of formal loyalty documents and the like. Secret clearance, top-secret clearance, you name it. Then they investigated us—boy, did they investigate. I got calls from ex-girlfriends twenty years removed: 'A bunch of suits were just here asking a lot of questions about you. What the hell did you do now, Singer?' " He laughed.

"So you've been here from the beginning," Carson said.

"That's right. Only the scientists have six-month tours. I guess they figure I don't do enough real work to get burnt out." He laughed. "I'm the old-timer here, me and Nye. And a few others, old Pavel and the fellow you just met, Mike Marr. Anyway, it's been much nicer since we went civilian. The military boys were a pain in the posterior."

"How did the changeover happen?" Carson asked.

Singer steered him through the smoked-glass door of a structure on the far side of the residency compound. A river of air-conditioning washed over them as the door hissed shut. Carson found himself in a vestibule, with slate floors, white walls, and taupe furniture. Singer led him toward another door.

"At first, we did strictly defense research. That's how we got these land parcels in the Missile Range. Our job was to look for vaccines, countermeasures and antitoxins to presumed Soviet biological weapons. When the Soviet Union fell apart, so did our brief. We lost the contract in 1990. We almost lost the lab, too, but Scopes did some quick lobbying behind closed doors. God knows how he did it, but we were able to get a thirty-year lease under the Defense Industry Conversion Act."

Singer opened a door into a long laboratory. A series of black tables gleamed under fluorescent lights. Bunsen burners, Erlenmeyer flasks, glass tubing, stereozoom microscopes and various other low-tech equipment sat in neat, spotless rows.

Carson had never seen a lab look so clean. "Is this the low-level facility?" he asked incredulously.

"Nope," Singer said. "Most of the real work is done on the inside, our next stop. This is just eye candy for congressmen and military brass. They expect to see an upscale version of their old university chem lab, and we give it to them."

They passed into another, much smaller room. A large, gleaming instrument sat in its center. Carson recognized it instantly.

"The world's best microtome: the Scientific Precision 'Ultra-Shave,' " Singer said. "That's what we call it, anyway. It's all computer controlled. A diamond blade that cuts a human hair into twenty-five hundred sections. Widthwise. This one's just for show, of course. We've got two identical units operating on the inside."

They walked back into the baking heat. Singer licked a finger and held it up. "Wind's from the southeast," he said. "As always. That's why they picked this place—always blowing from the southeast. The first town downwind of us is Claunch, New Mexico, population twenty-two. One hundred forty miles away. The Trinity Site, where they blew up the first A-bomb, is only thirty miles northwest of here. Good place to hide an atomic explosion. You couldn't find a more isolated place in the lower forty-eight."

"We called that wind the Mexican Zephyr," Carson said. "When I was a kid, I hated to go out in that wind more than anything. My dad used to say it caused more trouble than a rat-tailed horse tied short in fly time."

Singer turned. "Guy, I have no idea what you just said."

"A rat-tailed horse is a horse with a short tail. If you tie him short and the flies start tormenting him, he'll go crazy, tear down your fence and take off."

"I see," Singer said without conviction. He pointed over Carson's shoulder. "Over there are the recreational facilities—gymnasium, tennis courts, horse corral. I have a strong aversion to physical activity, so I'll let you explore those on your own." He patted his paunch affectionately and laughed. "And that awful-looking building is the air incinerator for the Fever Tank."

"Fever Tank?"

"Sorry," Singer said. "I mean the Biosafety Level-5 laboratory, where the really high-risk organisms are worked on. I'm sure you've heard of the Biosafety classification system. Level-1 is the safety standard for working with the least infectious, least dangerous microbes. Level-4 is for the most dangerous. There are two Level-4 laboratories in the country: the CDC has one in Atlanta, and the Army's got one at Fort Detrick. These Level-4 laboratories are designed to handle the most dangerous viruses and bacteria that exist in nature."

"But what's this Level-5? I've never heard of it."

Singer grinned. "Brent's pride and joy. Mount Dragon has the only Level-5 laboratory in the world. It was designed for handling viruses and bacteria *more* dangerous than anything naturally existing in nature. In other words, microbes that have been genetically engineered. Somebody christened it the Fever Tank years ago, and the name stuck. Anyway, all the air from the Level-5 facility is circulated through the incinerator and heated to one thousand degrees Celsius before being cooled and returned. Sterilized completely."

The alien-looking air incinerator was the only structure Carson had seen at Mount Dragon that was not pure white. "So you're working with an airborne pathogen?"

"Clever. Yes we are, and a very nasty one at that. I enjoyed it much more when we were working on PurBlood. That's our artificial blood product."

Carson glanced over in the direction of the corrals. He could see a barn, stalls, several turnouts, and a large fenced pasture beyond the perimeter fence.

"Can you ride outside the facility?" he asked.

"Of course. You just have to log out and log in." Singer glanced around and wiped his forehead with the back of his hand. "Christ, it's hot. I just never get used to it. Let's go inside."

"Inside" meant the inner perimeter, a large chain-linked area at the heart of Mount Dragon. Carson could see only one break in the inner fence, a small gatehouse directly in front of them. Singer led the way through the gate and into a large building on the far side. The doors opened to a cool foyer. Through an open door, Carson could see a row of computer terminals on long white tables. Two workers, ID cards hung around their necks, wearing jeans under white lab coats, were busily typing at terminals. Carson realized with surprise that, except for guards, these were the first workers he'd seen on the site.

"This is the operations building," Singer said, gesturing into the mostly empty room. "Administration, data processing, you name it. Our staff isn't large. There were never more than thirty scientists here at one time, even in our military days. Now the number is half that, all focused on the project."

"That's pretty small," Carson said.

Singer shrugged. "The human-wave approach just doesn't work in genetic engineering."

He gestured Carson out of the foyer into a large atrium paved in black granite and roofed with heavily tinted glass. The strong desert sun, attenuated to a pale light, fell on a small grouping of palm trees in the center. Three corridors branched out from the atrium. "Those lead to the transfection labs and the DNA-sequencing facility," he said. "You won't be spending much time there, but you can get somebody to take you through at your leisure, if you like. Our next stop's out there." He pointed at a window. Through it, Carson could make out a low, rhombus-like structure poking up from the desert.

"Level-5," Singer said unenthusiastically. "The Fever Tank."

"Looks pretty small," Carson said.

"Believe me, it feels small. But what you see is just the housing for the HEPA filters. The real lab's beneath that, underground. Added protection in case of an earthquake, fire, explosion." He hesitated. "Guess we might as well go in."

A slow descent in a cramped elevator deposited them in a long, white-tiled corridor lit by orange lights. Video cameras hung from the ceiling, tracking their progress. At the end of the corridor, Singer stopped at a gray metal door, its edges curved to fit the doorframe and sealed with thick black rubber.

To the right was a small mechanical box. Bending over, Singer spoke his name into the device. A green light came on above the door, and a tone sounded.

"Voice recognition," said Singer, opening the door. "It's not as good as hand-geometry readers or retinal scanners, but those don't work through biosuits. And this one, at least, can't be fooled by a tape recorder. You'll be coded this afternoon, as part of your entrance interview."

They moved into a large room, sparsely decorated with modern furniture. Along one wall was a series of metal lockers. On the far side stood another steel door, polished to a high gloss, marked with a bright yellow-and-red symbol. EXTREME BIOHAZARD, read a legend above the frame.

"This is the ready room," Singer said. "The bluesuits are in those lockers."

He moved toward one of the lockers, then paused. Suddenly he turned toward Carson. "Tell you what. Why don't I get someone who really knows the place to show you around?"

He pressed a button on the locker. There was a hiss as the metal door slid up, revealing a bulky blue rubber suit, carefully packed into a molded container that resembled a small coffin.

"You've never entered a BSL-4 facility, right?" Singer asked. "Then listen closely. Level-5 is a lot like Level-4, only more so. Most people wear scrub under the full-body suits for comfort, but it's not a requirement. If you wear your street clothes, all pens, pencils, watches, knives must come out of the pockets. Anything that could puncture the suit." Carson quickly turned his pockets inside out.

"No long fingernails?" Singer asked.

Carson looked at his hands. "Nope."

"That's good. I'm always worrying mine down to the quick, so I don't have a problem." He laughed. "You'll find a pair of rubber gloves in that lower left compartment. No rings, right? Good. You'll have to take off your boots and put on those slippers. And no long toenails. You'll find toenail clippers in one of the locker compartments, if you need them."

Carson removed his boots.

"Now step into the suit, right leg first, then left leg, and draw it up. But not all the way. Leave the visor open for now so we can talk more easily."

Carson fumbled with the bulky suit, drawing it over his clothes with difficulty.

"This thing weighs a ton," he said.

"It's fully pressurized. See that metal valve at your waist? You'll be on oxygen the entire time you're inside. You'll be shown how to move from station to station. But the suit itself contains ten minutes' worth of air, in case of emergencies." He walked toward an intercom unit, pressed a series of buttons. "Rosalind?" he asked.

There was a short pause. "What?" came the buzzing response.

"Could I trouble you to give our new scientist, Guy Carson, a tour of BSL-5?"

There was a longer silence.

"I'm in the middle of something," the voice came back.

"It'll just take a few minutes."

"Aw, for Chrissakes." The voice cut off immediately.

Singer turned to Carson. "That's Rosalind Brandon-Smith. She's a little eccentric, I guess you could say." He leaned toward Carson's open visor conspiratorially. "Actually, she's extremely rude, but don't pay any attention. She was instrumental in developing our artificial blood. Now she's wrapping up her part of the new project. She did a lot of work with Frank Burt, and they were pretty close, so she may not be too friendly to his replacement. You'll be meeting her inside, no reason for her to go through decontam twice."

"Who's Frank Burt?" Carson asked.

"He was a true scientist. And a fine human being. But he found conditions here a little too stressful. Had something of a breakdown recently. It's not uncommon, you know. About a quarter of the people who come to Mount Dragon can't finish their tour."

"I didn't know I was replacing anyone," Carson frowned.

"You are. I'll tell you about it later. You'll be filling some large shoes." He stepped back. "OK, finish up the zippers. Make sure you close and secure all three. We've got a buddy system here. After you suit up, someone else has to check over everything."

He did a careful inspection of the bluesuit, then showed Carson how to use the visor intercom. "Unless you're standing next to somebody, it's very hard to hear anything. Press this button on your forearm to speak over the intercom."

He waved toward the door marked EXTREME BIOHAZARD. "On the far side of the air lock is a chemical shower. Once you're inside, it starts automatically. Get used to it, there'll be a much longer one coming out. When the inner door opens, go on through. Be especially careful until you're used to the suit. Rosalind will be waiting for you on the far side. I hope."

"Thanks," said Carson, raising his voice to make sure it carried through the thick rubber of the suit.

"No problem," came the muffled response. "Sorry I won't be going in with you. It's just . . ." He hesitated. "Nobody goes into the Fever Tank unless they have to. You'll see why."

As the door hissed shut behind him, Carson walked forward onto a metal grating. There was a sudden rumble, and a yellow chemical solution spurted from shower heads in the ceiling, walls, and floor. Carson could feel the solution drumming loudly on his suit. In a minute it was over; the next door opened, and he stepped into a small antechamber. A motor began to rumble, and he could feel the pressure of a powerful air machine blowing at him from all directions. Inside his suit, the drying mechanism felt like a strange, distant wind: He was unable to tell whether the air was hot or cold. Then the inner door hissed open, and Carson found himself facing a short woman who was staring at him impatiently through the clear faceplate of her visor. Even compensating for the bulkiness of the suit, Carson estimated her weight at 250 pounds.

"Follow me," a voice inside his helmet said brusquely, and the woman turned away, moving down a tiled corridor so narrow that her shoulders brushed against both walls. The walls were smooth and slick, with no corners or projecting apparatus that might tear a protective suit. Everything—floors, wall tiles, ceiling—was painted a brilliant white.

Carson pressed the left button on his forearm, activating the intercom. "I'm Guy Carson," he said.

"Glad to hear it," came the reply. "Now, pay attention. See those air hoses overhead?"

Carson looked up. A number of blue hoses dangled from the ceiling, metal valves affixed to their ends.

"Grab one and plug it into your suit valve. Careful. Turn it to the left to lock it in. When you move from one station to the next, you'll have to detach it and plug into another hose. Your suit has a limited supply of air, so don't dawdle between hookups."

Carson followed her instructions, felt the snap as the valve seated itself, and heard the reassuring hiss of airflow. Inside the suit, he felt a strange sense of detachment from the world. His movements seemed slow, clumsy. Because of the multiple pairs of gloves, he could barely feel the air hose as he guided it into the attachment.

"Keep in mind that this place is like a submarine," came the voice of Brandon-Smith. "Small, cramped, and dangerous. Everything and everyone has its place."

"I see," said Carson.

"Do you?"

"Yes."

"Good, because sloppiness is death down here in the Fever Tank. And not just for you. Got that?"

"Yes," Carson repeated. *Bitch.*

They continued down the narrow hall. As he followed Brandon-Smith, trying to acclimate himself to the pressure suit, Carson thought he could hear a strange noise in the background: a faint drumming, almost more sensation than sound. He decided it must be the Fever Tank's generator.

Brandon-Smith's great bulk eased sideways through a narrow hatch. In the lab beyond, suited figures were working in front of large Plexiglas-enclosed tables, their hands stretched through rubber holes bored into the cases. They were swabbing petri dishes. The light was painfully bright, throwing every object in the lab into sharp relief. Small waste receptacles with biohazard labels and flash-incineration attachments stood beside each worktable. More ceiling-mounted video cameras swiveled, monitoring the scientists.

"Everybody," Brandon-Smith's voice sounded in the intercom. "This is Guy Carson. Burt's replacement."

Visors angled upward as people turned to get a look at him, and a chorus of greetings crackled in Carson's helmet.

"This is production," she said flatly. It wasn't a statement that invited questions, and Carson didn't ask any.

Brandon-Smith led Carson through a warren of other labs, narrow corridors, and air locks, all starkly bathed in the same brilliant light. *She's right,* Carson thought, looking around. *The place is like a submarine.* All available floor space was packed with fabulously expensive equipment: transmission and scanning electron microscopes, autoclaves, incubators, mass spectrometers, even a small cyclotron, all reengineered to allow the scientists to operate them through the bulky bluesuits. The ceilings were low, heavily veined with piping, and painted white like everything else in the Fever Tank. Every ten yards Brandon-Smith halted to hook up to a new air hose, then waited for Carson to do the same. The going was excruciatingly slow.

"My God," Carson said. "These safety measures are unbelievable. What have you got in here, anyway?"

"You name it," came the response. "Bubonic plague, pneumonic plague, Marburg virus, Hantavirus, Dengue, Ebola, anthrax. Not to mention a few Soviet biological agents. All currently on ice, of course."

The cramped spaces, the bulky suit, the stuffy air, all had a disorienting effect on Carson. He found himself gulping in oxygen, fighting down an urge to unzip the suit, give himself breathing room.

At last they stopped in a small circular hub from which several narrow corridors branched out like the spokes of a wheel. "What's that?" Carson pointed to a huge manifold over their heads.

"The air uptake," Brandon-Smith said, attaching another new hose to her suit. "This is the center of the Fever Tank. The entire facility has negative airflow controls. The air pressure decreases the further in you go. Everything flows to this point, then it's taken up to the incinerator and recirculated." She gestured at one of the corridors. "Your lab's down there. You'll see it soon enough. I don't have time to show you everything."

"And down there?" Carson pointed to a narrow tube at their feet containing a shiny metal ladder.

"There are three levels beneath us. Backup labs, security substation, CRYLOX freezers, generators, the control center."

She stepped a few feet down one of the hallways, stopping in front of another door.

"Carson?" she said.

"Yes."

"Last stop. The Zoo. Keep the hell away from the cages. Don't let them grab you. If they rip a piece off your suit, you'll never see the light of day. You'll be locked up in here and left to die."

"The Zoo—?" Carson began, but Brandon-Smith was already opening the door. Suddenly the drumming was louder, and Carson realized it was not a generator, after all. Muffled screams and hoots filtered through his pressure suit. Turning a corner, Carson saw that one wall of the room's interior was lined floor to ceiling with cages. Black beady eyes peered out from between wire mesh. The new arrivals in the room caused the noise level to increase dramatically. Many of the prisoners were now pounding on the floors of the cages with their feet and hands.

"Chimpanzees?" asked Carson.

"Good for you."

A small bluesuited figure at the far end of the row of cages turned toward them.

"Carson, this is Bob Fillson. He takes care of the animals."

Fillson nodded curtly. Carson could see a heavy brow, bulbous nose, and wet pendulous lip behind the faceplate. The rest was in shadow. The man turned and went back to work.

"Why so many?" Carson asked.

She stopped and looked at him. "They're the only animal with the same immunological system as a human being. You should know that, Carson."

"Of course, but why exactly—"

But Brandon-Smith was peering intently into one of the cages.

"Aw, for Chrissakes," she said.

Carson came over, keeping a respectful distance from the countless fingers poking through the mesh. A chimpanzee was lying on its side, trembling, oblivious of the commotion surrounding it. There seemed to be something wrong with its facial features. Then Carson realized that the creature's eyeballs seemed abnormally enlarged. Looking closer, he could see that they were actually bulging from its head, the blood vessels rupturing and hemorrhaging in the sclera. The animal suddenly jerked, opened its hairy jaws, and screamed.

"Bob," Carson could hear Brandon-Smith saying through the intercom, "the last of Burt's chimps is about to go."

With a notable lack of haste, Fillson came shuffling over. He was a very small man, barely five feet, and he moved with a slow deliberation that reminded Carson of a diver under water.

He turned to Carson, and spoke with a hoarse voice. "You'll have to go. You too, Rosalind. Can't open a cage when others are in the room."

Carson watched in horror as one of the eyeballs suddenly erupted from its socket, followed by a gush of bloody fluid. The chimp thrashed about silently, teeth snapping, arms flailing.

"What the hell?" Carson began, frozen in horror.

"Good-*bye*," Fillson said firmly, as he reached into a cabinet behind him.

"Bye, Bob," said Brandon-Smith. Carson noticed a distinct change of tone in her voice when she spoke to the animal handler.

The last thing Carson saw as they sealed the door was the chimp, rigid with pain, pawing desperately at its ruined face, as Fillson sprayed something from an aerosol can into the cage.

Brandon-Smith made her ponderous way down another corridor, not speaking.

"Are you going to tell me what was wrong with that chimpanzee?" Carson said at last.

"I thought it was obvious," she snapped. "Cerebral edema."

"Caused by what?"

The woman turned to look at him. She seemed surprised. "You really don't know, Carson?"

"No, I don't. And from now on, the name is Guy. Or Dr. Carson, if you prefer. I don't appreciate being called by my last name."

There was a silence. "Fine, *Guy*," she replied. "Those chimps are all X-FLU positive. The one you saw is in the tertiary stage of the disease. The virus stimulates massive overproduction of cerebrospinal fluid. In time, the pressure herniates the brain down through the foramen magnum. That's when the lucky ones die. A few hang on until the eyeballs are forced from their sockets."

"X-FLU?" Carson asked. He could feel the sweat trickling down his forehead and under his arms, dampening the inside of his suit.

This time Brandon-Smith stopped dead. There was a buzz of static and he heard her voice: "Singer, can you enlighten me as to why this joker doesn't know about X-FLU?"

Singer's voice came back. "I haven't briefed him yet on the project. That comes next."

"Mr. Ass-backwards, as usual," she said, then turned to Carson. "Let's go, *Guy*, the tour's over."

She left Carson at the exit air lock. He stepped through the access chamber into another chemical shower, waiting the required seven minutes as the high-pressure solution doused his suit. A few minutes later he was back in the ready room. He was vaguely annoyed to see Singer, cool and relaxed, doing the crossword of the local newspaper.

"Enjoy your tour?" Singer asked, looking up from the paper.

"No," said Carson, breathing deeply, trying to shake the oppressive feeling of the Fever Tank. "That Brandon-Smith is meaner than a sidewinder in a hot skillet."

Singer burst out laughing and shook his bald head. "A colorful way of putting it. She's the most brilliant scientist we've got at present. If we pull this project off, you know, we're all going to become rich. Yourself included. That's worth putting up with a Rosalind Brandon-Smith, don't you think? She's really just a frightened, insecure little girl underneath that mountain of adipose tissue."

He helped Carson out of his suit and showed him how to pack it back inside the locker.

"I think the time has come for me to hear about this mysterious project," Carson said, closing the locker.

"Absolutely. Shall we head back to my office for a cold drink?"

Carson nodded. "You know, there was a chimpanzee back there with its—"

Singer held up a hand. "I know what you saw."

"So what the hell was it?"

Singer paused. "Influenza."

"What?" Carson said. "The *flu?*"

Singer nodded.

"I don't know of any flu that pops your eyeballs out of your skull."

"Well," Singer said, "this is a very special kind of flu." Gripping Carson's elbow, he led him through the outer corridors of the maximum-security lab and back up into the welcoming desert sunlight.

At precisely two minutes to three in the afternoon, Charles Levine opened his door and ushered a young woman, clad in jeans and sweatshirt, back into his outer office.

"Thank you, Ms. Fields," he said, smiling. "We'll let you know if anything opens up for next term."

As the student turned to leave, Levine checked his watch. "That's it, right, Ray?" he said, turning to his secretary.

With an effort, Ray shifted his eyes from Ms. Fields's departing ass to the open appointment book on his desk. He smoothed his hand over his immaculate Buddy Holly haircut, his fingers dropping to scratch the heavily muscled chest beneath the sleeveless red T-shirt. "That's it, Dr. Levine," he said.

"Any messages? Sheriff's deputies bearing summonses? Offers of marriage?"

Ray grinned and waited until the outer door closed before answering. "Borucki called twice. Apparently that pharmaceutical company in Little Rock was unimpressed with last month's article. They're suing for libel."

"How much?"

Ray shrugged. "A million."

"Tell our legal friends to take the usual steps." Levine turned away. "No interruptions, Ray."

"Right."

Levine closed the door.

With his notoriety as Foundation for Genetic Policy spokesman growing, Levine found it increasingly difficult to maintain a routine existence as professor of theoretical genetics. The nature of the foundation made it a lightning rod for a certain kind of student: lonely, idealistic, in need of a burning cause. It also made him and his office the target of a great deal of anger from business concerns.

When his former secretary quit after receiving a number of threatening phone calls, Levine took two precautionary steps.

He had a new lock installed on his office door, and he hired Ray. Ray's office skills left a lot to be desired. But as an ex-Navy SEAL discharged because of a heart murmur, he was very good at keeping things peaceful. Ray seemed to spend most of his nonworking hours chasing women, but at the office he was serenely indifferent to all forms of intimidation, and for that alone Levine found him indispensable.

The heavy bolt of the lock slid home with reassuring finality. Levine tugged at the doorknob, then, satisfied, moved quickly between piles of term papers, scientific journals, and back issues of *Genetic Policy* to his desk. The affable, easygoing air he had maintained during his consultation hours quickly dissipated. Clearing the center of the desk with a sweep of his hand, he tugged his computer keyboard into typing range. Then he dug into a pocket of his briefcase and pulled out a black object the size of a cigarette box. A slender length of gray cable dangled from one end. Leaning forward in his chair, Levine disconnected his telephone, plugged the phone line into one end of the black box, and inserted the slender gray cable into the back panel of his laptop computer.

Even before his single-minded crusade to regulate genetic engineering made his name a foul word in a dozen top labs around the world, Levine had learned hard lessons about security. The black box was a dedicated cryptographic device for scrambling computer transmissions over telephone lines. Using proprietary public-key algorithms far more sophisticated than the DES standard, it was supposedly uncrackable even by government supercomputers. Mere possession of such devices was of questionable legality. But Levine had been an active member of the student antiwar underground before graduating from U.C. Irvine in 1971. He was no stranger to using unorthodox or even illegal methods to achieve his ends.

Levine switched on his PC, drumming his fingers on the desktop while the machine booted itself into consciousness. Typing rapidly, he brought up the communications program that would dial out over the phone lines to another computer, and another user. A very special user.

He waited while the call was rerouted, then rerouted again across the telephone long lines, threading a complex, untraceable path. At last, the call was answered by the hiss of another modem. There was a shrill squealing noise as the two computers negotiated; then Levine's screen dissolved into a now-familiar image: a figure, dressed in mime's costume, balancing the earth on one fingertip. Almost immediately the log-in device disappeared, and words appeared on Levine's screen: disembodied, as if typed by a ghost.

Professor! What up?

I need a line into GeneDyne's net, Levine typed.

The response was immediate. **Simple enough. What are we looking for today? Employee phone numbers? P&L sheets? The latest scores of the mailroom deathmatchers?**

I need a private channel into the Mount Dragon facility, Levine typed.

The next response was a little slower in coming. **Whoa! __Whoa!__Whose pair of balls have you strapped on today, monsieur le professor?**

Can't do it? Levine prodded.

Did I say I couldn't do it? Remember to whom you're speaking, varlet! You won't find the word 'can't' in my spell-checker. I'm not worried about me: I'm worried about__you__, my man. I hear that this guy Scopes is bad juju. He'd love to catch you cop-

ping a feel beneath his skirts. Are you sure you're ready to jack into prime time, professor?

You're worried about me? Levine typed. That's hard to believe.

Why, professor. Your callousness wounds me.

Do you want money this time? Is that it?

Money? Now I'm insulted. I demand satisfaction. Meet me at high noon in front of the Cyberspace Saloon.

Mime, this is serious.

I'm always serious. Of course I can handle your little problem. Besides, I've heard rumors of some truly girthy program Scopes has been working on. Something very hip, very interesting. But he's a jealous guy, supposedly, keeps a chastity belt around it. Perhaps while I'm taking care of business, I can pay a little visit to his private server. That's just the kind of deflowering I enjoy most.

What you do on your off time is your own affair, Levine typed irritably. Just make sure the channel is absolutely secure. Let me know when it's in place, please.

CID.

Mime, I don't understand. CID?

Bless me, I keep forgetting what a newbie you are. Out here in the electronic ether, we use acronyms to help keep our epistolary exchanges short and sweet. CID: 'Consider it done.' You long-winded academic types could take a page from our virtual book. Here's another: TTFN. Viz, 'ta-ta for now.' So TTFN, Herr Professor.

The screen went blank.

John Singer's office, which occupied the southwest corner of the administration building, was more living room than director's suite. A kiva fireplace was built into one corner, surrounded by a sofa and two leather wing chairs. Against one wall was an antique Mexican *trastero*, on which sat a battered Martin guitar and an untidy stack of sheet music. A Two Gray Hills Navajo rug lay on the floor, and the walls were lined with nineteenth-century prints of the American frontier, including six Bodmer images of Mandan and Hidatsa Indians on the Upper Missouri. There was no desk—only a computer workstation and telephone.

The windows looked over the Jornada desert, where the dirt road wandered off toward infinity. Sun streamed in the tinted window and across the room, filling it with light.

Carson seated himself in one of the leather chairs while Singer moved to a small bar on the far side of the room.

"Anything to drink?" he asked. "Beer, wine, martini, juice?"

Carson glanced at his watch. It was 11:45 A.M. His stomach still felt a little queasy. "I'll have some juice."

Singer returned with a glass of Cranapple in one hand and a martini in the other. He settled back on the sofa and propped his feet up on the table. "I know," he said, "drinking before noon. Very bad. But this is a special occasion." He raised his glass. "To X-FLU."

"X-FLU," Carson muttered. "That's what Brandon-Smith said killed the chimp."

"Correct," Singer took a sip, exhaling contentedly.

"Forgive my bluntness," said Carson, "but I'd really like to know what this project is all about. I still can't understand why Mr. Scopes chose me out of—what—five thousand scientists? And why did I have to drop everything, get my ass out here on five minutes' notice?"

Singer settled back. "Let me start at the beginning. Are you familiar with an animal called a bonobo?"

"No."

"We used to call them pygmy chimpanzees until we realized they were a completely different species. Bonobos are even closer to human beings than the more common lowland chimps. They are more intelligent, form monogamous relationships, and share ninety-nine-point-two percent of our DNA. Most importantly, they get all our diseases. Except one."

He paused, sipped his drink.

"They don't get the flu. All other chimps, as well as gorillas and orangs, get the flu. But not the bonobo. This fact came to Brent's attention about ten months ago. He sent us several bonobos, and we did some genetic sequencing. Let me show you what we discovered."

Singer opened a notebook lying on the coffee table, moving aside a malachite egg to make room. Inside, the sheets of paper were covered with strings of letters in complex ladder-like arrangements.

"The bonobo has a gene that makes it immune to influenza.

Not just one or two strains, but *all* sixty known varieties. We've named it the X-FLU gene."

Carson examined the printout. It was a short gene, going only to several hundred base pairs.

"How does the gene work?" Carson asked.

Singer smiled. "We don't really know. It would take years to figure it out. But Brent hypothesized that if we could insert this gene into human DNA, it would render humans immune to flu, as well. The initial in vitro tests we performed bore this out."

"Interesting," Carson replied.

"I'll say. Take the gene out of the bonobo, and insert it into yourself. Presto, you never get the flu again." Singer leaned forward and lowered his voice. "Guy, how much do you know about the flu?"

Carson hesitated. He actually knew quite a bit. But Singer didn't seem the type who'd appreciate a braggart. "Not as much as I should. People are too complacent about it, for one thing."

Singer nodded. "That's right. People tend to think of it as a nuisance. But it's not a nuisance. It's one of the worst viral diseases in the world. Even today, a million people die annually from the flu. It remains one of the top ten causes of death in the United States. During flu season, one *quarter* of the population falls ill. And that's in a good year. People forget that the swine flu epidemic of 1918 killed one person out of fifty worldwide. That was the worst pandemic in recorded history, worse than the Black Death. And it happened *in this century*. If it happened again today, we'd be almost as helpless now as we were then."

"Truly virulent flu mutations can kill in hours," Carson said. "But—"

"Just one moment, Guy. That word, *mutation*, is key. The serious pandemics occur when the flu virus undergoes significant mutation. It's already happened three times this century, most recently with the Hong Kong flu in 1968. We're overdue—we're *ripe*—for another pandemic right now."

"And because the coating of the viral particle keeps mutating," Carson said, "there's no permanent vaccine. A flu shot is just a cocktail of three or four strains, a guess on the part of epidemiologists as to what strain might be coming along in the next six months. Correct? They could guess wrong and you'd be just as sick."

Singer smiled. "Very good, Guy. We're well aware of the work you did with flu viruses at MIT. That's part of the reason we chose you."

He finished his drink with a short hard gulp. "One thing you may not have been aware of was that the world economy loses almost one *trillion* dollars a year in unrealized productivity to the flu."

"I didn't know that."

"Here's something else you may not know: the flu causes an estimated two hundred thousand birth defects annually. When a pregnant woman gets a fever above a hundred and four degrees, all kinds of developmental hell can break loose in the womb."

He inhaled slowly. "Guy, we're working on the last great medical advancement of the twentieth century. And now you're a part of it. You see, with the X-FLU gene inserted into his body, a human being will be immune to all strains of the flu. Forever. What's more, his children will inherit the immunity."

Carson slowly put down his drink and looked at Singer.

"Jesus," he said. "You mean, a gene therapy aimed at reproductive cells?"

"That's right. We're going to alter the germ cell line of the human race permanently. And you, Guy, are central to this effort."

"But my work with influenza was just preliminary," Carson said. "My main focus was elsewhere."

"I know," Singer replied. "Bear with me a moment longer. Our major obstacle has been getting the X-FLU gene into human DNA. It has to be done, of course, using a virus."

Carson nodded. He knew that viruses worked by inserting their own DNA into a host's DNA. That made viruses the ideal vector to exchange genes between distantly related species. As a result, most genetic engineering used viruses in this way.

"Here's how it will work," Singer continued. "We insert the X-FLU gene into a flu virus itself. Use the virus as a Trojan horse, if you will. Then we infect a person with that virus. As with any flu vaccine, the person will develop a mild case of influenza. Meanwhile, the virus has inserted the bonobo DNA into the person's DNA. When he recovers, he's got the X-FLU gene. And he'll never get the flu again."

"Gene therapy," Carson said.

"Absolutely," Singer replied. "It's one of the hottest things around today. Gene therapies are promising to cure all kinds of genetic diseases. Like Tay-Sachs disease, PKU syndrome, hemophilia, you name it. Someday, anyone born with a genetic defect will be able to get the right gene and live a normal life. Only in this case, the 'defect' is susceptibility to the flu. And the change is *inheritable*."

Singer mopped his brow. "I get pretty excited, talking about this stuff," he said, grinning. "I never dreamed I could change the world when I was teaching at CalTech. X-FLU made me believe in God again, it really did." He cleared his throat.

"We're very close, Guy. But there's one small problem. When we insert the X-FLU gene into the ordinary flu virus, it turns the ordinary virus virulent. Infinitely more virulent. And brutally contagious. Instead of being an innocuous messenger, the protein coat of the virus seems to mimic a hormone that stimulates the overproduction of cerebrospinal fluid. What you saw in the Fever Tank was the virus's effect on a chimpanzee. We don't quite know what it will do to a human being, but we know it won't be pleasant." He stood up and moved to a nearby window.

"Your job is to redesign the viral coat of the X-FLU 'messenger' virus. To render it harmless. To allow it to infect its human host without killing it, so that it can transport the X-FLU gene into human DNA."

Carson opened his mouth to speak, then shut it abruptly. He suddenly understood why Scopes had plucked him out of the mass of GeneDyne talent. Until Fred Peck had set him to doing make-work, his specialty had been altering the protein shells that surround a virus. He knew that the protein coat of a virus could be changed or attenuated using heat, various enzymes, radiation, even through the growing of different strains. He'd done it all himself. There were many ways to neutralize a virus.

"It sounds like a straightforward problem," he said.

"It should be. But it isn't. For some reason, no matter what you do, the virus always mutates back to its deadly form. When Burt was working on it, he must have inoculated an entire colony of chimps with supposedly safe strains of the X-FLU virus. Each time, the virus reverted, and, well, you've seen the grim result. Sudden cerebral edema. Burt was a brilliant scientist. If it wasn't for him, we'd have never been able to get PurBlood, our artificial blood product, stabilized and out the door. But the X-FLU problem drove him—" Singer paused. "He couldn't take the pressure."

"I can see why people avoid the Fever Tank," Carson said.

"It's horrible. And I have grave misgivings about using the chimps. But when you consider the benefits to humanity . . ." Singer fell silent, looking out over the landscape.

"Why the secrecy?" Carson finally asked.

"Two reasons. We believe that at least one other drug company is working along similar lines of research, and we don't want to tip our hand prematurely. But more importantly, there are a lot of people out there afraid of technology. I don't really blame them. With nuclear weapons, radiation, Three Mile Island and Chernobyl—they're suspicious. And they don't like the idea of genetic engineering." He turned toward Carson. "Let's face it, what we're talking about is a permanent alteration in the human genome. That could be *very* controversial. And if people object to genetically altered veggies, what are they going to make of this? We face the same problem with PurBlood. So we want to have X-FLU ready to go when it's announced to the world. That way, opposition won't have time to develop. People will see that the benefits far outweigh any irrational outcry of fear from a small segment of the public."

"That segment can be pretty vocal." Carson had sometimes passed groups of demonstrators outside the GeneDyne gates on his way to and from work.

"Yes. You have people out there like Charles Levine. You know his Foundation for Genetic Policy? Very radical organization, out to destroy genetic engineering in general and Brent Scopes in particular."

Carson nodded.

"They were friends in college, Levine and Scopes. God, that's quite a story. Remind me to tell you what I know of it someday. Anyway, Levine is a bit unbalanced, a real Don Quixote. Rolling back scientific progress has become his goal in life. It's gotten worse since the death of his wife, I'm told. And he's carried out a twenty-year vendetta against Brent Scopes. Unfortunately, there are many in the media who actually listen to him and print his garbage." He stepped away from the window. "It's much easier to tear something down than build it up, Guy. Mount Dragon is the safest genetic-engineering lab in the world. No one, and I mean *no* one, is more interested in the safety of his employees and his products than Brent Scopes."

Carson almost mentioned that Charles Levine had been one of his undergraduate professors, but thought better of it. Maybe Singer already knew. "So you want to present the X-FLU therapy as a fait accompli. And that's the reason for the rush?"

"That's partly the reason." Singer hesitated, then continued. "Actually, the truth is that X-FLU is very important to GeneDyne. In fact, it's critical. Scopes's corn royalty patent—GeneDyne's financial bedrock—expires in a matter of weeks."

"But Scopes only turns forty this year," Carson said. "The patent can't be that old. Why doesn't he just renew it?"

Singer shrugged. "I don't know all the details. I just know it's expiring, and it can't be renewed. When that happens, all those royalties will cease. PurBlood won't see distribution for a couple of months, and it will take years to amortize the cost of R and D anyway. Our other new products are still stuck undergoing the approval process. If X-FLU doesn't come through soon, GeneDyne will have to cut its generous dividend. That would have a catastrophic effect on the stock price. Your nest egg and mine."

He turned, beckoned. "Come over here, Guy," he said.

Carson walked to where Singer was standing. The window offered a sweeping view of the Jornada del Muerto desert, which stretched toward the horizon, dissolving in a firestorm of light where the sky met the earth. To the south Carson could barely make out the rubble of what looked like an ancient Indian ruin, several ragged walls poking above the drifted sand.

Singer placed a hand on Carson's shoulder. "These matters shouldn't be of any concern to you right now. Think about the potential that lies just beneath our fingertips. The average doctor, if he's lucky, may save hundreds of lives. A medical researcher may save thousands. But you, me, GeneDyne—we're going to save millions. Billions."

He pointed toward a low range of mountains to the northeast, rising above the bright desert like a series of dark teeth. "Fifty years ago, mankind exploded the first atomic device at the foot of those mountains. The Trinity Site is a mere thirty miles from here. That was the dark side of science. Now, half a century later, in this same desert, we have the chance to redeem science. It's really as simple and as profound as that."

His grip tightened. "Guy, this is going to be the greatest adventure of your lifetime. I think I can guarantee that."

They stood looking out over the desert, and as he stared, Carson could feel its vast intensity, a feeling almost religious in its force. And he knew Singer was right.

Carson rose at five-thirty. He swung his feet over the side of the bed and looked out the open window toward the San Andres Mountains. The cool night air flowed in, bringing with it the intense stillness of the predawn morning. He breathed deeply. In New Jersey, it was all he could do to drag himself out of bed at eight o'clock. Now, on his second morning in the desert, he was already back on his old schedule.

He watched as the stars disappeared, leaving only Venus in the cloudless eastern sky. The peculiar green color of the desert sunrise crept into the sky, then faded to yellow. Slowly, the outlines of plants emerged from the indistinct blueness of the desert floor. The wiry tangles of witch mesquite and the tall clumps of tobosa grass were widely scattered; life in the desert, Carson thought, was a solitary, uncrowded affair.

His room was sparsely but comfortably furnished: bed, matching sofa and chair, oversized desk, bookshelves. He showered, shaved, and dressed in white scrubs, feeling alternately excited and apprehensive about the day ahead.

He'd spent the previous afternoon being processed into the Mount Dragon workforce: filling out forms, getting voice-printed and photographed, and undergoing the most extensive physical he'd ever experienced. The site doctor, Lyle Grady, was a thin, small man with a reedy voice. He'd barely smiled as he typed notes into his terminal. After a brief dinner with Singer, Carson had turned in early. He wanted to be well rested.

The workday at GeneDyne began at eight o'clock. Carson did not eat breakfast—a holdover from the days when his father roused him early and made him saddle his horse in the dark—but he found his way to the cafeteria, where he grabbed a quick cup of coffee before heading toward his new lab. The cafeteria was deserted, and Carson remembered a remark Singer had made at dinner the night before. "We eat big dinners around here," he'd said. "Breakfast and lunch aren't too popular. Something about working in the Fever Tank that really curbs your appetite."

People were suiting up quickly and silently when Carson arrived at the Fever Tank. Everyone turned to look at the new arrival, some friendly, some frankly curious, some non-committal. Then Singer appeared in the ready room, his round face smiling broadly.

"How'd you sleep?" he asked, giving Carson a friendly pat on the back.

"Not bad," Carson said. "I'm anxious to get started."

"Good. I want to introduce you to your assistant." He looked around. "Where's Susana?"

"She's already inside," said one of the technicians. "She had to go in early to check some cultures."

"You're in Lab C," Singer said. "Rosalind showed you the way, right?"

"More or less," Carson said, pulling the bluesuit out of his locker.

"Good. You'll probably want to start by going over Frank Burt's lab notes. Susana will see that you have everything you need."

Completing the dressing procedure with Singer's help, Carson followed the others into the chemical showers, then again entered the warren of narrow corridors and hatches of the Biosafety Level-5 lab. Once again, he found it difficult to get used to the constricting suit, the reliance on air tubes. After a few wrong turns he found himself in front of a metal door marked LABORATORY C.

Inside, a bulky, suited figure was bent over a bioprophylaxis table, sorting through a stack of petri dishes. Carson pressed one of the intercom buttons on his suit.

"Hi. Are you Susana?"

The figure straightened up.

"I'm Guy Carson," he continued.

A small sharp voice crackled over the intercom. "Susana Cabeza de Vaca."

They clumsily shook hands.

"These suits are a pain in the butt," de Vaca said irritably. "So you're Burt's replacement."

"That's right," said Carson.

She peered into his visor. "*Hispano?*" she asked.

"No, I'm an Anglo," Carson replied, a little more hastily than he'd intended.

There was a pause. "Hmm," de Vaca said, looking at him intently. "Well, you sure *sound* like you could be from around here, anyway."

"I grew up in the Bootheel."

"I knew it! Well, Guy, you and I are the only natives here."

"You're a New Mexican? When did you come?" Carson asked.

"I got here about two weeks ago, transferred from the Albuquerque plant. I was originally assigned to Medical, but now I'll be replacing Dr. Burt's assistant. She left a few days after he did."

"Where're you from?" Carson asked.

"A little mountain town called Truchas. About thirty miles north of Santa Fe."

"Originally, I mean."

There was another pause. "I was born in Truchas," she said.

"Okay," Carson said, surprised by her sharp tone.

"You meant, when did we swim the Rio Grande?"

"Well, no, of course not. I've always had a lot of respect for Mexicans—"

"Mexicans?"

"Yes. Some of the best hands on our ranch were Mexican, and growing up I had a lot of Mexican friends—"

"My family," de Vaca interrupted frostily, "came to *America* with Don Juan de Oñate. In fact, Don Alonso Cabeza de Vaca and his wife almost died of thirst crossing this very desert. That was in 1598, which I'm sure was a lot earlier than when your redneck dustbowl family settled in the Bootheel. But I'm deeply touched you had Mexican friends growing up."

She turned away and began sorting through petri dishes again, typing the numbers into a PowerBook computer.

Jesus, thought Carson, *Singer wasn't kidding when he said everyone here was stressed.* "Ms. de Vaca," he said, "I hope you understand I was just trying to be friendly."

Carson waited. De Vaca continued to sort and type.

"Not that it matters, but I don't come from some dustbowl family. My ancestor was Kit Carson, and my great-grandfather homesteaded the ranch I grew up on. The Carsons have been in New Mexico for almost two hundred years."

"Colonel Christopher Carson? Well, whaddya know," she said, not looking up. "I once wrote a college paper on Carson. Tell me, are you descended from his Spanish wife or his Indian wife?"

There was a silence.

"It's got to be one or the other," she continued, "because you sure don't look like a white man to me." She stacked the petri dishes and squared them away, sliding them into a stainless-steel slot in the wall.

"I don't define myself by my racial makeup, Ms. de Vaca," Carson said, trying to keep an even tone.

"It's *Cabeza* de Vaca, not 'de Vaca,' " she responded, beginning to sort another stack.

Carson jabbed angrily at his intercom switch. "I don't care if it's Cabeza or Kowalski. I'm not going to take this kind of rude shit from you or that walking chuck wagon Rosalind or anyone else."

There was a momentary silence. Then de Vaca began to laugh. "Carson? Look at the two buttons on your intercom panel. One is for private conversation over a local channel, and one is for global broadcast. Don't get them mixed up again, or everyone in the Fever Tank will hear what you're saying."

There came a hiss on the intercom. "Carson?" Brandon-Smith's voice sounded. "I just want you to know I heard that, you bowlegged asswipe."

De Vaca smirked.

"Ms. *Cabeza* de Vaca," said Carson, fumbling with the intercom buttons. "I just want to get my job done. Got that? I'm not interested in petty squabbling or in sorting out your identity problem. So start acting like an assistant and show me how I can access Dr. Burt's lab notes."

There was an icy pause.

"Right," de Vaca said at last, pointing to a gray laptop stored in a cubbyhole near the entry hatch. "That PowerBook was Burt's. Now it's yours. If you want to see his entries, the network jacks are in that receptacle by your left elbow. You know the rules about notes, don't you?"

"You mean the pencil-and-paper directive?" Back in New Jersey, GeneDyne had a policy of discouraging the recording of any information except into company computers.

"They take it a step further here," de Vaca said. "No hard copy of *any* kind. No pens, pencils, paper. All test results, all lab work, *everything* you do and think, has to be recorded in your PowerBook and uploaded to the mainframe at least once a day. Just leaving a note on someone's desk is enough to get you fired."

"What's the big deal?"

De Vaca shrugged inside the confines of her suit. "Scopes likes to browse through our notes, see what we're up to, offer suggestions. He roams company cyberspace all night long from Boston, poking and prying into everyone's business. The guy never sleeps."

Carson sensed a note of disrespect in her voice. Turning on the laptop and plugging the network cable into the wall jack, he logged on, then let de Vaca show him where Burt's files were kept. He typed a few brief commands—annoyed at the pudgy clumsiness of his gloved fingers—and waited while the files were copied to the laptop's hard disk. Then he loaded Burt's notes into the laptop's word processor.

February 18. First day at lab. Briefed by Singer on PurBlood with other new arrival, R. Brandon-Smith. Spent afternoon in library, studying precedents for encapsulating naked hemoglobin. The problem, as I see it, is essentially one of . . .

"You don't want that stuff," de Vaca said. "That's the last project, before I came. Page ahead until you get to X-FLU."

Carson scrolled through three months' worth of notes, at last locating where Burt had completed work on GeneDyne's artificial blood and begun laying the groundwork for X-FLU. The story unfolded in terse, businesslike entries: a brilliant scientist, fresh from the triumph of one project, launching immediately into the next. Burt had used his own filtration process—a process that had made him a famous name within GeneDyne—to synthesize PurBlood, and his optimism and enthusiasm shone through clearly. After all, it had seemed a fairly simple task to neutralize the X-FLU virus and get on with human testing.

Day after day Burt worked on various angles of the problem: computer-modeling the protein coat; employing various enzymes, heat treatments, and chemicals; moving from one angle of attack to another with rapidity. Scattered liberally throughout the notes were comments from Scopes, who seemed to peruse Burt's work several times a week. The computer had also captured many on-line typed "conversations" between Scopes and Burt. As he read these exchanges, Carson found himself admiring Scopes's understanding of the technical aspects of his business, and envying Burt's easy familiarity with the GeneDyne CEO.

Despite Burt's ceaseless energy and brilliant attack, however, nothing seemed to work. Altering the protein capsule around the flu virus itself was an almost trivial matter. Each time, the coat remained stable in vitro, and Burt would then move toward an in vivo test—injecting the altered virus into chimpanzees. Each time, the animals lived for a while without obvious symptoms, then suddenly died hideous deaths.

Carson scrolled through page after page in which an increasingly exasperated Burt recorded continual, inexplicable failures. Over time, the entries seemed to lose their clipped, dispassionate tone, and become more rambling and personal. Barbed comments about the scientists Burt worked with— especially Rosalind Brandon-Smith, whom he detested— began to appear.

About three weeks before Burt left Mount Dragon, the poems began. Usually ten lines or less, they focused on the hidden, obscure beauty of science: the quaternary structure of a globulin protein, the blue glow of Cerenkov radiation. They were lyrical and evocative, yet Carson found them chilling, appearing suddenly between columns of test results, unbidden, like alien guests.

Carbon, one of the poems began,

> *Most beautiful of elements.*
> *Such infinite variety,*
> *Chains, rings, branches, buckyballs, side groups,*
>   *aromatics.*
> *Your index of refraction kills shahs and speculators.*
> *Carbon.*
> *You who were with us in the streets of Saigon,*
> *You were everywhere, floating in the air*
> *Invisible in the fear and sweat,*
> *The napalm.*
>
> *Without you we are nothing.*
> *Carbon we were and carbon we shall become.*

The entries quickly grew more sporadic and disjointed as the end drew near. Carson had increasing difficulty following Burt's logic from one thought to another. Throughout, Scopes had been a constant background presence; now his comments and suggestions became more critical and sarcastic. Their exchanges developed a distinct confrontational edge: Scopes aggressive, Burt evasive, almost penitent.

> *Burt, where were you yesterday?*
>
> *I took the day off and walked outside the perimeter.*
>
> *For every day this problem isn't solved, it's costing GeneDyne one million dollars. So Dr. Burt decides to take the day off for a one-million-dollar hike. Charming. Everybody's waiting on you, Frank, remember? The entire project's waiting on you.*

Brent, I just can't go on day after day. I've got to have some time to think and be alone.

So what did you think about?

I thought about my first wife.

Jesus Christ, he thought about his first wife. One million bucks, Frank, to think about your fucking first wife. I could kill you, I really could.

I just couldn't work yesterday. I've tried everything, including recombinant viral vectors. The problem isn't solvable.

Frank, I really hate you for even thinking that. No problem is insoluble. That's what you said about the blood, remember? And then you solved it. You did it, Frank, think about it! And I love you for it, Frank, I do. And I know you can do it again. There's a Nobel Prize in this for you, I swear.

Tempting me with glory won't help, Brent. Money won't, either. Nothing is going to make an impossible problem possible.

Don't say that, Frank. Please. It hurts me to hear you say that word, because it's always a lie. "Impossible" is a lie. The universe is strange and vast, and anything is possible. You remind me of Alice in Wonderland. You remember that exchange between Alice and the Queen about this very subject?

No, I don't. And I don't think Alice in Wonderland is going to help me believe in the impossible.

You son of a bitch, if I hear that word again I'll come out there and kill you with my bare hands. Look, I've given you everything you need. Please, Frank, just get back in there and do it. I have faith that you can do it. Look, why don't you just start over. Start with some other host, something really improbable, like a new virus, a macrophage. Or a reovirus. Something that will let you approach things from an entirely new direction. Okay?

All right, Brent.

Several days passed with no entries at all. Then, on June 29—just a fortnight past—came a rush of writing, full of apocalyptic imagery and ominous ramblings. Several times Burt mentioned a "key factor," never explaining what it was. Carson shook his head. His predecessor had obviously gone delusional, imagining solutions his rational mind had been unable to discover.

Carson sat back, feeling the trapped sweat collecting between his shoulder blades and around his elbows. For the first time, he felt a momentary thrust of fear. How could he succeed, when a man like Burt had failed—not only failed, but lost his mind in the process? He glanced up and found de Vaca looking at him.

"Have you read this?" he asked.

She nodded.

"How . . . I mean, how do they expect me to take this over?"

"That's your problem," she responded evenly. "I'm not the one with the degrees from Harvard and MIT."

Carson spent the rest of the day rereading the early experiments, staying away from the distracting convolutions of Burt's lab notes. Toward the end of the day he began to feel more upbeat. There was a new recombinant DNA technique he had worked with at MIT that Burt hadn't been aware of. Carson diagrammed the problem, breaking it down into its parts, then further breaking down those parts until it had been separated into irreducibles.

As the day drew to a close, Carson began to sketch out an experimental protocol of his own. There was, he realized, still a lot to work with. He stood up, stretched, and watched as de Vaca plugged her notebook into the network jack.

"Don't forget to upload," she said. "I'm sure Big Brother will want to check over your work tonight."

"Thanks," said Carson, scoffing inwardly at the thought that Scopes would waste time looking over his notes. Scopes and Burt had clearly been friends, but Carson was still just a grade-three technician from the Edison office. He uploaded the day's data, stored the computer in its cubbyhole for the night, then followed de Vaca as she made the long slow trip out of the Fever Tank.

Back in the ready room, Carson had unbuckled his visor and was unzipping the lower part of his biohazard suit when he glanced over at his assistant. She had already stowed her suit and was shaking out her hair, and Carson was surprised to see not the chunky *señorita* he had imagined underneath the bluesuit, but a slender, extremely beautiful young woman with long black hair, brown skin, and a regal face with two deep purple eyes.

She turned and caught his look.

"Keep your eyes to yourself, *cabrón*," she said, "if you don't want them to end up like one of those chimps in there."

She slung her handbag over her shoulder and strode out while the others in the ready room erupted into laughter.

The room was octagonal. Each of its eight walls rose ponderously toward a groined ceiling that hung fifty feet above, softly
illuminated by invisible cove lighting. Seven walls were covered with enormous flat-panel computer screens, currently
dark. The eighth wall contained a door, flush with the wall,
small but extremely thick to accommodate the room's external soundproofing. Although the room stood sixty stories
above the Boston harbor, there were no windows and no
views. The floor was laid in rare Tanzanian *mbanga* slate. The
colors were a spectrum of muted grays, ashes, and taupes.

The exterior of the door was made of a thick, banded metal
alloy. Instead of a handle, there was an EyeDentify retinal
scanner and a FingerMatrix hand geometry reader. Next to
the door, beneath a sterilizing ultraviolet light, sat a row of
foam slippers, their sizes imprinted in large numbers on the
toes. Below an overhead camera that swiveled ceaselessly to
and fro, a large sign read, SPEAK SOFTLY AT ALL TIMES PLEASE.

Beyond lay a long, dimly lit corridor leading to a security
station and an elevator bank. On either side of the corridor,
a series of closed doors led to the security offices, kitchens,
infirmary, air-purifying electrostatic precipitators, and ser-
vants' quarters necessary to fill the various requirements of
the octagonal room's occupant.

The door closest to the octagon was open. The room inside
was paneled in cherry, with a marble fireplace, a parquet floor
covered with a Persian rug, and several large Hudson River
School paintings on the wall. A magnificent mahogany desk
stood in the center of the room, its only electronic device an
old dial telephone. A suited figure sat behind the desk, writing
on a piece of paper.

Inside the huge octagonal room itself, a spotlight was recessed into the very point of the vaulted ceiling, and it
dropped a pencil beam of pure white light down to the mid-
point of the room. Centered in the pool of light was a battered
sofa of 1970s styling. Its arms were dark with use and wifts of

stuffing protruded from the threadbare nap. Silver duct tape sealed the front edge. As ugly and frayed as it was, the sofa had one essential quality: it was extremely comfortable.

Two cheap faux-antique end tables stood guard at either side of the sofa. A large telephone and several electronic devices in black brushed metal boxes stood on one of the end tables, and a video camera, affixed to one end, was pointed toward the sofa. The other end table was bare, but it bore the legacy of innumerable greasy pizza boxes and sticky Coke cans.

In front of the sofa sat a large worktable. In contrast to the other furniture, it was breathtakingly beautiful. The top was carved from bird's-eye maple, polished and oiled to bring out its fractal perfection. The maple was surrounded by a border of lignum vitae, black and heavy, in which was inlaid a strip of oyster walnut in a complex geometric pattern. This pattern showed the *naadaa*, the sacred corn plant, which was at the heart of the religion of the ancient Anasazi Indians. The kernels of this corn had made the room's occupant a very wealthy man. A single computer keyboard lay on the table, a short remote antenna jutting from its flank.

The rest of the vast room was clinically sterile and empty, the only exception being a large musical instrument that stood perched at the periphery of the circle of light. It was a six-octave, quadruple-string pianoforte, supposedly built for Beethoven in 1820 by the Hamburg firm of Otto Schachter. The shoulders and lyre of the piano's rosewood sound box were ornately carved in a rococo scene of nymphs and water gods.

A figure in a black T-shirt, blue jeans, and beaded Sioux Indian slippers sat hunched at the piano, head drooping, motionless fingers dead on the ivory keys. For several minutes, all was still. Then the profound silence was shattered with a massive diminished-seventh chord, sforzando, resolving to a melancholy C minor: the opening bars of Beethoven's last piano sonata, Opus 111. The maestoso introduction echoed upward into the great vaulted space. The introduction evolved into the allegro con brio ed appassionato, the first motive notes filling the room with sound, drowning out the beep of an incoming video call. The movement continued, the slight figure hunched over the keyboard, his untidy hair shaking with the effort. The beep sounded again, unnoticed, and finally one massive wall screen sprang to life, revealing a mud-streaked, rain-spattered face.

The notes suddenly stopped, the sound of the piano dying away quickly. The figure rose with a curse, slamming the keyboard cover shut.

"Brent," the face called. "Are you there?"

Scopes walked over to the battered couch, flounced down on it cross-legged, and dragged the computer keyboard into his lap. He typed some commands, then looked up at the vast image on the screen.

The mud-spattered face belonged to a man currently seated inside a Range Rover. Beyond the vehicle's rain-streaked windows lay a green clearing, a fresh gash in the flank of the surrounding Cameroon jungle. The clearing was a sea of mud, churned into lunar shapes by boots and tires. Scarred tree trunks were pulled up along the edges of the clearing. A few feet from the Range Rover, several dozen cages made of pipe and hog wire were stacked into rickety piles. Furry hands and toes poked from the hog wire, and miserable childlike eyes peered out at the world.

"How you doing, Rod?" Scopes said wearily, turning to face the camera on the end table.

"The weather sucks."

"Raining here too," Scopes said.

"Yeah, but you haven't seen rain until you've—"

"I've been waiting three days to hear from you, Falfa," Scopes interrupted. "What the hell's been going on?"

The face broke into an ingratiating smile. "We had problems getting gas for the trucks. I've had a whole village out in the jungle, at a dollar a day per person, for the last two weeks. They're all rich now, and we've got fifty-six baby chimps." He grinned and wiped his nose, which only served to smear more mud across his face. Or maybe it wasn't mud.

Scopes looked away. "I want them in New Mexico in six weeks. With no more than a fifty-percent mortality rate."

"Fifty percent! That'll be tough," Falfa said. "Usually—"

"Yo, Falfa!"

"Excuse me?"

"You think that's tough? See what happens to Rodney P. Falfa if more corpses than live bodies arrive in New Mexico. Look at them, sitting out there in the goddamn rain."

There was a silence. Falfa honked and an African face appeared in the window. Falfa cracked the window a half inch, and Scopes could hear the miserable screams of the animals beyond. "Hunter mans!" Falfa was saying in pidgin. "You cover up dat beef, you hear? For every beef dat ee go die, hunter mans get dashed out one shilling."

"Na whatee?" came the response from outside the Range Rover. "Masa promise de dash of—"

"Do it." Falfa snugged the window shut, locking out the man's complaints, and turned to Scopes with another grin. "How's that for prompt action?"

Scopes looked at him coldly. "Piss-poor. Don't you think those chimps need to be fed, too?"

"Right!" Falfa honked the horn again. Scopes pressed a button, cutting off the video communication, and sat back on the sofa. He typed a few more commands, then stopped. Suddenly, with another curse, he winged the keyboard angrily across the room. The keyboard hit the wall with a sharp cracking sound. A single key, jarred loose, rattled across the polished floor. Scopes flopped back onto the sofa, motionless.

A moment later the door hissed open and a tall man of perhaps sixty appeared. He was dressed in a charcoal suit, with a starched white shirt, wing-tip shoes, and a blue silk tie. Between graying temples, two fine gray eyes framed a small, chiseled nose.

"Is everything all right, Mr. Scopes?" the figure asked.

Scopes gestured toward the keyboard. "The keyboard is broken."

The figure smiled ironically. "I take it Mr. Falfa finally checked in."

Scopes laughed, rubbing his unruly hair. "Correct. These animal collectors are the lowest form of human being I've encountered. It's a shame the Mount Dragon appetite for chimps seems insatiable."

Spencer Fairley inclined his head. "I wish you would let somebody else handle these details, sir. You seem to find them so upsetting."

Scopes shook his head. "This project is too important."

"If you say so, sir. Can I get you anything else besides a new keyboard?"

Scopes waved his hand absently. As Fairley turned to go, Scopes suddenly spoke again. "Wait. There were two things, after all. Did you see the Channel Seven news last night?"

"As you know, sir, I don't care for television or computers."

"You crusty Beacon Hill fossil," Scopes said affectionately. Fairley was the only man in the company Scopes would allow to call him sir. "What would I do without you to show me how the electronically illiterate half live? Anyway, last night on Channel Seven they discussed a twelve-year-old girl who has leukemia. She wanted to go to Disneyland before she died. It's the usual exploitative crap we're fed on the evening news. I forget her name. Anyway, will you arrange for her and her family to go to Disneyland, private jet, all expenses paid, best hotels, limos, the works? And please, keep it strictly anonymous. I don't want that bastard Levine mocking me again, twisting it into something it isn't. Give them some money to help with the medical bills, say, fifty thousand. They seemed like nice people. It must be hell to have a kid die of leukemia. I can't even imagine it."

"Yes, sir. That's very kind of you sir."

"Remember what Samuel Johnson said: 'It is better to live rich, than die rich.' And remember: it's to be *anonymous*. I don't even want *them* to know who did it. All right?"

"Understood."

"And another thing. When I was in New York yesterday, this fucking cab nearly ran me over in a crosswalk. Park Avenue and Fiftieth."

Fairley's expression was inscrutable. "That would have been unfortunate."

"Spencer, you know what I like about you? You're so droll that I can never tell whether I'm being insulted or complimented. Anyway, the hack number on top of the cab was four-A-five-six. Get his medallion pulled, will you? I don't want the son of a bitch running over some grandmother."

"Yes, sir." As the small door hissed shut with a muffled click, Scopes stood up and made his way thoughtfully back toward the piano.

A loud tone sounded in his helmet, and Carson jerked up from his terminal screen with a start. Then he relaxed again. It was only his third day on-site; he assumed that eventually he'd get used to the 6 P.M. reminder. He stretched, looked around the lab. De Vaca was in pathology; he might as well wrap up for the day. He laboriously typed a few paragraphs into his laptop, detailing the day's events. As he connected the laptop to the network link and uploaded his files, he found himself unable to suppress a sense of pride. Two days of lab-work, and he knew exactly what had to be done. Familiarity with the latest lab techniques was the advantage he'd needed. Now, all that remained was to carry it out.

Then he hesitated. A message was flashing at the bottom of the screen.

> **John Singer@Exec.Dragon is paging.**
> **Press the command key to chat.**

Hurriedly, Carson went into chat mode and paged Singer. He hadn't been plugged into the network all day; there was no telling when Singer had originally requested to speak with him.

> **John Singer@Exec.Dragon ready to chat.**
> **Press the command key to continue.**

> **How are you, Guy?** came the words on Carson's screen.

> **Good,** Carson typed. **Just got your page now.**

> **You should get in the habit of leaving your laptop connected to the network the entire time you're in the lab. You might mention that to Susana, too. Could you spare me a few moments after dinner? There's something we need to discuss.**

> **Name the time and place,** Carson typed.

How about nine o'clock in the canteen? I'll see you then.

Wondering what Singer wanted, Carson issued the network logoff. The computer responded:

**One new message remains unread.
Do you want to read it now (Y/N)?**

Carson switched to GeneDyne's electronic messaging system and brought up the message. *Probably an earlier message from Singer, wondering where I am*, he thought.

> *Hello, Guy. Glad to see you in place and at work.*
> *I like what you've done with the protocol. It has the feel of a winner. But remember something: Frank Burt was the best scientist I've ever known, and this problem bested him. So don't get cocky on me, okay?*
> *I know you're going to come through for Gene-Dyne, Guy.*
> *Brent.*

A few minutes after nine, Carson helped himself to a Jim Beam from the canteen bar and stepped through the sliding glass doors onto the observation deck beyond. Early in the evening, the canteen—with its cozy coffeehouse atmosphere and its backgammon and chess boards—was a favorite hangout for lab people. But now it was almost deserted. The wind had died down, and the heat of the day had abated. The deck was empty, and he chose a seat away from the white expanse of the building. He savored the smoky flavor of the bourbon—drunk without ice, a taste he developed when he drank his dinner cocktail from a hip flask in front of a fire out on the ranch—and watched the last of the sun set over the distant Fra Cristóbal Mountains. To the northeast and the east the sky still held traces of a rich shade of pearly rose.

He tilted his head backward and closed his eyes a moment, inhaling the pungent smell of the desert air, chilled by sunset: a mixture of creosote bush, dust, and salt. Before he'd gone East, he had only noticed the odor after a rain. But now it was like new to him. He opened his eyes again and stared at the vast dome of night sky, smoking with the brilliance of stars already in place above his head: Scorpio clear and bright in the south, Cygnus overhead, the Milky Way arching over all.

The bewitching fragrance of the night desert combined with the familiar stars brought a hundred memories crowding back. He sipped his drink meditatively.

He brushed the thoughts away at the sound of footsteps. They came from one of the walkways beyond the canteen, and Carson assumed it was Singer, approaching from the residency compound. But the figure that came silently out of the dusk was not short and squat, but well over six feet, and impeccably dressed in a tailored suit. A safari hat sat incongruously atop hair that looked iron gray in the cold beam of the sodium walkway lights. A ponytail descended between his shoulder blades. If the man saw Carson he gave no sign, continuing past the balcony toward the limestone central plaza.

There was a thump behind him, then Carson heard Singer's voice. "Beautiful sunset, isn't it?" the director said. "Much as I hate the days here, the nights make up for it. Almost." He stepped forward, a mug of coffee steaming in one hand.

"Who's that?" Carson nodded toward the retreating figure.

Singer looked out into the night and scowled. "That's Nye, the security director."

"So that's Nye," Carson said. "What's his story? I mean, he looks a little strange out here, with that suit-and-pith-helmet getup."

"Strange isn't the word. I think he looks ridiculous. But I advise you not to tangle with him." Singer drew up a seat next to Carson and sat down. "He used to work at the Windermere Nuclear Complex, in the UK. Remember that accident? There was talk of employee sabotage, and somehow Nye, as security director, became the scapegoat. Nobody wanted to touch him after that, and he had to find work in the Middle East somewhere. But Brent has peculiar ideas about people. He figured that the man, always a stickler, would be extra careful after what happened, so he hired him for GeneDyne UK. He proved to be such a fanatic about security that Scopes brought him over here at start-up. Been here ever since. Never leaves. Well, that's not true, exactly. On the weekends, he often disappears for long rides into the desert. Sometimes he even stays out overnight, a real no-no around here. Scopes knows, of course, but he doesn't seem to mind."

"Maybe he likes the scenery," said Carson.

"Frankly, he gives me the willies. During the week, all the security personnel live in fear of him. Except Mike Marr, his assistant. They seem to be friends. But I suppose a facility such as ours needs a Captain Bligh for a security director."

He looked at Carson for a moment. "I guess you riled up Rosalind Brandon-Smith pretty good."

Carson glanced at Singer. The director was smiling again and there was a gleam of good humor in his eye.

"I pushed the wrong button on my intercom," said Carson.

"So I gather. She filed a complaint."

Carson sat up. "A complaint?"

"Don't worry," Singer said, lowering his voice, "you've just joined a club that includes me and practically everyone else here. But formality requires that we discuss it. This is my version of calling you on the carpet. Another drink?" He winked. "I should mention, though, that Brent places a high value on team harmony. You might want to apologize."

"*Me?*" Carson felt his temper rising. "I'm the one that should be filing a complaint."

Singer laughed and held up a hand. "Prove yourself first, then you can file all the complaints you want." He got up and walked to the balcony railing. "I suppose you've looked through Burt's lab journal by now."

"Yesterday morning," said Carson. "It was quite a read."

"Yes, it was," said Singer. "A read with a tragic end. But I hope it gave you a sense of what kind of man he was. We were close. I read through those notes after he left, trying to figure out what happened." Carson could hear a real sadness in his voice.

Singer sipped his coffee, looked out over the expanse of desert. "This is not a normal place, we're not normal people, and this is not a normal project. You've got world-class geneticists, working on a project of incalculable scientific value. You'd think people would only be concerned with lofty things. Not so. You wouldn't believe the kind of sheer pettiness that can go on here. Burt was able to rise above it. I hope you will, too."

"I'll do my best." Carson thought about his temper; he'd have to control it if he was going to survive at Mount Dragon. Already he'd made two enemies without even trying.

"Have you heard from Brent?" Singer asked, almost casually.

Carson hesitated, wondering if Singer had seen the e-mail message sent to him.

"Yes," he said.

"What did he say?"

"He gave me a few encouraging words, warned me against being cocky."

"Sounds like Brent. He's a hands-on CEO, and X-FLU is his pet project. I hope you like working in a glass house." He took another sip of coffee. "And the problem with the protein coat?"

"I think I'm just about there."

Singer turned, gave him a searching glance. "What do you mean?"

Carson stood up and joined the director at the railing. "Well, I spent yesterday afternoon making my own extrapolations from Dr. Burt's notes. It was much easier to see the patterns of success and failure once I'd separated them from the rest of his writings. Before he lost hope and began simply going through the motions, Dr. Burt was very close. He found the active receptors on the X-FLU virus that make it deadly, and he also found the gene combination that codes for the polypeptides causing the overproduction of cerebrospinal fluid. All the hard work was done. There's a recombinant-DNA technique I developed for my dissertation that uses a certain wavelength of far-ultraviolet light. All we have to do is clip off the deadly gene sequences with a special enzyme that's activated by the ultraviolet light, recombine the DNA and it's done. All succeeding generations of the virus will be harmless."

"But it's not done yet," said Singer.

"I've done it a hundred times at least. Not on this virus, of course, but on others. Dr. Burt didn't have access to this technique. He was using an earlier gene-splicing method that was a little crude by comparison."

"Who knows about this?" Singer asked.

"Nobody. I've only roughed out the protocol, I haven't

actually tested it yet. But I can't think of a reason why it wouldn't work."

The director was staring at him, motionless. Then he suddenly came forward, taking Carson's right hand in both of his own and crushing it in an enthusiastic handshake. "This is fantastic!" he said excitedly. "Congratulations."

Carson took a step backward and leaned against the railing, a little embarrassed. "It's still too early for that," he said. He was beginning to wonder whether he should have mentioned his optimism to Singer quite so soon.

But Singer wasn't listening. "I'll have to e-mail Brent right away, give him the news," he said.

Carson opened his mouth to protest, then shut it again. Just that afternoon, Scopes had warned him against being cocky. But he knew instinctively that his procedure would work. His dissertation research had proved it countless times. And Singer's enthusiasm was a welcome change from Brandon-Smith's sarcasm and de Vaca's brusque professionalism. Carson found himself liking Singer, this balding, fat, good-humored professor from California. He was so unbureaucratic, so refreshingly frank. He took another swig of the bourbon and glanced around the balcony, his eye lighting on Singer's old Martin guitar. "You play?" he asked.

"I try," said Singer. "Bluegrass, mostly."

"So that's why you asked about my banjo," Carson said. "I got hooked listening to performances in Cambridge coffee-houses. I'm pretty awful, but I enjoy mangling the sacred works of Scruggs, Reno, Keith, the other banjo gods."

"I'll be damned!" said Singer, breaking into a smile. "I'm working through the early Flatt and Scruggs stuff myself. You know, 'Shuckin' the Corn,' 'Foggy Mountain Special,' that kind of thing. We'll have to massacre a few of them together. Sometimes I sit out here while the sun sets and just pick away. Much to everyone's dismay, of course. That's one reason the canteen is so deserted this time of the evening."

The two men stood up. The night had deepened and a chill had crept into the air. Beyond the balcony railing, Carson could hear sounds from the direction of the residency compound: footsteps, scattered snatches of conversation, an occasional laugh.

They stepped into the canteen, a cocoon of light and warmth in the vast desert night.

Charles Levine pulled up in front of the Ritz Carlton, his 1980 Ford Festiva backfiring as he downshifted beside the wide hotel steps. The doorman approached with insolent slowness, making no secret of the fact that he found the car—and whoever was inside it—distasteful.

Unheeding, Charles Levine stepped out, pausing on the red-carpeted steps to pick a generous coating of dog hairs off his tuxedo jacket. The dog had died two months ago, but his hairs were still everywhere in the car.

Levine ascended the steps. Another doorman opened the gilt glass doors, and the sounds of a string quartet came floating graciously out to meet him. Entering, Levine stood for a moment in the bright lights of the hotel lobby, blinking. Then, suddenly, a group of reporters was crowding around him, a barrage of flashbulbs exploding from all sides.

"What's this?" Levine asked.

Spotting him, Toni Wheeler, the media consultant for Levine's foundation, bustled over. Elbowing a reporter aside, she took Levine's arm. Wheeler had severely coiffed brown hair and a sharply tailored suit, and she looked every inch the public-relations professional: poised, gracious, ruthless.

"I'm sorry, Charles," she said quickly, "I wanted to tell you but we couldn't find you *anywhere*. There's some extremely important news. GeneDyne—"

Levine spotted a reporter he recognized, and his face broke into a big smile. "Evening, Artie!" he cried, shrugging away from Wheeler and holding up his hands. "Glad to see the Fourth Estate so active. One at a time, please! And Toni, tell them to cut the music for a moment."

"Charles," Wheeler said urgently, "please listen. I've just learned that—"

She was drowned out by the reporters' questions.

"Professor Levine!" one person began. "Is it true—"

"*I* will choose the questioners," Levine broke in. "Now, all of you be quiet. You," he said, pointing to a woman in front. "You start."

"Professor Levine," the reporter called out, "could you elaborate on the accusations about GeneDyne made in the last issue of *Genetic Policy*? It's being said that you have a personal vendetta against Brentwood Scopes—"

Wheeler suddenly spoke up, her voice cutting through the air like ice. "One moment," she said crisply. "This press conference is about the Holocaust Memorial award Professor Levine is about to receive, not about the GeneDyne controversy."

"Professor, please!" cried a reporter, unheeding.

Levine pointed at someone else. "You, Stephen, you shaved off that magnificent mustache. An aesthetic miscalculation on your part."

A ripple of laughter went through the crowd.

"Wife didn't like it, Professor. It tickled the—"

"I've heard enough, thank you." There was more laughter. Levine held up his hand.

"Your question?"

"Scopes has called you—and I quote—'a dangerous fanatic, a one-man inquisition against the medical miracle of genetic engineering.' Do you have any comment?"

Levine smiled. "Yes. Mr. Scopes has always had a way with words. But that's all it is. Words, full of sound and fury . . . You all know how that line ends."

"He also said that you are trying to deprive countless people of the medical benefits of this new science. Like a cure for Tay-Sachs disease, for example."

Levine held up his hand again. "That is a more serious charge. I'm not necessarily against genetic engineering. What I am against is *germ-cell therapy*. You know the body has two kinds of cells, somatic cells and germ cells. Somatic cells die with the body. Germ cells—the reproductive cells—live forever."

"I'm not sure I understand—"

"Let me finish. With genetic engineering, if you alter the DNA of a person's somatic cells, the change dies with the body. But if you alter the DNA of someone's germ cells—in other words, the egg or sperm cells—the change will be inherited by that person's children. *You've altered the DNA of the human race forever.* Do you understand what that means? Germ-cell changes are passed along to future generations. This is an attempt to alter what it is that makes us human. And there are reports that this is what GeneDyne is doing at their Mount Dragon facility."

"Professor, I'm still not sure I understand why that would be so bad—"

Levine threw up his hands, throwing his bow tie seriously askew. "It's Hitler's eugenics all over again! Tonight, I'm going to receive an award for the work I've done to keep the memory of the Holocaust alive. I was born in a concentration camp. My father died a victim to the cruel experiments of Mengele. I know firsthand the evils of bad science. I'm trying to prevent all of you from learning it firsthand, as well. Look, it's one thing to find a cure for Tay-Sachs or hemophilia. But GeneDyne is going further. They're out to 'improve' the human race. They're going to find ways to make us smarter, taller, better-looking. Can't you see the evil in this? This is treading where mankind was never meant to tread. It is profoundly wrong."

"But Professor!"

Levine chuckled and pointed. "Fred, I'd better let you ask a question before you pull a muscle in your armpit."

"Dr. Levine, you keep saying there is insufficient government regulation of the genetic-engineering field. But what about the FDA?"

Levine scowled impatiently, shook his head. "The FDA doesn't even require approval of most genetically engineered products. On your grocery-store shelves, there are tomatoes, milk, strawberries and, of course, X-RUST corn—all genetically engineered. Just how carefully do you suppose they've been tested? It's not much better in medical research. Companies like GeneDyne can practically do as they please. These genetic-engineering firms are putting *human* genes into pigs and rats and even bacteria! They're mixing DNA from plants and animals, creating monstrous new forms of life. At any moment they could accidentally—or deliberately—create a new pathogen capable of eradicating the human race. Genetic engineering is far and away the most dangerous thing mankind has ever done. This is infinitely more dangerous than nuclear weapons. And nobody is paying attention."

The shouts began again, and Levine pointed at a reporter near the front of the crowd. "One more question. You, Murray, I loved your article on NASA in last week's *Globe*."

"I have a question that I'm sure we're all waiting to hear the answer to. How does it feel?"

"How does what feel?"

"To have GeneDyne suing you and Harvard for two hundred million dollars and demanding the revocation of your foundation's charter."

There was a short, sudden silence. Levine blinked twice, and it dawned on everyone that Levine had not known about this development. "Two hundred million?" he asked, a little weakly.

Toni Wheeler came forward. "Dr. Levine," she whispered, "that's what I was—"

Levine looked at her briefly and put a restraining hand on her shoulder. "Perhaps it's time that everything came out, after all," he said quietly. Then he turned back to the crowd. "Let me tell you a few things you don't know about Brent Scopes and GeneDyne. You probably all know the story about how Mr. Scopes built his pharmaceutical empire. He and I were undergraduates together at U.C. Irvine. We were . . ." He paused. "Close friends. One spring break he took a solo hike through Canyonlands National Monument. He returned to school with a handful of corn kernels he'd found in an Anasazi ruin. He succeeded in germinating them. Then he made the discovery that these prehistoric kernels were immune to the devastating disease known as corn rust. He succeeded in isolating the immunity gene and splicing it into the modern corn he labeled X-RUST. It's a legendary story; I'm sure you can read all about it in *Forbes*.

"But that story isn't quite accurate. You see, Brent Scopes didn't do it alone. *We did it together*. I helped him isolate the gene, splice it into a modern hybrid. It was our joint accomplishment, and we submitted the patent together.

"But then we had a falling-out. Brent Scopes wanted to exploit the patent, make money from it. I, on the other hand, wanted to give it to the world for free. We—well, let's just say that Scopes prevailed."

"How?" a voice urged.

"That's not important," Levine said very brusquely. "The point is that Scopes dropped out of college, and used the royalty income to found GeneDyne. I refused to have anything to do with it—with the money, the company, anything. To me, it's always seemed like the worst kind of exploitation.

"But in less than three months, the X-RUST hybrid patent

will expire. In order for GeneDyne to renew it, the patent renewal must be signed by two people: myself, and Mr. Scopes. *I will not sign that patent renewal.* No amount of bribes or threats will change my mind. When it expires, the rust-resistant corn will fall into the public domain. It will become the property of the world. The massive royalties GeneDyne receives every year will cease. Mr. Scopes knows this, but I am not sure the financial markets know it. Perhaps it is time analysts took another look at the high P/E ratio of GeneDyne stock. In any case, I believe this lawsuit isn't really about my recent article on GeneDyne in *Genetic Policy*. It's Brent's way of trying to pressure me to sign that patent renewal."

There was a brief silence, and a sudden hubbub of voices.

"But Dr. Levine!" one voice sounded over the crowd. "You still haven't said what you plan to do about the suit."

For a moment, Levine said nothing. Then he opened his mouth and began to laugh; a rich, full laugh that reached to the back of the lobby. Finally, he shook his head in disbelief, took out a handkerchief, and blew his nose.

"Your response, Professor?" the reporter urged.

"I just gave you my response," said Levine, stowing the handkerchief. "And now I believe I have an award to receive." He waved to the reporters with a final smile, took Toni Wheeler's arm, and headed across the lobby toward the open doors of the banquet hall.

Carson stood before a bioprophylaxis table in Lab C. The lab was narrow and cluttered, the lighting almost painfully bright. He was rapidly learning the countless nuisances, minor and major, of working in a biohazard environment: the rashes that developed where the inside of the suit rubbed against bare skin; the inability to sit down comfortably; the muscular tension that came with hours of slow, careful movement.

Worst of all was Carson's growing feeling of claustrophobia. He had always had a touch of it—he assumed it was growing up in the open desert spaces that made him susceptible—and this was just the kind of constricted environment he couldn't stand. As he worked, the memory of his first terrified elevator ride in a Sacramento hospital kept surfacing, along with the three hours he had once spent in a subway train disabled beneath Boylston Street. The Fever Tank emergency-procedure drills were a regular reminder of the dangerous surroundings, as were the frequent mutterings about a "terminal fumble": the dreaded accident that might someday contaminate the lab and all who worked in it. At least, Carson thought, he wouldn't be confined to the Fever Tank much longer. Provided, of course, that the gene splicing worked.

And it had worked perfectly. He had done it many times before, at MIT, but this had been different. This was no dissertation experiment; he was involved with a project that could save countless lives and, perhaps, win them a Nobel Prize. And he had access to finer equipment than even the best-equipped laboratory at MIT.

It had been easy. In fact, it had been a breeze.

He murmured a few words to de Vaca, and she placed a single test tube into the bioprophylaxis chamber. At the bottom of the tube, the crystallized X-FLU virus formed a white crust. Despite the elaborate safety measures that constrained his every movement, Carson still had trouble comprehending that this thin film of white substance was terrifyingly lethal. Sliding his hands into the chamber through the rubberized armholes, he took a syringe, filled it with viral transport medium, and gently swirled the tube. The crystallized mass gently broke up and dissolved, forming a cloudy solution of live virus particles.

"Take a look," he said to de Vaca. "This is going to make us all famous."

"Yeah, right," said de Vaca. "If it doesn't kill us first."

"That's ridiculous. This is the safest lab in the world."

De Vaca shook her head. "I have a bad feeling, working with a virus this deadly. Accidents can happen anywhere."

"Like what?"

"Like what if Burt had become homicidal instead of just stressed out? He could have stolen a beaker of this shit and—well, we wouldn't be here today, I can tell you that."

Carson looked at her for a moment, thought of a reply, then shelved it. He was rapidly learning that arguments with de Vaca were always a waste of time. He uncoupled his air hose. "Let's get this to the Zoo."

Carson alerted the medical technician and Fillson, the animal handler, through the global intercom, and they started the slow journey down the narrow corridor.

Fillson met them outside the holding area, glaring at Carson morosely through his visor as if annoyed to be put to work. As the door swung open, the animals began their piteous screaming and drumming, brown hairy fingers curling from the wire mesh of the cages.

Fillson walked down the line of cages with a stick, rapping on the exposed fingers. The screaming increased, but the banging of the stick had the desired effect and all the fingers vanished back into the cages.

"Ouch," said de Vaca.

Fillson stopped and looked toward her. "Excuse me?" he asked.

"I said 'ouch.' You were hitting their fingers pretty hard."

Uh-oh, thought Carson, *here we go.*

Fillson gazed at her for a few moments, his wet bottom lip moving slightly behind his visor. Then he turned away. He reached into the cabinet and removed the same pump canister Carson had seen him use before, shuffled over to a cage, and directed its spray inside. He waited a few minutes for the sedative to take effect, then unlocked the cage door and carefully removed the groggy occupant.

Carson came forward for a look. It was a young female. She squeaked and looked up at Carson, her terrified eyes barely open, half-paralyzed by the drug. Fillson strapped her to a small stretcher and wheeled it to an adjoining chamber. Carson nodded to de Vaca, who handed the test tube, encased in a shockproof Mylar housing, to the technician.

"The usual ten cc's?" the technician asked.

"Yes," said Carson. This was his first time directing an inoculation, and he felt a strange mixture of anticipation, regret, and guilt. Moving into the next chamber, he watched as the technician shaved a small round area on the animal's forearm and swabbed it vigorously with betadine. The chimpanzee drowsily watched the process, then turned and blinked at Carson. Carson looked away.

They were joined, silently, by Rosalind Brandon-Smith, who gave Fillson a broad smile before turning, stony-faced, toward Carson. One of her responsibilities was tracking the inoculated chimps and autopsying those who died of edema. So far, Carson knew, the ratio of inoculations to deaths had been 1:1.

The chimp didn't flinch as the needle slid home.

"You realize you need to inoculate two chimps," Brandon-Smith's voice sounded in Carson's headset. "Male and female."

Carson nodded without looking at her. The female chimp was wheeled back into the Zoo, and Fillson soon returned with a male. He was even smaller, still juvenile, with an owlish, curious face.

"Jesus," said de Vaca, "it's enough to break your heart, isn't it?"

Fillson glanced at her sharply. "Don't anthropomorphize. They're just animals."

"Just animals," de Vaca murmured. "So are we, Mr. Fill-son."

"These two are going to live," said Carson. "I'm sure of it."

"Sorry to disappoint you, Carson," said Brandon-Smith, with a snort. "Even if your neutralized virus works, they'll be killed and autopsied anyway." She crossed her arms and looked at Fillson, receiving a smile in return.

Carson glanced at de Vaca. He could see an angry blush collecting on her face—a look that was becoming all too familiar to him. But she remained silent.

The technician slid the needle into the male chimp's arm and smoothly injected ten cc's of the X-FLU virus. He slipped the needle out, pressed a piece of cotton on the spot, then taped the cotton to the arm.

"When will we know?" Carson asked.

"It can take up to two weeks for the chimps to develop symptoms," said Brandon-Smith, "although it often happens more quickly. We take blood every twelve hours, and anti-bodies usually show up within one week. The infected chimps go straight into the animal-quarantine area behind the Zoo."

Carson nodded. "Will you keep me posted?" he asked.

"Certainly," said Brandon-Smith. "But if I were you, I wouldn't wait around for the results. I'd assume it was a failure and proceed accordingly. Otherwise, you're going to waste a lot of time."

She left the room. Carson and de Vaca unhooked their air hoses and followed her out the hatch and back to their work area.

"God, what an asshole," said de Vaca as they entered Lab C.

"Which one?" Carson asked. Watching the inoculations, listening to Brandon-Smith's sarcasm, had left him feeling short-tempered.

"I'm not sure we have a right to treat animals like that,"

de Vaca said. "I wonder if those tiny cages meet federal regulations."

"It may not be pleasant," Carson said, "but it's going to save millions of lives. It's a necessary evil."

"I wonder if Scopes is really interested in saving lives. It seems to me he's more into the dinero. *Mucho dinero.*" She rubbed her gloved fingers together.

Carson ignored her. If she wanted to talk this way on a monitored intercom channel and get herself fired, that was her business. Maybe his next assistant would be a little more friendly.

He brought up an image of an X-FLU polypeptide and rotated it on his computer screen, trying to think of other ways it might be neutralized. But it was hard to concentrate when he believed that he had already solved the problem.

De Vaca opened an autoclave and started removing glass beakers and test tubes, racking them at the far end of the lab. Carson peered deep into the tertiary structure of the polypeptide, made up of thousands of amino acids. *If I could cut those sulfur bonds, there,* he thought, *we might just uncurl the active side group, make the virus harmless.* But then Burt would have thought of that, too. He cleared the screen and brought up the data from his X-ray diffraction tests of the protein coat. There was nothing else left to be done. He allowed himself to think, just briefly, of the accolades; the promotion; the admiration of Scopes.

"Scopes is smart," de Vaca continued, "giving all of us stock in the company. It stifles dissent. Plays to people's greed. Everyone wants to get rich. Whenever you get a big multinational corporation like this—"

His daydream rudely punctured, Carson turned on her. "If you're so set against it," he snapped into his intercom, "why the hell are you here?"

"For one thing, I didn't know what I'd be working on. I was supposed to be assigned to Medical, but they transferred me when Burt's assistant left. For another, I'm putting my money into a mental health clinic I want to start in Albuquerque. In the barrio."

She emphasized the word *barrio*, rolling the *r*s off her tongue in rich Mexican Spanish, which Carson found even more irritating, as if she were showing off her bilingual ability. He could speak reasonable *pocho* Spanish, but he wasn't about to try it and give her an opportunity for ridicule.

"What do you know about mental health?" he asked.

"I spent two years in medical school," said de Vaca. "I was studying to be a psychiatrist."

"What happened?"

"Had to drop out. Couldn't swing it financially."

Carson thought about that for a moment. It was time to call this bitch on something. "Bullshit," he said.

There was an electric silence.

"Bullshit, *cabrón?*" She moved closer to him.

"Yes, bullshit. With a name like *Cabeza* de Vaca, you could've gotten a full scholarship. Ever heard of affirmative action?"

There was a long silence.

"I put my husband through medical school," de Vaca said fiercely. "And when it was my turn he divorced me, the *canalla*. I lost more than a semester, and when you're in medical school—" She stopped. "I don't know why I'm bothering to defend myself to you."

Carson was silent, already sorry that he'd once again allowed himself to be drawn into an argument.

"Yeah, I could've gotten a scholarship, but not because of my name. Because I got fifteens on all three sections of my MCATs. Asshole."

Carson didn't believe the perfect score, but fought to keep his mouth shut.

"So you think I'm just some poor dumb *chola* who needs a Spanish surname to get into medical school?"

Shit, Carson thought, *why the hell did I start this?* He turned back to his terminal, hoping that by ignoring her she would go away.

Suddenly he felt a hand tighten on his suit, screwing a fistful of the rubber material into a ball.

"Answer me, *cabrón.*"

Carson raised a protesting arm as the pressure on his blue-suit increased.

The enormous figure of Brandon-Smith bulked in the hatchway, and a harsh laugh barked over the intercom.

"Forgive me for interrupting you two lovebirds, but I just wanted to let you know that chimps A-twenty-two and Z-nine are back in their cages, revived and looking healthy. For now, anyway." She turned abruptly and waddled out.

De Vaca opened her mouth as if to respond. But then she relaxed her hold on his suit, stepped away, and grinned.

"Carson, you looked a little nervous there for a moment."

He looked back at her, struggling to keep in mind that the tension and nastiness that overcame people down in the Fever Tank was just a part of the job. He was beginning to see what had driven Burt crazy. If he could just keep his mind on the ultimate goal . . . in six months, one way or another, it would be over.

He turned back to the molecule, rotating it another 120 degrees, looking for vulnerabilities. De Vaca went back to racking equipment out of the autoclave. Quiet once again settled on the lab. Carson wondered, briefly, what had happened to de Vaca's husband.

Carson awoke just before dawn. He glanced blearily at the electronic calendar set into the wall beside his bed: Saturday, the day of the annual Bomb Picnic. As Singer had explained it, the Bomb Picnic tradition dated back to the days when the lab did military research. Once a year, a pilgrimage was organized to the old Trinity Site, where the first atomic bomb had been exploded in 1945.

Carson got up and prepared to brew a cup of coffee. He liked the quiet desert mornings, and the last thing he felt like doing was making small talk in the dining hall. He'd stopped drinking the insipid cafeteria coffee after three days.

He opened a cupboard and took out an enameled coffeepot, battered by years of use. Along with his old set of spurs, the tin pot was one of the few things he had brought with him to Cambridge, and one of the only possessions that remained after the bank auctioned the ranch. It was his companion of many morning campfires on the range, and he had become almost superstitiously fond of it. He turned it over in his hands. The outside was dead black, covered with a crust of fire-hardened soot a bowie knife couldn't remove. The inside was still a cheerful dark blue enamel flecked with white, with the fat dent on the side where his old horse, Weaver, had kicked it off the fire one morning. The handle was mashed, again Weaver's doing, and Carson remembered the unbearably hot day when the horse had rolled in Hueco Wash with both saddlebags on. He shook his head. Weaver had gone with the ranch, just a goose-rumped Mexican grade horse worth a couple hundred bucks, tops. Probably got his ass sent straight to the knacker's.

Carson filled the pot with water from his bathroom sink, dumped in two fistfuls of coffee grounds, and placed it on a hot plate built into a nearby console. He watched it carefully. Just before it boiled over he plucked it from the heat, poured in a little cold water to settle the grounds, and put it back on to finish. It was the very best way to make coffee—far better than the ridiculous filters, plungers, and five-hundred-dollar espresso machines everyone had used in Cambridge. And this coffee had a kick. He remembered his dad saying that the coffee wasn't done until you could float a horseshoe in it.

As he was pouring the coffee he stopped, catching his reflection in the mirror above his desk. He frowned, remembering how dubious de Vaca had looked when he'd insisted he was Anglo. In Cambridge, women had often found something exotic in his black eyes and aquiline nose. Occasionally, he'd told them about his ancestor, Kit Carson. But he never mentioned that his maternal ancestor was a Southern Ute. The fact that he still felt secretive about it, so many years removed from the schoolyard taunts of "half-breed," annoyed him.

He remembered his great-uncle Charley. Even though he was half white, he looked like a full-blood and even spoke Ute. Charley had died when Carson was nine, and Carson's memories of him were of a skinny man sitting in a rocking chair by the fire, chuckling to himself, smoking cigars and spitting bits of tobacco off his tongue into the flames. He told a lot of Indian stories, mostly about tracking lost horses and stealing livestock from the reviled Navajos. Carson could only listen to his stories when his parents weren't around; otherwise they hustled him away and scolded the old man for filling the boy's head with lies and nonsense. Carson's father did not like Uncle Charley, and often made comments about his long hair, which the old man refused to cut, saying it would reduce rainfall. Carson also remembered overhearing his father tell his mother that God had given their son "more than his share of Ute blood."

He sipped his coffee and looked out the open window, rubbing his back absently. His room was on the second floor of the residency quarters, and it commanded a view of the stables, machine shop, and perimeter fence. Beyond the fence the endless desert began.

He grimaced as his fingers hit a sore spot at the base of his back where the spinal tap had been inserted the evening before. Another nuisance of working in a Level-5 facility, he'd discovered, were the mandated weekly physical exams. Just one more reminder of the constant worry over contamination that plagued workers at Mount Dragon.

The Bomb Picnic was his first day off since arriving at the lab. He'd discovered that the inoculation of the chimps with his neutralized virus was just the beginning of his assignment. Although Carson had explained that his new protocol was the only possible solution, Scopes had insisted on two additional sets of inoculations, to minimize any chance of erroneous results. Six chimpanzees were now inoculated with X-FLU. If they survived the inoculations, the next test would be to see if they had been given immunity to the flu.

Carson watched from his window as two workmen rolled a large galvanized stock tank over to a Ford 350 pickup and began wrestling it onto the bed. The water truck had arrived early and the driver was idling in the motor pool, too lazy to shut off his engine, sending up clouds of diesel smoke. The sky was clear—the late-summer rains wouldn't begin for another few weeks—and the distant mountains glowed amethyst in the morning light.

Finishing his coffee and going downstairs, he found Singer standing by the pickup, shouting directions at the workmen. He was wearing beach sandals and Bermuda shorts. A flamboyant pastel shirt covered his generous midriff.

"I see you're ready to go," Carson said.

Singer glanced at him through an old pair of Ray-Bans. "I look forward to this all year," he said. "Where's your bathing suit?"

"Under my jeans."

"Get in the spirit, Guy! You look like you're about to round up some cattle, not spend a day at the beach." He turned back to the workmen: "We leave at eight o'clock sharp, so let's get moving. Bring up the Hummers and get them loaded."

Other scientists, technicians, and workers were drifting down to the motor pool, burdened with beach bags, towels, and folding chairs. "How did this thing ever start?" Carson asked, looking at them.

"I can't remember whose idea it was," Singer said. "The government opens the Trinity Site once a year to the public. At some point we asked if we could visit the site ourselves, and they said yes. Then someone suggested a picnic, and someone else suggested volleyball and cold beer. Then someone pointed out what a shame it was we couldn't bring the ocean along. And that's when the idea of the cattle tank came up. It was a stroke of genius."

"Aren't people worried about radiation?" Carson asked.

Singer chuckled. "There's no radiation left. But we bring along Geiger counters anyway, to reassure the nervous." He looked up at the sound of approaching motors. "Come on, you can ride with me."

Soon a dozen Hummers, their tops down, were jostling over a faint dirt track that led like an arrow toward the horizon. The water truck followed last, trailing a firestorm of dust.

After an hour of steady driving, Singer pulled the lead Hummer to a halt. "Ground zero," he said to Carson.

"How can you tell?" Carson asked, looking around at the desert. The Sierra Oscura rose to the west: dry, barren desert mountains, run through with jagged sedimentary outcrops. It was a desolate place, but no more desolate than the rest of the Jornada.

Singer pointed to a rusted girder, twisting a few feet out of the ground. "That's what was left of the tower that held the original bomb. If you look carefully, you'll see that we're in a shallow depression scooped out by the blast. Over there—" Singer pointed to a mound and some ruined bunkers "—was one of the instrument observation posts."

"Is this where we picnic?" Carson asked a little uncertainly.

"No," said Singer. "We continue another half mile. The scenery's nicer there. A little nicer, anyway."

The Hummers halted at a sandy flat devoid of brush or cactus. A single dune, anchored by a cluster of soapweed yucca, rose above the flat expanse of desert. While the workmen wrestled the stock tank off the pickup, the scientists began staking out positions in the sand, setting up chairs and umbrellas and laying out coolers. Off to one side, a volleyball net was erected. A wooden staircase was shoved up against the tank; then the water truck maneuvered up to its rim and began filling it with fresh water. Beach Boys harmonies blared from a portable stereo.

Carson stood to one side, watching the proceedings. He'd spent most of his waking hours in Lab C, and he still did not know many of the people by name. Most of the scientists were well into their tours and had been working together for close to six months. Looking around, he noticed with relief that Brandon-Smith had apparently stayed behind in the air-conditioned compound. The previous afternoon, he'd stopped by her office for an update on the chimps, and she'd practically taken his head off when he accidentally disturbed the little knickknacks she'd obsessively arranged along the edge of her desk. *Just as well*, he thought, as the unwelcome image of the scientist in her bathing suit intruded into his imagination.

Singer caught sight of him and waved him over. Two senior scientists that Carson barely knew were sitting nearby.

"Have you met George Harper?" Singer asked Carson.

Harper grinned and held out his hand. "We bumped into each other in the Fever Tank," he said. "Literally. Two biosuits passing in the night. And, of course, I heard your fetching description of Dr. Brandon-Smith." Harper was lanky, with thinning brown hair and a prominent hooked nose. He slouched in his deck chair.

Carson winced. "I was just testing the global function of my intercom."

Harper laughed. "All work stopped for five minutes while everyone shut off their own intercoms to, ah . . ." He glanced at Singer. "Cough."

"Now, George," Singer smiled. He indicated the other scientist. "This is Andrew Vanderwagon."

Vanderwagon wore a conservative bathing suit, his sallow, sunken chest looking dangerously exposed to the sunlight. He scrambled to his feet, removing his sunglasses. "How do you do," he said, standing and shaking Carson's hand. He was short, thin, straight, and fastidious, with blue eyes bleached to faded denim by the desert light. Carson had noticed him around Mount Dragon, wearing a coat and tie and black wing tips.

"I'm from Texas," Harper said, putting on a thick accent, "so I don't have to get up. We don't got no manners. Andrew here is from Connecticut."

Vanderwagon nodded in return. "Harper only gets up when a bull deposits a load at his feet."

"Hell, no," Harper said. "We just nudge it out of the way with a boot."

Carson settled in a deck chair provided by Singer. The sun was brutal. He heard several shouts, then a splash; people were climbing up the stairs and jumping into the water. As he looked around he saw Nye, the security director, sitting well off to one side and reading the *New York Times* under a golf umbrella.

"He's as odd as a gelded heifer," Harper said, following Carson's gaze. "Look at him out there in his damn Savile Row suit, and it must be a hundred degrees already."

"Why did he come?" Carson asked.

"To watch us," said Vanderwagon.

"What exactly might we do that's dangerous?" Carson asked.

Harper laughed. "Why, Guy, didn't you know? At any moment one of us might steal a Hummer, drive to Radium Springs, and sprinkle a little X-FLU into the Rio Grande. Just to hell around a bit."

Singer frowned. "That kind of talk's not funny, George."

"He's like a KGB man, always hovering," said Vanderwagon. "He hasn't left the place since '86, and I guess it's queered him. I wouldn't be surprised if he bugged our rooms."

"Doesn't he have any friends here?" Carson asked.

"Friends?" Vanderwagon said, eyebrows raising. "Not that I'm aware of. Unless you count Mike Marr. No family, either."

"What does he do all day long?"

"He struts around in that pith helmet and ponytail," said Harper. "You should see the security staff when Nye is around, bowing and bending like a pig over a nut."

Vanderwagon and Singer laughed. Carson was a little startled to see the Mount Dragon director joining in the mockery of his own security director.

Harper settled back, throwing his hands behind his head, and sighed. "So you're from these here parts," he said, nodding at Guy with his eyes half closed. "Maybe you can tell us more about the Mondragón gold."

Vanderwagon groaned.

"The what?" Carson asked.

All three turned to look at him in surprise.

"You don't know the story?" Singer asked. "And you a New Mexican!" He dove into the cooler with both hands and pulled out a fistful of beers. "This calls for a drink." He passed them around.

"Oh, no. We're not going to hear the legend *again*," Vanderwagon said.

"Carson here has never heard it," Harper protested.

"As *legend* has it," Singer began with a humorous glance at Vanderwagon, "a wealthy trader named Mondragón lived outside old Santa Fe in the late sixteen hundreds. He was accused of witchcraft by the Inquisition and imprisoned. Mondragón knew the punishment would be death, and he managed to escape with the help of his servant, Estevánico. This Mondragón had owned some mines in the Sangre de Cristo Mountains, worked by Indian slave labor. Rich mines, they say, probably gold. So when he escaped from the Inquisition, he snuck back to his hacienda, dug up the gold, packed a mule, and fled with his servant along the Camino Real. Two hundred pounds of gold, all he could safely carry on one mule. A few days into the Jornada desert the two men ran short of water. So Mondragón sent Estevánico ahead with the gourd canteen to replenish their supply, while he stayed behind with one horse and the mule. The servant found water at a spring a day's ride ahead, then galloped back. But by the time he returned to the spot where he'd left Mondragón, the man was gone."

Harper took over the story. "When the Inquisition learned what had happened, they began searching the trail. About five weeks later, right at the base of Mount Dragon, they found a horse, tied to a stake, dead. It was Mondragón's."

"At Mount Dragon?" Carson asked.

Singer nodded. "The Camino Real, the Spanish Trail, ran right through the lab grounds and around the base of Mount Dragon."

"Anyway," Harper continued, "they looked everywhere for signs of Mondragón. About fifty yards from the dead cayuse, they found his expensive doublet lying on the ground. But no matter how hard they looked, they never found Mondragón's body or the mule laden with gold. A priest sprinkled the base of Mount Dragon with holy water, to cleanse the spot of Mondragón's evil, and they erected a cross at the top of the hill. The place became known as *La Cruz de Mondragón*, the Cross of Mondragón. Later, when American traders came down the Spanish Trail, they simplified the place-name to Mount Dragon." He finished his beer and exhaled contentedly.

"I heard a lot of buried-treasure stories growing up," Carson said. "They were as common as blue ticks on a red heeler. And all equally false."

Harper laughed. "Blue ticks on a red heeler! Someone else with a sense of humor around here."

"What's a red heeler?" Vanderwagon asked.

Harper laughed louder. "Why, Andrew, you poor damned ignorant Yankee, it's a kind of dog used to herd cattle. Chases their heels, so they call it a heeler. Like when you heel a calf with a rope." He pantomimed the whirling of a lasso; then he looked at Carson. "I'm glad there's someone around here who isn't just another greenhorn."

Carson grinned. "When I was a kid, we used to go out looking for the Lost Adams Diggings. This state's supposedly got more buried gold than Fort Knox. That is, if you believe the stories."

Vanderwagon snorted. "That's the key: *if* you believe the stories. Harper's from Texas, where the leading industry is the manufacture and distribution of bull shit. And now, I think it's time for a swim." He twisted his beer bottle into the sand and stood up.

"Me too," said Harper.

"Come on, Guy!" Singer called out as he followed the scientists to the tank, pulling off his shirt as he trotted.

"In a minute," Carson said, watching them crowd up the wooden stairs and jump in, jostling each other as they did so. He finished his beer and set it aside. It seemed surreal to be sitting in the middle of the Jornada del Muerto desert, a mile from ground zero, watching several of the most brilliant biologists in the world splashing about in a cattle tank like children. But the very unreality of the place was like a drug. This was, truly, how it must have felt working on the Manhattan Project. He pulled off his jeans and shirt and lay back in his swimming trunks, closing his eyes, feeling relaxed for the first time in days.

After several minutes, the merciless heat roused him and he sat up, digging in the cooler for another beer. As he cracked it, he heard de Vaca's laugh rise above the scattered conversations. She was standing on the far side of the tank, pulling her long hair back from her face and talking to some of the technicians, her white bikini in stark contrast to her tawny skin. If she saw Carson, she gave no sign.

As he watched, Carson saw another person join de Vaca's group. The odd hitch in the walk was familiar, and Carson realized it was Mike Marr, second-in-command of security. Marr began talking to de Vaca, his head thrown back, the wide languorous grin clearly visible. Suddenly he drew closer, whispered something in de Vaca's ear. All at once, de Vaca's expression grew dark, and she pulled away roughly. Marr spoke again, and in an instant de Vaca had slapped him hard across the face. The sharp sound reached across the desert sands to Carson. Marr jerked backward, his black cowboy hat falling in the dust. As he stooped to retrieve it, de Vaca spoke quickly, a scornful curl to her lip. Though Carson could not make out exactly what she was saying to Marr, the group of technicians burst into laughter.

The look that came over Marr, however, was alarming. His eyes narrowed, and the easy, amiable expression fled his features in an instant. With great deliberation, he placed the cowboy hat back on his head, his eyes on de Vaca. Then he turned quickly on his heels and strode away from the group.

"She's a firecracker, isn't she?" Singer chuckled as he returned with the others and noticed the direction of Carson's gaze. Carson realized Singer hadn't really witnessed the little scene that had just played out. "You know, she originally came out here to work in the medical department the week before you arrived. But then Myra Resnick, Burt's assistant, left. With Susana's strong background, I thought she'd make you a perfect assistant. Hope I wasn't wrong." He tossed a small pebble into Carson's lap.

"What's this?" The pebble was green and slightly transparent.

"Atomic glass," said Singer. "The Trinity bomb fused the sand near ground zero, leaving a crust of this stuff. Most of it's gone, but once in a while you can still find a piece."

"Is it radioactive?" Carson asked, holding it gingerly.

"Not really."

Harper guffawed. "Not *really*," he repeated, clearing a water-clogged ear with the tip of his little finger. "If you plan to have children, Carson, I'd get that thing away from your gonads."

Vanderwagon shook his head. "You're a vulgar sod, Harper."

Singer turned to Carson. "They're best friends, although you'd never know it."

"How did you get started at GeneDyne, anyway?" Carson asked, tossing the pebble back to Singer.

"I was the Morton Professor of Biology at CalTech. I thought I was at the top of the profession. And then Brent Scopes came along and made me an offer." Singer shook his head at the memory. "Mount Dragon was going civilian, and Brent wanted me to take over."

"Quite a change from academia," said Carson.

"It took me a while to adjust," Singer said. "I'd always looked down on private industry. But I soon came to realize the power of the marketplace. We're doing extraordinary work here, not because we're smarter, but because we have so much more money. No university could afford to run Mount Dragon. And the potential returns are so much greater. When I was at CalTech, I was doing obscure research on bacterial conjugation. Now I'm doing cutting-edge stuff that has the potential to save millions of lives." He drained his beer. "I've been converted."

"*I* was converted," Harper said, "when I saw the kind of dough an assistant professor makes."

"Thirty thousand," said Vanderwagon, "after six or eight years of graduate education. Can you believe it?"

"I remember when I was at Berkeley," said Harper. "All my research proposals had to go through this decrepit bureaucrat, the chairman of the department. The fossilized SOB was always grousing about cost."

"Working for Brent," Vanderwagon said, "is like night and day. He understands how science operates. And how scientists work. I don't have to explain or justify anything. If I need something, I e-mail him and it happens. We're lucky to be working for him."

Harper nodded. "Damn lucky."

At least they agree on something, thought Carson.

"We're happy to have you aboard, Guy," Singer said at last, nodding and raising his beer in salute. The others followed.

"Thanks," Carson smiled broadly, thinking about the quirk of fate that had suddenly landed him amongst the pride of GeneDyne.

Levine sat in his office, the door open, listening in silent fascination to a telephone conversation his secretary Ray was having in the outer office.

"I'm sorry, baby," Ray was saying, "I swear I thought you said the *Boylston* Street Theater, not the Brattle—"

There was a silence.

"I swear, I heard you say *Boylston*. No, I was there, at the front door, waiting for you. At the Boylston Theater, of course! No wait, hold on. Baby, no—"

Ray cursed and hung up the phone.

"Ray?" Levine said.

"Yes?" Ray appeared in the door, smoothing his hair.

"There *is* no Boylston Street Theater."

Comprehension dawned on Ray's face. "Guess that's why she hung up."

Levine smiled, shaking his head. "Remember the call I got from that woman at the Sammy Sanchez show? I want you to call her back, tell her they can book me after all. I'll appear at their earliest convenience."

"Me? What about Toni Wheeler? She won't like—".

"Toni wouldn't approve. She's a stick-in-the-mud about those kinds of television shows."

Ray shrugged. "Okay, you got it. Anything else?"

Levine shook his head. "Not for now. Just work on your excuses. And shut the door, please."

Ray returned to the outer office. Levine checked his watch, picked up the telephone for the tenth time that day, and listened. This time, he heard what he had been waiting for: the dial tone had changed from the usual steady tone to a series of rapid pulses. Quickly he hung up the phone, locked the office door, and connected his computer to the wall jack. Within thirty seconds, the familiar log-in device was on his screen once again.

Well, dust my broom, if it ain't the good professor-man, came the words on his screen. **How's my mean mistreatin' papa?**

Mime, what are you talking about? Levine typed.

Aren't you a fan of Elmore James?

Never heard of him. I got your signal. What news?

Good and bad. I've spent several hours poking around the GeneDyne net. It's quite a place. Sixty K worth of terminal IDs, connected above and below. You know, satellites and dedicated land lines, fiber-optic networks for asynchronous transfer videoconferencing. The architecture is impressive. I'm something of an expert in it now, of course. I could give tours.

That's good.

Yes. The bad news is that it's built like a bank vault. Isolated-ring design, with Brent Scopes at the center. Nobody except Scopes can see beyond their own profile, and he can see everything. He's Big Brother, he can walk the system at will. To para-phrase Muddy Waters, he's got his mojo working, but it just won't work for you.

Surely that isn't a problem for the Mime, Levine typed.

Have mercy! What a thought. I can stay cloaked without much effort, sipping a few milliseconds of CPU time here, a few there. But it's a problem for YOU, professor. Setting up a secure channel into Mount Dragon is a non-trivial undertaking. It means duplicating part of Scopes's own access. And that way danger lies, professor.

Explain.

Must I spell it out? If he happens to contact Mount Dragon while you're in the channel, his own access may be blocked. Then he'll probably run a blood-

hound program back over the wire, and it'll bay up
the good professor, not Mime. ISHTTOETOOYLS.

Mime, you know I don't understand your acronyms.

"I should have thought that obvious even to one of
your lame sensibilities." You won't be able to dawdle,
professor. We'll have to keep your visits short.

What about the Mount Dragon records? Levine
typed. If I could get at those, it would speed things
up considerably.

NFW. Locked up tighter than Queen Mary's corset.

Levine took a deep breath. Mime was unreadable, unmov-
able, infuriating. Levine wondered what he would be like in
person: no doubt the typical computer hacker, a nerdy guy
with thick glasses, bad at football, no social life, onanistic
tendencies.

Why, Mime, that doesn't sound like you, he typed.

Remember me? I'm the Monsieur Rick of cyberspace: I stick my neck out for no one. Scopes is too
clever. You remember that pet project of his I was
telling you about? Apparently, he's been programming some kind of virtual world for use as a network
navigator. He gave a lecture on it at the Institute for
Advanced Neurocybernetics about three years ago.
Naturally, I broke in and stole the transcripts and
screen shots. Very girthy, very girthy indeed. Ground-
breaking use of 3-D programming. Anyway, since
then Scopes has clamped the lid down tight. Nobody

knows exactly what his program is now, or what it can do. But even back then, he was showing off some heavy shit at that lecture. Believe me, this dude is no computer-illiterate CEO. I found his private server, and was tempted to take a peek inside. But my discretion bested my curiosity. And that's unusual for me.

Mime, it's vitally important that I gain access to Mount Dragon. You know my work. You can help me to ensure a safer world.

No mind trips, my man! If there's one thing I've learned, only Mime matters. The rest of the world means no more to me than a dingleberry on a dog's ass.

Then why are you helping me at all? Remember that it was you who approached me in the first place.

There was a pause in the on-line conversation.

My reasons are my own, Mime responded. But I can guess yours. It's the GeneDyne lawsuit. Not just for money this time, is it? Scopes is trying to hit you where you live. If he succeeds, you'll lose your charter, your magazine, your credibility. You were a little hasty there with your accusations, and now you need some dirt to prove them retroactively. Tut, tut, professor.

You're only half right, Levine typed back.

Then I suggest you tell me the other half.

Levine hesitated at the keyboard.

Professor? Don't force me to remind you of the two planks our deep and meaningful phriendship is built on. One: I never do anything that will expose myself. And two: my own hidden agenda must remain hidden.

There's a new employee at Mount Dragon, Levine typed at last. A former student of mine. I think I can enlist his help.

There was another pause. I'll need his name in order to set up the channel, Mime responded at last.

Guy Carson, Levine typed.

Professor-man, came the response, you're a sentimentalist at heart. And that's a major flaw in a warrior. I doubt you'll succeed. But I shall enjoy watching you try; failure is always more interesting than success.

The screen went blank.

Carson stood impatiently in the hissing chemical shower, watching the poisonous cleansing agents run down his faceplate in yellow sheets. He tried to remind himself that the feeling of choking, of insufficient oxygen, was just his imagination. He stepped through into the next chamber and was buffeted by the chemical drying process. Another air-lock door popped open and he walked into the blinding white light of the Fever Tank. Pressing the global intercom button, he announced his arrival: "Carson in." Few if any scientists were around to hear him, but the procedure was mandatory. It was all becoming routine—but a routine he felt he would never get used to.

He sat down at his desk and turned on his PowerBook with a gloved hand. His intercom was quiet; the facility was almost deserted. He wanted to get some work done and collect whatever messages might be waiting for him before de Vaca came.

When he had finished logging on, a line popped on the screen.

GOOD MORNING, GUY CARSON.
YOU HAVE 1 UNREAD MESSAGE.

He moused the e-mail icon, and the words came rushing onto the screen.

Guy—What's the latest on the inoculations? There's nothing new in the system. Please page me so we can discuss.
Brent.

Carson paged Scopes through GeneDyne's WAN service. The Gene Dyne CEO's response was immediate, as if he had been waiting for the message.

Ciao Guy! What's going on with your chimps?

So far so good. All six are healthy and active. John Singer suggested we cut the waiting period down to one week under the circumstances. I'll discuss it with Rosalind today.

Good. Give me any updates immediately, please. Interrupt me no matter what I'm doing. If you can't find me, contact Spencer Fairley.

I will.

Guy, have you had a chance to complete the white paper on your protocol? As soon as we're sure of success, I'd like you to get it distributed internally, with an eye toward eventual publication.

I'm just waiting for some final confirmations, then I'll é-mail a copy to you.

As they chatted, more people began to arrive in the lab, and the intercom became a busy party line, each person announcing his or her arrival. "De Vaca in," he heard, and "Vanderwagon in"; then "Brandon-Smith!" loud and in-your-face, as usual; and then the murmur of other arrivals and other conversations.

De Vaca soon appeared in the hatchway, silently, and logged on to her machine. The bulky bluesuit hid the contours of her body, which was fine with Carson. He didn't need any more distractions.

"Susana, I'd like to run a GEF purification on those proteins we discussed yesterday," he said, keeping his voice as neutral as possible.

"Certainly," said de Vaca crisply.

"They're in the centrifuge, labeled M-one through M-three."

There was one thing he was glad of: de Vaca was a damn good technical assistant, maybe the best in the entire lab. A true professional—as long as she didn't lose her temper.

Carson made the final additions to the write-up that documented his procedure. It had taken him the better part of two days, and he was pleased with the result; though he thought Scopes might be a bit hasty in requesting it, he was secretly proud. Near noon, de Vaca returned with photographic strips of the gels. Carson took a look at the strips and felt another flush of pleasure: one more confirmation of imminent success.

Suddenly Brandon-Smith was in the door.

"Carson, you got a dead ape."

There was a shocked silence.

"You mean, X-FLU?" Carson said, finding his voice. It wasn't possible.

"You bet," she announced with relish, unconsciously smoothing her generous thighs with thickly gloved hands. "A pretty sight, I assure you."

"Which one?" Carson asked.

"The male, Z-nine."

"It hasn't even been a week," Carson said.

"I know. You made pretty short work of him."

"Where is he?"

"Still in the cage. Come on, I'll show you. Besides the rapidity, there are some other unusual aspects you'd better see."

Carson rose shakily and followed Brandon-Smith to the Zoo. It was impossible that the cause had been X-FLU. Something else must have happened. The thought of reporting this development to Scopes came into his head like a dull pain.

Brandon-Smith opened the hatchway to the Zoo and motioned Carson inside. They entered the room, the incessant drumming and screaming again penetrating the thick layers of Carson's suit.

Fillson sat at the far end of the Zoo at a worktable, setting some instrument. He stood up and glanced over at them. Carson thought he could detect a flicker of amusement on the handler's knobby face. He unsealed the door to the inoculation area and ushered them in, pointing upward.

Z-nine was in the topmost row, in a cage marked with a yellow-and-red biohazard label. Carson was unable to see inside the animal's cage. The other five inoculated chimps, in cages on the first and second tiers, seemed to be perfectly healthy.

"What was strange, exactly?" Carson asked, reluctant to see the damage firsthand.

"Look for yourself," said Brandon-Smith, rubbing her gloves up and down her thighs again with a slow, deliberate motion. *Unpleasant mannerism*, Carson thought. It reminded him of the habitual movements of a severely retarded person.

A metal ladder, encased entirely in white rubber, was attached to the upper rack of cages. Carson mounted it gingerly while Fillson and Brandon-Smith waited below. He peered inside the cage. The chimp lay on its back, limbs splayed in obvious agony. The animal's entire brain case had split open along the natural sutures, large folds of gray matter pushing out in several places. The bottom of the cage was awash in what Carson assumed was cerebrospinal fluid.

"Brain exploded," said Brandon-Smith unnecessarily. "Must've been a particularly virulent strain you invented there, Carson."

Carson began to descend. Brandon-Smith had her arms crossed and was looking up at him. Through her visor, he could see a faint sarcastic smile playing about her lips. He paused on the step. Something—he wasn't sure what— seemed wrong. Then he realized: a cage door on the second tier had come ajar, and three hairy fingers were curling around its frame, pushing the faceplate away.

"Rosalind!" he cried, fumbling with his intercom button. "Get away from the cages!"

She looked at him, uncomprehending. Fillson, standing next to her, glanced around in alarm. Suddenly things began to happen very quickly: a hairy arm lashed out, and there was an odd tearing noise. Carson saw the chimp's hand, strangely human, waving a swatch of rubber material. Looking toward Brandon-Smith, Carson could see, to his horror, a ragged hole in her suit, and through the hole a pair of scrubs riding over an exposed roll of fat. Across the scrubs were three parallel scratches. As he watched, blood began to well up in long crimson lines.

There was a brief, paralyzing silence.

The ape burst from its cage, shrieking with triumph at the top of its lungs, brandishing the piece of biohazard suit like a trophy. It bounded into the Zoo and out the open hatchway, disappearing down the corridor.

Brandon-Smith began to scream. With her intercom off, the sound was muffled and strange, like someone being strangled at a great distance. Fillson stood immobile, riveted in horror.

Then she found the intercom button and hysterical screams erupted into Carson's suit, so loud they saturated the system and dissolved into a roar of static. Carson, at the top of the ladder, punched his intercom to global. "Stage-two alert," he yelled over the noise. "Integrity breach, Brandon-Smith, animal-quarantine unit."

A stage-two alert. Human contact with a deadly virus. It was the thing they most feared. Carson knew there was a very strict procedure for dealing with such emergencies: lockdown, followed by quarantine. He had been through the drill time and again.

Brandon-Smith, realizing what was in store for her, disconnected her air hose and began to run.

Carson jumped off the ladder after her, stopping briefly to disconnect his own air supply, and brushed past the frozen Fillson. He caught up with her outside the exit air lock, where she was screaming and pounding on the door, unable to force it open. Lockdown had already taken place.

De Vaca came up behind him. "What happened?" he heard

her ask. A moment later, the corridor was filled with scientists.

"Open the door," Brandon-Smith screamed on the global channel. "Oh God, please, *open the door!*" She sank to her knees, sobbing.

A siren began to wail, low and monotonous. There was a sudden movement down the hall, and Carson turned quickly, craning for a glimpse over the helmets of the other scientists. Suited forms Carson knew to be security guards were appearing out of the access tube from the lower levels, moving quickly toward the mass of scientists huddled by the air lock. There were four of them, wearing red suits that looked even more bulky than the normal gear, and Carson realized they must contain extended air supplies. Though he had known there was a security substation in the lower levels of the Fever Tank, the rapidity with which the guards arrived was astonishing. Two of them held short-barreled shotguns, while the others held strange curved devices equipped with rubber handles.

Brandon-Smith's reflexes were lightning fast. She leapt up and, scattering the scientists against the sides of the corridor, plowed past the guards in an attempt to escape. One of the guards was knocked to the ground, grunting in pain. Another spun around and tackled Brandon-Smith as she was about to push past. They hit the floor heavily, Brandon-Smith screaming and clawing at the guard. As they wrestled, one of the other guards approached cautiously and pressed the end of the device he was holding to the metal ring of her visor. There was a blue flash, and Brandon-Smith jerked and lay still, her screams stopping instantly. As the intercom cleared, a welter of voices could be heard.

One of the security officers stood up, his hands fumbling over his suit in a panic. "The fat bitch ripped my suit!" Carson heard him shout. "I can't believe it—"

"Shut up, Roger," said one of the others, breathing heavily.

"No fucking way am I gonna go into quarantine. It wasn't my fault—Jesus, what the hell are you doing?"

Carson watched the other security officer level his shotgun. "Both of you are going," he said. "Now."

"Wait, Frank, you're not going to—"

The guard pumped a shell into the chamber.

"Son of a bitch, Frank, you can't do this to me," the guard named Roger wailed.

Carson saw three more security guards appear from the direction of the ready room. "Get them both to quarantine," the guard named Frank said.

Suddenly, Carson heard de Vaca's voice. "Look. She's thrown up in her suit. She might be suffocating. Get her helmet off."

"Not until we get her to quarantine," the officer said.

"The hell with that," de Vaca shouted back. "This woman is badly injured. She needs hospitalization. We've got to get her out."

The guard looked around and spotted Carson at the front of the crowd. "You! Dr. Carson!" he called. "Get your ass over here and help!"

"Guy," came de Vaca's voice, suddenly calm. "Rosalind could die if she's left in here, and you know it."

By now the few scientists remaining in the far corners of the Fever Tank had arrived and were crowding the narrow corridor, watching the confrontation. Carson stood motionless, looking from the security guard to de Vaca.

With a sudden, swift movement, de Vaca shoved the security officer aside. She bent over Brandon-Smith and lifted her head, peering into her faceplate.

Vanderwagon suddenly spoke up. "I'm for getting them out of here," he said. "We can't put them in quarantine like apes. It's inhuman."

There was a tense silence. The security officer hesitated, uncertain how to handle the confrontation with the scientists. Vanderwagon moved forward and began unbuckling Brandon-Smith's helmet.

"Sir, I order you to stand fast," the officer finally said.

"Fuck you," said de Vaca, helping Vanderwagon remove the visor, then clearing Brandon-Smith's mouth and nose of vomit. The scientist gasped once, and her eyes fluttered and rolled.

"You see that? She would have suffocated. And you'd be in deep shit." De Vaca looked at Carson. "Are you going to help us get her out?" she asked.

Carson spoke very quietly. "Susana, you know the drill. Think a moment. She may well have been exposed to the virus. She could already be contagious."

"We don't know that!" de Vaca blazed, turning to stare up at him. "It's never been demonstrated in vivo."

Another scientist stepped forward. "It could be any one of us lying there. I'll help."

Brandon-Smith was reviving from the electrical stun, streaks of vomit clinging to her generous chin, her head almost comically small in the bulky suit. "Please," Carson could hear her say. "Please. Get me out." In the distance, Carson could see another guard approaching down the corridor, carrying a shotgun.

"Don't worry, Rosalind," de Vaca replied. "That's where you're going." She looked at Carson. "You're no better than a murderer. You'd leave her here in the hands of these pigs, to die. *Hijo de puta.*"

Singer's voice broke over the intercom. "What's going on in the Fever Tank? Why haven't I been briefed? I want an immediate—"

His voice was abruptly cut off by a global override. The clipped English tones of a voice Carson knew must be Nye's crackled over the intercom.

"In a stage-two alert the security director may, at his discretion, temporarily relieve the director of command. I hereby do so."

"Mr. Nye, until I see the emergency for myself I'm not relinquishing authority to you or anyone else," said Singer.

"Disconnect Dr. Singer's intercom," Nye ordered coolly.

"Nye, for Chrissakes—" came Singer's voice, before it was abruptly cut off.

"Get the two individuals to quarantine immediately," Nye said.

The command seemed to break the indecision of the guards. One stepped forward and prodded de Vaca aside with the butt of his shotgun. She shoved back with a curse. Suddenly, the newly arrived guard stepped forward, ramming her viciously in the gut with the butt of his shotgun. She writhed to the floor, her wind knocked out. The guard raised the butt of the shotgun, poised to strike again. Carson stepped forward, balling his fists, and the guard swiveled his barrel toward Carson's midsection. Carson stared back, and was shocked to see the face of Mike Marr staring back at him. A slow smile broke across Marr's features, and his hooded eyes narrowed.

Nye's voice came on again. "Everyone will remain where they are while the security officers bring the two individuals to quarantine. Any further resistance will be met with lethal force. You will not be warned again."

Two guards helped Brandon-Smith to her feet and began leading her down the hall, while another took charge of the guard with the torn suit. The remaining guards, including Marr, positioned themselves along the corridor, watching the crowd of scientists and technicians carefully.

Soon the two detainees and their party had disappeared down the tube leading to the lower levels. Carson knew their destination: a cramped series of rooms two decks below the animal-quarantine unit. There they would spend the next ninety-six hours, having their blood constantly tested for X-FLU antibodies. If they were clear, they would be released to the infirmary for a week of observation; if not—if antibodies showed up, indicating infection—they would be required to spend the rest of their short lives in the quarantine area as the first human casualties of the rogue flu.

Nye's brisk voice broke through again. "Mendel, get down to quarantine with a new helmet and reseal the suits. Dr. Grady will administer first aid and draw the blood samples. We will not evacuate Level 5 until everyone—I repeat, everyone—has had his suit pressure-checked for breach."

"Fascist asshole," said de Vaca on global.

"Anyone disobeying the orders of the security officers will be imprisoned in quarantine for the duration of the emergency," came the cool answer. "Hertz, find the renegade animal and kill it."

"Yes, sir."

The site physician, Dr. Grady, appeared at the far end of the hall, wearing a red emergency suit and carrying a large metal suitcase. He disappeared down the access tube toward quarantine.

"We will now check everyone in alphabetical order," came Nye's voice. "As soon as you are cleared to leave the facility, please go directly to the main conference room for debriefing. Barkley, step into the exit air lock."

The scientist named Barkley glanced around at the assembled people, then stepped quickly through the hatch.

"Carson next," said Nye sixty seconds later.

"No," said Carson. "This isn't right. Our suits will run out of air in a few minutes. The women should go first."

"Carson is next," the voice repeated, calm but with a threatening undertone.

"Don't be a sexist idiot," said de Vaca, who was sitting up and cradling her stomach. "Get your ass in there."

Carson hesitated a moment, then stepped into the air lock. A suited figure waiting in the access chamber visually inspected his suit, then attached a small hose to his air valve.

"I'm going to test your suit for leaks," the man said. There was a hiss of stale air and Carson felt the air pressure within the suit rise, causing his ears to pop.

"Clean," said the man, and Carson moved to the chemical shower beyond. As he emerged into the ready room, he noted that Barkley had soiled his suit, and he turned his back while grappling with his own.

As he was stowing his gear, de Vaca emerged from the Fever Tank. She pulled off her helmet.

"Wait, Guy," she said. "I just want to say—"

Carson shut the door on her sentence and headed for the conference room.

Within an hour, everyone had assembled. Nye stood near a large videoconferencing screen, Singer at his side. Mike Marr slouched against one wall, booted legs crossed, chewing the ever-present rubber band as he lazily surveyed the group. Fear and resentment hung like a pall of smoke. Without a word, the room darkened, and the face of Scopes appeared on the screen.

"I don't need a debriefing," he said. "Everything was captured on videotape. Everything."

There was a silence while Scopes's eyes moved back and forth behind his thick glasses as if looking around the room.

"I am very disappointed in some of you," he said at last. "You know the procedures. You've rehearsed them dozens of times."

He turned to Singer. "John, you know the rules better than anyone. Mr. Nye was on top of the situation and you were not. He was perfectly correct to assume responsibility during the emergency. In a situation like this, there's no room for confusion in the chain of command."

"I understand," Singer said, his face expressionless.

"I know you do. Susana Cabeza de Vaca?"

"What," said de Vaca defiantly.

"Why did you ignore protocol and try to release Brandon-Smith from Level 5?"

"So she could receive medical attention in a hospital," de Vaca said, "instead of being locked in a cage."

There was a long silence while Scopes gazed at her. "And if she by chance had been infected with X-FLU?" he asked at last. "What then? Would medical attention save her life?"

There was a long silence. Scopes sighed heavily. "Susana, you're a microbiologist. I don't need to give you a lesson in epidemiology. If you had succeeded in springing Rosalind from Level 5, and if she were infected, you might have started an epidemic unprecedented in the history of mankind."

She remained stubbornly silent.

"Andrew?" Scopes said, turning his eyes on Vanderwagon. "In such an epidemic, little children, teenagers, mothers, working men and women, rich and poor, doctors and nurses, farmers and priests, all would have died. Thousands of people, maybe millions, and maybe—" He paused. "—even billions." Scopes's voice had grown very soft. He allowed another long silence to pass.

"Somebody tell me if I'm wrong."

There was another excruciating silence.

"Damn it!" he barked. "There are *reasons* why we have safety rules in Level 5. You all are working with the most dangerous pathogen in existence. The whole world depends on you not fucking up. And you almost fucked up."

"I'm sorry," Vanderwagon blurted out. "I acted without thinking. All I could think of was that it could be me—"

"Fillson!" Scopes said abruptly.

The animal handler approached the screen, his hands

twitching nervously, his pendulous lower lip moist.

"By failing to latch the cage properly, you caused incalculable harm. And you also failed to keep the quarantined animals' nails trimmed, as per explicit instructions. You are, of course, fired. Furthermore, I have instructed our lawyers to initiate a civil lawsuit against you. If Brandon-Smith should die, her blood will be on your hands. In short, your unforgivable carelessness will haunt you legally, financially, and morally for the rest of your life. Mr. Marr, please see that Fillson is immediately escorted out of the premises and dropped off at Engle, to make his own way home."

Mike Marr pushed himself away from the wall, a smile playing about his lips, and sauntered over.

"Mr. Scopes—Brent—*please*," Fillson began as Marr grasped him roughly by the arm and pulled him through the door.

"Susana?" Scopes said.

De Vaca remained silent.

Scopes shook his head. "I don't want to fire you, but if you can't see the mistake you made, I'll have to. It's too dangerous. More than one life was at stake back there. Do you understand?"

De Vaca dropped her head. "Yes. I understand," she said finally.

Scopes turned to Vanderwagon. "I know that you and Susana both were motivated by decent human emotions. But you *must* have more discipline when dealing with a danger as great as this virus. Remember the phrase: 'If thy right eye offends thee, pluck it out.' You can't let such emotions, no matter how well intended, get the better of your reason. You are scientists. We will examine the consequences, if any, of this incident on your bonus package at a later time."

"Yes, sir," said Vanderwagon.

"And you too, Susana. You're both on probation for the next six weeks."

She nodded.

"Guy Carson?"

"Yes," Carson said.

"I'm more sorry than I can say that your experiment failed."

Carson said nothing.

"But I am proud of the way you acted this morning. You could have joined the rush to free Brandon-Smith, but you didn't. You stayed cool and used your head."

Carson remained silent. He had done what he thought was right. But de Vaca's withering insult, her branding him a murderer, had struck home. Somehow, hearing himself praised by Scopes like this, in front of everyone, made him uncomfortable.

Scopes sighed. Then he addressed the entire group. "Rosalind Brandon-Smith and Roger Czerny are receiving the best medical treatment possible, their suits have been resealed, and they are resting comfortably. They must remain in the quarantine unit for ninety-six hours. You all know the procedure and the reasons behind it. Level 5 will remain closed except to security and medical personnel until the crisis period is over. Any questions?"

There was a silence. "If they test X-FLU-positive—?" someone began.

A look of pain crossed Scopes's face. "I don't want to consider that possibility," he said, and the screen went black with a pop of static.

"Get some sleep, Guy. There's nothing more you can do here."

Singer, looking drawn and haggard, sat at one of the rolling chairs in the Monitoring Station, his eyes glancing over a bank of black-and-white video screens. Over the last thirty-six hours Carson had returned time and again to the station, gazing at the images on the video screens, as if the sheer force of his will could bring the two scientists out of quarantine. Now he picked up his laptop, said a reluctant good-bye to Singer, and left the subdued blue glow of the station for the empty halls of the operations building. Sleep was impossible, and he allowed his feet to take him to one of the aboveground labs beyond the inner perimeter.

Sitting at a long table in the deserted lab, he went over the failed experiment again and again in his head. He'd recently been told that the escaped chimp had tested positive for X-FLU. He could not forget, even for a moment, that if he had been successful this would not have been the case. To make things worse, the paternal, encouraging messages from Scopes had ceased. He had let everyone down.

And yet the inoculation *should* have worked. There was no flaw that he could find. All the preliminary tests had shown the virus altered in precisely the way he intended.

He powered up his computer and began listing the possible scenarios:

Possibility 1: An unknown mistake was made.
Answer: Repeat experiment.
Possibility 2: Dr. Burt got the gene locus wrong.
Answer: Find new locus, repeat experiment.
Possibility 3: Chimps already had dormant X-FLU when inoculated.
Answer: Monitor successive inoculatees for results.
Possibility 4: Viral product exposed to heat or some other mutagen.
Answer: Repeat experiment, taking paramount care with viral culture between gene splicing and in vivo trial.

It all boiled down to the same thing: repeat the damned experiment. But he knew he'd get the same results, because there was nothing that could be done any differently. Wearily, he called up Burt's notes and began going through the sections that dealt with the mapping of the viral gene. It was superb work, and Carson could hardly see where Burt had gone wrong, but it was worth going over again anyway. Maybe he should remap the entire viral plasmid from scratch himself, a process that he knew would take at least two months. He thought of spending two more months locked up in the Fever Tank. He thought of Brandon-Smith, somewhere in quarantine at this very moment, deep in the Tank. He remembered the blood welling from her raked side, the expression of fear and disbelief on her face. He remembered standing there, watching, while the guards dragged her away.

He worked in front of a large picture window that looked out over the desert. It was his only consolation. From time to time he stared out, watching the afternoon sun grow golden on the yellow sands.

"Guy?" he heard a voice say behind him. It was de Vaca. He turned and found her standing in the door, in jeans and T-shirt, her lab coat slung over her arm.

"Need any help?" she asked.

"No," he said.

"Look," she said, "I'm sorry about my comment in the Fever Tank."

He turned away silently. Talking with this woman only ended in grief.

He heard a rustle as she moved closer.

"I came to apologize," she said.

He sighed. "Apology accepted."

"I don't believe it," she said. "You still sound mad."

Guy turned toward her. "It's not just the comment in the Fever Tank. You bitch about everything I say."

"You say a lot of stupid things," de Vaca said, flaring up.

"That's just what I mean. You didn't come to apologize. You came to argue."

There was a silence in the empty lab.

De Vaca stood up. "We can at least maintain a professional relationship. We've got to. I need that bonus for my clinic. So the experiment failed. We'll try again."

Carson looked at her, standing illuminated in the picture window, her violet eyes darting at him, her long black hair flowing wild down her back and shoulders. He found himself holding his breath, she was so beautiful. It took all the steam out of his anger.

"What's going on with you and Mike Marr?" he asked.

She looked at him quickly. "That son of a bitch? He'd been coming on to me since day one. I guess he thought no woman could resist big black boots and a ten-gallon hat."

"You seemed to be resisting pretty well at the Bomb Picnic."

A rueful expression crossed de Vaca's face. "Yes, and he's not a man who likes to be crossed. He comes across all smiles and aw-shucks, but that's not how he really is, at all. You saw how he planted the butt of his shotgun in my gut, back there in the Fever Tank. There's something about him that scares the hell out of me, if you want to know the truth." She pulled her hair back brusquely with one finger. "Come on, let's get to it."

Carson exhaled deeply. "Okay. Take a look at my ideas, see if you can think of any other reasons for the failure." He pushed the PowerBook over, and she took the next stool at the lab table, reading the information on the screen.

"I have another idea," she said after a moment.

"What's that?"

She typed:

Possibility 5: Viral product contaminated with other strains of X-FLU or plasmid fragments.
Answer: Repurify and test results.

"What makes you think it was contaminated?" Carson asked.

"It's a possibility."

"But those samples were run with GEF. They're all cleaner than a Vatican joke."

"I just said it's a *possibility*," de Vaca repeated. "You can't always believe a machine. These X-FLU strains are very similar."

"OK, OK," Carson sighed. "But first, I want to double-check Burt's notes on the mapping of the X-FLU plasmid. I know it all by heart, but I want to go through it once more, just to be certain."

"Let me help you," said de Vaca. "Maybe between us, we can find something."

They began to read in silence.

Roger Czerny lay on his bed in the quarantine room, looking at Brandon-Smith sitting against the far wall. Pouting, as usual. He loathed the sight of her more deeply, more thoroughly, than he ever had any other person in his life. He loathed the fat dough-boy biohazard suit she wore, loathed the whining sarcastic voice, loathed the very sound of her breathing and whimpering through the intercom. Because of her, he might die. He was furious that he had to share the quarantine room with her. With all the money GeneDyne had, why hadn't they built two quarantine rooms? Why stick him in with this fat, ugly woman who bitched and moaned all day long? He was forced to watch her every bodily function, her eating, her sleeping, her emptying her shit bag, everything. It was intolerable. And everything was so complicated, just taking a piss or trying to eat dinner while maintaining the sterile environment. When he got out of here, he thought, unless they did something really nice for him—a hundred-grand bonus at least—he was going to sue their asses. They should have given him a rip-proof suit. It should have been part of the procedure. It didn't matter that they'd given them both fresh bluesuits. They had locked him in with his own would-be murderer. They were liable as hell, and they were going to pay.

On top of everything else, they wouldn't tell him the results of the frequent blood tests. The only way he'd know anything was when the ninety-six hour waiting period was up. If they let him out, he was clean. If not . . .

Shit, he thought, it was going to take two hundred to make up for this. Two-fifty. He'd get himself a good lawyer.

It was ten o'clock. The lighting was dim, so he knew it had to be evening, not morning. That was the only way he could tell in this prison. He thought, once again, of his one visit to a hospital, ten years earlier. Emergency appendectomy. This was like a hospital, only worse. Much worse. Here he was, a hundred feet below the ground, sealed in a small room, no way out, with a roommate that—He opened and closed his mouth several times, hyperventilating, trying to ease the panic that came bubbling toward the surface.

Slowly, his breathing returned to normal. He shifted on his bed and pointed a remote at the television that hung from the ceiling. "Three Stooges" reruns. Anything to get his mind out of there.

A soft beep sounded and a blue light began blinking high on the wall. There was a hiss of compressed air escaping; then the doctor, Grady, squeezed through the hatchway, the bulky red emergency suit hindering his movements. "That time again," he said cheerfully into the intercom. He took Brandon-Smith's blood first, inserting the needle through a special rubber-sealed grommet in the upper arm of her suit.

"I don't feel good," Brandon-Smith whined. It was what she said every time the doctor came. "I think I'm feeling a little dizzy."

The doctor checked her temperature, using the thermometer inserted in her suit.

"Ninety-eight point six!" he piped. "It's the stress of the situation. Try to relax."

"But I have a *headache*," she said again, for the twentieth time.

"It's not time yet for another shot of Tylenol," the doctor said. "Another two hours."

"But I have a headache *now*."

"Perhaps a half dose," said the doctor, fumbling in his suitcase with gloved hands and administering the injection.

"Just tell me, please, *please*, if I have it," she pleaded.

"Twenty-four more hours," the doctor said. "Just one more day. You're doing fine, Rosalind, you're doing beautifully. As I told you, I'm not being given any more information than you are."

"You're a liar," Brandon-Smith snapped. "I want to talk to Brent."

"*Relax.* Nobody's a liar. That's just the stress speaking."

The doctor came over to Czerny, who presented the side of his suit in resigned anticipation of having his blood drawn.

"Anything I can do for you, Roger?" the doctor asked.

"No," said Czerny. Even if he pushed past the doctor, he knew there were two of his fellow guards stationed directly outside the quarantine area.

The doctor drew the blood and left. The blue light stopped blinking as the hatchway was sealed. Czerny went back to the Three Stooges, while Brandon-Smith lay down, falling at last into a fitful sleep. At eleven, Czerny turned off the lights.

He awoke suddenly at two. Even though it was pitch black, he felt, with a shiver of horror, a presence hovering above his bed.

"Who is it?" he cried, sitting up. He fumbled for the light, then dropped his arm again when he realized the form at the end of his bed was Brandon-Smith.

"What do you want?" he said.

She did not answer. Her large frame was trembling slightly.

"Leave me alone!"

"My right arm," said Brandon-Smith.

"What about it?"

"It's gone," she said. "I woke up and it was gone."

In the dark, Czerny pawed at his sleeve, found the global emergency button and punched it savagely.

Brandon-Smith took a small step forward, bumping his bedframe.

"Get away from me!" Czerny shouted. He felt the bed vibrate.

"Now my left arm's going," she whispered, her voice strangely slurred. Her whole body began to shake. "This is strange. There's something crawling inside my head, like tapeworms." She fell silent. The trembling continued.

Czerny backed up against the wall. "Help me!" he cried into his intercom. "Somebody get the hell in here!"

Two recessed bulbs in the ceiling snapped on, soaking the chamber in a dim crimson light.

Suddenly Brandon-Smith screamed. "*Where are you? I can't see you! Please don't leave me!*"

Over his intercom, Czerny heard a peculiar wet sound that was almost instantly smothered by the dying buzz of a short circuit. Looking up in sudden horror, he saw wrinkled gray brain matter thrusting against the inside glass of Brandon-Smith's faceplate. And yet she remained standing for the longest time, still twitching, before she slowly began to topple forward onto his bed.

PART TWO

The horse barn stood at the edge of the perimeter fence, a modest metal building with six stalls. Four of the stalls held horses. It was an hour before dawn, and Venus, the morning star, shone brightly on the eastern horizon.

Inside the barn, Carson watched the horses drowsing in their stalls, heads drooping. He whistled softly and the heads jerked upward, ears perked.

"Which one of you ugly old cayuses wants to go for a ride?" he whispered. One horse nickered in return.

He looked them over. They were a motley lot, obviously locally purchased, ranch rejects. A goose-rumped Appaloosa, two old quarterhorses, and one grade horse of indeterminate breeding. Muerto, Nye's magnificent Medicine Hat paint gelding, was gone, apparently taken out by the Englishman on one of his mysterious rides even earlier that morning. *Guess he's had enough of the place, too,* Carson thought. Though it seemed a strange time for the security director to be leaving the grounds. Carson, at least, had an excuse: the Level-5 facility was still closed, and would remain so until an OSHA inspector arrived the following day. Carson couldn't work if he wanted to.

But even if the Fever Tank had been open for business, there was no way Carson was working this day. He grimaced in the dark, overripe air of the stable. Just when he'd decided it was irrational to blame himself for Brandon-Smith's accident, she'd died of exposure to X-FLU. Then Czerny had been removed in an ambulance, virus-free but incoherent. The entire Fever Tank had been decontaminated, then sealed. Now there was nothing to do but wait, and Carson had grown tired of waiting in the hushed, funereal atmosphere of the residency compound. He needed time to think about the X-FLU problem, to figure out what went wrong, and—perhaps most important—to recover his equilibrium. He knew no better tonic than a long ride on horseback.

The grade horse caught Carson's eye. He was a liver-colored bay with a head the size of a coffin. But he was young and tough-looking. He eyed Carson through a straggly lock of mane.

Carson stepped inside the stall and ran his hand along the horse's flank. The fur was tight and coarse, the skin tough as tripe. The horse didn't jerk or tremble; he merely turned his head and smelled Carson's shoulder. He had a calm, alert gleam in his eye that Carson liked.

He picked up the front leg. The hooves were good although the shoeing job was abysmal. The horse stood calmly while Carson cleaned the hoof with a penknife. He dropped the leg and patted the horse on the neck.

"You're a damn fine horse," Carson said, "but you sure are one ugly son of a bitch."

The horse nickered his appreciation.

Carson eased a halter over the animal's head and led him to a hitching post outside. It had been two years since he'd ridden, but already the old instincts were coming back. He went into the tack room and looked over Mount Dragon's saddle collection. It was obvious that most of the other residents were uninterested in riding. One of the saddles had a broken tree; another was just a screwed-together affair that would probably disintegrate the moment the horse broke into a trot. There was one old Abiquiu saddle with a high cantle that might do. Carson picked it up, grabbed a blanket and pad, and carried everything out to the hitching post. He buckled on his old spurs, noting that during the years of disuse one of the rowels had broken.

"What's your name?" he murmured softly while brushing out the horse's coat.

The horse stood there in the gathering light, saying nothing.

"Well then, I'm going to call you Roscoe." He folded the blanket, placed it on the horse's back, then added the pad and saddle. He looped the latigo through the rigging and tightened it, feeling the horse swell his belly with air in an attempt to trick Carson into leaving the cinch too loose.

"You're a rascal," said Carson. He hitched the breast collar and loosely buckled the flank cinch. When the horse wasn't paying attention he jabbed his knee in its belly and jerked the latigo tight. The horse flattened his ears.

"Gotcha," said Carson.

The light was now brighter in the east, and Venus had grown pale, almost invisible. Carson tied on the saddlebags containing his lunch, looped a gallon canteen over the horn, and swung up into the saddle.

No guard was on duty at the rear gate in the perimeter fence. Approaching the keypad, Carson leaned over and punched in the code, and the gate swung open.

He trotted out into the desert and took a deep breath. After almost three weeks of incarceration inside the lab, he was finally free. Free of the claustrophobic Fever Tank, free of the horror of the last few days. Tomorrow, the OSHA inspector would arrive and the grind would begin again. Carson was determined to make this day count.

Roscoe had a rough, fast trot. Carson turned the horse southward and rode toward the old Indian ruin that poked above the horizon, a few wrecked walls amid piles of rubble. He'd been a little curious since he'd first seen it from Singer's window.

He rode past at a distance. Most of the ruin was covered with windblown sand, but here and there he could make out the low outlines of collapsed walls and small room blocks. It looked like many of the old ruins that had dotted the landscape of his youth. Soon, it was nothing but a diminishing point behind him.

When he was several miles from the lab, Carson dropped the horse into a walk and looked around. Mount Dragon had shrunk to a white cluster to the north. The vegetation of the Jornada desert had changed subtly, and he found himself surrounded by creosotebush that marched toward the horizon with almost mathematical precision.

He continued south again, enjoying the familiar rocking of the horse. A pronghorn antelope paused on a rise and looked in his direction. It was joined by another. Suddenly, as if on cue, they wheeled about and fled; they had caught his scent. He rode through a curious stand of soapweed yucca, looking uncannily like a crowd of bowing people, and he remembered a story passed down in his family about how Kit Carson and a wagon train had circled and fired at a group of hostiles for fifteen minutes before realizing they were shooting at just such a yucca grove.

By noon, Carson reckoned he was about fifteen miles from Mount Dragon. He could just make out the cinder cone itself, a dark triangle on the northern horizon, but the laboratory had long sunk out of view. A low range of hills had appeared in the west, and he turned his horse toward them, eager to explore.

He came to the edge of a vast lava flow, black jagged rubble piled on the desert floor, covered with blooming ocotillo. This, Carson knew, was part of the vast lava formation known as El Malpaís, the Bad Country, which covered hundreds of square miles of the Jornada desert. The western hills were closer now, and Carson could see that, much like Mount Dragon, they were a chain of dead cinder cones.

Carson rode along the edge of the lava, winding in and out, following the irregular pattern of the flow. The lava had spread amoebalike across the desert, leaving a complicated maze of coves, islands, and lava caves.

As Carson rode, he watched a summer thunderstorm rapidly build over the hills. A great thunderhead began to rear against the tropopause, its bottom as flat and dark as an anvil. He smelled a change in the air, a freshening of the breeze, bringing with it the smell of ozone. The spreading cloud covered the sun, and a cathedral-like hush fell on the landscape. In a few minutes the cloud was dropping a column of rain the color of blued steel. Carson urged Roscoe into a trot, scanning the edge of the lava, figuring he could weather the coming storm in one of the caves that were usually found at the edges of the flows.

The column of rain thickened, and the wind began to push skeins of dust along the ground. Lightning flickered inside the cloud, the rumbling of thunder rolling across the desert like the sound of a distant battle. As the storm approached, a low moaning filled the air and the smell of wet sand and electricity became stronger.

Carson rounded a point of lava and saw a promising-looking cave among the mounds of twisted basalt. He dismounted, removed his saddlebags, and tied Roscoe to a rock by his lead rope. He climbed over the lava to the cave entrance.

The mouth was dark and cool, with a soft floor of wind-blown sand. He stepped inside just as the first heavy drops of rain slapped the ground. He could see Roscoe, on the long lead rope, turn his butt to the wind and hunker down. The saddle would get soaked. He should have brought it into the cave with him, but such a saddle didn't deserve special treatment. He would oil it when he got back.

The desert was suddenly engulfed in sheets of rain. The hills disappeared and the line of black lava faded into the gray torrent. Carson lay on his back in the dimness of the cave. His thoughts turned inevitably to Mount Dragon. Even here, he could not escape it. It still seemed unreal to him, this laboratory lost in the desert. And yet the death of Brandon-Smith was real enough. Once again, he tortured himself with the thought that if his genetic splicing had succeeded, she would be alive. In one sense, his overconfidence had killed her. Part of him realized this train of thought was irrational, and yet it kept returning to haunt him, again and again. He had done his best, he knew; Fillson's and Brandon-Smith's own inattention were responsible. Still, he couldn't shake the feeling of guilt.

He closed his eyes and forced himself to listen to the rain and wind. Finally, he sat up and stared out the cave opening. Roscoe stood silently, unafraid. He had seen it all before. Although Carson felt sorry for him, he knew it had been the lot of horses since time immemorial to stand in the rain while their masters took refuge in caves.

He eased back and absentmindedly ran his hands through the sand on the cave floor, waiting for the storm to pass. His fingers closed over something cool and hard, and he pulled it from the sand. It was a spearpoint, made from gray chert, as light and balanced as a leaf. He remembered finding a similar arrowhead once, out riding the range. When he brought it home his great-uncle Charley had become very excited by the find, saying that it was a powerful sign of protection and that he should carry it always. His great-uncle had made him a buckskin medicine bag for the spearpoint; then he had chanted and sprinkled pollen over it. His father had been disgusted by the whole proceeding. Later, Carson had thrown away the bag and told his great-uncle he had lost it.

He slid the spearpoint into his pocket, stood up, and walked to the cave entrance. Somehow, the find made him feel better. He would get through this; he would succeed in neutralizing X-FLU, if only to ensure that Brandon-Smith's death had not been in vain.

The storm eased, and Carson stepped out of the lava tube. Looking around, he saw a great double rainbow arching over the hills to the south. The sun began to break through the clouds. He collected Roscoe's lead rope, patted him and apologized, then wiped the seat dry and remounted.

Roscoe's hooves sank into the wet sand as Carson nosed the horse once again in the direction of the hills. In minutes the heat returned, the desert began steaming, and he felt thirsty. Not wanting to exhaust his water supply, he dug into his pocket for a stick of gum.

Topping a rise, he froze, the gum halfway to his mouth. Tracks crossed the sand directly before him: a mounted horse, showing evidence of the same poor shoeing job as Roscoe. The tracks were fresh, made after the rain.

Popping the gum into his mouth, Carson followed. At the top of a second rise he saw, in the distance, the horse and rider posting between two cinder cones. He immediately recognized the absurd safari hat and dark suit. There was nothing absurd, however, about the way the man handled his horse. Pulling Roscoe below the rise, Carson dismounted and peered over the top.

Nye was trotting at right angles to Carson, riding English. Suddenly he reined his horse to a stop and fished a piece of paper out of his breast pocket. He flattened it on the pommel and took out a sighting compass, orienting it on the paper and taking a bearing directly at the sun. He turned his horse ninety degrees, nudged him back into a trot, and soon disappeared behind the hills.

Carson remounted, curious. Confident in his own tracking skills, he let Nye gain some distance before easing his horse forward.

Nye was leaving a very peculiar trail. He rode in a straight line for a half mile, made another abrupt ninety-degree turn, rode another half mile, then continued the process, zigzagging across the desert in a checkerboard pattern. At each turn Carson could see, from the hoofprints in the sand, that Nye halted for a moment before continuing.

Carson continued tracking, fascinated by the puzzle. What the hell was Nye doing? This was no pleasure ride. It was getting late; clearly, the man was planning to spend the night out here, in these godforsaken volcanic hills twenty miles from Mount Dragon.

He dismounted again to examine the track. Nye was moving faster now, riding at a slow lope. He was riding a good horse, in better physical condition than Roscoe, and Carson realized he would not be able to follow indefinitely without exhausting his own horse. With a little exercise, Roscoe might be the equal of Nye's mount, but he was "barn sour" and they were still many miles from the lab. Even if Carson turned back, he would not get back before midnight. It was time to give up the chase.

He was preparing to mount when he heard a sharp voice behind him. Turning, he saw Nye approaching.

"What the bloody hell do you think you're doing?" the Englishman said.

"Out for a ride, same as you," Carson replied, hoping his voice didn't betray his surprise. Nye had obviously noticed he was being followed and doubled back in a classic move, tracking the tracker.

"You lying git, you were stalking me."

"I was curious—" Carson began.

Nye moved his horse closer and with invisible knee pressure turned him expertly on the forehand, at the same time laying his right hand on the butt of a rifle sheathed beside the saddle.

"A lie," he hissed. "I know what you're up to, Carson, don't play stupid with me. If I ever catch you following me again I'll kill you, you hear me? I'll bury you out here, and no one will ever know what happened to your stinking pishogue of a carcass."

Carson quickly swung up on his horse. "Nobody talks to me that way," he said.

"I'll talk to you any bloody way I like." Nye began to slide the rifle out of its scabbard.

Carson jabbed his horse in the flank and surged forward. Nye, taken off guard, jerked the rifle free and tried to swing it around. Roscoe slammed into Muerto and threw the security director sideways in the saddle; at the same instant, Carson dropped his reins and grabbed the barrel of the rifle with both hands, yanking it out of Nye's grasp with a sharp downward tug.

Keeping an eye on Nye, Carson opened the breech and removed the magazine, tossing it into the sand. Then he extracted the wad of gum from his mouth and jammed it deep into the chamber. He snapped the breech shut and winged the gun far down the hill.

"Don't ever unship a rifle in front of me again," he said quietly.

Nye sat on his horse, breathing hard, his face red. He moved toward the rifle but Carson spun his horse, blocking him.

"For an Englishman, you're a rude son of a bitch," Carson said.

"That's a three-thousand-dollar rifle," Nye replied.

"All the more reason not to wave it in people's faces."

Carson nodded down the hill. "If you try to use that gun now, it'll misfire and blow off your little ponytail. By the time you've cleaned it, I'll be gone."

There was a long silence. The late-afternoon sun refracted through Nye's eyes, giving them a strange dark gold color. Looking into those eyes, Carson saw that the fiery tints were not completely a trick of the sun; the man's eyes had a reddish cast, like the inward flames of a secret obsession.

Without another word Carson turned his horse and headed north at a brisk trot. After several minutes he stopped, looking back. Nye remained motionless on his mount, silhouetted against the rise, gazing after him.

"Watch your back, Carson!" came the distant voice. And Carson thought he heard a strange laugh drift toward him across the desert, before being whisked away by the wind.

The portable CD player sat on an outspread *Wall Street Journal* on a white table in the control room, exploded into twenty or thirty pieces. A figure wearing a dirty T-shirt was bent over it, the picture of concentration. The T-shirt's legend, VISIT BEAUTIFUL SOVIET GEORGIA, was proudly emblazoned over a picture of a grim, fortresslike government structure, the epitome of Stalinesque architecture.

De Vaca stood to one side of the immaculate control room, wondering if the T-shirt was a joke. "You said you've never fixed a CD player before," she said nervously.

"*Da*," the figure muttered without looking up.

"Well, then how do you . . . ?" She let the sentence hang.

The figure muttered again, then popped a chip out of a circuit board, holding it up with a pair of plastic-coated tweezers. "Hmmmph," he said, and tossed it carelessly on the newspaper. Working the tweezers again, he popped out a second chip.

"Maybe this wasn't such a good idea," said de Vaca.

The figure eyed her over a pair of reading glasses fallen halfway down his nose. "But is not fixed yet," he protested.

De Vaca shrugged, sorry she had ever brought the CD player to Pavel Vladimirovic. Though she'd been told he was some kind of mechanical genius, she'd seen no evidence of it so far. And the man had even admitted he had never even seen a CD player before, let alone fixed one.

Vladimirovic sighed heavily, dropped the second chip, and sat down heavily, pushing the glasses back up his nose.

"Is *broke*," he announced.

"I know," said de Vaca. "That's why I brought it to you."

He nodded and indicated with his palm for her to sit in a chair.

"Can you fix it or not?" de Vaca said, still standing.

He nodded. "*Da*, don't worry! I can fix. Is problem with chip that controls laser diode."

De Vaca took a seat. "Do you have a replacement?" she asked.

Vladimirovic nodded and rubbed his sweaty neck. Then he stood up, moved to a cabinet, and returned with a small box, green circuit boards peeping from its open top. "I put back together now," he nodded

De Vaca watched while, in a burst of activity, he cannibalized parts from the box full of circuit boards. In less than five minutes he had assembled the player. He plugged it in, inserted the CD that de Vaca had brought, and waited. The sound of the B-52s came roaring out of the speakers.

"Aiee!" he cried, turning it off. "*Nekulturny*. What is that noise! Must still be broke." He roared with laughter at his own joke.

"Thank you," de Vaca said, real delight in her voice. "I use this just about every evening. I was afraid I'd have to spend the rest of my time here without music. How'd you do it?"

"Here, many extra pieces from the fail-safe mechanism," Vladimirovic said. "I use one of those. Is nothing, very simple little machine. Not like this!" he gestured proudly at the rows of control panels, CRT screens and consoles.

"What do they all do?" de Vaca asked.

"Many things!" he cried, lumbering over to a wall of electronics. "Here, is control for laminar airflow. Air intake here, furnace is controlled by all these." He waved his hand vaguely. "And then all these control cooldown."

"Cooldown?"

"*Da.* You wouldn't want one-thousand-degree air going back in! Has to be cooled, the air."

"Why not just suck in fresh air?"

"If suck in fresh air, must vent old air. No good. This is *closed* system. We are only laboratory in world with such system. Goes back to fail-safe mechanism of military days, shunt hot air to Level-5."

"You mentioned that fail-safe system before," de Vaca asked. "I don't remember hearing about it."

"For stage-zero alert."

"There is no stage-zero alert. Stage one is the worst-case scenario."

"Back then, was stage-zero alert." He shrugged. "Maybe terrorists in Level-5, maybe accident with total contamination. Inject one-thousand-degree air into Level-5, make complete sterilization. Not only sterilization. Blow place up real *kharasho!* Boom!"

"I see," said de Vaca, a little uncertainly. "It can't go off by accident, this state-zero alert, can it?"

Pavel chuckled. "Impossible. When civilians took over, system was deactivated." He waved his hand at a nearby computer terminal. "Only work if put back on line."

"Good," said de Vaca, relieved. "I wouldn't want to be fried alive because someone tripped over the wrong switch up here."

"True," Pavel rumbled. "It's hot enough outside without making more heat, *nyet? Zharka!*" He shook his head, eyes staring absently at the newspaper. Then he stiffened. He picked up the rump end of the *Journal* and stabbed his finger at it.

"You see this?" he asked.

"No," said de Vaca. She glanced over at the columns of tiny numbers, thinking that he must have stolen the paper from the Mount Dragon library, which had subscriptions to a dozen or so newspapers and periodicals that were not available on-line. They were the only printed materials allowed on the site.

"GeneDyne stock down half point again! You know what this mean?"

De Vaca shook her head.

"We losing money!"

"Losing money?" de Vaca asked.

"*Da!* You own stock, I own stock, and this stock go down half point! I lose three hundred fifty dollars! What I could have done with that money!"

He buried his head in his hands.

"But isn't that to be expected?" de Vaca asked.

"*Shto?*"

"Doesn't the stock go up and down every day?"

"*Da*, every day! Last Monday I made six hundred dollars."

"So what does it matter?"

"Makes even worse! Last Monday, six hundred dollars richer I was. Now it's all gone! Poof!" He spread his hands in despair.

De Vaca tried to keep from laughing. The man must watch the movement of the stock every day, feeling elated on the days it went up—thinking how he was going to spend the money—and horrified on the days it went down. It was the price of employee ownership: giving stock to people who had never invested before. And yet, she was sure overall he must have made a large profit on his employee plan. She hadn't checked since arriving at Mount Dragon, but she knew the GeneDyne stock had been soaring in recent months, and that they all were getting richer.

Vladimirovic shook his head again. "And in last few days, worse, much worse. Down many points!"

De Vaca frowned. "I didn't know that."

"You not heard talk in canteen! It's that Boston professor, Levine. Always, he talking bad about GeneDyne, about Brent Scopes. Now he say something worse, I don't know what, and stock go down." He muttered under his breath. "KGB would know what to do with such a man."

He sighed deeply, then handed her the CD player.

"After hearing decadent counterrevolutionary music, I'm sorry I fixed it," he said.

De Vaca laughed and said good-bye. She decided the T-shirt had to be a joke. After all, the man must have had top secret clearance to work at Mount Dragon in the old days. She'd have to search him out in the canteen some evening and get the whole story, she decided.

The first heat of summer lay like a sodden blanket over Harvard Yard. The leaves hung limply on the great oaks and chestnut trees, and cicadas droned in the shadows. As he walked, Levine slipped out of his threadbare jacket and slung it over his shoulder, inhaling the smell of freshly cut grass, the thick humidity in the air.

In the outer office, Ray was at his desk, idly picking at his teeth with a paper clip. He grunted at Levine's approach.

"You got visitors," he said.

Levine stopped, frowned. "You mean, inside?" He nodded toward his closed office door.

"Didn't like the company out here," Ray explained.

As Levine opened the door, Erwin Landsberg, the president of the university, turned toward him with a smile. He held out his hand.

"Charles, it's been a long time," he said in his gravelly voice. "Much too long." He indicated a second man in a gray suit. "This is Leonard Stafford, our new dean of faculty."

Levine shook the limp hand that was offered, stealing a furtive glance around the office. He wondered how long the two had been there. His eyes landed on the laptop, open on one corner of the desk, telephone cord dangling from its side. Stupid, leaving it out like that. The call was due in just five minutes.

"It's warm in here," said the president. "Charles, you should order an air conditioner from Central Services."

"Air conditioners give me head colds. I like the heat." Levine took a seat at his desk. "Now, what's this about?"

The two visitors sat down, the dean glancing around at the disorderly piles with distaste. "Well, Charles," the president began. "We've come about the lawsuit."

"Which one?"

The president looked pained. "We take these matters very seriously." When Levine said nothing, he continued. "The GeneDyne suit, of course."

"It's pure harassment," Levine said. "It'll be dismissed."

The dean of faculty leaned forward. "Dr. Levine, I'm afraid we don't share that view. This is not a frivolous suit. GeneDyne is alleging theft of trade secrets, electronic trespass, defamation and libel, and quite a bit else."

The president nodded. "GeneDyne has made some serious accusations. Not so much about the foundation, but about your methods. *That's* what concerns me most."

"What about my methods?"

"There's no need to get excited." The president adjusted his cuffs. "You've been in hot water before, and we've always stuck by you. It hasn't always been easy, Charles. There are several trustees—very powerful trustees—who would much prefer if we'd left you outside for the vigilantes. But now, with the ethics of your methods being called into question . . . well, we have to protect the university. You know what's legal, and what isn't. Stay within those bounds. I know you understand." The smile faded slightly. "And that's why I'm not going to warn you again."

"Dr. Landsberg, I don't think you even *begin* to appreciate the situation. This is not some academic tiff. We're talking about the future of the human race." Levine glanced at his watch. Two minutes. *Shit.*

Landsberg raised a quizzical eyebrow. "The future of the human race?"

"We're at war here. GeneDyne is altering the germ cells of human beings, committing a sacrilege against human life itself. 'Extremism in the defense of liberty is no vice.' Remember? When they came to clear the ghettos, it was no time for worrying about ethics and the law. Now they're messing with the human genome itself. I have the proof."

"Your comparison is offensive," Landsberg said. "This is not Nazi Germany, and GeneDyne, whatever you think of it, is not the SS. You undermine the good work you've done in the name of the Holocaust by making such trivial comparisons."

"No? Tell me the difference, then, between Hitler's eugenics and what GeneDyne is doing at Mount Dragon."

Landsberg sat back in his chair with an exasperated sigh. "If you can't see the difference, Charles, you've got a warped moral view. I suspect this has more to do with your personal feud against Brent Scopes than with some high-flown worry about the human race. I don't know what happened between you two twenty years ago to start this thing, and I don't care. We're here to tell you to leave GeneDyne alone."

"This has *nothing* to do with a feud—"

The dean waved his hand impatiently. "Dr. Levine, you've got to understand the university's position. We can't have you running around like a loose cannon, involved in shady activities, while we're litigating a two-hundred-million-dollar lawsuit."

"I consider this to be interference with the autonomy of the foundation," Levine said. "Scopes is putting pressure on you, isn't he?"

Landsberg frowned. "If you call a two-hundred-million-dollar lawsuit 'pressure,' then, hell, yes!"

A telephone rang, then a hiss sounded as a remote computer connected to Levine's laptop. His screen winked on, and an image came into view: a figure, balancing the world on its fingertip.

Levine leaned back casually in his chair, obscuring their view of his computer screen. "I've got work to do," he said.

"Charles, I get the feeling that this isn't sinking in," the president said. "We can pull the foundation's charter any time we like. And we will, Charles, if you press us."

"You wouldn't dare," Levine said. "The press would hammer you like a nail. Besides, I have tenure."

President Landsberg abruptly stood up and turned to leave, his face livid. The dean rose more slowly, smoothing a hand over his suit front. He leaned toward Levine. "Ever heard the phrase 'moral turpitude'? It's in your tenure contract." He moved toward the door, then stopped, looking back speculatively.

The miniature globe on the screen began to rotate faster, and the figure balancing the earth began to scowl impatiently.

"It's been nice chatting with you," Levine said. "Please shut the door on your way out."

When Carson entered the Mount Dragon conference room, the cool white space was already packed with people. The nervous buzz of whispered conversations filled the air. Today, the banks of electronics were hidden behind panels, and the teleconferencing screen was dark. Urns of coffee and pastries were arrayed along one wall, knots of scientists gathered around them.

Carson spotted Andrew Vanderwagon and George Harper standing in one corner. Harper waved him over. "Town meeting's about to start," he said. "You ready?"

"Ready for what?"

"Hell if I know," Harper said, ruffling a hand through his thinning brown hair. "Ready for the third degree, I suppose. They say if he doesn't like what he finds here he might just shut the place down."

Carson shook his head. "They'd never do that over a freak accident."

Harper grunted. "I also heard that this guy has subpoena power and can even bring criminal charges."

"I doubt it," said Carson. "Where'd you hear these things?"

"The Mount Dragon rumor mill, of course: the canteen. Didn't see you there yesterday. Until they reopen Level 5 there's nothing else to do, unless you want to sit in the library or play tennis in the hundred-degree heat."

"I went for a ride," Carson said.

"A ride? You mean, on that hot young assistant of yours?" Harper cackled.

Carson rolled his eyes. Harper could be irritating. He had

already decided not to mention meeting Nye to anyone. It would just create more problems.

Harper turned to Vanderwagon, who was chewing his lip and staring expressionlessly into the crowd. "Come to think of it, I didn't see you in the canteen, either. Spend the day in your room again, Andrew?"

Carson frowned. It was obvious that Vanderwagon was still upset about what had happened in the Fever Tank, and about his dressing down by Scopes. By the look of his bloodshot eyes, he hadn't had much sleep. Sometimes Harper had the tact of a hand grenade.

Vanderwagon turned and eyed Harper as a sudden hush fell over the crowd. Four people had entered the room: Singer, Nye, Mike Marr, and a slight, stooped man in a brown suit. The stranger carried an oversized briefcase that bumped against his legs as he walked. His sandy hair was graying at the temples, and he wore black-rimmed glasses that made his pale skin look sallow. He radiated ill health.

"That must be the OSHA man," whispered Harper. "He doesn't look like much of a terror to me."

"More like a junior accountant," Carson replied. "He's going to get a nasty burn with that skin."

Singer went to the lectern, tapped the microphone, and held up his hand. His normally pleasant, ruddy face looked bone-tired. "As you all know," he said, "tragic accidents such as the one that occurred last week must be reported to the proper authorities. Mr. Teece here is a senior investigator from the Occupational Safety and Health Administration. He'll be spending a little time with us at Mount Dragon, looking into the cause of the accident and reviewing our safety procedures."

Nye stood next to Singer, silent, his eyes traveling over the assembled scientists. A knot in his jaw was working away, his powerful frame rigid in the tailored suit. Marr stood next to him, nodding his closely cropped head and smiling broadly beneath a hat brim so low it hid his eyes. Carson knew that in some ways, as director of security, Nye was ultimately responsible for the accident. He was obviously all too aware of it. The security director's gaze met Carson's for a moment before it moved on. *Perhaps that explains his paranoia out in the desert*, Carson thought. *But what the hell was he up to? Whatever it was must have been damn important, keeping him out overnight before a meeting like this.*

"Because industrial secrets of GeneDyne are involved, the specifics of our research will remain secret regardless of the outcome of the investigation. None of this will be reported to the press." Singer shifted at the podium. "I want to emphasize one thing: everyone at Mount Dragon will be expected to cooperate fully with Mr. Teece. This is an order that comes directly from Brent Scopes. I assume that's sufficiently clear."

There was a silence in the room. Singer nodded.

"Good. I think Mr. Teece would like to say a few words."

The frail-looking man walked up to the microphone, still carrying his briefcase.

"Hello," he said, his thin lips forming a fleeting smile. "I'm Gilbert Teece—please call me Gil. I expect to be here for the next week or so, poking and prying about." He laughed; a brief, dry chuckle. "This is standard procedure in a case such as this. I will be speaking to most of you individually, and of course I'll need your help understanding exactly what happened. I know this is very painful for all concerned."

There was a silence, and it seemed that Teece had already run out of things to say. "Any questions?" he finally asked.

There were none. Teece shuffled back.

Singer stepped back up to the lectern. "Now that Mr. Teece has arrived and decontamination is complete, we've agreed to reopen Level-5 without delay. As difficult as it will be, I expect to see everyone back at work tomorrow morning. We've lost a lot of time, and we need to make it up." He drew a hand across his forehead. "That's all. Thank you."

Teece suddenly stood up, his finger in the air. "Dr. Singer? May I have another word—?"

Singer nodded, and Teece stepped up to the podium again. "The reopening of Level-5 was not my idea," he said, "but perhaps it will aid the investigation, after all. I must say I'm a little surprised that we were not joined today by Mr. Scopes. It was my understanding he likes to be present—in an electronic sense, at least—at meetings of this sort." He paused expectantly, but neither Singer or Nye said a word.

"That being the case," Teece continued, "there's one question I'll offer up generally. Perhaps you'll offer me your thoughts on it when we do meet individually."

He paused.

"I'm curious to know why Brandon-Smith's autopsy was conducted in secrecy and her remains cremated with such unseemly haste."

There was another silence. Teece, still gripping his briefcase, gave another quick, thin-lipped smile and followed Singer out the door.

Although Carson took his time arriving at the ready room the following morning, he was not surprised to find most of the bluesuits still on their racks. Nobody was anxious to go back into the Fever Tank.

As he dressed, he felt a knot tighten slowly in his stomach. It had been almost a week since the accident. As much as he'd been haunted by it—those gashes in Brandon-Smith's suit, the red blood welling up through the rents in her scrubs—he'd blocked the Fever Tank itself from his mind.

Now it came back to him in a rush: the cramped spaces, the stale air of the suit, the constant sense of danger. He closed his eyes a moment, forcing fear and panic from his mind.

As he was about to duck his head into his helmet, the outer door hissed open and de Vaca entered through the air lock. She looked at Carson.

"You're not looking particularly chipper," she said.

Carson shrugged.

"Me neither, I suppose," she said.

There was an awkward silence. They had not spoken much since Brandon-Smith's death. Carson suspected that de Vaca, sensing his guilt and frustration, had given him a wide berth.

"At least the guard survived," said de Vaca.

Carson nodded. The last thing he wanted to do now was discuss the accident. The stainless-steel door with its oversized biohazard label loomed at the far end of the room. It reminded Carson of what he imagined a gas chamber to look like.

De Vaca began suiting up. Carson hung back, waiting for her, eager to get past the initial ordeal but somehow unable to go through the door.

"I went riding the other day," he said. "Once you get out of sight of Mount Dragon, it's actually very nice out there."

De Vaca nodded. "I've always loved the desert," she said. "People say it's ugly, but I think it can be the most beautiful place in the world. Which horse did you take?"

"The liver-colored gelding. He turned out to be a pretty good horse. One of my spurs was broken, but it turned out I didn't even need to use them. Good luck getting a spur rowel fixed around here."

De Vaca laughed, slinging her hair. "You know that old Russian guy, Pavel Vladimiro-something? He's the mechanical engineer, runs the sterilizing furnace and laminar-flow system. He can fix anything. I had a broken CD player that he opened up and fixed, just like that. He claimed he'd never seen one before."

"Hell," said Carson, "if he can fix a CD player, he could fix a rowel. Maybe I should go see him."

"Any idea when that investigator's going to get around to us?" de Vaca asked.

"Nope," said Carson. "Probably won't take him long, considering . . ." He stopped. *Considering I was instrumental to the cause of death.*

"Yamashito, the video technician, said the investigator was planning to spend the day watching security tapes," she said, twisting into the arms of her suit.

They donned their helmets, checked each other's suits, and went through the air lock. Inside decontam, Carson took a big swallow of air and fought down the nausea that inevitably rose as the poisonous yellow liquid cascaded down his faceplate.

Carson had hoped the elaborate decontamination procedures after the accident would have rearranged the interior spaces of the Fever Tank, made them look somehow different. But the lab seemed just as Carson had left it the minute Brandon-Smith walked in to announce the chimp's death. His seat was pulled away from the desk at the same angle, and his PowerBook was still open, plugged into the WAN socket and ready for use. He moved toward it mechanically and logged on to the GeneDyne network. The log-in messages scrolled past; then the word processor came up, displaying the procedure write-up he'd been finishing. The cursor came into focus at the end of an unfinished line, blinking, waiting with cruel detachment for him to continue. Carson slumped in his chair.

Suddenly, the screen went blank. Carson waited a moment, then hit a few keys. Getting no response, he swore under his breath. Maybe the battery had gone dead. He glanced over to the wall plug and noticed that the laptop was plugged in. *Strange.*

Something began to materialize on the screen. *Must be Scopes,* Carson thought. The GeneDyne CEO was known to play with other people's computers. Probably a prepared pep talk, some way to ease the transition back into the Fever Tank.

A small picture came into focus: the image of a mime, balancing the Earth on his finger. The Earth was slowly revolving. Mystified, Carson punched the Escape key without success.

The small figure suddenly dissolved into typed words.

Guy Carson?

Here, Carson typed back.

Am I speaking with Guy Carson?

This is Guy Carson, who else?

Well, looky here, Guy! It's about time you logged in. I've been waiting for you, partner. But first, I need you to identify yourself. Please enter your mother's birthday.

June 2, 1936. Who is this?

Thank you. This is Mime speaking. I have an important message from an old homeboy of yours.

Mime? Is that you, Harper?

No, it is not Harper. I would suggest that you clear your immediate area so that no one inadvertently sees the message I am about to transmit. Let me know when you're ready.

Carson glanced over at de Vaca, who was busy on the other side of the lab.

Who the hell is this? he typed angrily.

My, my! You had best not dis the Mime, or I might dis you back. And you wouldn't like that. Not one bit.

Listen, I don't like—

Do you want the message or not?

No.

I didn't think so. Before I send it, I want you to know that this is an absolutely secure channel, and that I, Mime, and none other, have hacked into the GeneDyne net. No one at GeneDyne knows about this or could possibly intercept our conversation. I have done this to protect you, cowboy. If anyone should happen by while you are reading the following message, press the command key and a fake screen of genetic code will pop up, hiding the message. Actually, it won't be genetic code, it will be the lyrics to Professor Longhair's "Ball the Wall," but the patterns will be correct. Press the command key again to return to the message. Whoopie-ki-yi-yo, and all that sort of thing. Now sit tight.

Carson again glanced in de Vaca's direction. Perhaps this was one of Scopes's jokes. The man had an odd sense of humor. On the other hand, Scopes hadn't sent a single message to the laptop in Carson's quarters since the accident. Perhaps Scopes was pissed off at him, and was testing his loyalty with some kind of game. Carson looked uneasily back at the laptop.

The screen went black for a moment, then a message appeared:

> *Dear Guy,*
> *This is Charles Levine, your old professor. Biochem 162, remember? I'll get right to the point, because I know you must feel compromised at the moment.*

Jesus, thought Carson. *Understatement of the year.* Dr. Levine, penetrating the GeneDyne network? It didn't seem possible. But if it *was* Levine, and if Scopes found out . . . Carson's finger moved quickly to the Escape key again, punching it several times without result.

> *Guy, I've heard rumors from a source in the regulatory agency. Rumors of an accident at Mount Dragon. The lid's been shut down tight, though, and all I've been able to learn is that someone was accidentally infected with a virus. Apparently it's quite a deadly virus, one that people are scared to death of.*
> *Guy, listen to me. I need your help. I need to know what's going on out there at Mount Dragon. What is this virus? What are you trying to do with it? Is it really as dangerous as the rumors imply? The people of this country have a right to know. If it's true—if you really are out in the middle of nowhere, messing with something far more dangerous than an atomic bomb—then none of us are safe.*
> *I remember you well from your days here, Guy.*

You were a truly independent thinker. A skeptic. You never accepted what I told you as given; you had to prove it for yourself. That is a rare quality, and I pray you haven't lost it. I would beg you now to turn that natural skepticism on your work at Mount Dragon. Don't accept everything they tell you. Deep inside, you know that nothing is infallible, that no safety procedure can ensure one hundred percent protection. If the rumors are true, you've learned this firsthand. Please ask yourself: Is it worth it?

I will be in contact with you again through Mime, who is an expert in matters of network security. Next time, perhaps we can talk on line: Mime wasn't willing to risk a live conversation initially.

Think about what I've said, Guy. Please.

Best regards,

Charles Levine

The screen went blank. Carson felt his heart pounding as he fumbled with the power switch. He should have turned the thing off immediately. Could it really have been Levine? His instincts told him that it was. The man must be insane to contact him like this, endangering his career. As Carson thought about it, anger began to take the place of shock. How the hell could Levine be so sure the channel was secure?

Carson remembered Levine well: stomping across the lectern, speaking impassionedly, suit lapels flapping, chalk screeching on the blackboard. Once he had been so engrossed in writing a long chemical formula that he shuffled off the edge of the lectern and fell to the floor. In many ways, he had been an outstanding professor: iconoclastic, visionary; but, Carson remembered, also excitable, angry, and full of hyperbole. And this was going too far. The man had obviously become a zealot.

He switched the PowerBook back on and logged in a second time. If he heard from Levine again, he'd tell him exactly what he thought of his methods. Then he'd turn the machine off before Levine had a chance to reply.

He turned back to the screen and his heart stopped.

Brent Scopes is paging.
Press the command key to chat.

Fighting back dread, Carson began typing. Had Scopes picked up the message?

Ciao, Guy.

Hello, Brent.

I just wanted to welcome you back. You know what T.H. Huxley said: 'The great tragedy of science is the slaying of a beautiful hypothesis by an ugly fact.' That is what has happened here. It was a beautiful idea, Guy. Too bad it didn't work out. Now, you've got to move on. Every day we go without results costs GeneDyne almost a million dollars. Everyone is waiting for the neutralization of the virus. We cannot continue until that step has been accomplished. Everyone's depending on you.

I know, Carson wrote. I promise I'll do my best.

That's a start, Guy. Doing you best is a start. But we need results. We've had one failure, but failure is an integral part of silence, and I know you can come through. I'm counting on you to come through. You've had almost a week to think about it. I hope you have some new ideas.

We're going to repeat the test, see if by chance we overlooked something. We're also going to remap the gene, just in case.

Very well, but do it quickly. I also want you to try something else. You see, we learned something crucial from this failure. I've got the autopsy results on Brandon-Smith in front of me. Dr. Grady did an excellent job. For some reason the strain you designed was even more virulent than the usual X-FLU strain. And more contagious, if our pathology tests are correct. It killed her so fast that antibodies to the virus had only been in her bloodstream a few hours when she died. I want to know why. We had the strain cultured from Brandon-Smith's brain matter prior to cremation, and I'm having it sent down to you. We're calling this new strain X-FLU II. I want you to dissect that virus. I want to know how it ticks. In trying to neutralize the virus, you fortuitously stumbled on a way to enhance its deadliness instead.

Fortuitously? I'm not sure I understand—

Jesus Christ, Guy, if you figure out what made it more deadly, maybe you can figure out how to make it LESS deadly. I'm a little surprised you didn't think of this yourself. Now get to work.

The communications window on the screen winked shut. Carson sat back, exhaling slowly. Clinically, it made sense, but the thought of working with a virus cultured from Brandon-Smith's brain chilled his blood.

As if on cue, a lab assistant stepped through the entranceway, carrying a stainless-steel tray loaded with clear plastic bioboxes. Each biobox was marked with a biohazard symbol and a simple label: X-FLU II.

"Present for Guy Carson," he said with a macabre chuckle.

The late-afternoon sun, streaming in the west-facing windows, covered Singer's office in a mantle of golden light. Nye sat on the sofa, staring silently into the kiva fireplace, while the director stood behind his workstation, back turned, looking out at the vast desert.

A slight figure with an oversized briefcase appeared in the doorway and coughed politely.

"Come in," Singer said. Gilbert Teece stepped forward, nodding to them both. His thinning wheat-colored hair imperfectly covered a scalp that gleamed a painful red, and his burnt nose was already peeling. He smiled bashfully, as if aware of his own inadequacy to the hostile environment.

"Sit down anywhere." Singer waved his hand vaguely over the office furniture.

Despite the empty wing chairs, Teece moved immediately toward Nye's sofa and sat down with a sigh of contentment. The security director stiffened and shifted, moving himself away.

"Shall we get started?" said Singer, sitting down. "I hate to be late for my evening cocktail." Teece, busy with his briefcase latch, looked up and flashed a quick smile. Then he slipped his hand inside the case and removed a microcassette player, which he laid carefully on the table in front of him.

"I'll keep this as short as possible," he said.

At the same time, Nye brandished his own recorder, laying it next to Teece's.

"Very good," said Teece. "Always a good idea to get things down on tape, don't you think, Mr. Nye?"

"Yes," came the clipped reply.

"Ah!" said Teece, as surprised as if he had not heard Nye speak before. "English?"

Nye slowly turned to look at him. "Originally."

"Myself as well," said Teece. "My father was Sir Wilberforce Teece, Baronet, of Teecewood Hall in the Pennines. My older brother got the title and the money and I got a ticket to America. Do you know it? Teecewood Hall, I mean."

"No," Nye said.

"Indeed?" Teece arched his eyebrows. "Beautiful part of the country. The Hall's in Hamsterley Forest, but Cumbria's so near by, you know. Lovely, especially this time of year. Grasmere, Troutbeck . . . Windermere Lake."

The atmosphere in the office grew suddenly electric. Nye turned toward Teece and focused his eyes on the man's smiling face. "I suggest, Mr. Teece, that we cut out the civilities and proceed with the interview."

"But, Mr. Nye," Teece cried, "the interview *has* started! As I understand it, you were once chief of safety operations at the Windermere Nuclear Complex. Late seventies, I believe. Then there was that dreadful accident." He shook his head at the memory. "I keep forgetting whether there were sixteen or sixty casualties. Anyway, before joining GeneDyne UK, you couldn't find work in your chosen field for nearly ten years. Am I right? Instead, you were employed by an oil company in a remote portion of the Middle East. The details of your job description there are, unfortunately, rather vague." He scratched the tip of his peeling nose.

"This has nothing whatsoever to do with your assignment," said Nye slowly.

"But it has a lot to do with the strength of your loyalty to Brent Scopes," Teece said. "And that loyalty, in turn, may have a bearing on this investigation."

"This is a farce," Nye snapped. "I intend to report your conduct to your superiors."

"What conduct?" Teece said with a faint smile. And then without waiting for an answer, he added, "And what superiors?"

Nye leaned toward him and spoke very softly. "Stop playing coy. You know perfectly well what happened at Windermere. You don't need to ask these questions, and you'll learn bugger-all from me about it."

"Now, wait a moment," Singer said with false heartiness. "Mr. Nye, we shouldn't—"

Teece held up his hand. "I'm sorry. Mr. Nye is right. I *do* know everything about Windermere. I just like to verify my facts. These reports"—he patted his massive briefcase—"are so often inaccurate. Government workers write them, and you never know what some witless bureaucrat might say about you, now do you, Mr. Nye? I thought you might appreciate the chance to set the record straight, erase any existing calumnies, that kind of thing."

Nye sat in rigid silence.

Teece shrugged, pulled a manila envelope out of his briefcase. "Very well, Mr. Nye. Let's proceed. Could you tell me, in your words, what happened on the morning of the accident?"

Nye cleared his throat. "At nine-fifty, I received word of a stage-two alert from the Level-5 facility."

"Lots of numbers. What do they all mean?"

"That an integrity breach had occurred. Someone's biohazard suit had been compromised."

"And who made this report?"

"Carson. Dr. Guy Carson. He reported it over the global emergency channel."

"I see," Teece nodded. "Proceed."

"I went immediately to the security station, assessed the

situation, then assumed command of the facility for the duration of the stage-two alert."

"Did you, now? Before informing Dr. Singer?" Teece looked toward the director.

"That is the protocol," said Nye flatly.

"And Dr. Singer, when you heard that Mr. Nye had put himself in charge you cheerfully agreed, naturally?"

"Naturally."

"Dr. Singer," said Teece a little more sharply. "I spent this afternoon reviewing videotapes of the accident. I've listened to most of the communications that took place. Now, would you care to answer the question again?"

There was a silence. "Well," Singer said at last, "the truth is, I wasn't too happy about it, no. But I went along."

"And Mr. Nye," Teece continued, "you say that assuming temporary command was company protocol. But according to my information, you're only supposed to do so if, in your judgment, the director is unable to appropriately discharge his duties."

"That is correct," said Nye.

"Therefore, I can only conclude that you had prior reason to think the director was not discharging his duties properly."

There was another long pause. "That is correct," Nye repeated.

"That's absurd!" Singer cried out. "There was no need for it. I had complete control of the situation."

Nye sat rigidly, his face a stone mask.

"So what was it," Teece continued placidly, "that led you to think Dr. Singer here wouldn't have been able to handle the emergency?"

This time, Nye didn't hesitate. "I felt Dr. Singer had allowed himself to become too close to the people he was supposed to be supervising. He is a scientist, but he is overly emotional and poor at handling stress. If the emergency had been left in his hands, the outcome might have been quite different."

Singer jumped to his feet. "What's wrong with being a little friendly?" he snapped. "Mr. Teece, it should be obvious even on such short acquaintance what kind of man you're talking to here. He's a megalomaniac. Nobody likes him. He disappears into the desert practically every weekend. Why Scopes keeps him on is a mystery to everyone."

"Ah! I see." Teece cheerfully consulted his folder, letting the uncomfortable silence lengthen. Singer returned to his original position at the window, his back to Nye. Teece took a pen from his pocket and made a few notations. Then he waggled it in front of Nye. "I understand these things are *streng verboten* around here. Good thing I'm exempt. I hate computers." He replaced the pen carefully.

"Now, Dr. Singer," he continued, "let's proceed to this virus you're working on. X-FLU. The documents I've been given are rather uninformative. What, exactly, makes it so deadly?"

"Once we've learned that," Singer said, "we'll be able to do something about it."

"Do something about it?"

"Make it safe, of course."

"Why are you working with such a terrifying pathogen to begin with?"

Singer turned to face him. "It wasn't our intention, believe me. The virulence of X-FLU is an unexpected side effect of our gene-therapy technique. The virus is in transition. Once the product is stabilized, this will no longer be a concern." He paused. "The tragedy is that Rosalind was exposed to the virus at this early stage."

"Rosalind Brandon-Smith." Teece repeated the name slowly. "We're not entirely happy with the way her autopsy was conducted, as you know."

"We followed all the standard guidelines," Nye interjected.

"The autopsy was conducted within the Level-5 facility, in security suits, and was followed by incineration of the corpse and decontamination of all laboratories within the secure perimeter."

"It's the brevity of the pathologist's report that concerns me, Mr. Nye," Teece said. "And brief as it is, there are several things that puzzle me. For example, as best as I can fathom, Brandon-Smith's brain essentially exploded. And yet at the time of death she was locked in the quarantine chamber, far from any medical help."

"We didn't know that she had contracted the disease," said Singer.

"How can that be? She was scratched by an infected chimpanzee. Surely she would have shown antibodies in her bloodstream."

"No. From the time the antibodies appear until time of death—well, it can obviously be very short."

Teece frowned. "Disturbingly short, it appears."

"You've got to remember, this is the first time a human being has been exposed to the X-FLU virus. And hopefully the last. We didn't know what to expect. And the X-FLU strain was particularly virulent. By the time the blood tests came back positive, she was dead."

"The blood. That's another strange thing in this report. Apparently, there was significant internal bleeding before death." Teece looked in his folder, and caressed the paragraph with his finger. "Look here. Her organs were practically awash in blood. Leakage from the blood vessels, it says."

"No doubt a symptom of the X-FLU infection," said Singer. "Not unheard of. The Ebola virus does the same thing."

"But the pathology reports I have on the X-FLU chimpanzees don't show any such symptom."

"Obviously the disease affects humans differently from chimps. Nothing remarkable about that."

"Perhaps not." Teece flipped pages. "But there are other

curious things about this report. For example, her brain shows high levels of certain neurotransmitters. Dopamine and serotonin, to be exact."

Singer spread his hands. "Another symptom of X-FLU, I'd expect."

Teece closed the folder. "Again, the infected chimps show no such elevated levels."

Singer sighed. "Mr. Teece, what's your point? We've all too aware of the dangerousness of this virus. Our efforts have been directed toward neutralizing it. We have a scientist, Guy Carson, devoted to nothing else."

"Carson. Yes. The one who replaced Franklin Burt. Poor Dr. Burt, currently residing in Featherwood Park sanatorium." Teece leaned forward and lowered his voice. "Now, that's another really odd thing, Doctor. I talked to a David Fossey, Franklin Burt's attending physician. Burt also has leaky blood vessels. And his levels of dopamine and serotonin are wildly elevated."

There was a shocked silence in the room.

"Jesus," said Singer. His eyes had taken on a faraway look, as if he was calculating something.

Teece held up a finger. "But! Burt exhibits no X-FLU antibodies, and it's been weeks since he was at Mount Dragon. So he can't have the disease."

There was a noticeable decrease of tension. "A coincidence, then," Nye said, sitting back in the sofa.

"Unlikely. Are you working on any other deadly pathogens here?"

Singer shook his head. "We have the usual stuff on ice— Marburg, Ebola Zaire, Lassa—but none of those would cause insanity."

"Quite right," said Teece. "Nothing else?"

"Absolutely not."

Teece turned toward the security director. "What exactly did happen to Dr. Burt?"

"Dr. Singer recommended his removal," Nye said simply.

"Dr. Singer?" Teece prompted.

"He was becoming confused, agitated." Singer hesitated. "We were friends. He was an unusually sensitive person, very kind and concerned. Though he didn't talk about it much, I think he missed his wife a great deal. The stress here is remarkable. . . . You need a certain kind of toughness, which he didn't have. It did him in. When I began to notice signs of incipient paranoia, I recommended he be taken to Albuquerque General for observation."

"The stress did him in," Teece murmured. "Forgive my saying so, Doctor, but what you describe doesn't sound like a garden-variety nervous breakdown to me." He glanced down at his open briefcase. "I believe Dr. Burt got his M.D./Ph.D. degree from Johns Hopkins in five years—half the time it normally takes."

"Yes," said Singer. "He was . . . is . . . a brilliant man."

"Then, according to the background sheet I was given, Dr. Burt did one of his medical rotations in the emergency room at the Harlem Meer Hospital, 944 East 155th Street. Ever seen that neighborhood?"

"No," said Singer.

"The police call people who live around there Dixie Cups. A macabre reference to the disposability of life in that neck of the woods. Dr. Burt's rotation was what interns call a thirty-six special. He was on call in the emergency room thirty-six hours straight, off for twelve, then back on for another thirty-six. Day after day, for three months."

"I didn't know that," Singer said. "He never talked much about his past."

"Then, during his first two years of residency, Dr. Burt managed to write a four-hundred-page monograph, *Metastization*. A superb piece of work. At the time he was also involved in a bitter divorce with his first wife."

Teece paused again, then spoke loudly. "And you're telling me this man couldn't handle *stress?*" He barked a laugh, but his face had lost its expression of mirth even before the sound of his laughter died.

Nobody spoke. After a moment, the inspector stood. "Well, gentlemen, I think I've taken up enough of your time for the present." He stuffed the cassette recorder and folder into his briefcase. "No doubt we'll have more to talk about once I've met with your staff." He scratched his peeling nose and grinned sheepishly.

"Some people tan, some burn," he said. "I guess I'm a burner myself."

Night had fallen on the white clapboard house that stood at the corner of Church Street and Sycamore Terrace in the Cleveland suburb of River Pointe. A soft May breeze rustled the leaves, and the distant barking of a dog and a lonely train whistle added a sense of mystery to the quiet neighborhood.

The light emanating from the gabled second-story window was not the warm yellow light found in the windows of other houses along the street. It was a subdued blue, similar to the glow of a television but unwavering in color or intensity. A passerby, stopping beneath the open window, could have heard a soft beeping sound, along with the faint slow clicking of computer keys. But no pedestrians were strolling along the quiet lane.

Inside the room sat a small figure. Behind the figure was a bare wall, into which a plain wooden door was set; the other walls were crowded with metal racks. Within the racks, rows of electronic circuit boards rose toward the ceiling with aching regularity. Among the circuit boards could be seen monitors, RAID fixed-disk systems, and equipment that numerous small governments would have liked to acquire: network sniffers, fax interception devices, units for the remote seizure of computer screen images, dedicated password breakers, cellular telephone scanner-interceptors. The room smelled faintly of hot metal and ozone. Thick bundles of cables hung drooping between the racks like jungle snakes.

The figure shifted, causing the wheelchair in which it sat to creak in protest. A withered limb rose toward the custom-made keyboard set along one arm of the wheelchair. A single crooked finger flexed itself in the blue light, then began pressing the soft-touch pads of the keyboard. There was the faint rapid tone of high-speed dialing. In one of the metal racks, a CRT sprang to life. A burst of computer code scrolled across the screen, followed by a small corporate logo.

The finger moved up to a row of oversized, color-coded keys and selected one.

Silent seconds stretched into minutes. The figure in the wheelchair did not believe in breaking into computer systems by methods as crude as brute-force attacks or algorithm reversals. Instead, his program inserted itself at the point where the external Internet traffic entered the corporation's private network, piggybacking onto the header packets entering at the gate machine and circumventing the password routines completely. Suddenly the screen flashed and a torrent of code began scrolling by. The withered arm raised itself again and began typing first slowly, and then somewhat more rapidly, tapping out chunks of hexadecimal computer code, pausing every so often to wait for a response. The screen turned red, and the words "GeneDyne Online Systems—Maintenance Subsection" appeared, followed by a short list of options.

Once again, he had penetrated the GeneDyne firewall.

The undeveloped arm raised a third time, initiating two programs that would work symbiotically. The first would place a temporary patch on one of the operating system files, masking the movements of the second by making it look like a harmless network maintenance agent. The second, meanwhile, would create a secure channel through the network backbone to the Mount Dragon facility.

The figure in the wheelchair waited patiently as the programs bypassed the network bridges and pipelines. At last came a low beep, then a series of routing messages scrolled across the screen.

The arm reached out to the keyboard again, and the hissing shriek of a modem filled the room. A second screen popped to life and a sentence, rapidly typed by an unseen hand, appeared on it.

> You said you'd call an hour ago! It's not easy, keeping my schedule clear while I wait to hear from you.

The shriveled finger pressed out a response on the padded keyboard: I love it when you get all righteous on me, professor-man. Testify! Write that funky formula for me one time!

> It's too late, he must have left the lab by now.

The finger tapped another message.

> O ye of little faith! No doubt Dr. Carson has another computer in his room. We should be able to gain his undivided attention there. Now remember the ground rules.

Right. Let's go.

The finger pressed a button, and another waiting subroutine began executing, sending an anonymous page across the Mount Dragon WAN to Guy Carson. Based on the previous encounter, Mime decided to dispense with his standard greeting card; Carson might turn off his computer if he saw Mime's introductory logo again. A moment passed; then a response appeared, out of the New Mexico desert:

Guy here. Who's this?

The finger pressed a single color-coded key, sending a pre-typed message across the network.

What it is! Let me introduce myself again: I am Mime, bearer of tidings. I give you Professor Levine. With the push of another key, the finger patched Levine into the secure channel.

Forget it, came Carson's response. Get off the system now.

Guy, please, this is Charles Levine. Wait a minute. Let me talk.

No way. I'm rebooting.

Mime pressed another button, and another message flashed on the screen.

Just a dern minute, pardner! This is Mime you're dealing with. We control the vertical, we control the horizontal. I've put a little snare on your network node, and if you cut our connection now you'll trigger the internal alarms. Then you'd have some fast talking to do to your dear Mr. Scopes. I'm afraid the only way to get rid of the Mime is to hear the good professor out. Now listen, cowboy. At the professor-man's request, I have set up a means by which you can call him. Should you ever wish to reach him, simply send a chat request to yourself. That's correct: to yourself. This will initiate a communications daemon I've hidden inside the net. The daemon will dial out and connect you with the good professor, as long as his trusty laptop is on-line. I now yield the floor to Professor Levine.

If you think this is the way to persuade me, Levine, you're mistaken. You're jeopardizing my whole career. I don't want anything to do with you and your crusade, whatever it is.

I have no choice, Guy. The virus is a killer.

We have the best safety precautions of any lab in the world—

Apparently not good enough.

That was a freak accident.

Most accidents are.

We're working on a medical product that will produce incalculable good, that will save millions of lives every year. Don't tell me what we're doing is wrong.

Guy, I believe you. Then why mess around with a deadly virus like this?

Look, that's the whole problem, we're trying to neutralize the virus, make it harmless. Now get off the net.

Not yet. What's this medical miracle you mentioned?

I can't talk about it.

Answer this: does this virus alter the DNA in human germ cells, or just in somatic cells?

Germ cells.

I knew it. Guy, do you really think you have the moral right to alter the human genome?

For a beneficial alteration, why not? If we can rid the human race of a terrible disease forever, where's the immorality?

What disease?

None of your business.

I get it. You're using the virus to make the genetic alteration. This virus, is it a doomsday virus? Could it destroy the human race? Answer that question and I'll get off.

I don't know. Its epidemiology in humans is mostly unknown, but it's been 100% lethal in chimpanzees. We're taking all precautions. Especially now.

Is it an airborne contagion?

Yes.

Incubation period?

One day to two weeks, depending on the strain.

Time between first symptoms and mortality?

Impossible to predict with any certainty. Several minutes to several hours.

Several minutes? Dear God. Mode of lethality?

I've answered enough questions. Get off.

Mode of lethality?

Massive increase in CSF, causing edema and hemorrhaging of the brain tissue.

That sure sounds like a doomsday virus to me. What's its name?

That's it, Levine. No more questions. Get the hell off the system and don't call again.

Back at the little house on the corner of Church and Sycamore, the arm gently pressed a few keys. One CRT screen showed the daemon program cutting communications and sneaking back out of the GeneDyne net. The other screen showed Levine's frantic message:

Damn! We were cut off. Mime, I need more time!

The finger pressed out a response:

> Chill, professor. Your zeal will do you in. Now, on to other business. Ready your computer, I'm going to be sending you an interesting little file. As you'll see, I was able to obtain the information you requested. Naturally. It posed a rather unique challenge, and you'd be astonished at the phone charges I rang up in the process. A certain Mrs. Harriet Smythe of Northfield, Minnesota, is going to be rather upset when she gets her long-distance bill next month, I'm afraid.

The finger pressed a few more keys and waited while the file was downloaded. Then both screens zapped to black. For a moment, the only sound in the room was the soft whine of the CPU fans, and, through the open window, a single cricket chirruping in the warm night. And then there came a low laugh, a rising wheeze of mirth that racked and rattled the wasted, shrunken body in the wheelchair.

The chef at Mount Dragon—an Italian named Ricciolini—always served the main course himself, in order to bask in the expected compliments, and as a result dinner service was execrably slow. Carson sat at a center table with Harper and Vanderwagon, battling a stubborn headache without success. Despite the pressure from Scopes, he'd been able to accomplish almost nothing that day, his mind full of Levine's message. He wondered how in hell Levine was able to get inside the GeneDyne net, and why Levine had picked him to contact. *At least*, he thought, *nobody noticed.* As far as he could tell.

The little chef laid the plates with a flourish at Carson's table and stepped back expectantly. Carson looked suspiciously at his serving. The menu called them sweetbreads but what arrived did not look like bread at all, but the mysterious inner part of some animal.

"Wonderful!" cried Harper, taking the cue. "A masterpiece!"

The Italian gave a quick half bow, his face a mask of delight.

Vanderwagon sat silently, polishing his silverware with a napkin.

"What is it, exactly?" inquired Carson.

"*Animella con marsala e funghi!*" the chef cried. "Sweetbreads with wine and mushrooms."

"Sweet bread?" Carson asked.

A puzzled expression came over the man's face. "Is not English? Sweetbreads?"

"What I mean is, exactly what part of the cow—?"

Harper clapped him on the back. " 'Tis better not to inquire too closely into some things, my friend."

The Italian gave a puzzled smile and returned to the kitchen.

"They should clean these dishes better," Vanderwagon muttered, wiping his wineglass, holding it up to the light, and wiping again.

Harper shot a look across the room, where Teece was eating at a table by himself. His fastidious manners were almost a caricature of perfection.

"Has he talked to you yet?" Harper whispered to Carson.

"No. You?"

"He buttonholed me this morning."

Vanderwagon turned. "What did he ask?"

"Just a lot of sly questions about the accident. Don't be deceived by his looks. That guy is no fool."

"Sly questions," Vanderwagon repeated, picking up his knife a second time and wiping it carefully. Then he laid it down and carefully squared it with his fork.

"Why the hell can't we have a nice steak once in a while?" Carson complained. "I never know what I'm eating."

"Think of it as experiencing international cuisine," said Harper, slicing open the sweetbreads and stuffing a jiggling piece into his mouth. "Excellent," he said, his mouth full.

Carson took a tentative bite. "Hey, these aren't bad," he said. "Not very sweet, though. So much for truth in advertising."

"Pancreas," said Harper.

Carson laid down his fork with a clatter. "Thanks a lot."

"What kind of sly questions?" Vanderwagon asked.

"I'm not supposed to say." Harper winked at Carson.

Vanderwagon turned sideways and gave Harper a penetrating stare. "About me."

"No, not about you, Andrew. Well, maybe a few, you know. You were, shall we say, in the thick of things."

Vanderwagon slid his uneaten plate away and said nothing.

Carson leaned over. "This is from the pancreas of a *cow?*"

Harper shoveled another mouthful in. "Who cares? That Ricciolini can cook anything. Anyway, Guy, you grew up eating Rocky Mountain oysters, right?"

"Never touched 'em," Carson said. "That was just something we served to the dudes as a joke."

"If thy right eye offends thee," Vanderwagon said.

The others turned to look at him.

"Getting religion?" Harper asked.

"Yes. Pluck it out," Vanderwagon said.

There was an uneasy silence.

"You all right, Andrew?" Carson asked.

"Oh, yes," said Vanderwagon.

"Remember Biology 101?" Harper asked. "The Islets of Langerhans?"

"Shut up," Carson warned.

"Islets of Langerhans," Harper continued. "Those clusters of cells in the pancreas that secrete hormones. I wonder if you can see them with the naked eye?"

Vanderwagon stared at his plate, then slowly brought his knife up and sliced neatly through the sweetbreads. He picked up the piece of organ with his fingers, looked carefully at the incision he'd made, then dropped the morsel again, sending sauce and pieces of mushroom flying onto the white table-cloth. He poured some water into his napkin, folded it, and carefully wiped his hands. "No," he said.

"No what?"

"They're not visible."

Harper snickered. "If Ricciolini saw us playing with our food like this, he'd poison us."

"What?" Vanderwagon said loudly.

"I was just kidding. Calm down."

"Not you," Vanderwagon said. "I was talking to *him*."

There was another silence.

"Yes sir, I will!" Vanderwagon shouted. He came to attention suddenly, knocking his chair over as he stood up. His hands were straight at his sides, fork in one and knife in the other. Slowly, he raised the fork, then swiveled it toward his face. Each movement was calculated, almost reverent. He looked as if he was about to take a bite from the empty fork.

"Andrew, what are you up to now?" Harper said, chuckling nervously. "Look at this guy, will you?"

Vanderwagon raised the fork several inches.

"For Chrissakes, sit down," Harper said.

The fork inched closer, the tines trembling slightly in Vanderwagon's hand.

Carson realized what the scientist was about to do the instant before it happened. Vanderwagon never blinked as he placed the tines of the fork against the cornea of one eye. Then he pressed his fist forward with slow, deliberate pressure. For a second, Carson could see, with horrifying clarity, the ocular membrane yielding under the tines of the fork; then there was the sound of a grape being stepped on and clear liquid sprayed across the table in a viscous jet. Carson lunged for the arm, jerking it back. The fork came out of the eye and clattered to the floor as Vanderwagon began to make a high, keening noise.

Harper leaped forward to help but Vanderwagon slashed with his knife and the scientist fell backward into his chair. Harper looked down in disbelief at the red stripe spreading across his chest. Vanderwagon lunged again and Carson moved in, bringing a fist up toward his gut. Vanderwagon anticipated the blow, jerked sideways, and Carson's hand glanced harmlessly off Vanderwagon's hipbone. A moment later, Carson felt a stunning blow to the side of his skull. He stumbled backward, shaking his head, cursing himself for underestimating the man. As his vision cleared he saw Vanderwagon bearing down on him and he swung with his right, connecting with the scientist's temple. Vanderwagon's head snapped sideways and he crashed to the floor. Grabbing the wrist that held the knife, Carson slammed it to the floor until the knife came free. Vanderwagon arched forward, screaming incoherently, fluid streaming from his ruined eye. Carson gave him a short, measured blow to the chin and he rolled sideways and lay still, his flanks heaving.

Carson eased back carefully, hearing for the first time the tremendous hubbub of voices around him. His hand began to throb in time with the beat of his heart. The rest of the diners had come forward, forming a circle around the table. "Medical's on the way," a voice said. Carson looked up at Harper, who nodded back. "I'm okay," he gasped, pressing a bloodied napkin against his chest.

Then there was a hand on Carson's shoulder and Teece's thin, peeling face passed his field of vision. The inspector knelt beside Vanderwagon.

"Andrew?"

Vanderwagon's good eye slid around and located Teece.

"Why did you do that?" Teece asked sympathetically.

"Do what?"

Teece pursed his lips. "Never mind," he said quietly.

"Always talking . . ."

"I understand," Teece said.

"Pluck out . . ."

"Who told you to pluck it out?"

"Get me out of here!" Vanderwagon suddenly screamed.

"We're going to do just that," said Mike Marr as he made his way through the circle of diners, pushing Teece aside. Two medical workers lifted Vanderwagon onto a stretcher. The investigator followed the group toward the door, leaning over the stretcher, crooning: "Who? Tell me who?"

But the medic had already sunk a needle in Vanderwagon's arm and the scientist's one good eye rolled up into his head as the powerful narcotic took effect.

The studio's Green Room wasn't green at all, but a pale yellow. A sofa and several overstuffed chairs were lined up against the walls, and in the center a scratched Bauhaus coffee table was piled high with copies of *People*, *Newsweek*, and *The Economist*. On a table in the far corner sat a pot of well-cooked coffee, a pile of Styrofoam cups, some elderly looking cream, and an untidy heap of sweetener packages.

Levine decided not to chance the coffee. He shifted on the sofa, glancing around again. Besides himself and Toni Wheeler, the foundation's media consultant, there was only one other person in the room, a sallow-faced man in a glen plaid suit. Feeling Levine's eyes on him, the man glanced up, then looked away, dabbing his sweaty forehead with a silk handkerchief. He was clutching a book: *The Courage to Be Different*, by Barrold Leighton.

Toni Wheeler was whispering into his ear, and Levine made an effort to listen.

"—a mistake," she was saying. "We shouldn't be here, and you know it. This isn't the kind of forum you should be seen in."

Levine sighed. "We've already been through this," he whispered back. "Mr. Sanchez is interested in our cause."

"Sanchez is only interested in one thing: controversy. Look, what's the point of paying me if you never take my advice? We need to be shoring up your image, making you look dignified, patrician. A statesman in the crusade against dangerous science. This show is exactly what you don't need."

"What I need is more exposure," Levine replied. "People know I speak the truth. And I've been making real progress in recent weeks. When they hear about this"—he patted his breast pocket—"they'll learn what 'dangerous science' really is."

Ms. Wheeler shook her head. "Our focus group research shows you're beginning to be perceived as eccentric. The recent lawsuits, and especially this thing with GeneDyne, are throwing your credibility into question."

"My credibility? Impossible." The perspiring man caught his eye again. "I'll bet that's Barrold Leighton himself," Levine whispered. "Here to promote his book, no doubt. Must be his first time on television. *The Courage to Be Different*, indeed. He's a poor choice to be hawking courage to the world."

"Don't change the subject. Your credibility is compromised. The Harvard chair, your work with the Holocaust Fund, just isn't enough anymore. We need to regroup, do damage control, alter your public perception. Charles, I'm asking you again. Don't do this."

A woman poked her head in the door. "Levine, please," she said in a flat voice.

Levine stood up, smiled and waved at his publicist, then followed the woman through the door and into Makeup. *Damage control, indeed*, Levine thought as a cosmetician placed him in a barber chair and began working his jawline with a crayon. Toni Wheeler sounded more like a submarine captain than a media consultant. She was clever and savvy, but she was a spin doctor at heart. She still didn't understand that it wasn't his nature to back down in the face of a struggle. Besides, he'd decided he *needed* a vehicle like this. The press had barely touched his account of the Novo-Druzhina accident. They thought it was too long ago and far away. "Sammy Sanchez at Seven" was based in Boston, but its broadcast feed was picked up by a string of independent stations across the country. Not "Geraldo," perhaps, but good enough. He felt inside his suit jacket for the two envelopes. He was confident, even buoyant. This was going to be very, very good.

Studio C was typical: a faux Victorian oasis of dark wallpaper and mahogany chairs surrounded by dangling lights, television cameras, and a hundred snaking cables. Levine knew the other two panelists well: Finley Squires, the pit-bull-in-a-suit of the pharmaceutical industry, and consumer activist Theresa Court. They'd already had the first segment of the show to themselves, but Levine relished the disadvantage. He stepped across the concrete floor, picking his way carefully over the cables. Sammy Sanchez himself sat in a swivel chair at the far side of the round table, his lean predatory face gazing at Levine. He motioned him to a seat as the countdown to the second segment began.

As the live feed started, Sanchez briefly introduced Levine to the other panelists and the estimated two million viewers, then turned the discussion over to Squires. From the monitor in the makeup room, Levine had seen Squires holding forth on the benefits of genetic engineering. Levine couldn't wait: he felt like a boxer in top shape, advancing into the ring.

"Do you have a baby with Tay-Sachs disease?" Squires was saying, "Or sickle-cell anemia? Or hemophilia?"

He gazed into the camera, his face full of concern. Then he gestured at Levine without looking at him. "Dr. Levine here would deny you the legal right to cure your child. If he has his way, millions of sick people, who *could* be cured of these genetic diseases, will be forced to suffer."

He paused, voice dropping.

"Dr. Levine calls his organization the Foundation for Genetic Policy. Don't be fooled. This is no foundation. This is a *lobbying* organization, which is trying to keep the miraculous cures offered by genetic engineering from you. Denying *your* right to choose. Making *your* children suffer."

Sammy Sanchez swiveled in his chair, raising one eyebrow in Levine's direction. "Dr. Levine? Is it true? Would you deny my child the right to such a cure?"

"Absolutely not," Levine said, smiling calmly. "I'm a geneticist by training. After all, as I recently made public, I was one of the developers of the X-RUST variety of corn, though I have refrained from profiting by it. Dr. Squires is grossly distorting my position."

"A geneticist by training, perhaps, but not by practice," Squires continued. "Genetic engineering offers hope. Dr. Levine offers despair. What he terms a 'cautious, conservative approach' is really nothing more than a suspicion of modern science so deep it's practically medieval."

Theresa Court began to say something, then stopped. Levine glanced at her without concern; he knew she'd side with the winner whichever way things shook out.

"I think that what Dr. Levine is advocating is greater responsibility on the part of the companies engaged in genetic research," Sanchez said. "Am I right, Doctor?"

"That's part of the solution," Levine replied, content for the time being to press his usual message home. "But we also need greater governmental oversight. Currently, corporations are seemingly free to tinker with human genes, animal and plant genes, viral genes, with little or no supervision. Pathogens of unimaginable virulence are being created in labs today. All it takes is one accident to cause a catastrophe with potentially worldwide implications."

At last, Squires turned his scornful gaze toward Levine. "More government oversight. More regulation. More bureaucracy. More stifling of free enterprise. That is precisely what this country does *not* need. Dr. Levine is a scientist. He should know better. Yet he persists in fostering these untruths, frightening people with lies about genetic engineering."

It was time. "Dr. Squires is attempting to portray me as deceitful," Levine said. He reached a hand inside his jacket, feeling for the inner pocket. "Let me show you something."

He slipped out a bright red envelope, holding it up to the cameras. "As a professor of microbiology, Dr. Squires is beholden to no one. He's only interested in the truth."

Levine shook the sealed envelope slightly, hoping that Toni Wheeler was watching from the Green Room. The red color had been a stroke of genius. He knew the cameras had focused on the envelope, and that countless viewers were now waiting for it to be opened.

"And yet, what if I told you that, in this envelope, I have proof that Dr. Squires has been paid a quarter of a million dollars by the GeneDyne Corporation? One of the world's leading genetic engineering firms? And that he has kept this employment secret, even from his own university? Would that, perhaps, call his motives into question?"

He laid the envelope in front of Squires.

"Open it, please," he said, "and show the contents to the camera."

Squires looked at the envelope, not quite comprehending the trap that was being set. "This is preposterous," he said at last, brushing the envelope to the floor.

Levine could hardly believe his luck. He turned to the camera with a triumphant smile. "You see? He knows exactly what's inside."

"This is grossly unprofessional," snapped Squires.

"Go ahead," Levine goaded. "Open it."

The envelope was now on the floor, and Squires would have to stoop to pick it up. In any case, Levine thought, it was too late for Finley Squires. If he had opened it immediately he might have maintained his credibility.

Sanchez was looking from one scientist to the other. It began to dawn on Squires what was happening. "This is the lowest form of attack I have ever witnessed," he said. "Dr. Levine, you ought to be ashamed of yourself."

Squires was on the ropes but still combative. Levine removed the second envelope from his pocket.

"And in this envelope, Dr. Squires, I have some information about recent developments at GeneDyne's secret genetic-engineering lab, the one known as Mount Dragon. These developments are extremely disturbing, and of interest to any scientist who has the greater interests of humanity at heart."

He laid the second envelope in front of Squires. "If you won't open the other, at least open this. Be the one to expose GeneDyne's dangerous activities. Prove that you have no interest in the company."

Squires sat very stiffly. "I will not be intimidated by intellectual terrorism."

Levine felt his heart racing. It was almost too good to be true: the man was *still* putting his foot into every trap.

"I can't open it myself," Levine said. "GeneDyne has sued my foundation for two hundred million dollars in an effort to silence me. Someone else must do it."

The envelope sat on the table, cameras focused upon it. Sanchez swiveled in his chair, gazing back and forth between the panelists.

Court reached over and snatched it up. "If no one else has the courage to open it, *I* will."

Good old Theresa, thought Levine; he knew she could not resist the opportunity to play a role in the drama.

Inside the envelope was a single sheet of white paper, containing a message in a simple, sober-looking typeface.

NAME OF VIRUS:	Unknown.
INCUBATION PERIOD:	One week.
TIME BETWEEN FIRST SYMPTOMS AND DEATH:	Five minutes to two hours.
MODE OF DEATH:	Aggravated cerebral edema.
INFECTIOUSNESS:	Spreads more easily than the common cold.
MORTALITY RATE:	100%—*all victims die*.
DANGER FACTOR:	A "doomsday virus": if released, accidentally or intentionally, it could destroy the human race.
CREATOR:	GeneDyne, Inc.
PURPOSE:	Unknown. It is a corporate secret protected by the privacy laws of the United States. Work on this virus is continuing, with minimal government oversight.

HISTORY: Within the last 2 weeks, this
                            virus infected an unidentified
                            scientist or technician at a
                            remote GeneDyne testing
                            facility. The technician was
                            apparently isolated before
                            additional exposures could
                            take place. The technician
                            was dead within three days.
                            Had quarantine procedures
                            been ineffective, the virus
                            could have escaped to the
                            populace at large. We might
                            all be dead.

Court read the document aloud, stopping several times to look incredulously at Levine. As she finished, Sanchez swiveled his chair toward Finley Squires.

"Any comment?" he asked.

"Why would I comment?" Squires said irritably. "I have nothing whatsoever to do with GeneDyne."

"Shall we open the first envelope?" Sanchez said, a faint but wicked smile appearing on his cadaverous face.

"Be my guest," said Squires. "Whatever's inside will undoubtedly be a forgery."

Sanchez picked up the envelope. "Theresa, you seem to be the one with the guts around here," he said, handing it to her.

She ripped it open. Inside was a computer printout indicating that the sum of $265,000 had been wired from GeneDyne Hong Kong to a numbered account at the Rigel Bancorp, Netherlands Antilles.

"There's no name on this account," said Sanchez, looking closer.

"Hold the second page up to the cameras," said Levine.

The second page was fuzzy but readable. It was a screen print, covertly seized from a live image on a computer terminal by an expensive and prohibited device. The screen contained wiring instructions from Finley Squires regarding an account at the Rigel Bancorp, Netherland Antilles. The account had the same number.

There was a chill silence, and Sanchez wrapped the segment, thanking the participants and asking the audience at home to stay tuned for Barrold Leighton.

The moment the cameras shut off, Squires stood up. "This charade will be met with massive legal reply," he said tersely, and strode off the set.

Sanchez swiveled toward Levine, his lips pursed appraisingly. "Cute act," he said. "I hope for your sake you can back it up."

Levine merely smiled.

Returning to his lab after retrieving some test results from Pathology, Carson moved awkwardly through the narrow crawl spaces of the Fever Tank. It was after six, and the facility was almost empty. De Vaca had left hours earlier to run some enzyme tests in the computer lab; it was time to close up shop and make the long slow trek toward the surface. But much as he hated the tight spaces of the Fever Tank, Carson found himself in no hurry to leave. He'd lost his dinner partners: Vanderwagon was gone, of course, and Harper would be in the infirmary for another day.

At the lab hatchway, he stopped short. A strange bluesuit was in his lab, poking around his worktable, turning over objects. Carson punched the intercom button on the sleeve of his suit. "Looking for something?" he asked.

The suit straightened up and swiveled toward him, and the painfully sunburnt face of Gilbert Teece came into view through the faceplate.

"Dr. Carson! How nice to make your acquaintance. I wonder if I could have a few words with you." The figure extended its hand.

"Why not," Carson said, feeling foolish as he shook the inspector's hand through several layers of rubber. "Have a seat."

The figure looked around. "I still haven't figured out how to do that while wearing this bloody suit."

"I guess you'll have to stand, then," said Carson, moving forward and taking a seat at the worktable.

"Just so," said Teece. "It's quite an honor, you know, speaking to the descendant of Kit Carson."

"Nobody else seems to think so," Carson said.

"You have your own modesty to thank for that," Teece said. "I don't think many people around here know. It's in your personnel file, of course. Mr. Scopes seemed very taken with the historical irony of it." Teece paused. "Quite a fascinating character, your Mr. Scopes."

"He's brilliant." Carson looked appraisingly at the investigator. "Why did you ask that question about Brandon-Smith's autopsy back in the conference room?"

There was a brief silence. Then Carson heard Teece's laughter crackling over the speaker in his headset. "You practically grew up among the Apache Indians, right? Then you may know one of their ancient sayings: 'Some questions are longer than others.' That question I asked in the conference room was very long." He smiled. "But you're a relatively recent arrival, and it was not aimed at you. I'd rather we talked about Mr. Vanderwagon for a moment." He caught Carson's grimace. "Yes, I know. Terrible doings. Did you know him well?"

"After I arrived here, we became fairly good friends."

"What was he like?"

"He was from Connecticut. Very preppie, but I liked him. Underneath that serious exterior he had a wicked sense of humor."

"Did you notice anything unusual prior to the incident in the dining room? Any strange behavior? Personality changes?"

Carson shrugged. "This last week, he seemed preoccupied, withdrawn. You'd speak to him and he wouldn't answer. I didn't think much about it, really, because we were all in shock after what happened. Besides, people often act a little strange around this place. The level of tension is unbelievable. Everyone calls it Mount Dragon fever. Like cabin fever, only worse."

Teece chuckled. "I'm feeling a bit of that myself."

"After what happened, Andrew was publicly reprimanded by Brent. I think he took it pretty hard."

Teece nodded. "If thy right eye offends thee," he murmured. "According to the tapes I watched, Scopes quoted that to Vanderwagon during his dressing-down in the conference room. Still, poking one's eye out is a rather extreme reaction to stress, in my book. What did Cornwall say in King Lear: 'Out, vile jelly. Where is thy lustre now?'"

Carson was silent.

"Do you know anything about Vanderwagon's past history at GeneDyne?" Teece asked.

"I know he was brilliant, very highly thought of. This was his second tour here. University of Chicago grad. But you must know all this."

"Did he speak to you about any troubles? Any worries?"

"None. Except the usual complaints about the isolation. He was a great skier, and there obviously isn't any skiing around here, so he used to complain about that. He was pretty liberal, and he and Harper used to argue politics a lot."

"Did he have a girlfriend?"

Carson thought a moment. "He did mention someone. Lucy, I think. She lives in Vermont." He shifted in the chair. "Look, where have they taken him, anyway? Have you learned anything yet?"

"He's undergoing tests. So far, we know very little. It's very difficult here, with no open phones to the outside. But already there are some perplexing developments, which I'd ask you to keep to yourself for the time being."

Carson nodded.

"Preliminary tests show Vanderwagon suffering from unusual medical problems: overly permeable capillaries and elevated levels of dopamine and serotonin in the brain."

"Permeable capillaries?"

"Leaky blood vessels. Somehow, a small percentage of his blood cells have disintegrated, releasing hemoglobin. This hemoglobin has leaked out of his capillaries and into various parts of his body. Naked hemoglobin, as you may know, is poisonous to human tissues."

"Did that contribute to his breakdown?"

"It's too early to say," Teece replied. "The elevated levels of dopamine, however, are very significant. What do you know about dopamine? Serotonin?"

"Not much. They're neurotransmitters."

"Correct. At normal levels, there's no problem. However, too much of either in the brain would dramatically affect human behavior. Paranoid schizophrenics have elevated levels of dopamine. LSD trips are caused by a temporary increase in the same neurotransmitter."

"What are you saying?" Carson asked. "That Andrew has elevated levels of these neurotransmitters in his brain because he's crazy?"

"Perhaps," Teece replied. "Or vice versa. But there really isn't any point in speculating until we know more. Let's move on to my original purpose here, and talk about this X-FLU strain you're working on. Perhaps you can tell me how, while you thought you were neutralizing the virus, you instead managed to make it more deadly."

"God, if I could answer that question . . ." Carson paused. "We don't really understand yet how X-FLU does its dirty work. When you recombine genes, you never really know what will happen. Suites of genes work together in complicated ways, and removing one or putting a new one into the mix often causes unexpected effects. In some ways, it's like an incredibly complex computer program that nobody fully understands. You never know what might happen if you plug in strange data or change a line of code. Nothing might happen. Or it might work better. Or the whole program might crash." He had the vague realization that he was being more frank with this OSHA investigator than Brent Scopes might like. But Teece was sharp; there was no point dissembling.

"Why not use a less dangerous virus as a vehicle for the X-FLU gene?" asked Teece.

"That's difficult to explain. You must know that the body is composed of two types of cells: somatic cells and germ cells. In order for X-FLU to be a permanent cure—one that would be passed on to descendants—we have to insert the DNA into germ-line cells. Somatic cells won't do. The X-FLU host virus is uniquely capable of infecting human germ cells."

"What about the ethics of altering germ cells? Of introducing new genes into the human species? Has there been any discussion of that at Mount Dragon?"

Carson wondered why this subject kept coming up. "Look," he said, "we're making the tiniest change imaginable: inserting a gene only a few hundred base pairs long. It will make human beings immune to the flu. There's nothing immoral in that."

"But didn't you just say that making a small change in one gene can have unexpected results?"

Carson stood up impatiently. "Of course! But that's what phased testing is all about—looking for unexpected side effects. This gene therapy will have to go through a whole gamut of expensive tests, costing GeneDyne millions of dollars."

"Testing on human beings?"

"Of course. You start with in vitro and animal tests. In the alpha phase you use a small group of human volunteers. The beta phase is larger. The tests will be done using an out-group monitored by GeneDyne. Everything is done with excruciating care. You know all this as well as I do."

Teece nodded. "Forgive me for dwelling on the subject, Dr. Carson. But if there are 'unexpected side effects,' wouldn't you be perpetuating these side effects in the human race if you introduce the X-FLU gene into the germ cells of even a few people? Creating, perhaps, a new genetic disease? Or a race of people different from the rest of humanity? Remember, it took just a single mutation in one person— *one person*—to introduce the hemophilia gene into the race. Now, there are countless thousands of hemophiliacs across the world."

"GeneDyne would never have spent almost half a billion dollars without working out the details," Carson snapped, uncertain why he was feeling so defensive. "You're not dealing with a start-up company here." He walked around the side of his worktable to face the investigator. "My job is to neutralize the virus. And believe me, that's more than enough. What they do with it once it's neutralized is not my concern. There are suffocating government regulations covering every inch of this problem. You, of all people, should know that. You probably wrote half the damn regulations yourself."

Three tones chimed in his headset. "We've got to leave," Carson said. "They're doing an early decontamination sweep tonight."

"Right," Teece replied. "Would you mind leading the way? I'm afraid I'd be lost within fifty feet."

* * *

Outside, Carson stood silently for a moment, shutting his eyes and letting the warm evening wind blow over him. He could almost feel the accumulated tension and dread dissipating on the desert breeze. He blinked his eyes open, noticed the unusual color of the sunset, and frowned. Then he turned to Teece.

"Sorry if I was a bit brusque back there," he said. "That place wears on me, especially by the end of the day."

"Perfectly understandable." The investigator stretched, scratched his peeling nose, and glanced around at the white buildings, thrown into dramatic relief by the sunset. "It's not so bad here, once that bloody great sun goes down." He looked at his watch. "We'd better hurry if we're going to catch dinner."

"I guess." Carson's tone betrayed his reluctance.

Teece turned to look at him. "You sound about as eager as I feel."

Carson shrugged. "I'll be all right by tomorrow. I just don't feel all that hungry."

"Me neither." The investigator paused. "So let's go have a sauna."

Carson turned his head in disbelief. "A *what?*"

"A sauna. I'll meet you there in fifteen minutes."

"Are you crazy? That's the last thing I—" Carson stopped when he caught the expression on Teece's face. Realizing it was an order, not an invitation, he narrowed his eyes.

"Fifteen minutes, then," he said, and headed for his room without another word.

When the plans for Mount Dragon were drawn up, the designers, realizing that the occupants would be virtually imprisoned by the vast desert around them, went to great lengths to add as many distractions and creature comforts as possible.

The recreation facility, a long low structure next to the residency compound, was better equipped than most professional health spas, boasting a quarter-mile track, squash and racquetball courts, swimming pool, and weight room. What the designers hadn't realized was that most of the scientists at Mount Dragon were obsessed with their work, and avoided physical exertion whenever possible. Practically the only residents who made use of the recreation center were Carson, who liked to run in the evenings, and Mike Marr, who spent hours working with the free weights.

Perhaps the most unlikely feature of the recreation center was the sauna: a fully equipped Swedish model with cedar walls and benches. The sauna was popular during the cold high-desert winters at Mount Dragon, but it was shunned by everyone in the summer.

As he approached the sauna from the men's locker room, Carson saw by the external thermometer that Teece was already inside. He pulled the door open, turning involuntarily from the blast of hot air that emerged. Stepping in, he saw through smarting eyes the pallid form of Teece, sitting near the bank of coals at the far end of the chamber, a white towel wrapped around his skinny loins. His pasty white complexion was in hilarious contrast to his burnt face. Sweat was pouring from his forehead and collecting at the end of his sun-abused nose.

Carson took a seat as far from the inspector as he could, gingerly settling the backs of his thighs against the hot wood. He breathed the fiery air in shallow gulps.

"All right, Mr. Teece," he said angrily. "What is this about?"

Teece looked at him with a wry smile. "You should see yourself, Dr. Carson," he panted. "All drawn up with righteous manly indignation. But don't get your knickers in a twist. I've asked you here for a very good reason."

"I'm waiting to hear it." Carson could already feel a sheen of sweat coating his skin. *Teece must have this thing cranked to a hundred and sixty*, he thought.

"There's something else I want to discuss with you," Teece said. "Mind if I add some steam?"

At some point, a Mount Dragon wag had replaced the usual wooden water dipper with a retort full of distilled water. Before Carson could protest, the investigator had picked up the retort and poured a pint of water onto the glowing coals. Clouds of steam rose immediately, filling the room with a scorching vapor.

"Why the hell did we have to come in here?" Carson croaked, head reeling.

"Mr. Carson, I don't mind sharing most of my discussions," came the disembodied voice through the steam. "In fact, more often than not it has served my own purposes. As with our talk in your lab this afternoon. But right now, what I want is privacy."

Comprehension came slowly to Carson's brain. It was commonly believed around Mount Dragon that any conversation taking place in the bluesuits was monitored. Obviously, Teece didn't want anybody else overhearing what he was about to say. But why not meet in the cafeteria, or the residency compound? Carson answered his own question: The canteen rumor mill suspected Nye of bugging the entire facility. Teece, apparently, believed the rumors. That left the sauna—with its corrosive heat and steam—as the only place where they could talk.

Or did it? "Why couldn't we have just taken a walk along the perimeter fence?" Carson gasped.

Teece suddenly materialized through the vapor. He took a seat next to Carson, shaking his head as he did so. "I have a horror of scorpions," he said. "Now, listen to me a moment. You're wondering why I asked you here, of all people. There are two reasons. First, I've watched your response to the Brandon-Smith emergency several times on tape. You were the one scientist who was intimately involved with the project, and with the tragedy, who behaved rationally. I may need that kind of impartiality in the days ahead. That's why I spoke with you last."

"You've talked to everyone?" Teece had been on-site only a few days.

"It's a small place. I've learned a great deal. And there is much else that I suspect, but do not yet know for certain." He wiped the sweat from his eyes with the back of his hand. "The second and most important reason involves your predecessor."

"You mean Franklin Burt? What about him?"

"In your lab, I mentioned that Andrew Vanderwagon was suffering from leaky blood vessels and overdrives of dopamine and serotonin. What I didn't tell you was that Franklin Burt is suffering from the same symptoms. And, according to the autopsy report, so to a lesser degree was Rosalind Brandon-Smith. Now, why would that be, do you suppose?"

Carson thought for a moment. It made no sense at all. Unless . . . Despite the heat of the sauna, a sudden thought chilled him.

"Could they be infected with something? A virus?" My God, he thought, could it be some long-gestating strain of X-FLU? Dread coursed through him.

Teece wiped his hands on his towel, grinning. "What's happened to your unswerving faith in safety procedures? Relax. You aren't the first to jump to that conclusion. But neither Burt nor Vanderwagon show any X-FLU antibodies. They're clean. Brandon-Smith, on the other hand, was riddled with them. So there's no commonality."

"Then I can't explain it," Carson said, expelling a pent-up breath. "Very strange."

"Yes, isn't it?" Teece murmured.

He added more water to the coals. Carson waited.

"I assume you studied Dr. Burt's work in detail when you first arrived," Teece went on.

Carson nodded.

"So you must have read his electronic notebook?"

"I have," said Carson.

"Many times, I imagine."

"I can recite it in my sleep."

"Where do you think the rest of it is?" asked Teece.

There was a short silence.

"What do you mean?" Carson asked.

"As I read the on-line files, something in them struck me as funny, like a melody that was missing some notes. So I did a statistical analysis of the entries, and I found that over the course of the last month the average daily entry dropped from over two thousand words to a few hundred. That led me to the conclusion that Burt, for whatever personal or paranoid reasons of his own, had started to keep a private notebook. Something Scopes and the others couldn't see."

"Hard copy is forbidden at Mount Dragon," Carson said, knowing he was merely stating the obvious.

"I doubt if rules meant much to Dr. Burt at that point. Anyway, as I understand it, Mr. Scopes likes to roam GeneDyne cyberspace all night long, poking and prying into everyone's business. A hidden journal is a logical response to that. I'm sure Burt wasn't the only one. There are probably several completely sane people here who keep private logs."

Carson nodded, his mind working fast. "That means—" he began.

"Yes?" Teece prompted, suddenly eager.

"Well, Burt mentioned a 'key factor' several times in his last on-line entries. If this secret journal exists, it might contain that key, whatever it is. I was thinking it might be the missing piece to solving the riddle of rendering X-FLU harmless."

"Perhaps," Teece said. Then he paused. "Burt worked on other projects before X-FLU, correct?"

"Yes. He invented the GEF process, GeneDyne's proprietary filtration technique. And he perfected PurBlood."

"Ah, yes. PurBlood." Teece pursed his lips distastefully. "Nasty idea, that."

"What do you mean?" Carson asked, mystified. "Blood substitutes can save countless lives. They eliminate shortages, the need for blood typing, protect against transfusions of tainted blood—"

"Perhaps," Teece interrupted. "Just the same, the thought of injecting pints of it into my veins isn't pleasant. I understand it's produced by a vat of genetically engineered bacteria that have had the human hemoglobin gene inserted into them. It's the same bacteria that exists by the trillions in . . ." His voice trailed off, and he added the word "dirt" almost soundlessly.

Carson laughed. "It's called *streptococcus*. Yes, it's the bacterium found in soil. The fact is, we at GeneDyne know more about *streptococcus* than any other form of life. It's the only organism other than *E. coli* whose gene we have completely mapped from beginning to end. So it's a perfect host organism. Just because it lives in dirt doesn't make it disgusting or dangerous."

"Call me old-fashioned, then," said Teece. "But I'm straying from our subject here. The doctor who's treating Burt tells me that he repeats an apparently nonsensical phrase over and over again: 'Poor alpha.' Do you have any idea what that might mean? Could it be the beginning of some longer sentence? Or perhaps his nickname for somebody?"

Carson thought a moment, then shook his head. "I doubt if it's anybody here."

Teece frowned. "Another mystery. Perhaps the notebook will shed light on this, as well. In any case, I have some ideas on how to go about searching for it. I plan to follow them up when I get back."

"When you get back?" Carson echoed.

Teece nodded. "I'll be leaving tomorrow for Radium Springs to file my preliminary report. Communication links to the outside world are practically nonexistent here. Besides, I need to consult with my colleagues. That's why I've spoken to you. You are the person closest to Burt's work. I'll be needing your full cooperation in the days to come. Somehow, I think Burt is the key to all this. We need to make a decision soon."

"What decision is that?"

"On whether or not to allow this project to continue."

Carson was silent. Somehow, he couldn't imagine Scopes allowing the project to be terminated. Teece was getting up, wrapping his towel tighter.

"I wouldn't advise it," Carson said.

"Advise what?"

"Leaving tomorrow. There's a big dust storm coming up."

"I didn't hear anything about it on the radio," Teece frowned.

"They don't broadcast the weather for the Jornada del Muerto desert on the radio, Mr. Teece. Didn't you notice the peculiar orange pall in the southern sky when we came out of the Fever Tank this evening? I've seen that before and it means trouble."

"Dr. Singer's lending me a Hummer. Those things are built like articulated lorries."

For the first time, Carson thought he saw a look of uncertainty in Teece's face. He shrugged. "I'm not going to stop you. But if I were you, I'd wait."

Teece shook his head. "What I've got to do can't wait."

The front had gathered its energy in the Gulf of Mexico, then moved northwestward, striking the Mexican coastline of Tamaulipas State. Once over land, the front was forced to rise above the Sierra Madre Oriental, where the moist air of the higher altitudes condensed in great thunderheads over the mountains. Vast quantities of rain fell as the front moved westward. By the time it descended on the Chihuahua desert, all moisture had been wrung from it. The front veered northward, moving laterally through the basin and range provinces of northern Mexico. At six o'clock in the morning it entered the Jornada del Muerto desert.

The front was now bone dry. No clouds or rain marked its arrival. All that remained of the Gulf storm was an enormous energy differential between the hundred-degree air mass over the desert and the sixty-five-degree air mass of the front.

All this energy manifested itself in wind.

As it moved into the Jornada, the front became visible as a mile-high wall of orange dust. It bore down across the land with the speed of an express train, carrying shredded tumbleweeds, clay, dry silt, and powdered salt picked up from playas to the south. At a height of four feet above the ground, the wind also included twigs, coarse sand, pieces of dry cactus, and bark stripped from trees. At a height of six inches, the wind was full of cutting shards of gravel, small stones, and pieces of wood.

Such desert storms, though rare enough to occur only once every few years, had the power to sandblast a car windshield opaque, strip the paint off a curved surface, blow roofs off trailer homes, and run horses into barbed-wire fences.

The storm reached the middle Jornada desert and Mount Dragon at seven o'clock in the morning, fifty minutes after Gilbert Teece, senior OSHA investigator, had driven off in a Hummer with his fat briefcase, heading for Radium Springs.

Scopes sat at his pianoforte, fingers motionless on the black rosewood keys. He appeared to be in deep thought. Lying beside the hand-shaped lid prop was a tabloid newspaper, torn and mangled, as if angry hands had crumpled it, then smoothed it again. The paper was open to an article entitled "Harvard Doc Accuses Gene Firm of Horror Accident."

Suddenly, Scopes stood up, walked into the circle of light, and flounced down on the couch. He pulled the keyboard onto his lap and typed a brief series of instructions, initiating a videoconference call. Before him, the enormous screen winked into focus. A swirl of computer code ran up along one edge, then gave way to the huge, grainy image of a man's face. His thick neck lapped over a collar at least two sizes too tight. He was staring into the camera with the bare-toothed grimace of a man unused to smiling.

"*Guten tag,*" said Scopes in halting German.

"Perhaps you would be more comfortable speaking in English, Mr. Scopes?" the man on the screen asked, tilting his head ingratiatingly.

"*Nein,*" Scopes continued in bad German. "I want to practice the German. Speak slowly and clearly. Repeat twice."

"Very good," the man said.

"*Twice.*"

"*Sehr gut, sehr gut,*" the man said.

"Now, Herr Saltzmann, our friend tells me you have clear access to the old Nazi files at Leipzig."

"*Das ist richtig. Das ist richtig.*"

"This is where the Lodz Ghetto files currently reside, is it not?"

"*Ja. Ja.*"

"Excellent. I have a small problem, an—how does one say it?—an *archival* problem. The kind of problem you specialize in. I pay very well, Herr Saltzmann. One hundred thousand Deutschmarks."

The smile broadened.

Scopes continued to talk in pidgin German, outlining his problem. The man on the screen listened intently, the smile slowly fading from his face.

Later, when the screen was blank once again, a soft chime, almost inaudible, sounded from one of the devices on the end table.

Scopes, who was still sitting on the decrepit sofa, keyboard in lap, leaned toward the end table and pressed a button. "Yes?"

"Your lunch is ready."

"Very well."

Spencer Fairley entered, the foam slippers on his feet in ludicrous contrast to the somber gray suit. He made no noise as he crossed the carpet and set a pizza and a can of Coca-Cola on the far end table.

"Will there be anything else, sir?" Fairley asked.

"Did you read the *Herald* this morning?"

Fairley shook his head. "I'm a *Globe* reader," he said.

"Of course you are," said Scopes. "You should try the *Herald* once in a while. It's much more lively than the *Globe.*"

"No, thank you," said Fairley.

"It's over there," Scopes said, pointing to the pianoforte.

Fairley went over and returned, holding the rumpled tabloid. "Unpleasant piece of journalism," he said, scanning the page.

Scopes grinned. "Nah. It's perfect. The crazy son of a bitch has put the knife to his own throat. All I need to do is give his arm a little nudge."

He pulled a rumpled computer printout from his shirt pocket. "Here's my charity list for the week. It's short, only one item: a million to the Holocaust Memorial Fund."

Fairley looked up. "Levine's organization?"

"Of course. I want it done publicly, but in a quiet, dignified way."

"May I ask . . . ?" Fairley raised an eyebrow.

". . . Why?" Scopes finished the sentence. "Because, Spencer, you old Brahmin, it's a worthy cause. And between you and me, they're shortly going to lose their most effective fundraiser."

Fairley nodded.

"Besides, if you thought about it, you would realize there are also strategic reasons to free Levine's pet charity from excessive dependence on him."

"Yes, sir."

"And Fairley, look, my jacket has a hole in the elbow. Would you like to go shopping with me again?"

A look of extreme distaste passed quickly across Fairley's face, then disappeared again. "No, thank you, sir," he said firmly.

Scopes waited until the door hissed shut. Then he laid the keyboard aside and lifted a slice of pizza from the box. It was almost cold, exactly the way he liked it. His eyes closed in enjoyment as his teeth met in the gooey interior of the pizza crust.

"*Auf wiedersehen*, Charles," he mumbled.

Carson emerged from the administration building at five o'clock and stopped in amazement. All around him, the buildings of Mount Dragon stood in the dim aftermath of the dust storm, dark shapes emerging from an orange pall. The landscape was deathly still. Carson breathed in gingerly, testing the air. It was arid, like brick dust, and strangely cold. As he stepped forward, his boot sank an inch into powdery dirt.

He'd gone to work very early that morning, before sunup, eager to get the analysis of X-FLU II out of the way. He worked diligently, almost forgetting the windstorm raging above the silent underground fastness of the Fever Tank. De Vaca arrived an hour later. She had beaten the storm, too, but just barely; her muttered curses, and the dirt-streaked face that scowled back at him through the visor, attested to that.

This must be what the surface of the moon looks like, he thought as he stood outside the administration building. *Or the end of the world.* He had seen plenty of storms on the ranch, but nothing like this. Dust lay everywhere, coating the white buildings, glazing the windows. Small drifts of sand had accumulated in long fins behind every post and vertical rise. It was an eerie, twilit, monochromatic world.

Carson started toward the residency compound, unable to see more than fifty feet ahead in the thick air. Then, hesitating a moment, he turned and headed instead for the horse corral. He wondered how Roscoe had fared. In a bad storm, he had known horses to go crazy in their stalls, sometimes breaking a leg.

The horses were safe, covered with dust and looking irritated but otherwise unhurt. Roscoe nickered a greeting and

Carson stroked his neck, wishing he had brought a carrot or a sugar cube. He looked the animal over quickly, then stood back with relief.

A sound from outside the paddocks, muffled and deadened by the dust, reached his ears. Glancing up, he saw a shadow looming out of the pall of dust. *Good God*, he thought, *there's something alive out there, something very large.* The shadow vanished, then reappeared. Carson heard the rattle of the perimeter gate. It was coming in.

He stared through the open door of the barn as the ghostly figure of a man on horseback materialized out of the dust. The man's head hung low on his shoulders, and the horse shuffled on trembling legs, exhausted to the point of collapse.

It was Nye.

Carson withdrew into the dim spaces of the barn and ducked into an empty stall. The last thing he wanted was another unpleasant encounter.

He heard the gate swing shut, then the sound of boots slowly crossing the sawdust floor of the barn. Squatting down, Carson peered through a knothole in the frame of the stall.

The security director was saturated, head to toe, in dun-colored dust. Only his black eyes and crusted mouth broke through the monotony of the powdery coat.

Nye stopped in front of the tack area and slowly untied his rifle boot and saddlebags, hanging them on a rack. He uncinched the saddle, jerked it off the horse, and set it on a carrier, slinging the saddle blankets on top. Every movement raised small mushroom clouds of gray dust.

Nye led the horse toward its stall, out of Carson's view. Carson could hear him brushing the horse down, murmuring soothing words. He heard the snip of a bale being cut, the thump of hay thrown into the stall and a hose filling the water bucket. In a few moments, Nye reappeared. Turning his back to Carson, he pulled out a heavy tack box from one corner of the barn and unlocked it. Then, moving to his saddle bags, he unbuckled one side and extracted what looked like two squares of clear stiff plastic, sandwiching a ragged—and completely unauthorized—piece of paper. Placing them on the floor of the tack area, Nye removed what looked like a wax pencil from the saddlebags, bent over the paper, and began making notations on the covering plastic. Carson pressed his eye to the crack, straining for a better view. The piece of paper looked old and well worn, and he could see a large, handwritten phrase across its upper border: *Al despertar la hora el águila del sol se levanta en una aguja del fuego,* "At dawn the eagle of the sun stands on a needle of fire." Beyond that he could make out nothing.

Suddenly, Nye sat up, alert. He looked around, craning his neck as if searching for the source of some noise. Carson shrank into the shadows at the back of the stall. He heard a shuffling sound, the click of a lock, the heavy clumping of feet. He peered out again to see the security director leave the barn, a gray apparition vanishing into the mist.

After a few moments, Carson got up and, eyeing the tack box curiously for a moment, moved over to the stall that held Muerto, Nye's horse. It stood spraddle-legged, a string of brown saliva hanging from its mouth. He reached down and felt the tendons. Some heat, but no serious inflammation. The corona was hot but the hooves were still good, and the horse's eye was clear. Whatever Nye had been doing, he had pushed the animal almost to its limit, maybe even as much as a hundred miles in the last twelve hours. The animal was still sound; there was no permanent damage and the horse would be back in form in a day or two. Nye had known when to quit. And he had a magnificent horse. A zero branded into its right jaw and a freeze brand high on its neck indicated it was registered with both the American Paint Horse Association and the American Quarter Horse Association. He patted its flank admiringly.

"You're one expensive piece of horseflesh," he said.

Carson left the stall and moved to the barn entrance, peering out into the dust that hung like smoke in the oppressive air. Nye was long gone. Closing the barn door quietly, Carson headed quickly for his room, trying to make sense of a man who would risk his life in a savage dust storm. Or a security director who would risk his job carrying around a piece of paper topped by a meaningless Spanish phrase at a place where paper was forbidden.

Carson passed through the canteen and out onto the balcony, the weathered banjo case knocking against his knees. The night was dark, and the moon obscured by clouds, but he knew that the figure sitting motionless by the balcony railing was Singer.

Since their first conversation on the balcony, Carson had often noticed Singer sitting out, enjoying the evening, fingering chords and runs on his battered guitar. Invariably, Singer had smiled and waved, or called out a cheerful greeting. But Singer seemed to change after the death of Brandon-Smith. He became quieter, more withdrawn. The arrival of Teece, and Vanderwagon's sudden fit in the dining room, seemed only to deepen Singer's mood. He still sat on the canteen balcony in the evenings, but now his head drooped in the desert silence, the guitar lying silent by his side.

During the first few weeks, Carson had often joined the director on the balcony for an evening chat. But as time went on and the pressure increased, Carson had found there was always more on-line research to be done, more lab notes to be recorded in the quiet solitude of his room after working hours. This evening, however, he was determined to find the time. He liked Singer, and didn't like to see him brooding, no doubt blaming himself unnecessarily for the recent troubles. Perhaps he could draw the man out of himself for a bit. Besides, the talk with Teece had left Carson with nagging doubts about his own work. He knew that Singer, with his unswerving faith in the virtues of science, would be the perfect tonic.

"Who's there?" Singer asked sharply. The moon passed out of the clouds, temporarily throwing the balcony into pale relief. Singer caught sight of Carson. "Oh," he said, relaxing. "Hello, Guy."

"Evening." Carson took a seat next to the director. Although the balcony had been swept clean of its mantle of dust, fresh clouds of the stuff rose dimly into view as he settled his weight into the chair. "Beautiful night," he said, after a pause.

"Did you see the sunset?" Singer asked quietly.

"Incredible." As if to make up for the fury of the dust storm, the desert sunset that evening had been a spectacular display of color against the smoky haze.

Without speaking further, Carson leaned over, unsnapped the case, and pulled out his Gibson five-string. Singer watched, a spark of interest kindling in his tired eyes.

"Is that an RB-3?" he asked.

Carson nodded. "Forty-hole tone ring. 1932 or thereabouts."

"It's a beauty," Singer said, squinting appraisingly in the moonlight. "My God. Is that the original calfskin head?"

"That's right." Carson drummed the dirty head lightly with the tips of his fingers. "They don't like desert conditions, and this one's always going flat. Some day I'll break down and buy a plastic one. Here, take a look." He handed the instrument to Singer.

The director turned it over in his hands. "Mahogany neck

and resonator. Original Presto tailpiece, too. The flange is pot-metal, I suppose?"

"Yes. It's warping a little."

Singer handed it back. "A real museum piece. How'd you come by it?"

"A ranch hand who worked for my grandfather. He had to leave our place in a hurry one day. This is one of the things he left behind. It sat for decades on top of a bookcase, collecting dust. Until I went to college, got the bluegrass bug."

As they spoke, Singer seemed to lose some of his funk. "Let's hear how it sounds," he said, reaching over and picking up his old Martin. He strummed it thoughtfully, tuned a string or two, then swung into the unmistakable bass line of "Salt Creek." Carson listened, nodding his head in time to the music as he vamped background chords. It had been months since he'd picked up the instrument, and his chops weren't what they had been at Harvard, but gradually his fingers limbered up and he tried some rolls. Then suddenly Singer was playing backup and Carson found himself taking a solo break, smiling almost with relief when he found that his pull-offs still sounded crisp and his single-string work was clean.

They finished with a shave-and-a-haircut tag and Singer launched immediately into "Clinch Mountain Backstep." Carson swung into the tune behind him, impressed by the director's virtuosity. Singer, meanwhile, seemed wholly engrossed, playing with the abandon of a man suddenly freed of a terrific burden.

Carson followed Singer through the strong, ancient changes of "Rocky Top," "Mountain Dew," and "Little Maggie," feeling more and more comfortable and at last allowing himself an up-the-neck break that brought a smile and a nod from the director. Singer moved into an elaborate ending tag, and they closed with a thunderous G chord. As the echoes died, Carson thought he heard the faint, brief sound of clapping from the direction of the residency compound.

"Thank you, Guy," Singer said, putting aside the guitar and wiping his hands together with satisfaction. "We should have done this a long time ago. You're an excellent musician."

"I'm not in your league," Carson said. "But thanks all the same."

A silence fell as the two men stared out into the night. Singer stood up and moved into the canteen to fix himself a drink. A disheveled-looking man walked by the balcony, counting imaginary numbers on his fingers and muttering loudly in what sounded like anguished Russian. *That must be Pavel*, Carson thought, *the one de Vaca told me about*. The man disappeared around a walkway corner into the night. A moment later, Singer returned from inside. His tread was slower now, and Carson sensed that whatever mantle of responsibility had temporarily been lifted was quickly settling again.

"So how've you been keeping, Guy?" Singer said, settling back into the chair. "We haven't really spoken for ages."

"I suppose Teece's visit kept you busy," Carson said. The moon had once again vanished behind thickening clouds, and he sensed, rather than saw, the director stiffen at the investigator's name.

"What a nuisance *that* turned out to be," Singer said. He sipped his drink while Carson waited. "Can't say I think much of Mr. Teece. One of those people who act like they know everything, but won't reveal any of it to you. He seems to get a lot of his information by setting people against each other. Know what I mean?"

"I didn't speak with him for very long. He didn't seem too pleased with the work we're doing," Carson said, choosing his words carefully.

Singer sighed. "You can't expect everyone to understand, let alone appreciate, what we're trying to do here, Guy. That's especially true of bureaucrats and regulators. I've met people like Teece before. More often than not, they're failed scientists. You can't discount the jealousy factor in people like that." He took a swallow. "Well, he'll have to give us his report sooner or later."

"Probably sooner," Carson replied, instantly sorry that he'd spoken. He felt Singer's eyes on him in the dark.

"Yes. He left here in an awful hurry. Insisted on taking one of the Hummers and driving himself to Radium Springs." Singer took another swallow. "You seem to be last one he spoke to."

"He said he wanted to save those closest to X-FLU for last."

"Hmm." Singer finished his drink and placed the glass heavily on the floor. He looked back again at Carson. "Well, he'll have heard about Levine by now. That won't make things any easier for us. He'll be back with a fresh set of questions, I'll bet money on it."

Carson felt a cold wave pass through him. "Levine?" he asked as casually as possible.

Singer was still looking at him. "I'm surprised you haven't heard, the rumor mill is full of it. Charles Levine, head of the Foundation for Genetic Policy. He said some pretty damaging things about us on national television a few days ago. GeneDyne stock is down significantly."

"It is?"

"Dropped another five and a half points today. The company has lost almost half a billion dollars in shareholders' equity. I needn't tell you what that does to our stock holdings."

Carson felt numb. He was not worried about the small amount of GeneDyne stock in his portfolio; he was worried about something entirely different. "What else did Levine say?"

Singer shrugged. "It doesn't really matter. It's all lies, anyway, all shitty lies. The problem is, people eat up that sort of stuff. They're just looking for something else to use against us, something to hold us back."

Carson licked his lips. He'd never heard Singer swear before. He wasn't very good at it. "So what's going to happen?"

A look of satisfaction surfaced briefly on Singer's features. "Brent will deal with it," he said. "That's just the kind of game he likes."

The helicopter approached Mount Dragon from the east, across the restricted airspace of the White Sands Missile Range, unmonitored by civilian air-traffic control. It was after midnight, the moon had disappeared, and the desert floor was an endless carpet of black. The helicopter's blades were of a noise-baffled military design, and the engine was equipped with pink-noise generators to minimize the aircraft's sound signature. The running lights and tail beacon were off, the pilot using downward-pointing radar to search for its target.

The target was a small transmitter, placed in the center of a reflective sheet of Mylar held down by a circle of stones. Next to the transmitter sat a Hummer, its engine and headlights off.

The helicopter eased down near the Mylar, the rotor wash tearing and shredding the material into confetti. As the runners settled on the desert floor, the dark figure of a man stepped out of the Hummer and ran toward the helicopter's hatch, an oddly shaped metal suitcase imprinted with the GeneDyne logo in one hand. The hatch opened, and a pair of hands reached out for the case. As soon as the hatch was secured, the helicopter lifted off, banked, and disappeared again into the blackness. The Hummer drove away, its shielded lights following the two tire tracks that had brought it. A single shred of Mylar, borne aloft in an updraft, curled and drifted away. Within moments, a bottomless silence had once again settled on the desert.

That Sunday, the sun rose to a flawless sky. At Mount Dragon, the Fever Tank was closed as usual for decontamination, and until the obligatory evening emergency drill, the science staff would be left to their own devices.

As his coffee brewed, Carson looked out his window at the black cone of Mount Dragon, just becoming visible in the predawn light. Usually, he spent his Sundays like the rest of the staff: isolated in his room, laptop for company, catching up on background work. But today, he would climb Mount Dragon. He'd been promising himself he'd do just that since first arriving at the site. Besides, the balcony session with Singer had whetted his appetite to play again, and he knew the sharp nasal sounds of the banjo strings echoing through the quiet residency compound would incite half a dozen irate e-mail messages through the lab net.

Dumping the coffee and grounds into a thermos, he slung his banjo over his shoulder and headed to the cafeteria to pick up some sandwiches. The kitchen staff, usually almost unbearably chipper, were morose and silent. They couldn't still be upset about what had happened to Vanderwagon. *Must be the early hour*, Carson thought. Everyone seemed to be in a bad mood these days.

Checking out with the perimeter guard, he set off down the dirt road that wound northeastward toward Mount Dragon. Reaching the base, he began the climb toward the summit, leaving the road in favor of a steep, narrow trail. The instrument felt heavy on his back, and the cinders slid under his feet as he climbed. Half an hour of hard work brought him to the top.

It was a classic cinder cone, its center scooped out by the ancient eruption. A few mesquite bushes grew along the rim. On the far side, Carson could see a cluster of microwave and radio towers, and a small white shed surrounded by a chain-link fence.

He turned around, breathing hard, ready to enjoy the view he'd worked hard for. The desert floor, at the precise instant of dawn, was like a pool of light, shimmering and swirling as if there were no surface at all, but merely a play of light and color. As the sun climbed fully over the horizon and flung a sheet of golden light across the ground, each solitary mesquite and creosotebush attached itself to shadows that ran endlessly toward the horizon. Carson could see the edge of light race across the desert, from east to west, etching the hills in light and the washes in darkness, until it rushed away over the curve of the earth, leaving a blanket of light in its wake.

Several miles away, he could see the wrecked outline of the old Anasazi pueblo—he now knew it was called Kin Klizhini—throwing shadows like black slashes across the dusty plain. Still farther away, the desert floor became black and mottled: the *Malpaís* lava flow.

He chose a comfortable spot behind a large block of tufa. Putting the banjo beside him, he stretched out and shut his eyes, enjoying the delicious solitude.

"Shit," came a familiar voice several minutes later.

Startled, Carson looked up and saw de Vaca standing over him, hands on her hips.

"What are you doing here?" she demanded.

Carson grabbed the handle of his banjo case. His day was already ruined. "What does it look like?" he asked.

"You're in my spot," she said. "I always come up here on Sundays."

Without another word, Carson heaved himself to his feet

and started to walk away. This was one day he was going to avoid an argument with his lab assistant. He'd take Roscoe out a good ten miles, do his playing out there.

He halted when he saw the expression on her face.

"Are you all right?" he asked.

"Why shouldn't I be?"

Carson looked at her. His instincts told him not to strike up a conversation, not to ask, just to get the hell out of there.

"You look a little upset," he said.

"Why should I trust you?" de Vaca asked abruptly.

"Trust me about what?"

"You're one of them," she said. "A *company* man." Beneath the accusatory tones, Carson sensed genuine fright.

"What is it?" he asked.

De Vaca remained silent for a long time. "Teece disappeared," she said at last.

Carson relaxed. "Of course he did. I talked to him the night before last. He was taking a Hummer to Radium Springs. He'll be back tomorrow."

She shook her head angrily. "You don't understand. After the storm, his Hummer was found out in the desert. Empty."

Shit. Not Teece. "He must have gotten lost in the sandstorm."

"That's what they're saying."

He turned toward her sharply. "What's that supposed to mean?"

De Vaca wouldn't look at him. "I overheard Nye. He was talking to Singer, saying that Teece was still missing. They were arguing."

Carson was silent. *Nye* . . . A vision came into his head: a vision of a man emerging from the sandstorm, encased in dust, his horse nearly dead from exhaustion.

"What, you think he was murdered?" he asked.

De Vaca did not reply.

"How far from Mount Dragon was the Hummer?"

"I don't know. Why?"

"Because I saw Nye return with his horse after the dust storm. He'd probably been out searching for Teece." He told her the story of what he'd seen in the stables two evenings before.

De Vaca listened intently. "You think he'd be out *searching* in a dust storm? Returning from burying the body, more likely. He and that asshole, Mike Marr."

Carson scoffed. "That's ludicrous. Nye may be a son of a bitch, but he's not a murderer."

"Marr *is* a murderer."

"Marr? He's as dumb as a lump of busted sod. He doesn't have the brains to commit murder."

"Yeah? Mike Marr was an intelligence officer in Vietnam. A tunnel rat. He worked in the Iron Triangle, probing all those hundreds of miles of secret tunnels, looking for Vietcong and their weapons caches and frying anybody they found down there. That's where he got his limp. He was down a hole, following a sniper. He triggered a booby trap and the tunnel collapsed on his legs."

"How do you know this?"

"He told me."

Carson laughed. "So you're friends, are you? Was this before or after he planted the butt of his shotgun in your gut?"

De Vaca frowned. "I told you, the scumbag tried to pick me up when I first got here. He cornered me in the gym and told me his life story, trying to impress me with what a bad dude he was. When that didn't work, he grabbed my ass. He thought I was just some kind of easy *Hispana* whore."

"He did? What happened?"

"I told him he was asking for a swift kick in the *huevos*."

Carson laughed again. "Guess it took that slap at the picnic to cool his ardor. Anyway, why would he or anybody else want to murder an OSHA inspector? That's insane. Mount Dragon would be shut down in an instant."

"Not it if looked like an accident," De Vaca returned. "The storm provided a perfect opportunity. Why did Nye take a *horse* out into the storm, anyway? And why haven't we been told about Teece's disappearance? Maybe Teece found out something that he wasn't supposed to know."

"Like what? For all we know, you could have misinterpreted what you heard. After all—"

"—I heard it, all right. Were you born yesterday, *cabrón*? There are billions at stake here. You think this is about saving lives, but it isn't. It's about money. And if that money is jeopardized . . ." She looked at him, eyes blazing.

"But why kill Teece? We had a terrible accident on Level-5, but the virus didn't escape. Only one person died. There's been no cover-up. Just the opposite."

" 'Only one person died,' " de Vaca echoed. "You ought to hear yourself. Look, something else is going on around here. I don't know what it is, but people are acting strange. Haven't you noticed? I think the pressure is driving people over the edge. If Scopes is so interested in saving lives, why this impossible timetable? We're working with the most dangerous virus ever created. One misstep, and *adiós muchachos*. Already, people's lives have been ruined by this project. Burt, Vanderwagon, Fillson the zookeeper, Czerny the guard. Not to mention Brandon-Smith. How many more lives?"

"Susana, you obviously don't belong in this industry," Carson replied wearily. "All great advances in human progress have been accompanied by pain and suffering. We're going to *save* millions of lives, remember?" Even as he spoke the words, they sounded hollow and clichéd in his ears.

"Oh, it all sounds noble enough. But is this really an advance? What gives us the right to alter the human genome? The longer I'm here, the more I see of what goes on, the more I believe what we're doing is fundamentally wrong. *Nobody* has the right to remake the human race."

"You're not talking like a scientist. We're not remaking the human race, we're curing people of the flu."

De Vaca was digging a trench in the cinders with short, angry movements of her heel. "We're altering human germ cells. We've crossed the line."

"We're getting rid of one small defect in our genetic code."

"*Defect.* What the hell is a defect exactly, Carson? Is having the gene for male pattern baldness a defect? Is being short a defect? Being the wrong skin color? Having kinky hair? What about being a little too shy? After we eradicate the flu, what comes next? Do you *really* think science is going to refrain from making people smarter, longer-lived, taller, handsomer, *nicer*? Particularly when there's billions of dollars to be made?"

"Obviously, it would be a highly regulated situation," Carson said.

"Regulation! And who is going to decide what's better? You? Me? The government? Brent Scopes? No big deal, let's just get rid of the unattractive genes, the ones nobody wants. Genes for fatness and ugliness and obnoxiousness. Genes that code for unpleasant personality traits. Take off your blinders for a moment, and tell me what this means for the integrity of the human race."

"We're a long way from being able to do all that," Carson muttered.

"Bullshit. We're doing it right now, with X-FLU. The mapping of the human genome is almost complete. The changes may start small, but they'll grow. The difference in DNA between humans and chimps is less than two percent, and look at the vast difference. It won't take big changes in the genome to remake the human race into something that we'd never even *recognize*."

Carson was silent. It was the same argument he had heard countless times before. Only now—despite his best efforts to resist—it was starting to make sense. Perhaps he was just tired, and didn't have the energy to spar with de Vaca. Or perhaps it was the look on Teece's face when he'd said, *What I've got to do can't wait.*

They sat silently in the shadow of the volcanic rock, looking down toward the beautiful cluster of white buildings that were Mount Dragon, trembling and insubstantial in the rising heat. Even as he fought against it, Carson could feel something crumbling inside him. It was the same feeling he'd had when, as a teenager, he had watched from a flatbed truck while the ranch was being auctioned off piece by piece. He had always believed, more firmly than he believed anything else, that the best hopes for mankind's future lay in science. And now, for whatever reason, that belief was threatening to dissolve in the heat waves rising from the desert floor.

He cleared his throat and shook his head, as if to dislodge the train of thought. "If your mind is made up, what do you plan to do about it?"

"Get the hell out of here and let people know what's going on."

Carson shook his head. "What's going on is one-hundred-percent legal, FDA-regulated genetic research. You can't stop it."

"I can if somebody was murdered. Something's not right here. Teece found out what it was."

Carson looked at her as she sat with her back against the rock, her arms wrapped around her knees, the wind whipping her raven hair away from her forehead. *Fuck it*, he thought. *Here goes.*

"I'm not sure what Teece knew," he said slowly. "But I know what he was looking for."

De Vaca's eyes narrowed. "What are you talking about?"

"Teece thinks Franklin Burt was keeping a private notebook. That's what he told me the night he left. He also said that Vanderwagon and Burt had elevated levels of dopamine and serotonin in their bloodstreams. So did Brandon-Smith, to a lesser extent."

De Vaca was silent.

"He thought that this journal of Burt's could shed light on whatever might be causing these symptoms," Carson added. "Teece was going to look for it when he got back."

De Vaca stood up. "So. Are you going to help me?"

"Help you what?"

"Find Burt's notebook. Learn the secret of Mount Dragon."

Charles Levine had taken to arriving at Greenough Hall very early, locking his office door, and leaving instructions for Ray that he was taking no calls and seeing no visitors. He had temporarily passed on his course load to two junior instructors, and he'd canceled his planned lecture schedule for the coming months. Those had been the last pieces of advice from Toni Wheeler before she resigned as the foundation's public-relations adviser. For once, Levine had decided to follow her suggestions. The internal pressure from the college trustees was growing, and the telephone messages left for him by the dean of faculty were becoming increasingly strident. Levine sensed danger, and—against his nature—had decided to lay low for a while.

So he was surprised to find a man waiting patiently in front of his locked office door at seven o'clock in the morning. Instinctively, Levine held out his hand, but the man only looked back at him.

"What can I do for you?" Levine said, unlocking the door and showing him in. The man sat down stiffly, gripping his briefcase across his lap. He had bushy gray hair and high cheekbones, and looked about seventy.

"My name is Jacob Perlstein," he said. "I am a historian

with the Holocaust Research Foundation in Washington."

"Ah, yes. I know your work well. Your reputation is without peer." Perlstein was known around the world for the unflagging zeal with which he brought to light old records from Nazi death camps and the Jewish ghettos of eastern Europe. Levine settled into his chair, puzzled by the man's hostile air.

"I will come to the point," the man said, his black eyes peering at Levine through contracted eyebrows.

Levine nodded.

"You have claimed that your Jewish father saved Jewish lives in Poland. He was caught by the Nazis and murdered by Mengele at Auschwitz."

Levine did not like the wording of the question, but he said nothing.

"Murdered through medical experimentation. Is that correct?"

"Yes," said Levine.

"And how do you know this?" the man asked.

"Excuse me, Mr. Perlstein, but I'm not sure I appreciate the tone of your questions."

Perlstein continued to stare at him. "The question is simple enough. I would like you to tell me how you know this."

Levine strove to conceal his irritation. He had told this story in countless interviews and at innumerable fund-raisers. Surely Perlstein had heard it before. "Because I did the research myself. I knew my father had died at Auschwitz, but that was all. My mother died when I was very young. I *had* to know what happened to him. So I spent almost four months in East Germany and Poland, combing Nazi files. It was a dangerous time, and I was doing dangerous work. When I found out—well, you can imagine how I felt. It changed my view of science, of medicine. It gave me deeply ambivalent feelings about genetic engineering, which in turn—"

"The files on your father," the man interrupted brusquely. "Where did you find them?"

"In Leipzig, where all such files are kept. Surely you already know this."

"And your mother, pregnant, escaped, and brought you to America. You took her name, Levine, rather than your father's name, Berg."

"That's correct."

"A touching story," said Perlstein. "Odd that Berg is not a commonly Jewish name."

Levine sat up. "I don't like the tone of your voice, Mr. Perlstein. I must ask you to say whatever it is you've come to say, and leave."

The man opened his briefcase and took out a folder, which he laid distastefully on the edge of Levine's desk. "Please examine these documents." He pushed the folder toward Levine with the edge of his fingers.

Opening the folder, Levine found a thin sheaf of photocopied documents. He recognized them immediately: the faded gothic typeface, the stamped swastikas, brought back memories of those horrible weeks behind the Iron Curtain, sifting through boxes of paper in damp archives, when only an overwhelming desire to know the truth had kept him going.

The first document was a color reproduction of a Nazi ID card, identifying one Heinrich Berg as an Oberstürmfuhrer in the *Schutzstaffel*—the German SS—stationed at the concentration camp of Ravensbrueck. The photograph still appeared to be in excellent shape, the family resemblance extraordinary.

He pawed through the rest of the papers quickly, in growing disbelief. There were camp documents, prison rosters, a report from the army company that liberated Ravensbrueck, a letter from a survivor bearing an Israeli postmark, and a sworn affidavit. The documents showed that a young woman from Poland named Miyrna Levine had been sent to Ravensbrueck for "processing." While there, she had come into contact with

Berg, become his mistress, and later been transferred to Auschwitz. There she had survived the war by informing on resistance movements within the camp.

Levine looked at Perlstein. The man was staring back, the eyes dry and accusatory.

"How dare you peddle these lies," Levine hissed when he had at last found his voice.

Perlstein's breath rasped inward. "So, you continue to deny. I expected as much. How dare *you* peddle *your* lies! Your father was an SS officer and your mother a traitor who sent hundreds to their deaths. You are not personally guilty of your parents' sins. But the lie you are living compounds their evil, and makes a mockery of the work you do. You claim to be searching for truth for everyone else, yet the truth doesn't apply to you. You—who allowed your father's name to be carved among the righteous at Yad Vashem: Heinrich Berg, an SS officer! It is an insult to the true martyrs. And this insult shall be made known." The man's hands trembled as they clutched the leather case.

Levine struggled to remain calm. "These documents are forgeries, and you are a fool to believe them. The East German communists were famous for faking—"

"Since this was brought to my attention several days ago, the originals have been examined by three independent experts in Nazi documents. They are absolutely genuine. There can be no mistake."

Suddenly, Levine was on his feet. "Get out!" he screamed. "You're just a tool for the revisionists. Get out, and take this filth with you!" He stepped forward, raising one arm threateningly above his head.

The elderly man tried to snatch the folder, ducking in alarm, and the contents spilled onto the floor. Ignoring them, he retreated to the outer office, then out into the corridor beyond. Levine slammed his office door and leaned against it, the pulse hammering in his head. It was an outrageous, vicious lie, and he would clear it up quickly . . . he had certified copies of the real documents, thank God . . . he would simply hire an expert to debunk the forgeries. The slander against his murdered father was like a stab through the heart, but this was not the first time he had been foully attacked and it would not be the last—

His eye fell on the folder, its documents and their filthy lies lying scattered across the floor, and a sudden, terrible thought struck him.

He rushed to a locked filing cabinet, jammed in a key, and reached for a folder marked, simply, "Berg."

The folder was empty.

"*Scopes,*" he whispered.

The next day, with a tone of infinite regret, the *Boston Globe* carried the story on the front page of its second section.

Muriel Page, a volunteer for the Salvation Army store on Pearl Street, watched the young man with the slept-on hair pawing through a rack of sport coats. It was the second time he had come in that week, and Muriel couldn't help feeling sorry for him. He didn't look like a self-medicator—he was clean and alert—no doubt just a young man down on his luck. He had a boyish, slightly awkward face that reminded her of her own grown son, married now and living in California. Except this young man was so *thin.* He certainly wasn't eating right.

The young man flipped through the rack at high speed, glancing at the jackets as they went by.

He stopped suddenly and pulled one out, sliding it on over his black T-shirt as he walked toward a nearby mirror. Muriel, watching out of the corner of her eye, had to admire the man's taste. It was a very nice jacket, with narrow lapels and little overlapping triangles and squares in red and yellow floating on a field of black. Probably dated from the early fifties. Very stylish, but not something—she thought a little mournfully—that most young men today would like. Clothes had been so much classier when she was a young lady.

The young man turned around, examined himself from various angles, and grinned. He came walking toward the counter, and Muriel knew she had a sale.

She removed the tag. "Five dollars," she said with a cheerful smile.

The young man's face fell behind the black glasses. "Oh," he said. "I was hoping . . ."

Muriel hesitated for just an instant. The five dollars probably represented several meals to him, and he looked hungry. She leaned forward and spoke conspiratorially. "I'll let you have it for three, if you won't tell anyone." She fingered the sleeve. "That's real wool, too."

The man brightened, smoothing his unruly cowlick with a self-conscious hand. "Very kind of you," he said, fishing in his pocket and removing three crumpled bills.

"It's a lovely jacket," Muriel said. "When I was a young lady, a man wearing a jacket like that . . . well!" She winked. The young man stared back at her, and instantly she felt silly. Briskly, she wrote out a receipt and handed it to him. "I hope you enjoy it," she said.

"I will."

She leaned forward again. "You know, just across the street we have a very nice place where you can get a bite of hot food. It's free and there are no strings attached."

The man looked suspicious. "No religious harangues?"

"None at all. We don't believe in forcing religion on people. Just a hot, nourishing meal. All we require is that you be sober and drug-free."

"Really?" he asked. "I thought the Salvation Army was a religious group of some kind."

"We are. But a hungry person isn't likely to be thinking about spiritual salvation, just his next meal. Feed the body and you free the soul."

The man thanked her and exited. Taking a covert peek out the window, she was gratified to see him head directly for the soup kitchen, take a tray at the door, and get in line, striking up a conversation with the man in front of him.

Muriel felt a tear well up in her eye. That absentminded, slightly lost expression was so much like her son's. She hoped that whatever had gone wrong in his life would straighten itself out before too long.

The following morning, the Pearl Street Salvation Army store and soup kitchen received an anonymous donation in the amount of a quarter of a million dollars, and no one was more surprised than Muriel Page when she was told it was in honor of her work.

Carson and de Vaca walked silently down the trail and back to the Mount Dragon complex. Outside the covered walkway leading to the residency compound, they stopped.

"So?" de Vaca prompted, breaking the silence.

"So what?"

"You still haven't told me if you're going to help me find the notebook," she said in a fierce whisper.

"Susana, I've got work to do. So do you, for that matter. That notebook, if it exists, isn't going anywhere. Let me think about this a while. OK?"

De Vaca looked at him for a moment. Then she turned

without a word and walked into the compound.

Carson watched her walk away. Then, with a sigh, he climbed the staircase to the second floor, stepping through the doorway into the cool, dark corridor beyond. Maybe Teece had been right about Burt's secret notebook. And maybe de Vaca was right about Nye. In which case, what Teece thought didn't matter as much anymore. But what concerned Carson most was that horrible moment on top of Mount Dragon, when he'd suddenly felt the strength of his convictions turn soft. Since his father died and the last ranch had failed, Carson's love of science—his faith in the good it could accomplish—had meant everything to him. Now, if . . .

But he wouldn't think about it any more today. Maybe tomorrow, he'd have the strength to face it again.

Back in his room, Carson stared at the drab white walls for a minute, summoning the energy to switch on his laptop and begin sorting through the X-FLU II test data. His eye fell upon the battered banjo case.

Hell with it, he thought. He'd play a little; without picks, to keep the noise down. Just five minutes, maybe ten. Get his mind off all this. Then he'd get to work.

As he lifted the five-string from the case, his eye fell on a folded piece of paper lying on the yellowing felt beneath. Frowning, he picked it up and unfolded it on his knee.

Dear Guy,

I've always hated this infernal instrument. For once, however, I hope you practice with regularity. You've apparently already left for the morning, and I can't delay my departure any further. This seems the best—indeed, only—way to contact you.

As you know, I'll be gone for a couple of days. Since we spoke, I have tried without success to learn where Burt might have hidden his notebook. You know the Mount Dragon com-

plex, you know the surrounding area, and—most importantly—
you know Burt's work. It's quite possible that, perhaps inadvertently, Burt left behind a clue to the whereabouts of the
notebook. Would you please look through Burt's electronic
notes and see if you can find such a clue?

Do not, however, try to find the notebook yourself. Let me
do that when I return from my journey. Meanwhile, please
don't mention this to anyone.

Had I felt there was more time, I would not have burdened
you with this. I have a feeling you are someone I can trust. I
hope I am not mistaken.

Yours,
Gil Teece

Carson reread the hastily scrawled note. Teece must have
come looking for him the morning of the dust storm and, not
finding him, left the message in the one place Carson would
be most likely to find it. When he'd opened the case on the
canteen balcony, the night had been dark and he hadn't seen
the note. He felt a momentary anxious stab as he thought
about how easily the paper could have fallen unnoticed to
the floor of the balcony, to be discovered later by Singer. Or
maybe Nye.

He angrily shook aside the thought. *Another couple of days
and I'll be as paranoid as de Vaca. Or even Burt.* Shoving the
note into his back pocket, he punched de Vaca's extension
on the residency intercom.

"So this is where you live, Carson? It figures they'd give you one of the better views. All I see from my room is the back end of the incinerator."

De Vaca moved away from the window. "They say the way a person decorates their own space is a good barometer of personality," she went on, scanning the bare walls. "Figures."

She leaned over his shoulder while he booted up his residency laptop.

"About a month before he left Mount Dragon, Burt's entries began to grow shorter," Carson said as he logged in. "If Teece is right, that's the time he started keeping the illegal journal. If there are any clues as to its whereabouts in Burt's on-line notes, that's where I figure we should start looking."

He began paging through the log. As the formulas, lists, and data scrolled by, Carson was reminded irresistibly of the first time he had read the journal, a lifetime ago, on his first workday in the Fever Tank. His heart sank as he skimmed yet again the failed experiments, the recordings of hopes that were alternately lifted, then shattered. It all felt uncomfortably close to home.

As he scrolled on, the scientific notes were increasingly leavened by conversations with Scopes, personal entries, even dreams.

May 20

I dreamt last night that I was wandering, lost, in the desert. I walked toward the mountains, and it grew darker and darker. Then a great light appeared, like a second dawn, and a vast mushroom cloud rose from behind the mountain range. I knew I was witnessing the Trinity explosion. I saw the wave of overpressure bearing down on me, and then I woke up.

"Damn," Carson said, "if he confides stuff like this to his on-line notes, why would he bother keeping a secret diary?"

"Keep going," urged de Vaca.

He continued scanning.

June 2

    When I shook out my shoes this morning, a little scorpion fell out and landed on the floor all in a tizzy. I felt sorry for him and brought him outside. . . .

"Keep going, keep going," de Vaca repeated impatiently.

Carson continued scrolling. Poetry began appearing among the data tables and technical notes. Finally, as Burt's madness emerged, the log degenerated into a confusing welter of images, nightmares, and meaningless phrases. Then there was the last horrifying conversation with Scopes; a burst of apocalyptic mania; and the end-of-file marker was reached.

They sat back and looked at each other.

"There's nothing here," Carson said.

"We're not thinking like Burt," de Vaca said. "If you were Burt, and you wanted to plant a clue in the record, how would you do it?"

Carson shrugged. "I probably wouldn't."

"Yes, you would. Teece was right: subconscious or conscious, it's human nature. First, you'd have to assume that Scopes was going to read everything. Right?"

"Right."

"So what would Scopes be *least* likely to read in here?"

There was a silence.

"The poetry," they both said at once.

They scrolled back to the point in the journal where the poems first appeared, then paged slowly forward. Most, but not all, were on scientific subjects: the structure of DNA, quarks and gluons, the Big Bang and string theory.

"You notice that these poems start around the same time the journal entries get shorter?" Carson asked.

"No one's ever written poetry quite like this before," de Vaca replied. "In its own way, it's beautiful." She read aloud:

> There is a shadow on this glass plate.
> A long exposure in the emission range
> Of alpha hydrogen
> Yields satisfactory results.
> M82 was once ten billion stars,
> Now it has returned to the slow lazy dust of creation.
> Is this the mighty work
> Of the same God who fires the Sun?

"I don't get it," she said.

"Messier 82 is a very strange galaxy in Virgo. The whole galaxy blew up, annihilating ten billion stars."

"Interesting," said de Vaca. "But I don't think it's what we're looking for."

They scrolled on.

> Black house in the sheeted sun
> The ravens rise as you approach,
> They circle and float, crying at the trespass,
> Waiting for emptiness to return.
> The Great Kiva
> Is half-filled with sand,
> But the sipapu
> Lies open.
> It empties its silent cry into the fourth world.
> When you leave
> The ravens settle back,
> Croaking with satisfaction.

"Beautiful," said de Vaca. "And somehow familiar. I wonder what this black house is?"

Carson suddenly sat up. "Kin Klizhini," he said. "It's

Apache for 'Black House.' He's writing about the ruin just south of here."

"You know Apache?" de Vaca asked, looking at his curiously.

"Most of our ranch hands were Apache," Carson said. "I picked up some stuff from them when I was a kid."

There was a silence while they read the poem again.

"Hell," said Carson. "I don't see anything here."

"Wait." De Vaca held up her hand. "The Great Kiva was the underground religious chamber of the Anasazi Indians. The center of the kiva contained a hole, called the *sipapu*, that connected this world with the spirit world below. They called that world the Fourth World. We live in the Fifth World."

"I know that," Carson said. "But I still don't see any clues here."

"Read the poem again. If the kiva was filled with sand, how could the *sipapu* be open?"

Carson looked at her. "You're right."

She looked at Carson and grinned. "At last, *cabrón*, you learn to speak the truth."

They decided to take the horses, in order to be back in time for the evening emergency drill. The sun had passed the meridian and the day was at its hottest.

Carson watched de Vaca throw a saddle on the rat-tailed Appaloosa. "I guess you've ridden before," he said.

"Damn right," de Vaca replied, buckling the flank cinch and looping a canteen over the horn. "You think Anglos have a monopoly? When I was a kid, I had a horse named Barbarian. He was a Spanish Barb, the horse of the Conquest."

"I've never seen one," Carson said.

"They're the best desert horse you can find. Small, stout, and tough. My father got some from an old Spanish herd on the Romero Ranch. Those horses had never interbred with Anglo horses. Old Romero said he and his ancestors always shot any damn *gringo* stallions that came sniffing around their mares." She laughed and swung herself into the saddle. Carson liked the way she sat a horse: balanced and easy.

He mounted Roscoe and they rode to the perimeter gate, punched in the access code, then reined toward Kin Klizhini. The ancient ruin reared up on the horizon about two miles away: two walls poking up from the desert floor, surrounded by mounds of rubble.

De Vaca tilted her head back, gave her hair a shake. "In spite of everything that's happened, I never get tired of the beauty of this place," she said as they rode.

Carson nodded. "When I was sixteen," he said, "I spent a summer on a ranch at the northern end of the Jornada, called the Diamond Bar."

"Really? Is the desert up there like it is down here?"

"Similar. As you move northward, the Fra Cristóbal Mountains come around in an arc. The rain shadow from the mountains falls across there and it gets a little greener."

"What were you, a ranch hand?"

"Yeah, after my dad lost the ranch I cowboyed around for the summer before going to college. That Diamond Bar was a big ranch, about four hundred sections between the San Pascual Mountains and the Sierra Oscura. The real desert started at the southern edge of the ranch, at a place called Lava Gate. There's a huge lava flow that runs almost to the foot of the Fra Cristóbal Mountains. Between the lava flow and the mountains is a narrow gap, maybe a hundred yards across. The old Spanish trail used to go through there." He laughed. "Lava Gate was like the gates of hell. You didn't want to go south from there, you might never come back. And now here I am, right in the middle of it."

"My ancestors came up that trail with Oñate in 1598," said de Vaca.

"*Up* the Spanish trail?" Carson asked. "They crossed the Jornada?"

De Vaca nodded, squinting against the sun.

"How did they find water?"

"There's that doubting look on your face again, *cabrón*. My grandfather told me they waited until dusk at the last water, and then drove their stock all night, stopping at about four in the morning to graze. Farther on, their Apache guide brought them to a spring called the Ojo del Aguila. Eagle Spring. Its location is now lost. At least, that's what my grandfather said."

There was a question Carson had been curious about for some time, but had been afraid to ask. "Where, exactly, did you get the name Cabeza de Vaca?"

De Vaca looked at him truculently. "Where'd you get the name Carson?"

"You have to admit, 'Head of Cow' is a little odd for a name."

"So is 'Son of Car' "

" 'Forgive me for asking," Carson said, mentally reprimanding himself for not knowing better.

"If you knew your Spanish history," de Vaca said, "you'd know about the name. In 1212, a soldier in the Spanish army marked a pass with a cow skull, and led a Spanish army to victory over the Moors. That soldier was given a royal title and the right to use the name 'Cabeza de Vaca'. "

"Fascinating," Carson yawned. *And probably apocryphal*, he thought.

"Alonso Cabeza de Vaca was one of the first European settlers in America in 1598. We come from one of the most ancient and important European families in America. Not that I pay any attention to that kind of thing."

But Carson could see from the proud look on her face that she paid a great deal of attention to that kind of thing.

They rode for a while, saying nothing, enjoying the heat of the day and the gentle roll of the horses. De Vaca rode slightly ahead, her lower body moving with the horse, her torso relaxed and quiet, left hand on the reins and right hooked in her belt loop. As they approached the ruin, she stopped, waiting for him to catch up.

He drew alongside and she looked at him, an amused gleam in her violet eyes.

"Last one there is a *pendejo*," she said suddenly, leaning forward and spurring her horse.

By the time Carson could recover and urge Roscoe forward, she was three lengths ahead, the horse going at a dead run, its head down, ears flattened, hooves throwing gravel back into Carson's face. He urged Roscoe on with urgent, light heel jabs.

Carson edged up on her and the two horses raced alongside, leaping the low mesquite bushes, the wind roaring in their ears. The ruin loomed closer, the great stone walls etched against the blue sky. Carson knew he had the better mount, yet he watched in disbelief as de Vaca leaned close to her horse's ear, urging him forward in a low but electric voice. Carson jabbed and shouted in vain. They flashed between the two ruined walls, de Vaca now half a length ahead, her hair whipping like a black flame behind her. Ahead of them, Carson saw a low wall rise suddenly out of the brown sands. A group of ravens burst upward with a raucous crying as they both took the wall at a leap and were suddenly past the ruin. They slowed to a lope, then a trot, turning the horses back, cooling them off.

Carson looked over at de Vaca. Her face was flushed, and her hair wild. A fleck of foam from the sweaty horse lay across her thigh. She grinned. "Not bad," she said. "You almost caught me."

Carson flicked his reins. "You cheated," he said, hearing the peevishness in his own voice. "You got the jump on me."

"You have the better horse," she said.

"You're lighter."

She smirked. "Face it, *cabrón*, you lost."

Carson smiled grimly. "I'll catch you next time."

"Nobody catches me."

Reaching the ruin, they dismounted, tying their horses to a rock. "The Great Kiva was usually in the very center of the pueblo, or else far outside its borders," de Vaca said. "Let's hope it hasn't collapsed completely."

The ravens circled far overhead, their distant cries hanging in the dry air.

Carson looked around curiously. The walls were formed from stones of shaped lava, cemented together with adobe. Walls and room blocks rose on three sides of the U-shaped ruin, the fourth side opening onto a central plaza. Potsherds and pieces of flint littered the ground beneath their feet. Much of it was covered by sand.

They walked into the plaza, long overgrown with yucca and mesquite. De Vaca knelt down by a large fire-ant hill. The ants had fled inside to escape the noonday heat, and she carefully smoothed the gravel with her fingers, examining it closely.

"What are you doing?" Carson asked.

Instead of answering, de Vaca picked something off the mound and held it between thumb and forefinger. "Take a look," she said.

She placed something in his palm, and he squinted at it: a perfect little turquoise bead, with a hole no wider than a human hair drilled through its center.

"They polished their turquoises using blades of grass," she said. "No one is really sure how they got the holes so small and perfect, without the use of metal. Perhaps by twirling a tiny sliver of bone against the turquoise for hours." She stood up. "Come on, let's find that kiva."

They moved to the center of the plaza. "There's nothing here," Carson said.

"We'll separate and search beyond the perimeter," de Vaca replied. "I'll take the northern semicircle, you take the southern."

Carson moved out beyond the edge of the ruin, tracing a widening arc, scanning the desert as he did so. The huge storm and drying winds had erased any signs of footprints; it was impossible to tell whether Burt had been there or not. Centuries before, the subterranean kiva would have had a roof flush with the desert floor, with only a smoke hole on the surface revealing its presence. While it was likely the roof had collapsed long ago, there was a chance that it had remained intact and was now completely concealed by the shifting sands.

Carson found the kiva about one hundred yards to the southwest. The roof had collapsed, and the kiva was now nothing but a circular depression in the desert, thirty feet across and perhaps seven feet deep. Its walls were of shaped rock, from which projected a few stubs of ancient roof timbers. De Vaca came running at his call, and together they stood at its edge. Near the bottom, Carson could make out places where the walls were still plastered in adobe mud and red paint. At the base, the wind had piled up a crescent of sand, completely burying the floor.

"So where's this sipapu?" Carson asked.

"It was always in the exact center of the kiva," said de Vaca. "Here, help me down." She scrambled down the side, paced off the center, then knelt, digging in the sand with her fingers. Carson dropped down and began to help. Six inches into the sand, their hands scraped against flat rock. De Vaca brushed the sand away excitedly, moving the stone aside.

There, in the sipapu hole, sat a large plastic specimen jar, its GeneDyne label still intact. Inside the jar was a small book with dented corners, bound in a stained, olive-colored canvas.

"*Madre de Dios*," de Vaca whispered. She lifted the jar out of the sipapu, pried open the lid, and pulled out the journal, opening it as Carson looked on.

The first page was headed *May 18*. Below the date, the page was covered in dense, precise handwriting, so tiny that two lines were written in each ruled space.

Carson watched as de Vaca flipped through the pages incredulously. "We can't bring this back to Mount Dragon," he said.

"I know. So let's get started."

She turned to the beginning.

May 18

Dearest Amiko,

I write to you from the ruins of a sacred Anasazi kiva, not far from my laboratory.

When we were packing my things, that last morning before I flew to Albuquerque, I stuck this old journal into the pocket of my jacket, on impulse. I'd always planned to use it for bird sightings. But I think now I've found a better use for it.

I miss you so terribly. The people here are friendly, for the most part. Some, like the director, John Singer, I think I can even count as friends. But we are associates before we are friends here, all pushing toward one common goal. There is pressure upon us; tremendous pressure to move ahead, to succeed. I feel myself drawing inward under such pressure. The endless desolation of this awful desert magnifies my loneliness.

It is as if we have stepped off the edge of the world.

Paper and pencil are forbidden here. Brent wants to keep track of everything we do. Sometimes, I believe he even wants to keep track of what we think. I'll use this small journal as my lifeline to you. There are things I want to tell you, in good time. Things that will never appear in the on-line records at GeneDyne. Brent is, in many ways, still a boy, with boyish ideas; and one of those ideas is that he can control what others do and think.

I hope you will not worry when I tell you such things. But I forget; when you read this, it will be with me by your side. And these will be but memories. Perhaps the passage of time will allow me to laugh at myself and my petty complaints. Or feel pride at what we have accomplished here.

It's a long walk out to this kiva, and you know how poor a rider I am. But I think it does me good, to spend this time with you. The journal will be safe here, under the sand. Nobody leaves the facility except the security director, and he seems to have his own strange desert business to attend to.

I will come again, soon.

May 25

My darling wife,

It is a terribly hot day. I keep forgetting how much water one needs in this frightful desert. I will have to bring two canteens next time.

It is no wonder, in this waterless landscape, that the entire religion of the Anasazi was directed at the control of nature. Here, in the kiva, is where the rain priests called on the Thunderbird to bring the rain.

Oh, male divinity!
With your moccasins of dark cloud, come to us,
With the zigzag lightning flung out on high over your head, come to
    us soaring,

*With these I wish the foam floating on the flowing water over the roots
of the great corn,*
Happily abundant dark clouds I desire,
Happily abundant dark mists I desire,
Happily may fair blue corn, to the ends of the earth, come with you.

This was how they prayed. It is a very ancient desire, this
thirst for knowledge and power, this hunger to control the
secrets of nature, to bring the rain.

But the rain did not come. Just as it does not come today.

What would they think if they could see us now, laboring
day after day, in our warrens beneath the earth, working not
only to control nature, but to shape it to our will?

I can write no more today. The problem I've been given is
demanding all my time and energy. It's hard to escape it, even
here. But I will return soon, my love.

June 4

Dearest Amiko,

Please forgive my long absence from this place. Our schedule in the laboratory has been fiendish. Were it not for the
requisite decontaminations, I believe Brent would have us
working round the clock.

Brent. How much have I told you about him?

It's strange. I never knew that I could feel such profound
respect for a man, and yet dislike him at the same time. I
suppose I might even hate him. Even when he's not actually
pushing me to work faster, I can still see his face, frowning,
because the results are not as he would like. I hear him whispering in my ear: *Just five more minutes. Just one more test series.*

Brent is probably the most complex person I've ever met.
Brilliant, silly, immature, cool, ruthless. He has an enormous
internal storehouse of witty aphorisms which he brings forth
for any occasion, quoting them with great delight. He gives
away millions while arguing bitterly over hundreds. He can

be suffocatingly kind to one person and unbearably cruel to the next. His knowledge of music is extraordinary. He owns Beethoven's last and finest piano, the one that supposedly prompted him to write his final three sonatas. I can only guess at the price.

I'll never forget the first time I spoke to him. It was when I was still working in GeneDyne Manchester, shortly after my breakthrough with GEF, the filtration system. Our preliminary results were excellent, and everyone was excited. The system promised to cut production time in half. The team in the transfection lab were beside themselves. They told me they were going to nominate me for president.

That's when the call came from Brent Scopes. I assumed it was congratulatory; perhaps another bonus. But instead, he asked me to come to Boston, on the next plane. I had to drop everything, he said, to assume leadership of a critical GeneDyne project. He didn't even allow me to finish the final tests on GEF; I had to leave that to my staff at Manchester.

You remember my trip to Boston. I'm sure I must have seemed evasive on my return, and for that I am sorry. Brent has a way of pulling you in behind his banner, of electrifying you with his own enthusiasm. But there seems no reason not to tell you about it now. It will be in all the newspapers in a matter of months, anyway.

My task—putting it simply—was to synthesize artificial blood. To use the vast resources of GeneDyne to genetically engineer human blood. The preparatory work had already been done, Brent said. But he wanted someone with my background, and my expertise, to see it through. My work on the GEF filtration process made me the perfect choice.

It was a noble idea, I admit, and Brent's delivery was superb. Never again would hospitals suffer from blood shortages and emergencies, he said. No longer would people have to fear contaminated transfusions. No longer would people with rare blood types die for lack of a match. GeneDyne's artificial blood would be free of contamination, would match all types, and would be available in limitless quantities.

And so I left Manchester—I left you, our home, everything I hold dear—and came to this desolate place. To pursue a dream of Brent Scopes, and, with any luck, make the world a better place. The dream lives. But its cost is very high.

June 12

Dearest Amiko,

I have decided to use this journal to continue the story I began in my last entry. Perhaps that was my purpose all along. All I can tell you is that, after leaving this kiva on my last visit, I felt a tremendous sense of release. So I will continue, for my own sake if not for posterity.

I remember one morning, perhaps four months ago. I was holding a flask of blood. It was the blood of a human being, yet it had been manufactured by a form of life as far removed from human as possible: *streptococcus*, the bacterium that lives in the soil, among other places. I had spliced the human hemoglobin gene into *strep* and forced it to produce human hemoglobin. Vast quantities of human hemoglobin.

Why use *streptococcus*? Because we know more about *strep* than about almost any other form of life on the planet. We have mapped its entire genome. We know how to snip apart its DNA, tuck in a gene, and sew everything back together.

You will forgive me if I simplify the process. Using cells taken from the lining of a human cheek (my own), I removed a single gene located on the fourth chromosome, 16s rDNA, locus D3401. I multiplied it a millionfold, inserted the copies into the *strep* bacteria, and grew them in large vats filled with a protein solution. Despite how it sounds, my dear, this part wasn't difficult. It has been done many times before with other genes, including the gene for human insulin.

We made this bacterium—this extremely primitive form of life—ever so slightly human. Each bacterium carried a tiny, invisible piece of a human being inside it. This human piece, in essence, took over the functions of the bacterium and forced it to do one thing: produce human hemoglobin.

And that, to me, is the magic—the irreducible truth of genetics, the promise that will never grow stale.

But this is also where the difficult work really began.

Perhaps I should explain. The hemoglobin molecule consists of a protein group, called a globin, with four heme groups riding shotgun on it. It collects oxygen in the lungs, exchanges this oxygen with carbon dioxide in the tissues, and then dumps carbon dioxide into the lungs to be exhaled.

A very clever, very complicated molecule.

Unfortunately, hemoglobin by itself is deadly poisonous. If you injected naked hemoglobin into a human being, it would probably be fatal. The hemoglobin needs to be enclosed in something. Normally, this would be a red blood cell.

We therefore had to design something that would seal up the hemoglobin, make it safe. A microscopic sack, if you will. But something that would "breathe," that would allow oxygen and carbon dioxide to pass through.

Our solution was to create these little "sacks" out of pieces of membrane from ruptured cells. I used a special enzyme called lyase.

Then came the final problem: to purify the hemoglobin. This may sound like the simplest problem of all.

It was not.

We grew the bacteria in huge vats. As the amount of hemoglobin produced by the bacteria built up, it poisoned the vat. Everything died. We were left with a soup of crap: molecules of hemoglobin mixed with dead and dying bacteria; bits of DNA and RNA; chromosomal fragments; rogue bacteria.

The trick was to purify this soup—to separate the healthy hemoglobin from all the junk—so that we would end up with pure human hemoglobin and nothing else. And it had to be *extremely* pure. Getting a blood transfusion is not like taking a tiny pill. Many *pints* of this substance might go inside a human being. Even the slightest impurities, multiplied by those quantities, could cause unpredictable side effects.

It was around this time that we got word of what was going on back in Boston. The marketing people were already studying—in great secrecy—how to market our genetically engineered blood. They assembled focus groups of ordinary citizens. They discovered that most people are terrified of getting a blood transfusion because they fear contamination: from hepatitis, from AIDS, from other diseases. People wanted to be reassured that the blood they were receiving was pure and safe.

So our unfinished product was dubbed *PurBlood*. And the decree came down from corporate headquarters: henceforth, in all papers, journals, notes, and conversations, the product would be called PurBlood. Anyone calling it by its trade name, Hemocyl, would be disciplined. In particular, the marketing decree stated, any use of the word "genetic engineering" or "artificial" was *verboten*. The public did not like the idea of genetically engineered *anything*. They didn't like genetically engineered tomatoes, they didn't like genetically engineered milk; and they *really* hated the phrase "genetically engineered artificial human blood." I guess I can't blame them, really. The thought of having such a substance pumped into something as inviolate as one's own veins has to be disturbing to a layman.

My love, the sun is growing low in the sky, and I must leave. But I will return tomorrow. I'll tell Brent I need a day off. It's not a lie. If you only knew how pouring out my soul to you on these pages has lifted a great weight from my shoulders.

June 13

Dearest Amiko,

I come now to the most difficult part of my story. The part, in fact, that I was not sure until now I could bring myself to tell you. I may yet burn these pages, if my resolve weakens. But it is a secret I can no longer keep within myself.

. . . So I began the purification process. We fermented the solution to free the hemoglobin from its bacterial prison. We centrifuged it to clear out the refuse. We forced it through ceramic micron filters. We fractionated it. To no avail.

You see, hemoglobin is extremely delicate. You cannot heat it; you cannot use overly strong chemicals; you cannot sterilize or distill it. Each time I attempted to purify the hemoglobin, I ended up destroying it. The molecule lost its delicate structure: it "denatured." It became useless.

A more delicate purification process was required. And so Brent suggested we try my own GEF filtration process.

I realized immediately that he was right. There was no reason not to. It must have been misplaced modesty on my part that kept it from occurring to me before.

The process I'd been working on in Manchester was a type of modified gel electrophoresis, an electric potential that drew precisely the correct molecular weight molecule through a set of gel filters.

Setting up the process took time, however—time during which Brent grew increasingly impatient. At last, I was able to purify six pints of PurBlood using the gel process.

The GEF process was successful beyond my wildest hopes. Using four of the six pints as samples, I was able to prove the mixture was pure down to sixteen parts per million. Thus, out of one *million* hemoglobin molecules, there were no more than sixteen foreign particles. And probably less.

This may sound pure. And it *is* pure enough for most drugs. But, in this case, it was not. The FDA had decided, with typical capriciousness, that 100 parts per billion would be safe.

Sixteen parts per million was not. The number 16—it will haunt me forever. In scientific terms, a purity of 1.6×10^{-7}.

Please don't misunderstand. I believed—and I still believe—that PurBlood is much purer than that. I just couldn't *prove* it. The difference is crucial. But to me, the distinction was unfair and artificial.

There was one test for purity—the ultimate test—that I had not performed, because it was discouraged under FDA regulations. I secretly performed that test. Please forgive me, my love—one night, in the low-security lab, I opened a vein in my arm and bled out a pint. Then I replaced it with a transfusion of PurBlood.

It was rash, perhaps. But PurBlood passed with flying colors. Nothing happened to me, and all medical tests proved it was safe. Naturally, I couldn't report the results of that test, but it satisfied *me* that PurBlood was pure.

So I did something else. I infinitesimally diluted my last pint of PurBlood with distilled water, two hundred to one, and ran the array of tests that automatically calculated and recorded purity. The result was, of course, a purity of 80 parts per billion. Well within the FDA safety range.

That was all I had to do. I did *not* make a report, I did *not* change figures or falsify data. When Scopes downloaded the test results that night, he knew what they meant. The next day he congratulated me. He was beside himself.

The question I now ask myself—the question you may ask me—is why did I do it?

It wasn't for the money. I have never really cared that much about money. You know that, my darling Amiko. Money is more trouble than it's worth.

It wasn't for fame, which is a terrific nuisance.

It wasn't to save lives, although I have rationalized that this was the reason.

I think perhaps it was pure, naked desire. A desire to solve this last problem, to take that final step to completion. It is the same desire that led Einstein to suggest the terrible power of the atom in a letter to Roosevelt; it is the same desire that led Oppenheimer to build the bomb and test it not thirty miles from here; it is the same desire that led the Anasazi priests to meet in this stone chamber and exhort the Thunderbird to send the rain. It was the desire to conquer nature.

But—and this is what haunts me, what has driven me to commit this all to paper—the success of PurBlood does not alter the fact that I cheated.

I am only too well aware of this. Especially now . . . now that PurBlood has gone on to large-scale production, and I am banging my head against another, even more insoluble problem.

Anyway, dearest one, I hope you can find it in your heart to understand. Once I am free of this place, I will make it my life's resolve never to be apart from you again.

And perhaps that will be sooner than you think. I'm beginning to suspect certain people here of—but more on that some other time. I had best end this for today.

You will never know what being able to speak this secret has done for me.

June 30

It took me a long time to get here today. I had to take a special route, a secret route. The woman who cleans my room has been looking at me strangely, and I don't want her following me. She'll talk to Brent about it, just as my lab assistant and the network administrator have done.

It's because I've discovered the key. And now I must be ceaselessly vigilant.

You can tell them by the way they leave things on their desks. Their messiness gives them away. And they are polluted with germs. Billions of bacteria and viruses hiding in every crevice of their bodies. I wish I could speak of it to

Brent, but I must continue as if nothing had happened, as if all were normal.

I don't think I had better come here again.

Carson was silent. The sun settled toward the horizon, its shape ballooning in the layers of air. The old stone walls of the ruin smelled of dust and heat, mingled with the faint scent of corruption. One of the horses whinnied with impatience, and the other answered.

At the sound of the horses, de Vaca started. Then she quickly stuffed the journal in the container, placed it into the sipapu, covered the hole with the flat rock, and smoothed the warm concealing sand over the spot.

She straightened up, brushing off her jeans. "We'd better get back," she said. "There'll be questions if we miss the emergency drill."

They climbed out of the ruined kiva, mounted their horses, and reined slowly in the direction of Mount Dragon.

"Burt, of all people," de Vaca muttered as they rode. "Faking his data."

Carson was silent, lost in thought.

"And then using himself as guinea pig," de Vaca went on.

Carson roused himself, startled by a sudden realization. "I guess that's what he meant by 'poor alpha,'" he said.

"What?"

"Teece told me that Burt has been raving about 'poor alpha, poor alpha.' I guess he meant himself, as the alpha test subject." He shrugged. "I wouldn't call him a guinea pig, though. Making himself the alpha was very much in character. A man like Burt wouldn't deliberately risk thousands of lives on unproven blood. He was under incredible time pressure to prove its safety. So he tested it on himself. It's not unheard of. It isn't exactly illegal to do something like that, either." He looked at de Vaca. "You have to admire the guy for putting his life on the line. And he had the last laugh. He proved the blood was safe."

Carson fell silent. Something was teasing the back of his mind; something that had surfaced as they read the journal. Now it remained just out of the reach of consciousness, like a forgotten dream.

"Sounds like he's still having the last laugh. In a nuthouse somewhere."

Carson frowned. "That's a pretty callous remark, even for you."

"Maybe so," de Vaca replied. Then she paused. "I guess it's just that everyone talks about Burt like he was larger than life. This is the guy who invented GeneDyne's filtration process, synthesized PurBlood. Now we find he faked his data."

There it was again. Suddenly, Carson realized what it was in the journal that had raised an unconscious flag. "Susana, what do you know about GEF?"

She looked back at him, puzzled.

"The filtration process Burt invented when he was working at Manchester," Carson went on. You just mentioned it. We've always simply *assumed* the filtration process works on X-FLU. What if it doesn't?"

De Vaca's look of puzzlement turned to scorn. "We've tested X-FLU again and again to make sure that the strain coming out of the filter is absolutely pure."

"Pure, yes. But is it the *same* strain that went in?"

"How could the filtration process change the strain? It makes no sense."

"Think about how GEF works," Carson replied. "You set up an electrical field that draws the heavy protein molecules through a gel filter, right? The field is set precisely to the molecular weight of the molecule you want. All the other molecules are trapped in the gel, while what you want emerges from the other end of the filter."

"So?"

"What if the weak electrical field, or the gel itself, causes subtle changes in the protein structure? What if what comes out is different from what went in? The molecular weight would be the same, but the structure would be subtly altered. A straightforward chemical test wouldn't catch it. All it takes is the tiniest change in the surface protein of a virus particle to create a new strain."

"No way," said de Vaca. "GEF is a patented, tested process. They've already used it to synthesize other products. If there was anything wrong, it would've shown up a long time ago."

Carson reined in Roscoe and stood motionless. "Have any of the tests for purity we've done looked at that possibility? That *specific* possibility?"

De Vaca was silent.

"Susana, it's the only thing we haven't tried."

She look at him for a long moment.

"All right," she said at last. "Let's check it out."

The Dark Harbor Institute was a large, rambling Victorian house perched on a remote headland above the Atlantic. The institute counted one hundred and twenty honorary members on its rolls, although at any given time only a dozen or so were actually in residence. The responsibility of the people who came to the institute was to do only one thing: to think. The requirements for membership were equally simple: genius.

Members of the institute were very fond of the rambling Victorian mansion, which 120 years of Maine storms had left without a single right angle. They especially liked the anonymity, since even the institute's closest neighbors—mostly summer visitors—did not have the vaguest idea of who those bespectacled men and women were who came and went so unpredictably.

Edwin Bannister, associate managing editor of the *Boston Globe*, checked out of his inn and directed the placing of his bags into the back of his Range Rover, his head still throbbing from the effects of the bad bordeaux he'd been served at the previous evening's dinner. Tipping the porter, he walked around the Rover, eyeing as he did so the little town of Dark Harbor, with its fishing boats and church steeple and salt air. Very quaint. Too damn quaint. He preferred Boston, and the smoke-filled atmosphere of the Black Key Tavern.

He slid behind the wheel and consulted the hand-drawn map that had been faxed to him at the newspaper. Five miles to the institute. Despite the assurances, a part of him still doubted whether or not his host would really be there.

Bannister accelerated through a yellow light and swung onto County Road 24. The car lurched over one pothole, then another, as it left the tiny town behind. The narrow road headed due east to the sea, then ran along a series of high bluffs over the Atlantic. He rolled down the window. From below, he could hear the distant thunder of the surf, the crying of gulls, the dolorous clang of a bell buoy.

The road ran into a stand of spruce, then emerged at a high meadow covered with blueberry bushes. A log fence ran across the meadow, its rustic length interrupted by a wooden gate and shingled guardhouse. Bannister stopped at the gate and powered down his window.

"Bannister. With the *Globe*," he said, not bothering to look at the guard.

"Yes sir." The gate hummed open, and Bannister noted

with amusement that the rustic logs of the gate were backed with bars of black steel. *No car bombers crashing this party*, he thought.

The mansion's oak-paneled foyer seemed empty, and Bannister walked through to the lounge. A fire blazed in an enormous hearth, and a long series of casement windows looked out over the sea, sparkling in the morning light. The faint sound of music could be heard in the background.

At first, Bannister thought he was alone. Then, in a far corner, he spotted a man in a leather armchair, drinking coffee and reading a paper. The man was wearing white gloves. The newspaper rustled between them as its pages were turned.

The man looked up. "Edwin!" he said, smiling. "Thank you for coming."

Bannister immediately recognized the unkempt hair, the freckles, the boyish looks, the retro sports jacket over black T-shirt. So he *had* come, after all.

"Good to see you, Brent," Bannister said, taking the proffered armchair. He automatically glanced around for a waiter.

"Coffee?" Scopes asked. He had not offered to shake hands.

"Yes, please."

"We help ourselves here," Scopes said. "It's over by the bookcase."

Bannister hauled himself to his feet again, returning with a cup that promised to be less than satisfactory.

They sat in silence for a moment, and it dawned on Bannister that Scopes was listening to the music. He sipped his coffee and found it surprisingly good.

The piece ended. Scopes sighed with satisfaction, folded the newspaper carefully, and placed it next to an open briefcase beside his chair. He removed his ink-stained reading gloves and placed them on top of the paper.

"Bach's *Musical Offering*," he said. "Are you familiar with it?"

"Somewhat," said Bannister, hoping that Scopes wouldn't

ask a question that would reveal the lie. Bannister knew next to nothing about music.

"One of the canons of the *Offering* is entitled 'Quaerendo Invenietis.' 'By seeking, you will discover.' It was Bach's puzzle, asking the listener to see if he could tell what intricate canonical code was used to create the music."

Bannister nodded.

"I often think of this as a metaphor for genetics. You see the finished organism—such as a human being—and you wonder what intricate genetic code was used to create such a marvelous thing. And then you wonder, of course: If you were to change a tiny piece of this intricate code, how would that translate into flesh and blood? Just as changing a single note in a canon can sometimes end up transforming the entire melody."

Bannister reached into his jacket pocket, pulled out a tape recorder, and showed it to Scopes, who nodded his approval. Turning on the device, Bannister settled back in his chair, his hands folded.

"Edwin, my company is in a bit of a predicament."

"How so?" Bannister already knew this was going to be good. Anything that brought Scopes out of his aerie had to be good.

"You know about the attacks Charles Levine has been making against GeneDyne. I hoped that people would recognize him for what he is, but that's been slow to happen. By hiding under the skirts of Harvard University, he acquired a credibility I wouldn't have thought possible." Scopes shook his head. "I've known Dr. Levine for over twenty years. I was once a close friend of his, in fact. It pains me a great deal to see what has happened to him. I mean, all those claims about his father, and then it turns out he was an SS officer. Now, I don't begrudge a man for protecting the memory of his father, but did he have to lionize him with such an offensive story? It just shows that this man holds truth secondary to achieving his own ends. It shows that one must scrutinize every word he utters. The press hasn't really done that. Except for the *Globe*, thanks to you."

"We never publish anything without verifying the facts."

"I know, and I appreciate that. And I'm sure the people of Boston appreciate it, given that GeneDyne is one of the state's larger employers."

Bannister inclined his head.

"In any case, Edwin, I can't sit still and take these scurrilous attacks any longer. But I need your help."

"Brent, you know I can't *help* you," Bannister said.

"Of course, of course," Brent waved his hand dismissively. "Here's the situation. Obviously, we're working on a secret project at Mount Dragon. It isn't secret because of any particular danger factor, but because we face tremendous competition. We're in a winner-take-all business. You know how it works. The first company to patent a drug makes billions, while the rest eat their R-and-D investments."

Bannister nodded again.

"Edwin, I want to assure you—as someone whose judgment I respect—that nothing uncommonly dangerous is going on at Mount Dragon. You have my word on that. We have the only Level-5 facility in existence, and our safety record is the best of any pharmaceutical company in the world. Those are facts of record. But don't take my word for it."

He slid a file out of his briefcase and placed it before Bannister.

"This folder contains the entire safety record of GeneDyne. Normally, this information is proprietary. I want you to have it for your story. Just remember: It didn't come from me."

Bannister looked at the file without touching it. "Thanks, Brent. You know, however, that I can't just take your word for it that you aren't working on dangerous viruses. Dr. Levine's charges—"

Scopes chuckled. "I know. The *doomsday* virus." He leaned

forward. "And that's the primary reason I've asked you here. Would you care to know just what this terrible, inconceivably deadly, virus is? The one that Dr. Levine says may end the world?"

Bannister nodded, the many years of professionalism successfully concealing his eagerness.

Scopes was looking at him, grinning mischievously. "Edwin, this is off the record, of course."

"I would prefer—" Bannister began.

Scopes reached over and turned off the tape recorder. "There is a Japanese corporation working on a very similar line of research. On this particular type of germ-line research, they're actually ahead of us. If they realize its ramifications before we do, then we're dead. Winner take all, Edwin. We're talking about a fifteen-*billion*-dollar annual market here. I'd hate to see the Japanese increase their trade deficit with us, and have to close down GeneDyne Boston, all because Edwin Bannister at the *Globe* revealed what virus we were working with."

"I see your point," Bannister said, swallowing hard. Sometimes it was necessary to work off the record.

"Good. It's called *influenza.*"

"What is?" Bannister said.

Scopes's grin widened. "We're working with the flu virus. And that is the *only* virus we are working with at Mount Dragon. *That* is Levine's so-called doomsday virus."

Scopes sat back with a look of triumph.

Bannister felt the sudden, desperate emptiness of a lead story disappearing beneath his fingers. "That's it? Just flu viruses?"

"That's right. You have my solemn promise. I want you to be able to write with a clear conscience that GeneDyne is not working with dangerous viruses."

"But why the *flu?*"

Scopes looked surprised. "Isn't it obvious? Countless dollars in productivity are lost every year because of flu. We are working on a *cure* for the flu. Not like these flu shots that you have to take every year, and that don't work half the time. I'm talking about a permanent, onetime cure."

"My God," said Bannister.

"Just think what that will do to our stock price if we succeed. Those who own GeneDyne stock are going to become rich. Especially considering how cheap the stock has become recently, thanks to our friend Levine. Not rich tomorrow, but in a few months, when we announce the discovery and go into phased FDA testing." Scopes smiled, and his voice dropped to a whisper. "And we're *going to succeed.*" Then he reached over and switched on the tape recorder.

Bannister said nothing. He was trying to imagine just how large a number fifteen billion was.

"We are taking vigorous action against Dr. Levine and his libelous statements," Scopes continued. "You've done an excellent job so far in reporting our lawsuits against Dr. Levine and Harvard. I have news on that front. Harvard has revoked the university charter for Levine's foundation. They've been keeping the revocation under wraps, but it's about to be made public. I thought you might be interested. We will be dropping our lawsuit against Harvard, of course."

"I see," said Bannister, thinking quickly. *There might be a way to salvage this, after all.*

"The Faculty Committee on Tenure is reviewing Dr. Levine's contract. There is a clause in all university contracts allowing tenure to be revoked in cases of 'moral turpitude.'" Scopes laughed softly. "Sounds like something out of the Victorian Age. But it's cooked Levine's goose, I can tell you."

"I see."

"We're not yet sure how he did it, but certain grains of truth in his otherwise false allegations prove he used illegal, not to mention unethical, methods to gain confidential information from GeneDyne." Scopes slid another folder toward Bannister. "You'll find the details in here. I'm sure you will find out more in your own fashion. Obviously, my name must not appear in connection with any of this. I'm only telling you this because you're the one reporter whose ethics I most respect, and I want to help you write a balanced, fair article. Let the other newspapers write down everything Levine says without fact-checking. I know the *Globe* will be more careful."

"We *always* check our facts," said Bannister.

Scopes nodded. "I'm counting on you to set the record straight."

Bannister stiffened slightly. "Brent, all you can count on is a story that presents a strictly objective, accurate rendition of the facts."

"Exactly," Scopes said. "That is why I'm going to be totally honest with you. There is one charge Levine made that is partially true."

"And that is—?"

"There *was* a death at Mount Dragon recently. We were keeping the matter quiet until the family could be notified, but Levine somehow found out about it." Scopes paused, his face growing serious at the memory. "One of our best scientists was killed in an industrial accident. As you'll see in the first folder I gave you, certain safety procedures were not followed. We immediately notified the necessary authorities, who dispatched inspectors to Mount Dragon. It's a formality, of course, and the lab remains open."

Scopes paused. "I knew the woman well. She was—how shall I say it?—an original. Dedicated to her work. In certain ways, perhaps a bit difficult. But undeniably brilliant. You know, it's very difficult to be a brilliant woman in science, even today. She had a rough time of it until she got to GeneDyne. I lost a friend as well as a scientist." He looked briefly at Bannister, then dropped his eyes. "The CEO is ultimately responsible. This is something I'll have to live with for the rest of my life."

Bannister watched him, genuinely moved. "How did she—?" he began.

"She died of a head injury," Scopes said. Then he looked at his watch. "Damn! I'm running late. Anything else you'd care to ask, Edwin?"

Bannister picked up his tape recorder. "Not at the moment—"

"Good. I hope you'll excuse me. Call me if you have any questions."

Bannister watched the thin, slight figure of Scopes walk out of the room, toes pointing toward the walls, lugging the briefcase that seemed three sizes too large for him. An amazing fellow. Worth an amazing amount of money.

As Bannister wound his way back along the Atlantic headlands, he kept returning to that fifteen-billion-dollar figure, and what such an announcement would do to the value of GeneDyne stock. He wondered what GeneDyne was trading at right now. Come to think of it, he'd have to check that out. It wouldn't hurt to put in a call to his broker and stick his money in something a little more exciting than tax-free munis.

Carson glanced up, peering through his visor at the oversized clock on the lab wall. The amber LED display read 10:45 P.M.

An hour earlier, the Fever Tank had been full of frenzied sound, as the shriek of the alert siren sounded the drill and the suited bodies tramped down the low corridors. Now the lab was once again deserted and almost preternaturally quiet, the only audible sound the whisper of air in Carson's bluesuit and the faint hum of the negative-airflow system. The chimpanzees, disturbed by the drill, had finally ceased their hooting and screaming and had fallen into troubled sleep. Outside his own brightly lit lab, the corridor glowed a subdued red, and the cramped spaces of the Fever Tank were full of shadows.

Because the Fever Tank was decontaminated each weeknight and again over the weekend, Carson had rarely been inside this late. Although the red nocturnal illumination was creepy and a little disorienting, he preferred it to what had come just before. The full-scale stage-one alert drills—which had begun to supplant the less severe stage-two and stage-three drills since Brandon-Smith's death—were grim affairs. Nye was now personally supervising the drills, directing events from the security substation on the bottom level of the Fever Tank, and his brusque tones had rung irritatingly through Carson's headset.

The one advantage of the frequent drills was that Carson had become more adept at moving around the Fever Tank in his bluesuit. He found that he could maneuver quickly through the corridors and around the labs, avoiding protrusions deftly, hooking and unhooking his air hoses to his suit instinctively, like breathing.

He looked away from the clock toward de Vaca, who was staring skeptically back at him.

"Just how do you plan to test this theory of yours?" came her voice over the private channel.

Instead of taking the time to answer, Carson turned to the small lab freezer, dialed its combination, and removed two small test tubes containing X-FLU samples. The tops of the test tubes were covered with thick rubber seals. The virus existed as a small white crystalline film at the bottom of each tube. *If I handle this stuff a million times*, he thought, *I'll never get used to the fact that it's potentially more lethal to the human race than the largest hydrogen bomb*. He placed both tubes inside the bioprophylaxis table and sealed it carefully, waiting for the samples to reach room temperature.

"First," he said, "we're going to split open the virus and get rid of the genetic material."

Moving to a silver cabinet on the far wall of the lab, he removed some reagents and two sealed bottles labeled DE-OXYRIBASE.

"Give me a number-four Soloway, please," he said to de Vaca.

Since hypodermics were considered too dangerous for anything other than animal inoculation in the Fever Tank, other devices for transferring materials had to be used. The Soloway Displacer, named after its inventor, used blunt-ended plastic vacuum-needles to siphon liquid from one container to another.

Carson waited for de Vaca to place the instrument inside the bioprophylaxis table. Then, moving his gloves through the rubber openings in the front end of the table, he inserted one nozzle of the Soloway device into a reagent and the other through the rubber seal in one of the two test tubes. A cloudy liquid squirted into the tube. Gingerly, Carson swirled the tube in one gloved hand. The liquid became clear.

"We just killed a trillion viruses," Carson said. "Now to undress them. Take off their protein coats."

Using the device, Carson added a few drops of a blue liquid through the rubber seal, then removed .5 cc's of the resulting solution, injecting it into the deoxyribase container. He waited while the enzyme broke up the viral RNA, first into its base pairs, then into nucleic acids.

"Now, to get rid of the nucleic acids." He tested the precise acidity of the solution, then performed a remote-assist titration with a high-pH chemical. Then he drained off the solution, centrifuged out the precipitate, and transferred the pure, unfiltered X-FLU molecules that remained to a small flask.

"Let's see what this little old molecule looks like," he said.

"X-ray diffraction?"

"You got it."

Carson carefully placed the X-FLU flask into a yellow bio-box and sealed it. Then, holding the box carefully in front of him, he removed his air hose and followed de Vaca down the corridor toward the central hub of the Fever Tank, ducking at last through a hatchway into a deserted lab. A single red light glowed from the ceiling. Already small, the compartment was cramped by the eight-foot stainless-steel column that dominated the center of the room. Next to the column was an instrument housing that contained a computer workstation. There were no knobs, switches or dials on the column; the diffraction machine was controlled entirely by computer.

"Warm it up," Carson said. "I'll prepare the specimen."

De Vaca sat down at the workstation and began typing. There was a click and a soft, low hum that gradually increased in pitch until it disappeared into inaudibility, followed by the hiss of air being evacuated from the interior of the column. De Vaca typed in additional commands, tuning the diffraction beam to the correct wavelength. In a few moments, the terminal beeped its readiness.

"Open the mount, please," Carson said.

De Vaca typed a command, and a titanium-alloy stage mount slid out of the base of the column. It contained a small removable well.

Using a micropipette, Carson removed a single drop of the protein solution and placed it in the well. The stage mount slid shut with a hiss.

"Chill."

There was a loud drumming noise as the machine froze the drop of solution, lowering its temperature toward absolute zero.

"Vacuum."

Carson waited impatiently as the air was removed from the specimen chamber. The resulting vacuum would force all water molecules from the solution. As it did so, a faint electromagnetic field would allow the protein molecules to settle into a lowest-energy configuration. What remained would be a microscopic film of pure protein molecules, spaced with mathematical regularity on the titanium plate, held steady at two degrees above absolute zero.

"We're green," de Vaca said.

"Then let's go."

What happened next always seemed like magic to Carson. The huge machine began to generate X-rays, shooting them at the speed of light down the vacuum inside the column. When the high-energy X-rays struck the protein molecules, they would be diffracted by the crystal lattice structures. The scattered beams would be digitally recorded with an array of CCD chips and sent, as an image, to the computer screen.

Carson watched as a blurred image appeared on the screen, bands of dark and light. "Focus, please," he said.

Using an optical mouse, de Vaca manipulated a series of diffraction gratings inside the column, which tuned and focused the X-rays onto the specimen at the bottom. Slowly, the blurred image came into focus: a complicated series of dark and light circles, reminding Carson of the surface of a pond stippled with rain.

"Great," he said softly. "Easy does it."

The X-ray diffraction machine took just the right touch, Carson knew, and de Vaca had that touch.

"That's as sharp as it gets," she said. "Ready for film and data feed."

"I want sixteen angles, please," Carson said.

De Vaca typed in the commands, and the CCD chips captured the diffraction pattern from sixteen separate angles.

"Series complete," she said.

"Let's feed this into the central computer."

The machine's computer began loading the diffraction data into the GeneDyne net, where it was sent across a dedicated land line at 110,000 bits per second to the GeneDyne supercomputer in Boston. All Mount Dragon jobs had high priority, and the supercomputer immediately began translating the X-ray diffraction pattern into a three-dimensional model of the X-FLU molecule. For over a minute, those working late in the GeneDyne home office noticed a perceptible slowdown while several trillion floating-point operations were performed and fed back to Mount Dragon, where the image was reassembled on the diffraction machine's workstation.

An image appeared on the workstation screen: a breathtakingly complex cluster of vibrantly colored spheres, glowing in rainbows of rich purples, reds, oranges, and yellows: the protein molecule that made up the viral coat of X-FLU.

"There it is," Carson said, peering at the image over de Vaca's shoulder.

"The cause of such terrible suffering and death," came de Vaca's voice in his headset. "And look how beautiful it is."

Carson continued gazing at the image for a moment, mesmerized. Then he straightened up. "Let's purify the second test tube with the GEF filtration process. It's almost decontam time, we have to vacate the Tank for an hour or two anyway. Then we'll come back, take another look at it, and see if the molecule has changed."

"Lots of luck," de Vaca grumbled. "But I'm too tired to object. Let's go."

By the time the second, filtered X-FLU molecule crystallized on the computer screen, dawn was breaking over the desert floor fifty feet above their heads. Once again Carson marveled at the beauty of the molecule: how surreal it was, and how deadly.

"Let's compare the two molecules side by side," he said.

De Vaca split the screen into two windows and called up

the image of the unfiltered X-FLU molecule from the computer's memory, displaying it side by side with the filtered molecule.

"They look the same to me," she said.

"Rotate them both ninety degrees along the X axis."

"No difference," de Vaca said.

"Ninety degrees along the Y axis."

They watched as the images rotated on the computer screen. Suddenly, the silence turned electric.

"*Madre de Dios*," breathed de Vaca.

"Look how one of the tertiary folds of the filtered molecule has uncoiled!" said Carson excitedly. "The weak sulfur bonds along the entire side have become unstuck."

"Same molecule, same chemical composition, different shape," said de Vaca. "You were right."

"What's that?" Carson asked, looking at her with a grin.

"Okay, *cabrón*. You win this one."

"And it's the *shape* of a protein molecule that makes all the difference." Carson stepped away from the diffraction machine. "Now we know why X-FLU keeps mutating back to its deadly form. The last thing we always do before the in vivo test is to purify the solution using the GEF process. And it's the GEF process *itself* that causes the mutation."

"Burt's original filtration technique was to blame," de Vaca answered. "He was doomed from the beginning."

Carson nodded. "Yet nobody, least of all Burt, thought the process itself could be flawed. It's been used before without any problems. And here we've been banging our heads against the wrong door all this time. The gene splicing, everything else, was fine to begin with. It's like sifting through the wreckage of a plane crash to determine the cause of an accident, when in reality the problem was faulty directions from the control tower."

He leaned wearily against a cabinet. The full significance of the discovery began to sink in, like a flame in his gut. "Hot damn, Susana," he breathed. "After all this time, we've solved it at last! All we need to do is change the filtration process. It may take some time to correct, but we know the real culprit now. X-FLU is as good as manufactured." He could almost picture the expression on Scopes's face.

De Vaca was silent.

"You agree, don't you?" Carson prompted.

"Yes," said de Vaca.

"So what's the problem? Why the long face?"

She looked at him for a long moment. "We know the flaw in the filtration process causes mutations in the X-FLU protein coat. What I want to know is, what the hell does it do to PurBlood?"

Carson stared back at her, not comprehending. "Susana, who cares?"

"What do you mean, who cares?" de Vaca said, flaring up. "PurBlood could be dangerous as hell!"

"It's not the same thing at all," Carson replied. "We don't know that the filtration flaw would affect anything other than the X-FLU molecule. And besides, the kind of purity necessary for X-FLU doesn't necessarily apply to hemoglobin."

"Easy for you to say, *cabrón*. You're not putting the stuff into your veins."

Carson fought to keep his temper. This woman was attempting to spoil the greatest triumph of his life. "Susana, think a moment. Burt tested it on himself, and he survived. It's been in phased FDA testing now for months. If anybody had become sick, we'd have heard of it. Teece would have known. And, believe me, the FDA would have yanked it."

"Nobody getting sick? So tell me, where's Burt now? In a fucking hospital, that's where he is!"

"His nervous breakdown came *months* after he tested himself with PurBlood."

"There still might be a connection. Maybe it breaks down in the body, or something." She looked at him defiantly. "I want to know what the GEF process does to PurBlood."

Carson sighed deeply. "Look. It's seven-thirty in the morning. We've just made one of the biggest breakthroughs in the history of GeneDyne. And I'm dead on my feet. I'm going to report this to Singer. Then I'm going to take a shower, and get some well-deserved rest."

"Go ahead and get your gold star," de Vaca snapped. "I'm going to stay here and finish what we started."

She switched off the machine, disconnected the air hose from her suit valve with an angry yank, then turned and marched out of the compartment. As he watched her go, Carson heard other voices on the intercom, people announcing their arrival in the lab. The workday was beginning. He wearily pushed himself away from the cabinet. God, he was tired. De Vaca could tinker with PurBlood as much as she liked. He was going to spread the good news.

Carson stepped outside, breathing in the cool morning air with relish. He was tired, but elated. While there might be other snags ahead, he knew that this, at long last, was the home stretch.

Ducking back into the administration building, he bounded up the stairs and headed for Singer's corner office. At the far end of the main hall, he could see the director's door standing open, the light reflecting brilliantly off the white surfaces.

As he entered the office, Carson saw Singer sitting near the kiva fireplace. Another man stood before Singer, his back to Carson; a man with a ponytail, wearing a safari hat.

Singer looked up. "Ah, Guy. Mr. Nye and I were just about to have a private meeting."

Carson stepped forward. "John, there's something you'll be—"

Nye swiveled toward him, then waved his hand impatiently, cutting him off.

Singer leaned over the coffee table, adjusting a magazine. "Guy, another time, please."

"Dr. Singer, it's extremely important."

Singer looked up again, staring at him, a puzzled expression on his face. Carson was shocked at how bloodshot his eyes were, and at the faint cast of yellow in the whites. Singer didn't appear to have heard. Carson watched as the director plucked a malachite egg from the coffee table and began turning it over and over in his hands.

Nye glowered at Carson, arms crossed, a dark expression on his face. "Well?" he said. "What's so bloody important, then?"

Carson watched as Singer replaced the egg on the coffee table, adjusting its position carefully. Then the director's hands slowly passed over each item on the table, unconsciously adjusting them, lining and squaring them up.

"Carson?" Nye spoke again, more sharply.

The director looked up at Carson as if he had forgotten he was there. His eyes were watering.

In an instant, other images forced their way into Carson's consciousness. Brandon-Smith's mannerism of rubbing her hands along her thighs time and again. The way the knickknacks on her desk were so carefully arranged. The way Vanderwagon had carefully polished and lined up the tableware at dinner that night, just before putting out his own eye.

His eye. That was another thing: They all had bloodshot eyes.

Suddenly, everything became perfectly, terribly clear.

"It can wait," Carson said, backing out the door.

Nye watched him closely as he left. Then, without a word, he stepped forward and shut the door.

In the darkness of his suite at the institute, Scopes washed his hands meticulously. Then he paced restlessly, awaiting the helicopter that would return him to Boston. His front room boasted a spectacular view of the stormy Atlantic, but the heavy curtains were closed.

Abruptly, Scopes paused in his pacing. Then he moved quickly toward his PowerBook, plugging its thin cable into a wall jack. He knew the institute had a dedicated link into Flashnet, and from there, with his access key, he could enter the GeneDyne network.

There was something that had been tugging at the back of his mind for days; something his discussion with the *Globe* reporter had at last made clear. It had been obvious from the start, given the quality of Levine's data on Brandon-Smith and X-FLU, that the information had come from within GeneDyne, rather than from sources in the FDA or OSHA. But what had escaped Scopes's attention was the *timing* of Levine's information.

Levine had known details about X-FLU that even the nosy bastard Teece, the investigator, couldn't have learned until arriving at Mount Dragon. Levine had aired his dirt on the Sammy Sanchez show while Teece was still nosing around in New Mexico. And there were no standard long-distance lines out of Mount Dragon. Scopes knew that the only communications out of Mount Dragon were across the GeneDyne net. He knew it, because he had seen to it himself.

That meant Levine must not only have obtained his information from a source within GeneDyne—he must have obtained it from a source *within Mount Dragon*. And that meant Levine had gained unprecedented access to GeneDyne cyberspace.

Once inside the GeneDyne net, Scopes worked silently and intently. Within minutes, he was within a region that he and he alone had access to. Here, his finger was on the pulse of the entire organization: terabytes of data covering every word of every project, e-mail, program file, and on-line chat generated by GeneDyne employees over the last twenty-four hours. With the click of a few more keys, Scopes moved through his personal region of the network to a dedicated server containing a single massive application, which he had called, whimsically, Cypherspace.

Slowly, a strange landscape materialized on his small computer screen. It was like no landscape on earth, and too complex and symmetrical to have been conceived solely by a human mind. This was the virtual landscape of GeneDyne cyberspace. The Cypherspace application used direct links into the GeneDyne operating system to transform datastreams, memory contents, and all active processes into shapes, surfaces, shadows, and sounds. A strange sighing sound, like sustained musical notes, vibrated from the laptop's speaker. To a layman such a landscape would appear surreal and bizarre, but to Scopes, who loved to wander through this strange junglescape late at night, it was as familiar as the backyard of his childhood.

Scopes wandered through the landscape, looking, listening, watching. For a moment, he was tempted to go to a special place in this landscape—a secret among secrets—but he realized there was no time.

Suddenly Scopes sat up and breathed out. In the landscape, there was something that was not right. It was a thread, invisible of itself, manifest only by what it obscured. As Scopes crossed the invisible thread, the strange music dropped to silence. It was a tunnel of nothing, an absence of data, a black hole in cyberspace. Scopes knew what it must be: a hidden data channel, visible only because it had been hidden a little too well. Whoever had programmed this back channel was transcendentally clever. It couldn't have been Levine. Levine was brilliant, but Scopes knew that Levine's computer abilities had always been his weakest suit.

Levine had help.

Accessing his bag of digital tricks, Scopes selected a transparent relay, readying it for insertion in the channel. Then, slowly, with infinite care, he began to follow the thread, twisting and turning in its mazy path, losing it, picking it up again, working methodically back toward its hidden target.

Carson found de Vaca at work in Lab C. She had a small flask of PurBlood, still smoking from the deep freeze, sitting on the bioprophylaxis table.

"You've been gone for eight hours," came her voice over the private channel. "What, did they fly you to Boston for your awards ceremony?"

Carson moved toward his stool and sat down numbly. "I was in the library archives," he replied.

De Vaca swiveled her computer screen toward him. "Take a look at this."

Carson sat still for a long moment. Finally, he turned toward the screen. More than anything, he did not want to know what de Vaca might have discovered.

On her screen were two images of phospholipid capsules, side by side. One was smooth and perfect. The other was ragged, full of ugly holes and tears where molecules had obviously been displaced from their normal order.

"The first image shows an unfiltered PurBlood 'cell.' This

second image shows what happens to PurBlood after it passes through the GEF filtration." The excitement in de Vaca's voice was clear even through the speaker in Carson's headset. Mistaking his silence for disbelief, she continued. "Listen. You remember how PurBlood is made. Once the hemoglobin has been encapsulated, it has to be purified of all manufacturing by-products and any toxins produced by the bacteria. So they used Burt's GEF filtration on the hemoglobin to—"

De Vaca stopped, looking at Carson. He had positioned himself between her and the lab's video camera, blocking its view. He was moving his gloved hands downward in a suppressing motion. Through the visor, she could see him shaking his head and silently mouthing the word *stop*.

De Vaca frowned. "What's up?" she asked. "Been chewing peyote buttons, *cabrón?*"

Carson brusquely motioned her to wait. Then he looked around the lab as if searching for something. Suddenly he reached for a cabinet, pulled out a large vial of disinfectant powder, and sprinkled a light dusting of it on the glass surface of the bioprophylaxis table. Shielding his actions from the camera, he formed letters in the white dust with a gloved finger:

Don't use intercom.

De Vaca stared at the words for a moment. Then, extending a gloved finger, she formed a large question mark in the powder.

Tell me the rest HERE, Carson wrote.

De Vaca paused, looking narrowly at Carson. Then she wrote out the message: *PurBlood contaminated by GEF filtration. Burt used himself as alpha tester. That's what's wrong with him.*

Carson quickly smoothed out the message and sprinkled a little more disinfectant on the surface. He quickly wrote: *THINK. If Burt was alpha tester, who were the beta testers?*

He saw a look of fear spread slowly across her face. She was mouthing words but he could not hear them.

He wrote: *Library. Half hour.* After waiting for her to nod agreement, he erased the tracings with a sweep of his glove.

The Mount Dragon library was an oasis of rusticity in a high-tech desert: its yellow, gingham-checked curtains, rough-hewn roof beams, and coarse floorboards were designed to resemble an oversized Western lodge. The intent of the designers had been to provide relief from the sterile white corridors of the rest of the facility. However, given the moratorium on paper products at Mount Dragon, the library contained mostly electronic resources, and in any case few members of the overworked Mount Dragon staff had time to enjoy its solitude. Carson himself had only been in the library twice before: once when poking around the facility during his initial explorations, and again just a few hours before, immediately after leaving Singer and Nye to themselves.

As he closed the heavy door behind him, he was glad to see that de Vaca was the library's only occupant. She was sitting in a white Adirondack chair, dozing despite herself, long black hair fallen carelessly across her face. She looked up at his approach.

"Long day," she said. "And long night." She looked at him speculatively. "They're going to wonder why we left the Fever Tank early," she added in a lower tone.

"*They* would have wondered a lot more if I'd let you keep running your mouth," Carson muttered back.

"Hell, and I thought *I* was paranoid. You really think somebody listens to all those monitor tapes, *cabrón?*"

Carson gave a short shake of the head. "We can't take that chance."

De Vaca stiffened slightly. "Don't pull a Vanderwagon on me, Carson. Now, what's this about beta testers for Pur-Blood?"

"I'll show you." He motioned her over to a data terminal in a far corner of the library. Pulling up two chairs, he put the terminal's keyboard on his lap, entering his employee ID at the waiting prompt.

"What research have you done on PurBlood since you got here?" he asked, turning to her.

De Vaca shrugged. "Not much. The later lab reports of Burt's. Why?"

Carson nodded. "Exactly. The same kind of materials I examined: sample runs, lab notes Burt made while he was transferring his attention to X-FLU. The only reason we were interested in PurBlood at all was because Burt had worked on it prior to getting involved with our own project, X-FLU."

He punched keys. "I did see Singer this morning. But I didn't really speak with him. I came here instead. I remembered what you'd said about PurBlood, and I wanted to learn a little more about its development. Look what I found."

He gestured at the screen:

mol_desc_one	vcf	10,240,342	11/1/95
mol_desc_two	vcf	12,320,302	11/1/95
bipol_symmetr	vcf	41,234,913	12/14/95
hemocyl_grp_r	vcf	7,713,653	01/3/96
diffrac_series_a	vcf	21,442,521	02/5/96
diffrac_series_b	vcf	6,100,824	02/6/96
pr	vid	940,213,727	02/27/96
transfec_locus_h	vcf	18,921,663	03/10/96

"These are all the video files in the PurBlood research archives," he went on in a low tone. "Most of them are the usual: animations of molecules and the like. But look at the second from the last on the list, the one called *pr*. Notice its extension: it's a digital dump from a video camera, not the video compression format used in computer animations. And look at its huge size: almost a gigabyte."

"What is it?" de Vaca asked.

"It's a rough-cut video, unreleased, probably created for public-relations purposes." With a few more keystrokes, he called up a multimedia software object to play back the video file. An image appeared in a window on the terminal screen, grainy but perfectly distinct.

"You'll have to watch closely," he said. "There's no associated audio file."

A caravan of Hummers is approaching across the desert. The camera zooms out briefly to show the Mount Dragon complex, the white buildings, the blue New Mexico sky.

The camera returns to the caravan, now parked at the Mount Dragon motor pool. The passenger door of the lead vehicle opens, and a man emerges. He stands on the tarmac, waving, grinning, and shaking hands.

"Scopes," Carson murmured.

The entire Mount Dragon staff are on hand to greet him. There is much backslapping and grinning.

"Looks like a camp meeting," said de Vaca. "Who's that big-nosed guy standing next to Singer?"

"Burt," Carson replied. "It's Franklin Burt."

Now Burt is standing next to Scopes on the tarmac, talking to the crowd. Scopes puts his arm around him, and they raise hands in a victory gesture. The camera pans across the crowd.

The scene shifts to the Mount Dragon gymnasium. It has been cleared of all equipment, and in the center are two rows of chairs, carefully arranged. They are occupied by what appears to be the entire Mount Dragon staff. The camera, positioned on the balcony running track, now focuses on a temporary stage built at one end of the gym. Scopes is giving a talk to the enthusiastic crowd.

As Scopes continues, the camera pans the crowd again. Several of the faces seem to have grown somber, even uncertain.

A nurse comes from offstage, dressed in white, wheeling a stretcher with an IV rack. The rack holds a single unit of blood.

Scopes sits on the edge of the stretcher and the nurse rolls up his left sleeve. Franklin Burt now mounts the stage and begins to talk passionately, moving back and forth across the stage.

The camera zooms in as the nurse swabs Scopes's arm and slides in the IV. Then she hooks up the pint of blood and turns a plastic stopcock, starting the flow. While Scopes receives the blood, Burt talks to him, obviously monitoring his vital signs.

"Jesus Christ," de Vaca said. "He's getting PurBlood, isn't he?"

The camera makes a few cuts and in a few minutes the pint of blood is empty. The nurse removes the IV, places a gauze patch on the arm, and folds the arm up to seal the vein.

Scopes stands with a grin and holds up his other arm in a victory salute.

The camera turns to the audience. Everyone is clapping; some enthusiastically, others with more reserve. One scientist stands up. Then another. Soon the group is giving Scopes a standing ovation. Another nurse comes onstage, wheeling two large IV racks, each holding two dozen or so pints of blood.

Nye strides up to the stage. He shakes Scopes's hand and rolls up his left sleeve. The nurse inserts an IV into his arm and starts a unit of blood.

Another scientist comes forward, then a maintenance worker. Then Singer himself begins to approach the stage, and the audience breaks into another round of applause. The camera focuses on

Singer's plump face. It is white, and beads of sweat stand out on his brow. Yet he, too, sits down on a cot and rolls up his sleeve, and soon the blood is flowing into his veins.

After that, the audience stands in unison. Within moments, a line has formed from the stage, snaking back toward the rows of chairs.

"Look," de Vaca whispered. "There's Brandon-Smith. There's Vanderwagon and Pavel what's-his-name. And there's—oh, my God."

Abruptly, Carson halted the video, logged off the network, and cut the terminal's power.

"Let's take a walk," he said.

"They were the beta testers," said de Vaca, as they walked slowly around the inner perimeter fence. "They all got it, didn't they?"

"Every single one," said Carson. "From the custodians to Singer himself. Everybody except us. We're the only new arrivals since February 27th, the date of that file."

"How exactly did you figure this out?" de Vaca was hugging herself tightly as she walked, seemingly chilled despite the late-afternoon heat.

"When I went to see Singer this morning, I saw him lining up the objects on his coffee table. There was something very obsessive about his movements that struck me as unusual, out of character. I remembered how Vanderwagon had acted just before he put his eye out, and Brandon-Smith's obsessive habits in the last days. And then I noticed Singer's bloodshot eyes, with the yellow cast in the whites. It was just what Vanderwagon's eyes looked like. And Nye. Think about it. Don't a lot of the people here seem to have bloodshot eyes these days? I assumed it was the stress." He shrugged. "So I spent the day in the library, looking through the research files."

"And found that tape," de Vaca said.

"Yes. It must have been Scopes's brainchild, having the rest of the Mount Dragon team be the beta test subjects for PurBlood. It's a common enough thing in certain pharmaceutical companies, you know, to draw the volunteer pool from the company itself. They must have filmed it, thinking it would make good press later on."

"Only some of the volunteers didn't look too pleased about it," de Vaca said wryly.

Carson nodded. "Scopes is a brilliant speaker. Between him, Burt, and peer pressure, sure, it's not hard to see why everyone fell in line."

"But what the hell is happening to them *now*?" De Vaca struggled to keep the sound of panic out of her voice.

"Obviously, the PurBlood is breaking down in their bodies, having a toxic effect. Perhaps impurities got into the phospholipid capsule, DNA mutations occurred. We don't have the time to find out exactly. As the capsule decays, it's all released."

"How can you be sure it's PurBlood?" De Vaca frowned.

"What else could it be? They all received transfusions. And they're all beginning to show the same symptoms."

De Vaca was murmuring to herself. "Dopamine. What was it Teece told you about dopamine?"

"He said that Burt and Vanderwagon were suffering from overdrives of dopamine and serotonin. Brandon-Smith, too, to a lesser degree." Carson turned to her. "He told me that too much of those neurotransmitters in the brain can cause paranoia, delusions, psychotic behavior. You took two years of med school. Is he right?"

De Vaca stopped.

"Keep walking. Is he right?"

"Yes," she replied at last. "The production of bodily chemicals is very carefully balanced. If mutated DNA in PurBlood is instructing the body to pump out large amounts of . . ."

She paused, thinking, then began again. "Mental distress and disorientation would develop, perhaps combined with obsessive-compulsive behavior. If the overdrives were sufficiently great, the result would be extreme paranoia and fulminant psychosis."

"And the leaky blood vessels Teece described must be another symptom," Carson added.

"Naked hemoglobin, permeating through the capillary walls, would just make a bad situation worse. Poison the whole body. Bloodshot eyes would be the least of the problems."

They walked for several minutes in silence. "Burt was the alpha test subject," Carson said at last. "It makes sense he would be the first one affected. Then, last week, he was followed by Vanderwagon. Have you noticed any other odd behaviors?"

De Vaca thought. Then she nodded. "Yesterday at breakfast, that technician from the sequencing lab yelled at me for sitting in her chair. I got up and moved, but she wouldn't let up. She's normally such a mousy thing. I thought the pressure was getting to her."

"Obviously, people are affected at different rates. But it's only a matter of time until—"

He stopped. It wasn't necessary to finish the sentence. *Until the entire staff of this laboratory—this remote laboratory, in the middle of the desert, guardians of a virus that could destroy the human race—goes insane.*

Suddenly, another thought struck him. He turned to de Vaca. "Susana, do you know when PurBlood is scheduled for general distribution?"

She shook her head.

"I read several memos about it in the library this morning. GeneDyne marketing has organized a massive media event. There's going to be a big rollout, with all sorts of fanfare. They've chosen four wards across the country. One hundred hemophiliacs and children undergoing operations will be the first to receive PurBlood."

"When is this scheduled to happen?" de Vaca asked.

"August third."

De Vaca's hands flew to her mouth. "But that's this Friday!"

Carson nodded. "We have to warn the authorities. Get them to stop the PurBlood rollout, and get help for the people here."

"And how the hell are we supposed to do that? The only long-distance phone lines out of here are the dedicated network leased lines to Boston. Even if we could get to those, who'd believe us?"

Carson thought. "Maybe Scopes is already suffering the effects."

De Vaca snorted. "Even if he was, nobody would connect that with anything happening here."

He turned to her. "Maybe we're worrying unnecessarily. If there's a developing paranoia among all the Mount Dragon residents, wouldn't it turn them against each other, canceling the threat?"

She shook her head. "In this atmosphere? Not likely. Especially with someone as charismatic as Scopes running things. It's a textbook setting for folie à deux."

"What?"

"Shared insanity. Everyone acting out the same twisted fantasy. Or, as we called it in med school, a double-nut fruitcake."

Carson grimaced. "Great. That leaves us only one option. Get the hell out of here."

"How?"

"I don't know."

De Vaca smirked, started to speak. Then she stopped and nudged his elbow. "Look over there."

Carson looked. Ahead of them lay the motor pool: half a

dozen white Hummers in a gleaming row, standing like sentries and casting long shadows across the graveled lot.

They walked closer to the vehicles with feigned nonchalance. "First," Carson whispered, "we'd have to find the keys. Then, we'd have to drive out of the compound without anyone noticing."

Suddenly, de Vaca knelt beside him in the dust.

"What are you doing?"

"Tying my shoe."

"You're wearing slip-ons!"

De Vaca stood up. "I know that, idiot." She dusted one knee, shook her hair back from her head and looked at him. "There isn't a car made that I can't hot-wire."

Carson looked at her.

"I used to steal them."

"I believe it."

"Just for fun," she added defensively.

"Uh-huh. But these were once military vehicles, and this was once a top-secret facility. It won't be like breaking into a Honda Civic."

De Vaca frowned, kicking the dust at her feet with the heel of one shoe.

Carson spoke again. "On my first day here, Singer implied that the security is better than it looks. Even if we did bash through the perimeter fence, they'd be after us in a second and would just run us into the earth."

There was a long silence.

"There are two other possibilities," de Vaca said. "We could take the horses. Or we could walk."

Carson looked out over the vast, endless desert. "Only a fool would attempt something like that," he said quietly.

They both stood silently, looking out into the desert. Carson realized that, for the moment, he felt no fear: just an oppressive weight on his shoulders, as if he were supporting a terrific burden. He did not know if that meant he was brave or simply exhausted.

"Teece was no fan of the product," he said at last. "He told me as much in the sauna. I'll bet his hasty departure had something to do with PurBlood. He probably had enough doubts about X-FLU to want to stall the release of our other products, at least until he was satisfied there was no flaw in our procedures. Or until he'd learned more about Burt."

As he was speaking, he noticed de Vaca suddenly become rigid. "Someone's coming," she whispered.

There was the sound of footsteps; then the figure of Harper came down the covered walkway leading from the residency. Carson noticed a bulge under the scientist's shirt where a large bandage was attached.

Harper stopped. "Heading to dinner?" he asked.

"Sure," said Carson after a brief hesitation.

"Come on, then."

The dining hall was crowded, and only a few tables remained vacant. Carson looked around him as they took their seats. Since Vanderwagon's departure, Carson had taken to dining alone, well past the peak hour for dinner. Now he felt uneasy, seeing such a large number of Mount Dragon workers together at once. *Could all these people really* . . . He pushed the thought from his mind.

A waiter approached their table. As they gave their drink orders, Carson watched the waiter continually smooth an imaginary mustache: first the left side, then the right side, then the left, then the right. The skin of the man's upper lip was red and raw from being continuously pawed at.

"So!" said Harper as the waiter walked away. "What have you two been up to?"

Carson barely heard the question. He had realized what else was contributing to his uneasiness.

The atmosphere in the dining hall seemed hushed, almost furtive. The tables were full, people were eating, yet there were very few conversations going on. The diners seemed to be simply going through the motions of eating, as if from habit rather than hunger. The dying echoes of Harper's question seemed to ring in three dozen water glasses. *Christ, have I been asleep?* Carson asked himself. *How could I have missed this?*

Harper accepted his beer, while Carson and de Vaca drank club sodas.

"On the wagon?" Harper asked, taking a long pull at his beer.

Carson shook his head.

"I still haven't had an answer to my question," Harper asked, smoothing his thinning brown hair with a restless hand. "I asked what you two have been up to lately." He looked back and forth between them, his red eyes blinking rapidly.

"Oh, nothing much," said de Vaca, sitting very stiffly and looking down at her empty plate.

"Nothing much?" repeated Harper, as if the words were new to him. "Nothing much. That seems odd. We're working on the biggest project in GeneDyne's history, and you guys haven't been up to anything much."

Carson nodded, wishing Harper wouldn't talk so loudly. Even if they could steal a Hummer, what would they say when they got to civilization? Who would believe two wild-eyed people, driving out of the desert? They needed to download proof onto some kind of transportable media and take it with them. But did they dare leave X-FLU in the hands of a lot of people who were going insane by degrees? Not that there was much good they could do if they stayed. Unless they could somehow get the proof to *Levine*. Of course, it wouldn't be possible to transmit gigabytes of data across the net, it would be noticed, but—

He felt a hand twisting the material of his shirtfront. Harper had balled it into his fist.

"I'm talking to you, asshole," he said, pulling Carson forward in his seat.

Carson began to rise in protest when he felt a meaningful pressure on one forearm.

"Sorry," he mumbled. De Vaca's pressure on his forearm eased.

"Why are you ignoring me?" Harper asked loudly. "What is it you aren't telling me?"

"Really, George, I'm sorry. I was just thinking about other things."

"We've been so busy recently," said de Vaca, desperately trying to put a bright note in her voice. "We've got a lot to think about."

Carson felt the grip tighten further. "You just said you were doing nothing much. You said it, I know you said it. So which is it?" Carson glanced around. People at nearby tables were looking at them, and though the gazes were dull and vacant, they still held the kind of slack anticipation he hadn't seen since a bar fight he'd witnessed a long time ago.

"George," de Vaca said, "I heard you made an important breakthrough the other day."

"What?" Harper asked.

"That's what Dr. Singer told me. He said you'd made extraordinary progress."

Harper dropped his hand, immediately forgetting Carson. "John said that? I'm not surprised."

De Vaca smiled and laid her hand on Harper's arm. "And you know, I was very impressed with how you handled Vanderwagon."

Harper sat back, looking at her. "Thanks," he said at last.

"I should have mentioned it earlier. It was thoughtless of me not to. I'm so sorry."

Carson watched as de Vaca looked into Harper's eyes, an expression of sympathy and understanding on her face. Then, significantly, her eyes dropped to Harper's hands. Unaware of the suggestion she was planting, Harper looked down and began examining his nails.

"Look at that," he said. "There's dirt here. Shit. With all the germs in this place, you have to take precautions."

Without another word, he pushed his chair back and headed for the men's room.

Carson breathed out. "Jesus," he whispered. The scientists at the surrounding tables had returned to their meals, but a strange feeling remained in the air: a close, listening silence.

"I guess coming here was a bad idea," de Vaca murmured. "I'm not hungry, anyway."

Carson tried to steady his breathing, closing his eyes for a moment. As soon as he did so, the world seemed to sink away beneath his feet. Christ, he was tired.

"I can't think any more," he said. "Let's meet in the radiology lab at midnight. Meanwhile, try to get some sleep."

De Vaca snorted. "Are you crazy? How can I sleep?"

Carson glanced at her. "You aren't going to get another chance," he said.

Charles Levine stared at the blue folder in his hand, lavishly stamped and embossed, a large signature scrawled across the seal. He began to open it, then stopped. He already knew what it would say. He turned to throw it in the wastebasket, but realized that, too, was unnecessary. Destroying the document would not make its substance go away.

He looked out of his open door, past the boxes and moving crates, into the empty outer office. Just a week before, Ray had been sitting there, calmly fielding calls and turning away the zealots. Ray had been loyal to the end, unlike so many of his other colleagues and foundation members. How could his life's work be compromised so utterly, eclipsed in such a short space of time?

He sat down in his chair, gazing with vacant eyes at the single unpacked item on his desk: his notebook computer, still powered up and connected to the campus network. Not so many days before, he'd cast his line into the deep, cold waters of that network, fishing for help in his crusade. Instead, he'd hooked a leviathan; a murderous kraken that had devastated everything he cared about.

His biggest mistake had been underestimating Brent Scopes. Or, perhaps, overestimating him. The Scopes he knew would not have fought him in this way. Perhaps, Levine thought, he himself *had* been guilty—guilty of hyperbole, of leaping to conclusions, perhaps even unethical conduct, breaking into the GeneDyne net as he had. He had provoked Scopes. But for Scopes to calculatingly sully the memory of his murdered father—it was inexcusable, sociopathic. Always, in the back of his mind, Levine had kept the memory of their friendship—a friendship of profound, intellectual intensity that he could never replace. He had never gotten over the loss, and somehow he believed Scopes felt the same way.

But it was now obvious that he must have been wrong.

Levine's eyes wandered over the empty shelves, the open filing cabinets, the gray clouds of disturbed dust settling sluggishly through the still air. Losing his foundation, his reputation, and his tenure changed everything. It had made his choices very simple; it had, in fact, narrowed them to one. And out of that choice, the outline of a plan began to take shape in his mind.

After dark, Mount Dragon became home to a thousand shadows. The covered walkways and stark multifaceted buildings glowed a pale blue in the light of a setting crescent moon. The rare footfall, the crunch of gravel, served only to magnify the silence and utter loneliness. Beyond the thin necklace of lights that illuminated the perimeter fence, a vast darkness took over, flowing on for a hundred miles in all directions, unvexed by light or campfire.

Carson moved through the shadows toward the radiology lab. Nobody was outside, and the residency compound was quiet, but the silence only increased his nervousness. He had chosen the radiology lab because it had been supplanted by new facilities inside the Fever Tank and was hardly ever used, and because it was the only low-security lab with full network access. But now he wasn't so sure his choice had been a good one. The lab was off the normal track, behind the machine shop, and if he ran into anyone he'd have a difficult time explaining his presence.

He cracked open the door to the lab, then paused. A pale light glowed from inside the room, and he heard the rustle of movement.

"Jesus, Carson, you scared the shit out of me." It was de Vaca, a pallid phantom silhouetted in the glow of the computer screen. She motioned him inside.

"What are you doing?" he whispered, slipping into a seat next to her.

"I got here early. Listen, I thought of a way we could check all this out. See if we're really right about PurBlood." She was whispering fast as she typed. "We get weekly physicals, right?"

"Don't remind me."

De Vaca looked at him. "Well? Don't you get it? We can check the taps."

Comprehension dawned on Carson. The physicals included spinal taps. They could check the cerebrospinal fluid for elevated levels of dopamine and serotonin.

"But we can't access those records," he objected.

"*Cabrón*, you're miles behind. I already have. I worked in Medical my first week here, remember? My network privileges for the medical file servers were never revoked." In the reflected light of the terminal, her cheekbones were two sharp ridges of blue against black. "I began by checking a few records, but there's just too much data to poke around in. So I ran an SQL query against the medical database."

"What does it do? List the amount of dopamine and serotonin in everyone's system?"

De Vaca shook her head. "Neurotransmitters wouldn't show up in a spinal tap. But their breakdown products—their major metabolites—would. Homovanillic acid is the breakdown product of dopamine, and 5-hydroxyindoleacetic acid is the breakdown product of serotonin. So I told the program to look for those. And, just as a control, I told the program to tabulate MHPG and VMA, which are the breakdown products of another neurotransmitter, norepinephrine. That way, we'll have something to measure the results against."

"And?" Carson prompted.

"Don't know yet. Here it comes now."

The screen filled.

	MHPG	HVA	VMA	5-HIAA
Aaron	1	6	1	5
Alberts	1	9	1	10
Bowman	1	12	1	9
Bunoz	1	7	1	6
Carson	1	1	1	1
Cristoferi	1	8	1	5
Davidoff	1	8	1	8
De Vaca	1	1	1	1
Donergan	1	10	1	8
Ducely	1	7	1	9
Engles	1	7	1	6

MORE SCREENS AVAILABLE

"My God," Carson muttered.

De Vaca nodded grimly. "Look at the HVA and 5-HIAA counts. In every case, levels of dopamine and serotonin in the brain are many times above normal."

Carson paged down through the rest of the list. "Look at Nye!" he said suddenly, pointing to the screen. "Dopamine metabolites, fourteen times normal. Serotonin metabolites, twelve times normal."

"With levels like that, dangerously paranoid, perhaps presenting as schizophrenia," de Vaca said. "I'll bet he perceived Teece as a threat to Mount Dragon—or perhaps to himself—and set a trap for him out in the desert. I wonder if that bastard Marr was in on it. You were right when you said killing Teece was crazy."

Carson glanced at her. "How come these abnormal readings weren't flagged before?"

"Because you wouldn't be checking levels of neurotransmitters in a place like Mount Dragon. They look for antibodies, viral contamination, stuff like that. Besides, we're talking about nanograms per milliliter. Unless you're specifically looking for these metabolites, you aren't going to find them."

Carson shook his head in disbelief. "Isn't there anything we could do to counteract the adverse effects?"

"Hard to say. You could try a dopamine receptor antagonist, like chlorpromazine. Or imipramine, which blocks the transport of serotonin. But with levels this high, I doubt you'd see much improvement. We don't even know if the process can be reversed. And that's assuming there were sufficient stocks of both drugs on hand, and we found a way to administer it to every person on-site."

Carson continued to stare at the screen in horrified fascination. Then, suddenly, his hands moved onto the keyboard, copying the data to a file on the terminal's local drive. Then he cleared the screen and quit the program.

De Vaca turned. "What the hell are you doing?" she hissed.

"We've seen enough," Carson replied. "Scopes was a beta-tester too, remember? If he sees us at this, we're cooked." He logged de Vaca off the terminal and entered his own password at the GeneDyne security screen. As he waited for the log-on messages to scroll past, he fished two writeable compact discs from his pocket.

"I went back to the library and downloaded the most important data onto these CDs: the video, the filtration data, my on-line X-FLU logs, Burt's notes. Now, I'm going to add this CSF data to—"

He stopped, staring at the screen.

GOOD EVENING, GUY CARSON.
YOU HAVE 1 UNREAD MESSAGE

Quickly, Carson brought up the waiting electronic mail.

Ciao, Guy.

I couldn't help but notice the hellacious CPU time you soaked up, running that modeling program early this morning. It warms my heart to see you burning the midnight oil, but it wasn't clear, from the on-line logs, exactly what you were doing

I'm sure you wouldn't be wasting your time, or mine, without good reason. Does this mean you've made a breakthrough? I hope so for both our sakes. I don't need pretty pictures, I need results. Time is growing cruelly short.

Oh, yes. I almost forgot. Why this sudden interest in PurBlood?

I await your reply.

Brent

"Jesus, look at that," de Vaca said. "I can almost feel his breath on the back of my neck."

"Time is cruelly short, all right," Carson muttered. "If only he knew." He slid one of the CDs into the terminal's drive bay and copied the cerebrospinal-fluid results onto it. Then he initiated the network's chat mode.

"Are you crazy?" de Vaca hissed. "Who the hell are you going to page?"

"Shut up and watch," Carson said, as he continued to type.

**Chat target: Guy
Carson@Biomed.Dragon.GeneDyne**

"Now I know you're crazy," de Vaca said. "Requesting to chat with yourself."

"Levine told me that, if I ever needed to reach him, I should send a chat request across the network, using myself as the recipient as well as the sender," Carson said. "That would initiate a communications agent he'd planted, to connect with his computer."

"You're going to send him the data on PurBlood," de Vaca said.

"Yes. He's the only person that can help us."

Carson waited, fighting to keep calm. He imagined the small communications daemon burrowing secretly through the GeneDyne net, out into a public-access service, and then to Levine's computer. Somewhere, Levine's laptop would be flashing a message now. Assuming it was connected to the network, and Levine was around to hear it. *Come on. Come on.*

Suddenly the screen went blank.

Hello. I've been expecting your call.

Carson typed frantically.

Dr. Levine, pay careful attention. There is a crisis here at Mount Dragon. You were right about the virus. But it's more than that, much more. We can't do anything about it here, and we need your help. It is of the utmost importance that you act quickly. I am going to transmit to you a document I've prepared that explains the situation, along with files of supporting information. There is one other thing I must add: Please do what you can to get us out of here as soon as possible. I believe we are in real danger. And do whatever you must to get the stocks of X-FLU safely out of the hands of the Mount Dragon staff. As you will learn from the data I'm transmitting, they all need immediate medical attention. I'm commencing data transmission now, using standard network protocols.

He initiated the upload with a few keystrokes, and an access light on the terminal's faceplate lit up. Carson sat back gingerly, watching the data feed. Even with maximum compression and at the widest bandwidth the network would allow, it would take almost forty minutes to transmit the data. It was all too likely that the next time Scopes came nosing around, he'd notice the heavy use of resources. Or one of his network lackeys would point it out to him. And how the hell was he going to reply to Scopes's e-mail?

Suddenly the datastream was interrupted.

Guy? Are you there?

We're here. What's wrong?

Who is this 'we'? Is someone else there with you?

My lab assistant is also aware of the situation.

Very good. Now, listen to me. Is there anyone else on site who can help you?

No. We're on our own. Dr. Levine, let me continue the upload.

There's no time for that. I've received enough already to see what the problem is, and what I don't have I can get from the GeneDyne net. Thank you for trusting me with this. I'll see that the proper authorities are immediately called in to handle the situation.

Listen, Dr. Levine, we need to get out of here. We believe the OSHA investigator who came here may have been killed.

Of course. Getting you out will be my highest priority. You and de Vaca keep on as you have been and don't make any attempts to escape. Just stay calm. Okay?

Okay.

Guy, your work has been brilliant. Tell me how you stumbled across this.

As Carson prepared to type his response, a sudden chill shot through him.

You and de Vaca stay calm. But he had never spoken of de Vaca to Levine.

Who is this? he typed.

Suddenly the pixels on the screen began to dissolve into a snowstorm of white and black. The speaker next to the terminal came to life with a squeal of static. De Vaca gasped in surprise. Carson, rooted to his chair, watched the screen in disbelief, despair turning his limbs to lead. Was that the sound of raucous laughter, blending with the squeal of static in an infernal fugue? Was that a face, forming slowly out of the chaos on the screen: a face with jug ears, thick glasses, and impertinent cowlick?

Suddenly, the screen went blank, and the hiss of static abruptly cut off. The room was plunged in silent darkness. And then Carson heard the lonesome wail of the Mount Dragon alarm, rising in intensity across the desert sands.

PART THREE

Carson met de Vaca's eyes.

"Let's go," he hissed, powering down the terminal with a stab of his finger.

They eased out of the radiology lab, closing the door quietly behind them. Quickly, Carson scanned the immediate area. Quartz emergency beacons had come up along the perimeter fence. As he watched, Carson saw klieg lights snap into ivory brilliance, first in the front guard tower, then in the rear. The twin beams began slowly scanning the compound. There was no moon, and large sections of the facility were sunken in pools of impenetrable darkness. He urged de Vaca forward into the shadow of the machine shop. They crept along the base of the building and around a corner, then scurried across a walkway to a dark area behind the incinerator building.

They heard a shout and the distant running of feet.

"It'll take them a few minutes to get organized," Carson said. "This is our chance to get the hell out." He patted his pocket, ensuring that the CDs and the evidence they contained were still safe. "Looks like you'll get a chance to test your hot-wiring skills, after all. Let's grab a Hummer while we still can."

De Vaca hesitated.

"Let's move!" he urged.

"We can't," she whispered fiercely in his ear. "Not without destroying the stocks of X-FLU first."

"Are you crazy?" Carson snapped.

"If we leave X-FLU in the hands of these nuts, we won't survive even if we do escape. You saw what happened to Vanderwagon, what was happening to Harper. All it takes is one person to walk out with a vial of X-FLU, and you can kiss your ass good-bye."

"We sure as hell can't take them with us."

"No, but listen. I know how we can destroy X-FLU and escape at the same time."

Carson saw dark figures running across the compound, guards holding ugly-looking assault weapons. He pulled de Vaca farther into the shadows.

"We have to enter the Fever Tank to do it," de Vaca continued.

"The hell with that. We'll be trapped like rats."

"Listen, Carson, that's the *last* place they'll be looking for us."

Carson thought for a moment. "You're probably right," he said. "Even a madman wouldn't go back in there right now."

"Trust me." De Vaca grabbed his hand and pulled him around the far side of the incinerator.

"Wait, Susana—"

"Move your ass, *cabrón*."

Carson followed her across a dark courtyard to the inner perimeter. They dropped into the shadows of the operations building, breathing heavily.

Suddenly a shot rang out, cracking across the desert night. Several others followed in rapid succession.

"They're shooting at shadows," Carson said.

"Or perhaps each other," came the reply. "Who knows how far gone some of them are?"

A klieg light was making a slow arc toward them, and they ducked into the darkened operations building. After a hurried reconnoiter, they ran down the deserted hall and into the elevator that led to the BSL-5 entrance.

"I think you'd better tell me your plan," said Carson as they descended.

She looked at him, violet eyes wild. "Listen carefully. Remember old Pavel, who fixed my CD player? I've been meeting him in the canteen for backgammon. He likes to talk, probably more than he should. He told me that, back when the military funded this site, they insisted on the installation of a fail-safe device. Something to safeguard against a catastrophic release of a hot agent within the Fever Tank. It was taken off-line after Mount Dragon went private, but the mechanisms were never actually dismantled. Pavel even explained how easily it could be reactivated."

"Susana, how could—"

"Shut up and listen. We're gonna blow this whole *chingadera* up. The fail-safe device was called a stage-zero alert. It *reversed* the laminar airflow of the air incinerator, flooding the Fever Tank with thousand-degree air, sterilizing everything. Only a few of the old-timers, like Singer and Nye, know about it." She smirked in the dim light of the elevator. "When that superheated air hits all the combustibles in there, it should make a nice explosion."

"Yeah, right. And fry us, too."

"No. It'll take several minutes for the airflow to reverse. All we have to do is set the alert, get out, and wait for the explosion. Then we can snag a Hummer in the uproar."

The elevator door whispered open on a shadowy corridor.

They moved quickly to the gray metal door leading into the Fever Tank. Carson spoke his name into the voice-recognition box and the door clicked open.

"You know, they could be watching us right now," he said as he struggled into his bluesuit.

"They could," de Vaca said. "But considering all the hell that's breaking loose up there, I think they have more important cameras to monitor."

They checked each other's suits for safety, then stepped into decontam. As Carson stood in the sheets of poisonous liquid, staring at the dim alien figure of de Vaca standing beside him, a sense of unreality began to creep over him. *There are people looking for us. Shooting at us. And we're walking into the Fever Tank.* He felt the creeping claustrophobic fear settling around his chest once again, squeezing him like a vise. *They'll find us. We'll be trapped like rats, and . . .* He sucked at his air hose, filling his lungs with panicked gasps.

"You all right, Carson?" The calm voice of de Vaca over the private intercom channel shamed him into rationality. He nodded, stepping into the antechamber that housed the drying mechanism.

Two minutes later, they entered the Fever Tank. The global alarm droned quietly in the empty corridors, and the distant drumming of the chimps sounded like a muffled riot. Carson looked up at the white walls, searching for a clock: almost twelve-thirty. The corridor lights were on low, and would stay that way until the decontamination crew entered at 2 A.M. Only this time—with a little luck—there wouldn't be anything left to decontaminate.

"We have to access the security substation," came de Vaca's voice. "You know where it is, right?"

"Yeah." Carson knew only too well. The Level-5 security substation was located on the lowest level of the Fever Tank. Directly below the quarantine area.

They moved quickly through the corridors to the central

core. Carson let de Vaca descend first, then grabbed the handrails and went down the tube himself. Above his head he could see the huge uptake manifold that, in a few minutes, might be spewing superheated air throughout the facility.

The substation was a cramped circular room with several swivel chairs and a low ceiling. Five-inch terminal screens marched in orderly rows around the curve of the walls, showing a hundred views of the empty Fever Tank. Beneath them, a command console jutted into the room.

De Vaca took a seat in front of the console and began typing, slowly at first, then more rapidly.

"Now what the hell do we do?" Carson asked, thrusting a fresh air hose into the valve of his suit.

"Hold your water, *cabrón*," de Vaca said, lifting one gloved hand to press her communications button. "It's just like Pavel said it would be. All the safeguards here are to prevent a breach from occurring. They never thought to install safeguards against someone *deliberately* triggering a false alarm. Why should they? I'm going to bring the stage-zero crisis parameters back on-line, and then initiate the alert."

"And then we'll have *how* long to get out?"

"Plenty of time, believe me."

"How long is that, exactly?"

"Stop bothering me, Carson. Can't you see I'm busy? Just a few more commands, and we're in business."

Carson watched her type. Then he spoke again, more quietly. "Susana, let's think about this a moment. Is this really what we want to do? Destroy the entire Level-5 facility? The chimps? Everything we've worked for?"

De Vaca stopped typing and turned to face him. "What other choice do we have? The chimps are goners anyway, they're all exposed to X-FLU. We'll be doing them a favor."

"I know that. But a lot of good has come out of this facility. It would take years to reproduce the work that's been done in here. We *know* what's wrong with X-FLU now, we can correct the process."

"If we get our asses shot off, who's going to fix X-FLU?" came de Vaca's angry voice in his headset. "And if some nut gets his hands on the stuff, who's going to care about the damage we do to GeneDyne's bottom line? I'm going to—"

"Carson," came the severe tone of Nye. "De Vaca. Listen to me carefully. Effective immediately, your employment at GeneDyne is terminated. You are now trespassers on GeneDyne property, and your presence in the Level-5 facility must be assumed a hostile act. If you decide to surrender, I can guarantee your safety. If not, you will be hunted down and dealt with. There is no possibility of escape."

"So much for the video cameras," de Vaca muttered.

"He might be monitoring the private channel," Carson replied. "Say as little as possible."

"Doesn't matter. I'm there." De Vaca's typing slowed. Then she reached over and, lifting a hinged security grille protecting a bank of black switches, flipped the topmost switch.

Immediately, a loud tone sounded above the wail of the emergency siren, and an array of warning lights in the ceiling began to blink.

Attention, came a calm feminine voice in his headset that Carson had not heard before. *A stage-zero alert will initiate in sixty seconds.*

De Vaca threw a second switch, then stood back, kicking over the console with one gloved foot for good measure. A shower of sparks leapt across her suit.

Fail-safe activated, the feminine voice said. *Alert commit sequence bypassed.*

"Now you've done it," Carson said.

De Vaca punched the emergency global button on the communications panel of her bluesuit, broadcasting her words across the Mount Dragon PA system. "Nye? I want you to listen to me very carefully."

"There's nothing for you to say except yes or no," Nye replied coolly.

"Listen up, *canalla*! We're in the security substation. We've initiated a stage-zero alert. Total, unprejudiced sterilization."

"De Vaca, if you—"

"You can't back it down, I've already initiated the commit. Do you understand? In a few minutes Level-5 will be flooded with thousand-degree air. The whole damn place will go up like a Viking funeral. Anyone within a three-hundred-yard radius will turn into beef jerky."

As if in punctuation, the calm voice returned on the global channel: *Stage-zero alert initiated. You have ten minutes to evacuate the area.*

"Ten minutes?" Carson said. "Jesus."

"De Vaca, you're more insane than I thought," came the voice of Nye. "You can't succeed. Do you hear me?"

De Vaca barked a laugh. "You're calling me insane?" she said. "I'm not the one out there every day in the desert, in pith helmet and ponytail, bobbing up and down like a god damn dragoon."

"Susana, shut up!" Carson barked.

There was dead silence over the intercom.

De Vaca turned toward him, brows knitted in anger. Then her expression quickly changed.

"Guy, look at that," she said on the private channel, pointing over his shoulder.

Turning, Carson faced the wall of video monitors. He scanned the countless small black-and-white images, uncertain of what had caught de Vaca's attention. The laboratories, passages, and storage areas were still and deserted.

Except one. In the main corridor just beyond the entrance port, a single figure was moving. There was a stealth and deliberation to the figure's movements that chilled Carson's blood. He moved closer to the monitor, staring intently. The figure was wearing the kind of bulky biosuit with extended internal oxygen used exclusively by the security staff. In one hand was a long black object that looked like a policeman's nightstick. As the bulky biosuit moved closer, walking directly beneath the camera, Carson could see that the object was a double-barreled pistol-grip shotgun.

Then he noticed the figure's gait. Every now and then there was an odd hitch in the walk, as if a leg joint had momentarily come loose.

"Mike Marr," de Vaca murmured.

Carson moved his glove to his sleeve to reply, then stopped. His instincts told him that something else was wrong; terribly wrong. He stood motionless, trying to figure out what had triggered his subconscious alarm.

Then the realization hit him like a hammer.

Throughout the countless hours he'd spent in the Fever Tank—through all the many communications beeps, tones, and voices that had sounded in his headset—there had run one steady, continuous sound: the reassuring hiss of the air hose connected to his suit.

Now the hiss was gone.

Reaching down quickly, Carson disconnected the air hose from his suit valve, grabbed for another line, snapped it home. Nothing.

He turned to de Vaca, who had been watching his movements. Comprehension grew in her eyes.

"The bastard's turned off the air supply," came her voice.

You have nine minutes to evacuate the area.

Carson held a gloved finger up in front of his visor to simulate silence.

How long, he mouthed.

De Vaca held up a single hand, the fingers splayed. Five minutes of reserve air in their bluesuits.

Five minutes. Christ, it took that long just to decontaminate.

. . . Carson struggled to push back the panic that was growing inside him. He glanced back at the video screens, searching for Marr. He spotted the security officer again, moving now through the production area.

He realized they had only one chance.

Disconnecting the useless air hose from his suit, Carson gestured for de Vaca to follow him out of the security substation and back to the central core. Carson grabbed the metal rungs of the ladder, craning his neck upward. He could make out the huge uptake manifold five levels above, hovering like a grim promise at the very pinnacle of the Fever Tank. No sign yet of Marr. Grabbing the rungs of the ladder, Carson climbed as quickly as he could, past the generators and backup labs to the second-level storage facility. With de Vaca at his heels, he ducked quickly behind an oversized freezer bay.

Turning toward de Vaca, he made a suppressing movement with his hands, then concentrated on slowing his own breathing, trying to conserve his dwindling oxygen supply. He peered out from the darkness of the storage area toward the central core ladder.

Carson knew there was no way to leave the Fever Tank without passing through decontam. Marr would know this, also. He'd look for them first at the exit hatchway. Finding they weren't there, he would assume they were still in the security substation. After all, Marr knew that nobody would be foolish enough to waste time in any other section of the Fever Tank, with their air supply running out and a massive explosion due within minutes.

At least, Carson hoped Marr knew that.

You have eight minutes to evacuate the area.

They waited in the darkness, eyes riveted to the core ladder. Carson felt de Vaca nudge him urgently from behind, but he motioned her to stay still. He wondered, idly, what terrifying pathogen was stored in the freezer that stood mere inches from him. The seconds continued to tick by. He began taking shallow breaths, wondering if his plan had condemned them both to death.

Suddenly, a red-suited leg came into view on the ladder. Carson pulled de Vaca deeper into the shadows. The figure came fully into view. It paused at the second level, looking around. Then it continued downward toward the security sub-station.

Carson waited as long as he dared. Then he moved forward into the dim red light, de Vaca behind him. He cautiously peered over the edge of the central core: empty. Marr would be on the lower level by now, approaching the security sub-station. He'd be moving slowly, on the chance that Carson was armed. That gave them a few more seconds.

Carson urged de Vaca up the ladder to the main floor of the Fever Tank, motioning her to wait for him by the exit air lock. Then he moved quickly down the corridor toward the Zoo.

The chimps were in a frenzy, keyed to a fever pitch by the incessant droning of the alarms. They looked at him with angry red eyes, hammering on their cages with a terrifying ferocity. Several empty cages stood as mute testimony to recent victims of the virus.

Carson moved closer to the rack of cages. Then, careful to avoid the thrusting, probing hands, he pulled the cotter pins from the cage doors one by one and loosened the faceplates. Enraged by his proximity, the creatures redoubled their banging and screaming. Carson's suit seemed to vibrate with their desperate screams.

You have seven minutes to evacuate the area.

Carson raced from the Zoo and down the hall to the exit air lock. Seeing him approach, de Vaca opened the rubber-sealed door, and the two moved quickly into the decontamination chamber. As the sterilizing agents began to rain down on them, Carson stood near the hatchway door, looking through the glass plate back into the Fever Tank. By now, he knew, the force of the chimps' pounding would have shaken free the faceplates and opened the cage doors. He imagined the creatures, sick and angry, racing through the darkened facility, over lab tables, along corridors . . . down ladders . . .

You have five minutes to evacuate the area.

Suddenly, Carson realized his lungs were no longer drawing in air. He turned to de Vaca and made a chopping movement across his neck. If they continued trying to breathe, they would simply inspire carbon dioxide.

The yellowish bath stopped and the far hatchway opened. Carson moved into the next air lock, struggling against an overwhelming desire to breathe. As the immense driers roared into life, a terrible need for oxygen set fire to his lungs. He looked over at de Vaca, leaning weakly against the wall. She shook her head.

Was that a shotgun blast? Over the hum of the drying mechanism, Carson couldn't be sure.

Suddenly the last air lock opened and they tumbled into the ready room. Carson helped de Vaca remove her helmet, then tugged desperately at his own, dropping it to the floor and gulping in the fresh, sweet air.

You have three minutes to evacuate the area.

They struggled out of their bluesuits, then left the ready room, moving down the hallway and into the elevator leading up to the operations building. "They may be waiting for us outside," Carson said.

"No way," de Vaca gasped as she gulped in large lungfuls of air. "They're going to be running like hell to the other side of the compound."

The hallways of the operations building remained dark and empty. They raced down the corridor and through the atrium, pausing briefly at the front entrance. As Carson cracked the door open, the frantic blatting of emergency sirens rushed in to meet them. He looked around, then moved quickly into the shadows outside, motioning de Vaca to follow him.

Mount Dragon was in chaos. Carson could see several small knots of people huddled together, talking or yelling among themselves. In a pool of light outside the residency compound, several scientists were standing—some clad in pajamas—talking excitedly. Carson could see Harper among them, shaking a raised fist. Figures could be seen, marching and sometimes running between the probing beams of the klieg lights.

They moved quickly through the deserted inner perimeter gate and into the shadow of the incinerator. As Carson scanned the far end of the compound, his eyes fell on the motor pool. Half a dozen armed guards surrounded the Hummers, brilliantly spotlighted in a bank of lights. In the center of the group stood Nye. Carson saw the security director gesture in the direction of the Fever Tank.

"The stables!" Carson shouted in de Vaca's ear.

They found the horses standing in their stalls, restless, alert to the excitement. De Vaca led the horses to the tack room while Carson ran ahead to secure the blankets and saddles.

As Carson turned toward Roscoe, saddle in both hands, the earth suddenly shuddered beneath his feet. Then a flash of intense light illuminated the inside of the stables in a stark, unyielding glare. The explosion began as a muffled thump, followed by an endlessly building roar. Carson felt the wave of overpressure rock the stables, and the windows along the far wall burst inward, scattering shards of wood and glass across the barn floor. De Vaca's Appaloosa reared in terror.

"Easy, boy," said de Vaca, catching the reins and stroking the animal's neck.

Carson looked quickly around the stables, saw Nye's saddlebags, grabbed them and tossed them to de Vaca. "There should be canteens inside. Fill them in the horse trough!" he shouted, throwing on the blankets and reaching for the saddles.

When she raced back, he was tightening Roscoe's flank cinch. Carson slapped the saddlebags on the skirts and tied them with the saddle strings as de Vaca mounted.

"Wait a minute," Carson said. He ran back and grabbed two riding hats from their pegs in the tack room. Then, returning, he climbed onto Roscoe and they moved through the open door.

The heat of the fire slapped against their faces as they stared at the devastation outside. The low filtration housing that marked the roof of the Fever Tank was now a ruined crater from which gouts of flame licked skyward. The concrete roof of the operations building had buckled, and a reddish glow rose from its interior. In the residency compound, curtains whipped crazily through a hundred shattered windows. An intense fire roared out of the incinerator, coloring the surrounding sand a brilliant orange.

The path of the blast had cut a swath of destruction through the compound, peeling back the roof of the canteen and flattening a large section of the perimeter fence. "Follow me!" Carson shouted, giving his horse the heel. They raced through the smoke and fire to the blowdown, jumped the twisted wreckage of the perimeter fence, and galloped across the desert toward the welcoming darkness.

When they were half a mile from the compound and beyond the glow of the fire, Carson slowed his horse to a trot.

"We've got a long way to go," he said as de Vaca pulled up alongside. "We'd better take it easy on these horses."

As he spoke, another explosion rocked the ruins of the operations building, and a massive fireball arose from the hole in the ground that had been the Fever Tank, roiling toward the sky. Several secondary blasts slapped the darkness like aftershocks: the transfection lab crumbled into nothingness, and the walls of the residency compound shuddered, then collapsed.

The lights of Mount Dragon winked out, leaving only the

lambent flickering of the burning buildings to mark the remains of the complex.

"There goes my pre-war Gibson flathead," Carson muttered.

As he turned Roscoe back into the well of blackness ahead, he saw pencil beams of light begin to stab across the desert. The beams seemed to be moving toward them, blinking in and out of sight as they followed the bumpy terrain. Suddenly, powerful spotlights snapped on, illuminating the desert in long yellow lances.

"*Qué chinga'o*," said de Vaca. "The Hummers survived the explosion. We'll never outrun those bastards in this desert."

Carson said nothing. With any luck, they could evade the Hummers. He was thinking, instead, about their almost total lack of water.

Scopes sat alone in the octagon, examining his state of mind.

Carson and de Vaca were all but taken care of. Escape was impossible.

He had intercepted their transmission and cut off Carson's data feed almost immediately. True, the transparent relay he'd used as an alarm would not have stopped the initial part of the data transmission. It was within the realm of possibility that Levine—or whoever Levine was using to hack into the GeneDyne net—would pick up the aborted transmission. But Scopes had already taken the steps to ensure that such unauthorized entry would not happen again. Drastic steps, perhaps, yet necessary. Especially at this delicate time.

In any case, very little of the intended download had gotten through. And what Carson had sent seemed to make little sense. It was all about PurBlood. Even if Levine received the data, he would have learned nothing of value about X-FLU. And he was now so thoroughly discredited that no one would pay attention to any story of his, whatever it might be.

All bases had been covered. He could proceed as planned. There was nothing to worry about.

So why the strange, subtle, anxious feeling?

Sitting on his comfortably battered couch, Scopes probed his own mild anxiety. It was a foreign feeling to him, and the study of it was very interesting. Perhaps it was because he had misjudged Carson so thoroughly. De Vaca's treachery he could understand, especially after that incident in the Level-5 facility. But Carson was the last person he would have suspected of industrial espionage. Another might have felt terrible, even overwhelming anger at such a betrayal. But Scopes felt merely sorrow. The kid had been bright. Now he would have to be dealt with by Nye.

Nye—that reminded him. A Mr. Bragg from OSHA had left two messages earlier in the day, inquiring as to the whereabouts of that investigator, Teece. He'd have to ask Nye to look into it.

He thought again about the data file Carson had tried to send. There wasn't much, and he hadn't looked it over carefully. Just a few documents related to PurBlood. Scopes remembered that Carson and de Vaca had been messing around in the PurBlood files just the other day. Why the sudden interest? Were they planning to sabotage PurBlood, as well as X-FLU? And what was all this Carson had said about everyone needing immediate medical attention?

It bore closer looking into. In fact, it would probably be prudent for him to examine the aborted download more carefully, along with Carson's on-line activities of the last several days. Perhaps he could find the time after the evening's primary order of business.

At this new thought, Scopes's eyes moved toward the

smooth, black face of a safe set flush against the lower edge
of a far wall. It had been built, to his own demanding speci-
fications, into the structural steel of the building when the
GeneDyne tower was constructed. The only person who
could open it was himself, and if his heart stopped beating
there would be no way to open it short of using enough dynamite to vaporize every trace. As he pictured what lay
within, the odd sense of anxiety quickly melted away. A single
biohazard box—recently arrived via military helicopter from
Mount Dragon—and inside, a sealed glass ampule filled with
neutral nitrogen gas and a special viral transport medium. If
Scopes looked closely at the ampule, he knew he would be
able to make out a cloudy suspension in the fluid. Amazing
to think such an insignificant-looking thing could be so valuable.

He glanced at his watch: 2:30 P.M., eastern time.

A tiny chirrup came from a monitor beside the couch, and
a huge screen winked into life. There was a flurry of data as
the satellite downlink was decrypted; then a brief message
appeared, in letters fifteen inches tall:

**TELINT-2 data link established, lossy-bit en-
cryption enabled. Proceed with transmission.**

The message disappeared, and new words appeared on the
screen:

**Mr. Scopes: We are prepared to tender an offer of
three billion dollars. The offer is non-negotiable.**

Scopes pulled his keyboard over, and began typing. Com-
pared to hostile corporations, the military were pansies.

**My dear General Harrington: All offers are negotia-
ble. I'm prepared to accept four billion for the product**

we've discussed. I'll give you twelve hours to make
the necessary procurements.

Scopes smiled. He'd carry out the rest of the negotiations
from a different place. A secret place in which he was now
more comfortable than he was in the everyday world.

He resumed typing, and as he issued a series of commands
the words on the giant screen began to dissolve into a strange
and wondrous landscape. As he typed, Scopes recited, almost
inaudibly, his favorite lines from *The Tempest*:

> *Nothing of him that doth fade*
> *But doth suffer a sea-change*
> *Into something rich and strange.*

Charles Levine sat on the edge of the faded bedspread, staring
at the telephone propped on the pillow in front of him. The
phone was a deep burgundy color, with the words PROPERTY
OF HOLIDAY INN, BOSTON, MA stamped in white across the
back of the receiver. For hours he had spoken into the mouthpiece of that receiver, shouting, coaxing, begging. Now he
had nothing more to say.

He rose slowly, stretched his aching legs, and moved to the
sliding glass doors. A gentle breeze billowed the curtains. He
stepped out to the balcony railing and breathed deeply of the
night air. The lights of Jamaica Plain glittered in the warm
darkness, like a mantle of diamonds thrown casually across
the landscape. A car nosed by on the street below, its head-

lights illuminating the shabby working-class storefronts and deserted gas stations.

The telephone rang. In his shock at hearing an incoming call—after so many excuses, so many curt rejections—Levine stood motionless a moment, looking over his shoulder at the telephone. Then he stepped inside and picked up the receiver.

"Hello?" he said in a voice hoarse from talking.

The unmistakable rumble of a modem echoed from the tiny speaker.

Quickly, Levine hung up, transferred the jack from the telephone to his computer, and powered up the laptop. The phone rang again, and there was a flurry of noise as the machines negotiated.

How-do, professor-man. The words rushed immediately onto the screen without the usual introductory logo. I assume it's still appropriate to call you professor, is it not?

How did you find me? Levine typed back.

Without much problem, came the reply.

I've been on the telephone for hours, talking to everyone I can think of, Levine typed. Colleagues, friends in the regulatory agencies, reporters, even former students. Nobody believes me.

I believe you.

The job was too thorough. Unless I can prove my innocence, my credibility will be gone forever.

Don't fret, professor. As long as you know me, you can be assured of a good credit rating, if nothing else.

There's only one person I haven't spoken to: Brent Scopes. He's my next stop.

Just a minute, my man! came Mime's response. Even if you could talk to him, I doubt he'd be interested in hearing from you right about now.

Not necessarily. I have to go now, Mime.

One moment, professor. I didn't contact you just to present my condolences. A few hours ago, your Western homeboy Carson tried to send you an emergency transmission. It was almost immediately interrupted, and I was only able to retrieve the initial section. I think you need to read this. Are you ready to receive?

Levine replied that he was.

Okay, came the response. Here it comes.

Levine checked his watch. It was ten minutes to three.

Carson and de Vaca rode through the velvety blackness of the Jornada del Muerto, a vast river of stars flowing above their heads. The ground sloped downward from the compound and they soon found themselves in the bottom of a dry wash, the horses sinking to their fetlocks in the soft sand. The light of the stars was just enough to illuminate the ground beneath their feet. Any moon, Carson knew, and they would have been dead.

They rode down the wash while he thought.

"They'll expect us to head south, toward Radium Springs and Las Cruces," he said at last. "Those are the closest towns besides Engle, which belongs to GeneDyne anyway. Eighty miles, more or less. It takes time to track someone in this desert, especially across lava. So if I were Nye, I'd follow the track until I was sure it was heading south. Then I'd fan out the Hummers until the quarry was intercepted."

"Makes sense," came the voice of de Vaca in the gloom.

"So we'll oblige him. We'll head south, like we're going to Radium Springs. When we hit the Malpaís, we'll ride up onto the lava where tracking is difficult. Then we'll make a ninety-degree turn east, ride a few miles, and reverse direction. We'll head north instead."

"But there's no town to the north for at least a hundred and forty miles."

"That's exactly why it's the only way we can go. They'd never look for us in that direction. But we won't have to ride as far as a town. Remember the Diamond Bar ranch I told you about? I know the new ranch manager. There's a line camp at the southern edge of the ranch we can head for. It's called Lava Camp. I'd say it's about a hundred and ten miles from here, twenty or thirty miles north of Lava Gate."

"Can't the Hummers follow us onto the lava?"

"The lava's sharp, it would tear any ordinary tires to ribbons," Carson said. "But the Hummers have something called a central tire inflation system that can raise or lower tire pressure. The tubes are specially made to allow miles of continued travel after a puncture. Even so, I doubt if they could stay on the lava for long. Once they're sure of our direction, they'll get off the lava, move ahead to the far side and try to cut us off."

There was a silence. "It's worth a try," de Vaca said at last.

Carson turned his horse southward and de Vaca followed. As they came over the rise on the far side of the wash, they could still see, in the distance to the north, the flickering yellow glow of the burning complex. Midway across the dark sands, the circles of light had grown measurably closer.

"I think we'd better make tracks," Carson said. "Once we've thrown them we can rest the horses."

They urged their horses into a hand gallop. In five minutes, the jagged outline of the lava flow loomed up before them. They dismounted and led their horses up into the flow.

"If I remember correctly, the lava veers around to the east," Carson said. "We'd better follow it for a couple of miles before turning north."

They walked their horses through the lava, moving slowly, allowing the animals time to pick a trail through the sharp rubble. *It's damn lucky*, Carson thought, *that horses have much better night vision than humans*. He couldn't even make out the shape of the lava beneath Roscoe's hooves; it was as black as the night itself. Only scattered yucca plants, patches of lichen and windblown sand, and clumps of grass growing from cracks gave him an idea of the surface. Difficult as it was, movement was easier here near the edge of the flow. Farther in, Carson could see great blocks of lava, sticking up into the night sky like basaltic sentries, blotting out the stars.

Glancing back again, Carson could see the lights of the Hummers rapidly approaching. Periodically the lights would pause—presumably when Nye got out to check the tracks. The lava would slow them, but it wouldn't stop them.

"What about water?" de Vaca spoke suddenly out of the immense darkness. "Is this going to be enough?"

"No," Carson said. "We'll have to find some."

"But where?"

Carson was silent.

Nye stood in the empty motor pool, alone, looking out into the darkness, his fiery shadow playing across the desert sands. The ruined hulk of Mount Dragon burned out of control behind him, but he ignored it.

A security officer came running up, gasping and out of breath, his face smeared with soot. "Sir, the water pressure in the hoses will be exhausted within five minutes. Should we switch to the emergency reserves?"

"Why not?" Nye replied absently, not bothering to look at the man.

He had failed massively; he knew that. Carson had slipped from between his fingers, but not before he'd destroyed the very facility Nye had been charged with protecting. Briefly, he thought of what he could say to Brent Scopes. Then he pushed the thought from his mind. This was a failure like none other in his career, even worse than that other, the one that he no longer allowed himself to think about. There was no possibility of redemption.

But there was the possibility of revenge. Carson was responsible, and Carson would pay. And the Spanish bitch, as well. They would not be allowed to escape.

He watched the lights of the Hummers recede into the desert, and his lip curled with contempt. Singer was a fool. It was impossible to track anything from inside a Hummer. One had to keep stopping, getting out, and scouting the trail; it would be even slower than going on foot. Besides, Carson knew the desert. He knew horses. He probably knew a few simple tracking tricks. There were lava flows in the Jornada so mazelike that it would take years to explore every island, every "hole in the wall." There were sandy flats where a horse's track would be all but erased by the wind in just a few hours.

Nye knew all these things. He also knew that it was virtually impossible to completely erase a trail in this desert. There was always a trace left, even on rock or in sand. His ten years working an Arabian security detail in the *Rub' al-Khali*, the Empty Quarter, had taught him all any man could know about the desert.

Nye tossed his now-useless radio communicator into the sand and turned toward the stables. As he walked, he paid no heed to the desperate cries, the rushing sound of flame, the shriek of collapsing metal. Something new had occurred to him. If Carson had escaped, perhaps the man was more clever than he'd suspected. Perhaps he had been smart enough to steal or even disable his horse, Muerto, on the way out. The security director quickened his pace.

As he walked through the shattered barn door, he glanced automatically toward the locked tack box where he kept his rifle. It was still there, untouched.

Suddenly Nye froze. The nails that normally held his old McClellan saddlebags were empty. Yet the saddlebags had hung there yesterday. A red mist crept in front of his eyes. Carson had taken the bags and their two gallon canteens; a pitiful amount of water against the Jornada del Muerto, the Journey of Death. Carson was doomed by that fact alone.

It was not the loss of the canteens that bothered him. Something else was missing; something far more important. He had always believed that the saddlebags had provided an unobtrusive hiding spot for his secret. But now Carson had stolen them. Carson had destroyed his career, and now he was going to take from him the last thing he had left. For a moment, the white heat of Nye's anger rooted him, motionless, to the spot.

Then he heard the familiar whinny. And, despite his rage, Nye's lip curled in a half smile. Because he knew now that revenge was not only a possibility, but a certainty.

As they moved eastward, Carson noticed the lights of the Hummers drifting farther to their left. The vehicles were approaching the Malpaís. At that point, with any luck, they would lose the trail. It would take an expert tracker, moving on foot, to follow them through the lava. Nye was good, but he wouldn't be good enough to follow a horse trail through lava. When he lost the trail, Nye would assume they had taken a shortcut across the lava and were still heading south. Besides, with the tainted PurBlood working its way through his veins, Nye was probably becoming less and less of a threat to anyone but himself. In any case, Carson thought, he and de Vaca would be free. Free to get back to civilization and warn the world about the planned release of PurBlood.

Or free to die of thirst.

He felt the heavy cold canteen on his saddle horn. It contained four quarts of water—very little for a person crossing the Jornada del Muerto. But he realized this was only a secondary problem.

Carson halted. The Hummers had stopped at the edge of the lava flow, perhaps a mile away.

"Let's find a low spot and hide these horses," Carson said. "I want to make sure those Hummers keep going south."

They led the horses down a rubble-strewn crevasse in the

lava. De Vaca held the reins while Carson climbed to a high point and watched.

He wondered why his pursuers hadn't turned off their lights. As it was, they stuck out like a cruise ship on a moonless ocean, visible for ten miles or more. Odd that Nye hadn't thought of that.

The lights were stationary for a minute or two. Then they began moving up on to the lava flow, where they paused again. For a moment Carson worried they might somehow pick up his trail and come toward him, but instead they continued southward, at a faster clip now, the lights bouncing and sweeping over the lava.

He climbed back down.

"They're going south," he said.

"Thank God for that."

Carson hesitated. "I've done some thinking," he said at last. "I'm afraid we're going to have to save this water for the horses."

"What about us?"

"Horses require twelve gallons of water a day in desert conditions. Seven, if they ride only at night. If those horses collapse, we're finished. It won't matter how much water we've got, we wouldn't get five miles in lava or deep sand. But if we save this for the horses, even a little bit does some good. They'll be able to go an extra ten or twenty miles. That will give *us* a better chance to find water."

In the darkness, de Vaca was silent.

"It's going to be extremely hard to avoid drinking when we get thirsty," Carson said. "But we must save it for the horses. If you want, I'll take your canteen when the time comes."

"So you can drink it yourself?" came the sarcastic remark.

"It will take great discipline when it starts to get bad. And, believe me, it's going to get bad. So before we continue, there's another rule about thirst you should know. Never, *ever* mention it. No matter how bad it gets, don't talk about water. Don't *think* about water."

"Does this mean we're going to have to drink our pee?" de Vaca asked. In the darkness, Carson couldn't tell if she was serious or merely baiting him again.

"That only happens in books. What you do is this: When you feel like urinating, hold it in. As soon as your body realizes it's getting thirsty, it will automatically reabsorb the water. And your desire to urinate will vanish. Eventually you'll have to, of course, but by that time there will be so much salt in the urine it'll be useless to drink, anyway."

"How do you know all this?"

"I grew up in this kind of desert."

"Yeah," said de Vaca, "and I bet being part Ute helps, too."

Carson opened his mouth to retort, then decided against it. He'd save the arguments for later.

They continued eastward through the lava for another mile, moving slowly, leading the horses by the reins and letting them pick their own way. Occasionally a horse would stumble in the lava, its shoes sending out small flashes of sparks. From time to time, Carson stopped to climb a lava formation and look south. Each time, the Hummers had receded farther into the distance. At last, the lights disappeared completely.

As he climbed down for the last time, Carson wondered if he should have told de Vaca the worst news of all. Even with the two gallons all to themselves, the horses could barely make half the distance they needed to go. They were going to have to find water at least once along the way.

Nye tightened the cinch on Muerto and checked the horse's saddle rigging. Everything was in order. The rifle was snug in its boot, slung under his right leg where he could extract it with one smooth motion. The metal tube carrying his USGS 1:24,000 topographical maps was secure.

He tied the extra saddlebags behind the cantle and began packing ammunition into them. Then he filled two five-gallon flaxen desert water bags, tied them together, and slung them over the cantle, one on each side. It was an extra forty pounds of weight, but it was essential. Chances are it wouldn't be necessary for him to bother tracking Carson. Carson's having a mere two gallons of water would do the job for him. But Nye had to be sure. He wanted to see their dead, desiccated bodies, to reassure himself that the secret was once again his and his alone.

To the saddle horn, he tied a small sack containing a loaf of bread and a four-pound wax-covered wheel of cheddar cheese. He tested his halogen flashlight, then placed it in the saddlebags, along with a handful of extra batteries.

Nye worked methodically. There was no hurry. Muerto was trained as an endurance horse, and was in far better shape than the two specimens Carson had taken. Carson had probably pushed his horses in the beginning, galloping or loping to escape the Hummers. That would start them off badly. Only fools and Hollywood actors galloped their horses. If Carson and the woman expected to get across the desert, they would have to take it slow. Even so, as their horses began to suffer from the lack of water, they would start lagging. Nye figured that without water, traveling only at night, they could go perhaps forty-five miles before collapsing. If they attempted daytime travel, they'd make perhaps half that. Any animal lying motionless on the desert sands—or even one that was moving slowly or erratically—immediately attracted a spiraling column of vultures. He could find them by that alone.

But he wouldn't need vultures to tell him where they were.

Tracking was both an art and a science, like music or nuclear physics. It required a large volume of technical knowledge and an intuitive brilliance. He had learned a great deal about it during his time in the Empty Quarter. And years of searching the Jornada del Muerto desert had honed that knowledge.

He gave his outfit a final check. Perfect. He lofted himself into the saddle and rode out of the barn, following Carson and de Vaca's hoofprints in the glow of the fire. As he moved into the desert and away from the burning complex, the glow lessened. From time to time he switched on his flashlight, as he traced their route southward. Just as he thought: they had been running their horses. Excellent. Every minute of galloping here would be a mile lost at the far end. They had left a trail that any moron could follow. *A moron is following it,* Nye thought with amusement, as he saw the myriad tire tracks crisscrossing in confusion as they pursued the hoofprints southward.

He paused for a moment in the darkness. A voice had suddenly murmured his name. He swiveled in his saddle, scanning the infinite desert around him for its source. Then once again he urged his horse into a slow trot.

Time, water, and the desert were all on his side.

Carson paused at the far edge of the lava flow and looked northward. The great arm of the Milky Way stretched across the sky, burying itself at last below the far horizon. They were adrift in a sea of blackness. The faintest reddish glow to the north marked Mount Dragon. The blinking lights atop the microwave tower had long since disappeared, winking out when the generators failed.

He inhaled the fragrance that surrounded them: dry grasses and chamisa, mixed with the coolness of the desert night.

"We'll need to erase our tracks coming off the lava," he said.

De Vaca took the reins of both horses and, walking ahead, led them down off the lava and into the darkness. Carson followed her to the edge of the flow; then, turning around and removing his shirt, he got down on his hands and knees and began crawling backward on the sand. With each step he swept the sand before him clean with his shirt, obliterating both the hoofprints and his own marks. He worked slowly and carefully. He knew that nothing could completely erase marks in the sand. But this was pretty damn good. A Hummer would drive right past without seeing a thing.

He continued for over a hundred yards, just to make sure. Then he stood up, shook out his shirt, and buttoned it on. The job had taken ten minutes.

"So far so good," he said, catching up with de Vaca and climbing into his saddle. "We'll head due north from here. That'll give us a three-mile berth around Mount Dragon."

He looked into the sky, locating the North Star. He urged his horse into a slow, easy trot—the most efficient of gaits. Beside him, de Vaca did the same. They moved in silence through the velvety night. Carson glanced at his watch. It was one o'clock in the morning. They had four hours to dawn; that meant twenty-four miles, if they could keep up the pace. That would put them twenty-odd miles north of Mount Dragon, with close to another hundred still ahead of them. He smelled the air again, more carefully this time. There was a sharpness that indicated the possibility of a dew before dawn.

Traveling during the heat of the day was out of the question. That meant finding a low place to hide the horses, where they could move around and do a little grazing.

"You said your ancestors came through here in 1598," Carson spoke into the darkness.

"That's right. Twenty-two years before the Pilgrims landed at Plymouth Rock."

Carson ignored that. "Didn't you mention something about a spring?" he asked.

"The Ojo del Águila. They started across the Jornada and ran out of water. An Apache showed them this hidden spring."

"Where was it?"

"I don't know. The location was later lost. In a cave, I think, at the base of the Fra Cristóbal Mountains."

"Jesus, the Fra Cristóbals are sixty miles long."

"I wasn't planning to make a land survey at the time I heard the story, all right? It was in a cave, I remember my *abuelito* saying, and the water flowed back into the cave and disappeared."

Carson shook his head. The lava and the mountains were riddled with caves. They would never find a spring that didn't surface to the light of day, where it would generate some form of green plant life.

They continued to trot, the only sounds the clink of the saddle rigging and the low creak of leather. Once again, Carson glanced up at the stars. It was a beautiful, moonless night. Under any other circumstances, he might have enjoyed this ride. He inhaled again. Yes, there would definitely be a dew. That was a stroke of good fortune. He mentally added ten miles to the distance they could travel without water.

Levine skimmed the last, incomplete page of Carson's transmission, then quickly saved the data.

Mime, are you sure about this? he typed.

Yup, came the response. Scopes was very clever. Humblingly so. He discovered my access and grafted a transparent software relay onto it. The relay triggered an alarm when Carson attempted to access us.

Mime, speak English.

The wily bastard rigged a tripwire across my secret path, and Carson tripped over it, falling flat on his virtual face. However, his aborted data feed remained on the net. I was able to retrieve it.

Any chance you were discovered? Levine typed.

Discovered? Me? ⟨ROFL⟩

⟨ROFL⟩? I don't understand.

'Rolling on floor, laughing.' I am too well hidden. Any attempt would bog down in a maze of packet-switching. But Scopes does not appear to be trying to find me. Quite the opposite. He's put a moat around GeneDyne.

What do you mean, a moat? Levine asked.

He's physically cut off all network traffic out of GeneDyne headquarters. There's no way to dial into the building by phone, fax, or computer. All remote sites have been cut off.

If this transmission is true, PurBlood is contaminated in some terrible way, and Scopes himself is a victim. Do you suppose he knows? Is that why he sealed off the access?

Not likely, came Mime's response. See, when I realized Carson was trying to reach us, I entered GeneDyne cyberspace myself. A few moments later, I saw what had gone down. I realized our access had been discovered. I couldn't log out without making my presence known. So I put my ear to the door, listening to all the unprotected net chatter. I learned some very interesting things before Scopes cut off all outside links.

Such as?

Such as Carson seems to have had the last laugh on Scopes. At least, that's what I think. Fifteen minutes after Scopes terminated the data feed, there was a big ugly net crash and all communications from Mount Dragon ceased. A real patty melt.

Scopes shut down all communication with Mount Dragon?

Au contraire, professor-man. The head office tried frantically to reestablish communications. A facility such as Mount Dragon would have redundant emergency backups up the ying-yang. Whatever happened was so devastating it knocked out everything at once. Heap bad medicine. Once Scopes realized that he could not get through to Mount Dragon, he broke off the GeneDyne net.

But I _must_ communicate with Scopes, Levine typed. It's vital that he stop the release of PurBlood. Nobody on the outside will believe me. It's critical that I convince him.

You ain't been listening, professor-man. Scopes has physically severed all links. Until he decides the emergency is over, there's no way to call into the building. You can't hack across clear air, professor. Except . . .

What?

Except that there is ONE channel out of GeneDyne Boston. I discovered its data signature as I was poking around the edges of the moat. It is a dish uplink from Scopes's personal server to the TELINT-2 communications satellite.

Any chance you can use that satellite to get me in contact with Scopes?

No way. It's a dedicated two-way link. Besides, whoever Scopes is chatting with is using a highly unusual encryption scheme. Some kind of end-to-end block cipher that stinks like military to me. Whatever it is, I wouldn't go near it with anything short of a Cray-2. And if it's a prime factorial code, all the CPU time in the universe wouldn't crack the mother.

Is there traffic on the link?

A wee bit here and there. A few thousand bytes at irregular intervals.

Levine looked curiously at the words on the screen. Though the insolence still shone through, the prancing, boastful Mime he usually encountered was abnormally muted. He sat back a moment, thinking. Could Scopes have shut everything down because of PurBlood? No, that didn't make sense. What was happening at Mount Dragon? What of that other dangerous virus Carson had been working on?

There was no way around it: he *had* to speak to Scopes, warn him about PurBlood. Whatever else he might do, Scopes would never allow the intentional release of a dangerous medical product. It would destroy his company. And then, of course, if Scopes had been a beta-tester himself, he might need immediate medical treatment.

It is imperative that I communicate with Scopes, Levine wrote. How can I do that?

Only one chance. You'll have to physically get inside the building.

But that's impossible. The security on that building must be massive.

No doubt. But the weakest element of any security system is the people. I assumed you might make this request, and I've already begun making preparations. Months ago, when I first began hacking the Gene-Dyne net for you, I downloaded their network and security blueprints. If you can get your ass into the building, you may be able to reach Scopes. But I'll need to take care of a little business first.

I'm no hacker, Mime. You've got to come in with me.

I can't.

You must be in North America. Wherever you are, you can be on a plane and in Boston in five hours. I'll pay for your ticket.

No.

Why the hell not?

I just can't.

Mime, this isn't a game anymore. Thousands of lives depend on it.

Listen to me, professor. I'll help you get into the building. I'll show you how to contact me once inside. There are numerous security systems that will have to be compromised if you want to get close to Scopes. Forget doing it in real space. You'll have to make the trip by cyberspace, professor-man. I'll send you a series of attack programs I've written explicitly for GeneDyne. They should get you inside the net.

I need you there with me, not as some long-distance support service. Mime, I never thought you were the cowardly type. You've got to—

The screen went blank. Levine waited impatiently, wondering what hacker game Mime was playing now.

Suddenly, a picture materialized:

Levine stared blankly at the screen. The image was so unexpected that it took him several seconds to realize he was looking at the structural formula for a chemical. It took significantly less time to realize what the compound was.

"My God," he whispered. "Thalidomide. A thalidomide baby."

It was suddenly clear to him why Mime could not possibly come to Boston. And it was also clear—for the first time— why Mime hacked the big pharmaceutical companies with such vengeance; why, in fact, Mime was helping him at all.

There was a rap on the hotel-room door.

Levine opened it to see a disheveled-looking valet in a red suit that was several sizes too small. The valet held up a hanger containing two pieces of dark brown clothing, wrapped in protective plastic.

"Your uniform," he said.

"I didn't—" Levine began, then stopped. He thanked the valet and closed the door. He had not ordered any dry cleaning.

But Mime had.

From the welter of tracks at the edge of the lava flow, Nye could see that Singer and his Hummers had stopped and milled about. For quite some time, apparently; they had managed, in their ineptitude, to obscure Carson's and de Vaca's own tracks. Then the vehicles had moved up onto the lava itself, scraping and scratching along. The bloody yob didn't know the first rule of the tracker was never disturb the track one is following.

Nye stopped, waiting. Then he heard the voice again, clearer now, murmuring out of the lovely darkness. Carson hadn't continued straight south. Once on the lava, he had either gone east or west, hoping to shake his pursuers. Then he would have doubled back north, or doglegged south again.

Nye gave Muerto the whispered order to stand. Dismounting, he climbed onto the lava, flashlight in hand. He walked a hundred yards west of the mess left by the Hummers, then turned and cut for sign, playing his beam among the lava rocks, looking for the telltale marks of shoe iron on rock.

No track. He would try the other side.

And there he saw it: the whitish crushed edge of a lava rock, the fresh mark of a shoe. To make sure, he continued searching until he found another whitish streak against the black lava, and then another, along with an overturned stone. The horses had stumbled here and there, striking the rocks with their iron shoes, leaving an unmistakable trail. Carson and the woman had made a ninety-degree turn and were heading east.

But for how long? Would they turn south again, or double back north? There was no water in either direction. The only time Nye had seen any water in the Jornada was in the temporary playas that formed after heavy thundershowers. Except for the freak rain shower on that day he'd first suspected Carson was after his secret, there hadn't been any rain in months. There probably wouldn't be any more until the rainy season began in late August.

South seemed the obvious route, since the northward journey would be much longer and would cross more lava fields.

No doubt that's what Carson thought his pursuers would assume.

North, said the voice.

Nye stopped and listened. It was a familiar voice, cynical and high, laced with the salty Cockney tones that no amount of Home Counties public schooling could erase. Somehow, it seemed perfectly natural that it should be speaking to him. He wondered, in a detached way, whose voice it was.

He returned to Muerto and remounted. It was better to be absolutely sure of Carson's intentions. The two would have to come down off the lava field at some point. And that's where Nye knew he could pick up the track.

He decided to ride along the northern edge of the lava first. If he didn't pick up the trail, he'd cross the lava field and ride along its southern edge.

Within half an hour he had found the pathetic marks in the sand where Carson had tried to brush away their tracks. So the voice was right: They had turned north, after all. There was a regularity to Carson's sweepings that set them apart from the irregular patterns of windblown sand. Nye painstakingly traced the brushed marks back to where the trail began again, as clear in the deep sand as highway markers, heading straight for the North Star.

This would be easier than he thought. He'd catch Carson around sunrise. With the Holland & Holland, he could take Carson down from a quarter mile. The man would be dead before he even heard the shot. There would be no final confrontation, no desperate pleading. Just a clean shot from six hundred yards, and a second one for the bitch. Then he would finally be free to find the one thing that meant anything to him now: the Mount Dragon gold.

Once again, he did the calculations. He had done them innumerable times before, and they felt comfortable and familiar in his head. The amount of gold that could be carried on a pack mule was between 180 and 240 pounds, depending on the mule. In either case, well over one million in bullion alone. But the gold would probably be in the Pre-Revolt stamped bullion bars and coinage of New Spain. That would drive its worth up ten times or more.

He was free of Mount Dragon now; free of Scopes. Only Carson—Carson the traitor in the dark, Carson the sneak thief—stood in his way. And a bullet would take care of that.

By three in the morning, the sharpness in the air had intensified. Carson and de Vaca came over a rise and rode down into what appeared to be a broad, grassy basin. It had been almost two hours since they passed the glow of Mount Dragon on the horizon, heading north. They had seen no sign of lights behind them. The Hummers were gone for good.

Carson drew to a halt. He dismounted and bent down, feeling the blades of grass. Side oats grama, high in protein: excellent for the horses.

"We'll stop here for a couple of hours," he said. "Let the horses graze."

"Shouldn't we keep going while it's still dark?" de Vaca asked. "They might send helicopters."

"Not over the Missile Range," Carson said. "In any case,

we won't travel far in daylight without finding a place to hole up. But we have to take full advantage of this dew. You'd be surprised how much water the horses can take in grazing dewy grass. We can't afford to let this pass. An hour spent here will give us an extra ten miles, even more."

"Ahh," said de Vaca. "A Ute trick, no doubt."

Carson turned toward her in the darkness. "It wasn't funny the first time. Having a Ute ancestor doesn't make me an Indian."

"A Native American, you mean," came the teasing reply.

"For Chrissakes, Susana, even the Indians came from Asia. *Nobody's* a 'Native American.'"

"Do I detect defensiveness, *cabrón?*"

Carson ignored her and removed the lead rope from Roscoe's halter. He wrapped the cotton rope around Roscoe's front hoof, tied a knot, gave it two tight twists and looped it around the other hoof, tying a second knot. He did the same to the other horse. Then he took off the flank cinches and looped them through the O-rings on the halters, so that the buckled ends dangled loosely together.

"That's a clever way to hobble them," de Vaca said.

"The best way."

"What's the *cincha* for?"

"Listen."

They were silent a moment. As the horse began to graze, there was a faint sound as the two buckles of each cinch clinked together.

"Usually I bring a cowbell with me," said Carson. "But this works almost as well. In the still of the night, you can hear that clinking three hundred yards off. Otherwise, those horses would just vanish in the blackness and we'd never find them."

He sat back in the sand, waiting for her to say something more about Ute Indians.

"You know, *cabrón,*" de Vaca said, her disembodied voice coming to him out of the darkness, "you surprise me a little."

"How's that?"

"Well, you're a hell of a fine person to cross the Jornada del Muerto with, for one thing."

Carson blinked in surprise at the compliment, wondering for a moment whether she was being sarcastic. "We've still got a long way to go. We're barely one-fifth across."

"Yeah, but I can already tell. Without you along, I wouldn't have had a chance."

Carson didn't respond. He still felt there was less than a fifty-percent chance they'd find water. That meant a less than fifty-percent chance of survival.

"So you used to work on a ranch up there?" De Vaca spoke again.

"The Diamond Bar," said Carson. "That was after my dad's ranch went broke."

"Was it big?"

"Yep. My father fancied himself a real wheeler-dealer, always buying up ranches, selling them, buying them back. Usually at a loss. The bank foreclosed on fourteen sections of patent land that had been in my family for a hundred years. Plus, they got grazing leases on two hundred sections of BLM land. It was a hell of a big spread, but most of it was pretty burnt up. My father's fancy cattle and horses just couldn't survive in it."

He lay back. "I remember riding fence as a kid. The outside fence alone was sixty miles, and there were two hundred miles of interior fencing. It took me and my brother the whole summer to ride fence, fixing it as we went. Damn, that was fun. We each had a horse, plus a mule to pack the roll of wire, staples, and stretcher. And our bedrolls and some food. That jack mule was a mean son of a bitch. His name was Bobb. With two bs."

De Vaca laughed.

"We'd camp out as we went along. In the evening, we'd hobble the horses and find a low spot to lay out our bedrolls and light a fire. The first day out we always had a big steak, carried frozen in the saddlebags. If it was big enough, it'd just be thawed out by dinnertime. From then on, it was beans and rice. After dinner we'd lie around, faces to the stars, drinking camp coffee as the fire died down."

Carson stopped talking. It seemed like a vague dream of centuries ago, those memories. And yet the same stars he'd looked at as a kid were still there, above his head.

"It must've been really hard, losing that ranch," de Vaca said quietly.

"It was about the hardest thing that ever happened to me. My whole body and soul was part of that land."

Carson felt a twinge of thirst. He grubbed around in the sand and found a small pebble. He rubbed it on his jeans, then placed it in his mouth.

"I liked the way you lost Nye and those other *pendejos* in the Hummers," de Vaca said.

"They're idiots," Carson replied. "Our real enemy is the desert."

The offhand comment made him think. It had been an easy task to lose the Hummers. Surprisingly easy. They hadn't turned off their lights while tracking him. They hadn't even divided up to search for the track when they reached the edge of the lava flow. Instead they had just barreled southward like lemmings. It surprised him that Nye could be so stupid.

No. Nye wouldn't be so stupid.

For the first time, Carson wondered if Nye was with the Hummers at all. The more he thought about it, the less likely it seemed. But if he wasn't leading the Hummers, then where the hell *was* he? Back at Mount Dragon, managing the crisis?

He realized, with a dull cold thrust of fear, that Nye would be out hunting them. Not in a loud, ungainly Hummer, but on that big paint horse of his.

Shit. He should have taken that horse himself, or, at the very least, driven a nail deep into his hoof.

Cursing his own lack of foresight, he looked at his watch. Three-forty- five.

Nye stopped and dismounted, examining the tracks as they headed north. In the strong yellow glow of his flashlight, he could see the individual grains of sand, almost microscopic in size, piled up at the edges of the tracks. They were fresh and precarious, and no breath of wind had disturbed them. The track could not be more than an hour old. Carson was moving ahead at a slow trot, making no further attempt to hide or confuse his trail. Nye figured the two were about five miles ahead. They would stop and hide at sunrise, someplace where they could rest the horses during the heat of the day.

That's when he would take them.

He remounted Muerto and urged him into a fast trot. The best time to catch them would be just at dawn, before they even realized they were being followed. Hang back, wait for enough light for a clean shot. His own mount was doing fine, a little damp from the exertion but nothing more. He could maintain this pace for another fifty miles. And there were still ten gallons of water.

Suddenly he heard something. He quickly switched off his light and stopped. A gentle breeze blew out of the south, carrying the sound away from him. He stilled his horse, waiting. Five minutes passed, then ten. The breeze shifted a little, and he heard voices raised in argument, then the faint tinking of something that sounded like saddle rigging.

They had stopped already. The fools figured they had shaken their pursuers and could relax. He waited, hardly breathing. The voice—the *other* voice—said nothing.

Nye dismounted and led his horse back behind a gentle ridgeline, where he would be hidden and could graze unmolested. Then he crept back to the lip of the basin. He could hear the murmuring voices in the pool of darkness below.

He lay on his stomach at what he estimated was three hundred yards. The voices were clearer now; a few yards closer and he'd be able to make out what they were saying. Perhaps they were planning how to dispose of the gold. *His* gold. But he wasn't going to let curiosity spoil everything.

But even if they saw him, where were they going to go? At some earlier time, he might actually have enjoyed alerting them to his presence. They would have to run off immediately, of course, with no chance to retrieve their horses. The chase would make good, if brief, sport. There was no better shooting than in an open desert like this. It was little different from hunting ibex in the Hejaz. Except that an ibex moved at forty-five miles an hour, and a human at twelve.

Hunting down that bastard Teece had proved to be excellent sport, much better than he could have anticipated. The dust storm had provided an interesting element of complication, and—when he'd left Muerto standing riderless in the path of the oncoming Hummer—made it easier for him to hide while enticing the investigator to leave his vehicle for a moment. And Teece himself had been an unexpected surprise. The scrawny-looking fellow proved much more resilient than Nye expected, taking cover in the storm, running, resisting to the end. Perhaps he'd been expecting an ambush. In any case, there had been no death-fear in his eyes to savor, no groveling pleas for mercy, there at the end. Now the nancy-boy was safely under several feet of sand, deeper than any vulture's beak or coyote's paw could ever probe. And his filthy sneaking secrets were entombed with him. They would never reach their intended destination.

But all that had taken place a lifetime ago. Before Carson had escaped with his forbidden knowledge. Nye's unique brand of loyalty to GeneDyne, his blind dedication to Scopes, had been incinerated with the explosion. Now, no distractions remained for him.

He checked his watch. Three-forty-five. An hour to first light.

GeneDyne Boston, the headquarters of GeneDyne International, was a postmodern leviathan that towered over the waterfront. Although the Boston Aquarium complained bitterly about being in its shadow throughout most of the daylight hours, the sixty-story tower of black granite and Italian marble was considered one of the finest designs in the city. During the summer months, its atrium was crowded with tourists having their pictures taken beneath the Calder *Mezzoforte*, largest free-hanging mobile in the world. On all but the coldest days, people would line up in front of the building's facade, cameras in hand, to watch five fountains trade arching jets of water in a complex and computerized ballet.

But the biggest draw of all was the virtual-reality screens arranged along the walls of the public lobby. Standing twelve feet high and employing a proprietary high-definition imaging system, the panels displayed pictures of various GeneDyne sites throughout the world: London, Brussels, Nairobi, Budapest. When combined, the displays formed one massive landscape, breathtaking in its realism. Since the images were computer-controlled, they were not static: trees waved in the breeze in front of the Brussels research facility, and red double-decker buses rumbled in front of the London office. Clouds moved across skies that lightened and darkened with the passing of the day. The displays were the most public example of Scopes's advocacy of emerging technologies. When the landscapes were changed, on the fifteenth of each month, the local news broadcasts never failed to run a story on the new images.

From his parking place in the access road along the rear of the tower, Levine craned his neck upward, gazing at the spot where the unbroken facade suddenly receded, in a maze of cubes, toward the building's summit. Those upper floors of the building, he knew, were Scopes's personal domain. No camera had penetrated them since a photo spread in *Vanity Fair* five years earlier. Somewhere, on the sixtieth floor, beyond the security stations and the computer-controlled locks, was Scopes's famous octagonal room.

He continued to look speculatively upward. Then he ducked his head back inside the van and resumed reading a heavy paperbound manual titled *Digital Telephony*.

True to his word, Mime had spent the last two hours preparing Levine, turning to his connections within the byzantine hacker community, reaching out into remote information banks, threading mysterious datastreams. One by one, like some modern-day league of Baker Street Irregulars, strangers had arrived at Levine's hotel-room door. Boys, mostly; urchins and orphans of the hacker underground. One had brought him an ID card, identifying him as one Joseph O'Roarke of the New England Telephone Company. Levine recognized the photo on the card as one of himself that had appeared in *Business Week* two years before. The card attached to a clip on the front pocket of the phone-company uniform that the valet had delivered earlier.

A kid with an impudent curl to his lip had delivered a small piece of electronic equipment that looked somewhat like a garage-door opener. Another had brought several technical manuals—forbidden bibles within the phone phreaking community. Lastly, a slightly older youth had brought him the keys to a telephone-company van waiting below in the lot of the Holiday Inn. Levine was to leave the keys under the dashboard. The youth had said he'd be needing the van around seven in the morning; for what, he had not said.

Mime had remained in frequent modem contact: downloading the building blueprints to Levine and walking him through such security arrangements as he'd been able to ascertain, providing background on the cover Levine would use to gain access to the building. Finally, he'd transmitted a lengthy program to Levine's computer, with instructions on its use.

But now, Levine's laptop was on the seat next to him, powered down, and Mime was in some remote unguessable location. Now, there was nobody but Levine himself.

He shut the manual and closed his eyes a moment, whispering a brief prayer to the close and silent darkness. Then he picked up his laptop, stepped out of the van, and shut its door loudly, walking away without glancing back. The brisk harbor air had a faint overlay of diesel. He tried to move at the ambling, unhurried pace of technicians everywhere. The weight of the orange line-testing telephone bounced awkwardly against his hip. In his hand, he once again went over the various paths the upcoming conversation could take. Then he swallowed hard. There were so many possibilities, and he was prepared for so few.

Stepping up to an unmarked door in the building's backside, he pressed a buzzer. There was a long silence in which Levine struggled to keep from walking away. Then came a squawk of static and a voice said, "Yes?"

"Phone company," Levine said in what he hoped was a flat voice.

"What is it?" the voice did not sound particularly impressed.

"Our computers show the T-1 lines as being down at this location," Levine said. "I'm here to check it out."

"All external lines are down," came the voice. "It's a temporary condition."

Levine hesitated a moment. "You can't shut down leased lines. It's against regulations."

"It's a done deal."

Shit. "What's your name, son?"

Long silence. "Weiskamp."

"All right, Weiskamp. Regulations require that leased point-to-point communications be kept open once established. But listen, I'll tell you what. I don't want to have to go back and fill out a lot of paperwork on you. And I know you and your supervisor don't want to give a long explanation to the FCC. So I'll put a temporary terminator on the lines. Once you bring the system back up, the sites will be reopened automatically." Levine hoped he sounded more convincing to the disembodied voice inside than he did to himself.

No response.

"Otherwise, we're going to have to pull those circuits manually, from the external junction. And they won't be there when you go live again."

A sound like a sigh came through the small speaker beside the buzzer. "Let's see some ID." Levine looked around, spotted a camera lens set inconspicuously above one edge of the doorframe, and angled the badge hanging from his breast pocket in its direction. As he waited, Levine wondered idly why he'd been given the name O'Roarke. He hoped to hell that a Jewish professor from Brookline could imitate a Boston Irish drawl.

There was a loud click, followed by the sound of something heavy being rolled back. The door opened and a tall man peered out, long blond curls falling onto the collar of his gray-and-blue GeneDyne uniform.

"This way," the man said, nodding Levine inside.

Cradling his laptop carefully, Levine followed the guard down a long flight of corrugated iron stairs. From below his feet came the throaty hum of a huge generator. The concrete walls sweated in the humid air.

The guard opened a door marked AUTHORIZED ACCESS ONLY, then stood back, letting Levine enter first. Levine walked into a room crammed floor to ceiling with what he assumed to be digital switches and network relays. Banks of MAUs were arrayed in countless rows on metal racks. Although he knew that the real brain of GeneDyne—the massively-parallel supercomputer that fed the monstrous global network—was housed elsewhere, this room held the guts of the system, the ethernet cables that allowed the building's occupants to interconnect in one vast electronic nervous system.

Up ahead, he saw the outlines of the central relay console. Another guard was sitting at one end of the console, staring at a monitor built into its frame. He turned as Levine stepped in. "Who's this?" he asked, frowning and looking from Levine to Weiskamp.

"Who do you think, fuckin' Tinkerbell?" Weiskamp replied. "He's here about the leased lines."

"I've got to put a temporary terminator on them," Levine said, placing his laptop on the terminal and scanning the complex controls for the jack Mime had told him was sure to be there.

"I never heard nothing about that," the guard said.

"You've never cut them off before," Levine retorted.

The guard mumbled something threatening about "cutting them off," but made no move to stop him. Levine continued to scan the controls, a small warning tone sounding in his head as he did so. This second guard was trouble.

There it was: the network access port. Mime had told him the GeneDyne headquarters was so heavily networked that even the bathroom stalls sported outlet jacks for busy executives to use. Quickly, Levine turned on his laptop and connected it to the access port.

"What are you doing?" the guard at the terminal said suspiciously. He stood up and began to walk toward the laptop.

"Running the termination program," Levine replied.

"Never seen one of you guys use a computer before," the guard said.

Levine shrugged. "You change with the times. Now, you can just send a termination signal down the line to the control unit. Completely automatic."

A phone-company logo popped up on the laptop screen, followed by scrolling lines of data. Despite his nervousness, Levine suppressed a smile. Mime had thought of everything. While the screen was busy displaying complicated nonsense to entertain the guards, a program of Mime's own design was being inserted into the GeneDyne network.

"I think we'd better tell Endicott about this," the suspicious guard said.

The alarm began to ring louder in Levine's head.

"Put a sock in it, will you?" Weiskamp said irritably. "I've heard enough of your noise."

"You know the drill, pal. Endicott is supposed to okay any maintenance work being done on the system from outside."

The laptop chirped, and the phone company logo reappeared. Levine quickly yanked the cable out of the network jack.

"See?" Weiskamp said. "He's done."

"I'll see myself out," Levine said as the other guard reached for an internal phone. "Accounting will send a completed work order once you go back on-line."

Levine returned to the hallway. Weiskamp had not followed him. That was good; one less role he'd have to play later on.

But that other guard, the suspicious one, was probably calling Endicott. And that was bad. If Endicott—whoever he was—decided to call the phone company and check out an employee named O'Roarke . . .

At the top of the stairs, Levine turned right, then moved down a short hallway. The bank of service elevators lay directly ahead, just as Mime had assured him they would.

He entered the nearest service elevator and took it to the second floor. The door whisked open onto an entirely different world. Gone were the drab concrete spaces, the four-foot lengths of fluorescent tubes suspended from the ceilings. Instead, a plush indigo carpet rolled back from the elevator doors and along an elegant corridor. Small violet lights in the ceiling threw colored circles on the thick nap. Levine noticed large black squares lining the walls at regular intervals. He was puzzled until he realized the black squares were actually flat-panel displays, currently dark. During the day, the panels no doubt displayed digitized works of art, floor directories, stock-market quotations—almost anything imaginable.

He stepped out of the elevator, down a deserted corridor, and around another corner to the public elevators. As he pressed the Up button, a chime sounded and one of the bank of black elevator doors whispered open. Looking around one last time, he stepped in. The elevator was carpeted in the same lustrous indigo as the hallway. The side walls were lined in a light, dense wood Levine assumed was teak. The rear wall was glass, affording a spectacular pre-dawn view of Boston Harbor. Countless lights shimmered far below his feet.

Floor, please, said the elevator.

He had to work quickly now. Locating the network hub beneath the emergency telephone, he plugged his laptop into the metal receptacle. Quickly, he turned on the computer's power and typed a short command: curtain.

He waited as Mime's program disconnected the video feed for his elevator's security camera, recorded ten seconds of the adjoining car's video, and patched it in as a loop. Now the security camera would show an empty elevator: appropriate for one that was about to be placed out of service.

Floor, please, said the elevator.

Levine typed another command: cripple.

The elevator lights dimmed, then brightened again. The doors hissed shut. Levine watched the passing floors light up above the door. As the seventh floor slid by, the elevator coasted to a stop.

Attention, please, the voice announced smoothly. *This elevator is out of service.*

Unclipping the portable orange phone from his belt, Levine sat down, his back against the elevator door, the laptop balanced on his knees. Reaching into a pocket, he brought out the odd-looking device the hacker had given him earlier in the evening and attached it to the serial port of the computer. From one end of the device, he untelescoped a short antenna. Then he typed another command: sniff.

The screen cleared, and the response came almost immediately. My main man! I assume that all has gone well and you are now safe in the elevator, between floors seven and eight.

I'm between floors seven and eight, Levine typed back, but I'm not sure all has gone well. Somebody named Endicott may have been alerted to my presence.

I've seen that name before, came the response. I think he's head of security. Just a moment. Once again, the screen went blank.

I've done a brief survey of net activity within the GeneDyne building, Mime replied after several minutes. All seems quiet in the enemy's camp. Are you ready to proceed?

Against his better judgment, Levine replied: Yes.

Very good. Remember what I told you, professor-man. Scopes, and Scopes alone, controls the computer security of the upper floors of the building. That means you have to sneak into his personal cyberspace. I've told you what I know about it. It will be like nothing you could possibly imagine. Nobody knows much about Scopes's cyberspace beyond the few working images he showed years ago at the Center for Advanced Neurocybernetics. At the time, he spoke of a new technology he was developing called 'cypherspace.' It's some kind of three-dimensional environment, his private home base from which he can surf his network at will. Since then, nada. I guess the thing was so bodacious he wanted to hog it all for himself. I've determined from the compiler logs that the program runs to fifteen million lines of code. It's the Big Kahuna of coding, professor-man. I know where the cypherspace server is located, and I can provide a navigation tool that will allow you access to it. But nothing more. You need to be physically inside the building to jack in.

But can't I bring you along, using this remote link?

NFW, came the response. The omnidirectional infrared unit attached to your laptop allows us to communicate only through the standard net, and only from a roaming-enabled access point. GeneDyne's internal transceiver is located on the seventh floor, within spitting distance of your elevator. That's why I parked you there.

Isn't there anything else you can tell me?

I can tell you that the computing resources this
Scopes program soaks up makes the SAC missile-
trajectory routines look like bean-counters. And it
takes up entire terabytes of data storage. Only massive video archives would require that. It may well be
much more real than you can imagine.

Not likely, on a nine-inch laptop screen, Levine replied.

Have you been sleeping through my lectures, professor-man? Scopes is working with much larger
canvases in his headquarters. Or hadn't you noticed?

Levine started blankly at the words. Then he realized what
Mime meant.

He looked up from the laptop. The view out of the elevator
was breathtaking. But there was something odd that, in his
haste, he hadn't noticed when he first entered. The stars in
the eastern sky hung over the quiet scene. He could see the
harbor spread out below him, a million tiny pinpoints of light
in the warm Massachusetts darkness.

Yet he was only on the seventh floor. The view he was
seeing should be from a much higher vantage point.

It was no wall of glass he was staring out of. It was a wall-
sized flat-panel display, currently showing a virtual image of
an imaginary view outside the GeneDyne building.

I understand, he typed.

Good. I have marked your elevator as being out of
service and under repair. That should keep prying
eyes away. However, I would not stay longer than
necessary. I'll remain on the net here as long as I

can, updating its repair status from time to time, to avoid any suspicion. That's all, I'm afraid, that I can do to protect you.

Thank you, Mime.

One more word. You said something about this not being a game. I would ask you to remember your own advice. GeneDyne takes a dim view of intruders, within cyberspace or without. You're embarked on an extremely dangerous journey. If they find you, I will be forced to flee. There will be nothing I can do for you, and I have no intention of being a martyr a second time. You see, if they find me, they'll take my computers. If that happens, I might as well be dead.

I understand, Levine typed again.

There was a pause. It is possible that we may never speak again, professor. I would like to say that I have valued this acquaintance with you.

And I as well.

MTRRUTMY;MTWABAYB;AMYBIHHAHBTDKYAD.

Mime?

Just a sentimental old Irish saying, Professor Levine. Good-bye.

The screen winked to black. There was no time now to decipher Mime's parting acronym. Taking a deep breath, Levine typed another brief command:

Lancet.

"What is it?" de Vaca asked as Carson sat up abruptly.

"I just smelled something," he whispered. "I think it's a horse." He licked his finger and held it up in the drifting air.

"One of ours?"

"No. The wind's from the wrong direction. I swear to God, I just smelled a sweaty horse. From behind us."

There was a silence. Carson felt a sudden cold feeling in the pit of his stomach. It was Nye. There was no other explanation. And the man was very close.

"Are you sure—?"

Quickly, Carson covered her mouth with one hand, and with the other drew her ear close to his lips.

"Listen to me. Nye is waiting out there somewhere. He didn't go with the Hummers. Once dawn breaks, we're dead. We've got to get out of here, and we've got to do it in utter silence. Do you understand?"

"Yes," came the strained reply.

"We'll move toward the sound of our horses. But we'll have to walk by feel. Don't just plant one foot in front of the other; let it rest an inch above the ground until you're sure you have a clear step. If we step on some dry grass or a piece of brush, he'll hear it. We'll have to untie the hobbles without making a sound. Don't get on your horse at first—lead it away. We'd better go east, back toward the lava fields. It's our only hope of losing him. Head ninety degrees to the right of the North Star."

He felt, more than saw, de Vaca's head rise and fall in a vigorous nod.

"I'll be going the same way, but don't try to follow me. It's too dark for that. Just try to maintain as straight a course as possible. Keep low, because he might glimpse you moving against the stars. We'll be able to see each other at first light."

"But what if he hears—?"

"If he comes after us, run like hell for the lava. When you get there, ditch your horse, whack him on the ass, and hide as best you can. Like as not he'll follow your horse." He paused. "That's the best I can do. Sorry."

There was a brief silence. Carson realized that de Vaca was trembling slightly, and he released her. His hand groped for hers, found it, squeezed.

They moved slowly toward the tinking sound of the horses. Carson knew that their chances of survival, never good, were now minute. It had been bad enough without Nye. But the security director had found them. And he'd found them very quickly—he hadn't been fooled for a moment by their detour on the lava. He had the better horse. And that damned wicked rifle.

Carson realized he had grossly underestimated Nye.

As he crept across the sand, a sudden image of Charley, his half-Ute great-uncle, came back into his mind. He wondered what synaptic trick had brought Charley to mind, now of all times.

Most of the old man's stories had been about a Ute ancestor named Gato who had undertaken numerous livestock raids against the Navajos and U.S. cavalry. Charley had loved to recount those raids. There were other stories about Gato's tracking exploits, his skill with a horse. And the various tricks he'd used to throw off pursuers, usually of the official variety. Charley had recounted all these stories with quiet relish, there in the rocking chair before the fire.

Carson found Roscoe in the dark and began untying his hobbles, whispering soothing words to forestall any inquiring whinnies. The horse stopped grazing and pricked up his ears. Carson gently stroked the horse's neck, slipped off the lead rope, and carefully removed the cinch from the halter. Then, with infinite care, he clipped the bullsnap on the halter and looped the lead rope around the saddle horn. He stopped to listen: the silence of the night was absolute.

Guiding the horse by the halter strap, Carson led him westward.

One of his legs had gone to sleep, and Nye carefully shifted position, cradling the rifle between his arms as he did so. The faintest glow was appearing in the east, over the Fra Cristóbal Mountains. Another ten minutes, maybe less. He glanced around into the darkness, satisfying himself once again that he was well hidden. He looked back behind the rise and saw the dim outlines of his horse, still standing at attention, awaiting his next command. He smiled to himself. Only the English really knew how to train their horses. This American cowboy mystique was bollocks. They knew next to nothing about horses.

He turned his attention back to the broad, shallow hollow. In a few minutes the ambient light would show him what he needed to see.

With infinite care he slid back the safety on the Holland & Holland. A stationary, perhaps sleeping, target at three hundred yards. He smiled at the thought.

The light grew behind the Fra Cristóbals, and Nye scanned the basin for dark shapes that would indicate horses or people. There was a scattering of soapweed yucca, looking damnably like people in the half light. But he could see nothing large enough to be a horse.

He waited, hearing the slow strong beat of his heart. He was pleased at the steadiness of his breathing, at the dryness of his palm against the rifle's buttstock.

It slowly began to dawn on him that the basin was empty.

And the voice came again: a low, cynical snicker. He turned, and there was a shadow in the half light.

"Who the hell are you?" Nye murmured.

The chuckle built in intensity, until the laughter echoed across the landscape. And Nye recognized the laugh as being remarkably like his own.

In an instant, Boston faded to black.

The breathtaking view from the elevator was gone. The landscape had seemed so real that, for a horrible instant, Levine wondered if he had suddenly been struck blind. Then he realized the subdued lights of the elevator were still on, and it was merely the wall-sized display in front of him that had gone dark. He stretched his hand forward to touch the surface. It was hard and opaque, similar to the panels he had seen in the GeneDyne corridor but much larger.

Then, suddenly, the elevator was twice as large as it had been. Several businessmen in suits, briefcases in hand, stared down at him. Levine almost knocked the computer from his lap and jumped to his feet before he realized that, again, this was simply an image projected on the display: an image that made the elevator deeper, and populated it with imaginary GeneDyne staffers. Levine marveled at the video resolution necessary to create such a lifelike image.

Then the image changed again, and the blackness of space yawned before him. Below, the gray surface of the moon spun lazily in the clear ether, revealing its pocked surface without shame. Behind it, Levine could see the faint curve of the Earth, a blue marble hanging in the distant black. The sensation of depth was profound; Levine had to close his eyes for a minute to allow the vertigo to pass.

He realized what was happening. As Mime's lancet program drilled into Scopes's private server, it must have interrupted the normal routine of the software bindery controlling the elevator images. Temporarily without control, the various available images were being displayed one by one, like a fantastically expensive slide show. Levine wondered what other vistas Scopes had programmed into the display for the amusement or consternation of the elevator passengers.

The image changed again, and Levine found himself staring at a bizarre landscape: a three-dimensional construction of walkways and buildings, rising from a vast, apparently bottomless space. He appeared to be gazing at this landscape from a terrazzo platform, tiled in muted browns, reds, and yellows. From the end of the platform, a series of bridges and walkways led in many directions: some up, some down, and some continuing horizontally, falling away in various directions to spaces inconceivably vast. Rising among the walkways were dozens of enormous structures, dark with countless tiny illuminated windows. Running between the buildings were great streams of colored light that forked and flickered into the distance, like lightning.

The landscape was beautiful, even awe-inspiring in its complexity, but in a few minutes Levine grew impatient, wondering what was taking Mime's program so long to access GeneDyne cyberspace. He shifted his position on the floor of the elevator.

The landscape moved.

Levine looked down. He realized that he had inadvertently

moved the rolling trackball that was built into the keyboard of his laptop. Placing his hand on the trackball, he rolled it forward.

Immediately, the terrazzo surface in front of him fell backward, and he found himself balanced on the very edge of space, a slender walkway ahead of him, floating like gossamer in the black void. The smoothness of the video response on the huge display made the sense of forward motion almost unbearably real.

Levine took a deep breath. He wasn't simply looking at a video image this time: he was inside Scopes's cyberspace.

Levine removed his hands from the laptop for a minute, steadying himself. Then, carefully, he placed one hand on the trackball and the other on the cursor keys of his laptop. Painstakingly, he began the task of learning how to control his own movement within the bizarre landscape. The immensity of the elevator screen—and the remarkably lifelike resolution of the image itself—made comprehension difficult. Always, he was troubled by vertigo. Though he knew he was only in cyberspace, the fear of falling off the terrazzo platform into the depths below kept his movements excessively slow and deliberate.

At last, he set the laptop aside and massaged his back. Idly, he glanced at his watch, and was shocked to learn that an hour had gone by. One hour, and he hadn't moved from the platform he'd started on. The fascination of this computer environment was both amazing and alarming. But it was time to find Scopes.

As his hands returned to the laptop, Levine became aware of a low, sighing sound, almost like singing. It was coming from the same speakers the elevator had used to announce the floors. When it had started, Levine could not say; perhaps it had been there all along. He was unable to take even a remote guess at its purpose.

Levine found himself growing concerned. He had to find

Scopes in this three-dimensional representation of GeneDyne cyberspace, reason with him, explain the desperate situation. But how? Clearly this cyberspace was too vast to just wander around in. And even if he found Scopes, how would he recognize him?

He had to think the problem through. Vast and complex as this landscape was, it had to serve some purpose, have some design. In the past several years, Scopes had been extremely secretive about his cyberspace project. Little was known beyond the fact that Scopes was creating it to make his own extensive journeys through the interconnected network of GeneDyne computers easier.

Yet it seemed obvious that everything—the surfaces, shapes, and perhaps sounds—represented the hardware, software, and data of the GeneDyne computer network.

Levine took a walkway at random and moved carefully along it, trying to accustom himself to the bizarre sense of motion imparted by the vast screen in front of him. He was on a bridge without a railing, tiled in its own complicated pattern. The pattern would mean something, but he had no idea what: different byte configurations, or sequences of binary numbers?

The walkway snaked between several buildings of differing shapes and sizes, ending at last in a massive silver door. He moved to the door and tried to go through it. The eerie, floating music seemed to get louder, but nothing happened. He returned to an intersection and took another walkway, which crossed one of the rivers of colored light that streamed between the buildings. He stepped into the river, and it became a torrent of hexadecimal code, streaming past at a dizzying rate. He quickly stepped out of the stream.

He had discovered one thing: The streams of light were data-transfer operations.

So far, he had used only the trackball and cursor keys of his laptop. The cypherspace program would certainly recognize keystrokes of one form or another: mnemonics, commands, or shortcuts. He typed the sentence universally used by coders trying out new computer languages: Hello, world.

When he hit the enter key, the words "Hello, world" sang out in a musical whisper from the speakers. They echoed and reechoed through the vast spaces until dying away at last beneath the strange musical sighing.

There was no answer.

Scopes! he typed. The word rang out, dying away like a cry. Again, no answer.

Levine wished Mime were there to help him. He looked at his watch again; another hour had passed, and he was just as lost now as he'd been at the beginning. He looked away from the screen, and around the tiny elevator. He did not have unlimited time to explore. He'd wandered about long enough. Now he had to think fast.

What did one do when one was stuck in an application? Or in a computer game?

One asks for help.

Help, he typed.

Ahead of him, the landscape changed subtly. Something formed out of nothing, appearing at the far end of the walkway. It circled, then stopped, as if noticing Levine. Then, it began moving toward him with remarkable speed.

When he felt he had put sufficient distance between himself and the basin, Carson released Roscoe's halter and climbed into the saddle. He found himself going over, again and again, his first confrontation with Nye in the desert. He remembered the cruel laughter that had floated over the sands toward him.

He found himself waiting to hear that laugh again—much closer now—and the sharp sound of a rifle bullet snugging into its chamber. To distract himself he turned his thoughts back to his great-uncle and his stories about Gato. He remembered a story about his ancestor and the telegraph. When at last he'd figured out how it worked, Gato cut the wires, then strung them back up with tiny thongs of leather to conceal the break. It had driven the cavalry crazy, his great-uncle told him.

Gato had a lot of tricks to throw off trackers. He would ride down streams and then ride out of them backward. He would make phony horse trails across slickrock and into dangerous trap canyons. Or over cliffs, using a horseshoe and a stone . . .

Carson racked his brains. *What else?*

It was growing light in the eastern sky. At any moment Nye would discover them gone. That gave them a half hour's lead, at most. Unless Nye had learned of their deception already. He was too damn close; they *had* to make time.

As the light came up he scanned the horizon. With enormous relief, he made out the small figure of de Vaca, gray against black, trotting perhaps a quarter mile ahead of him. He turned toward her, urging Roscoe into an easy lope.

The real problem was that, even in lava, iron horseshoes left clear impressions on the stones. A horse weighed half a ton, and was balanced on four skinny iron shoes that left sharp white marks all over the rock. Once you knew what to look for, it didn't take any special talent to track a horse over rock; it was far easier, for example, than tracking a horse in shortgrass prairie. Nye had already demonstrated he had more than enough talent. But at least the lava would slow Nye down.

Carson slowed, matching the gait of de Vaca's horse. The image of his great-uncle returned: old Charley's face, laughing in the glow of the fire as he rocked back and forth. Laughing about Gato. Gato, the trickster. Gato, the bedeviler of white men.

"God, am I glad to see you," de Vaca said. She grabbed his hand briefly as they trotted.

The warmth of her hand, the touch of another person after the long creeping journey in the dark, brought a surge of renewed hope to his soul. He scanned the lava flow that lay before them, a black, jagged line against the horizon.

"Let's move well into that lava," he said. "I think I have an idea."

The object stopped directly in front of him. Levine noticed with disbelief that it seemed to be a small dog, apparently a miniature collie. Levine stared, fascinated, marveling at the lifelike way with which the computer-generated animal wagged its tail and stood at attention. Even the black nose glistened in the otherworldly light that surrounded it.

Who are you? Levine typed.

Fido, the voice said. It raised its head, displaying a collar from which a small name tag hung. Looking closer, Levine saw the engraved words: PHIDO. PROPERTY OF BRENTWOOD SCOPES. Almost despite himself, Levine smiled. Scopes's interests, after all, had a lot in common with hackers and phone phreaks.

I'm looking for Brent Scopes, Levine wrote.

I see, said the voice.

Can you take me to him?

No.

Why not?

I don't know where he is.

What are you?

I am a dog.

Levine gritted his teeth.

What kind of program are you? he asked.

I am the front end for an AI-based help system. However, the help system was never enabled, so I'm afraid I really can't provide any assistance at all.

Then what is your purpose?

Are you interested in my functionality? I am a program, written by Brent Scopes in his own version of C++, which he calls C³. It is an object-oriented language with visual extensions. It is primarily used for three-dimensional modeling, with built-in hooks for polygon shading, light-sourcing, and various rendering tools. It also directly supports wide-area network communications, using a variant of the TCP/IP protocol.

This was getting Levine nowhere. *Why can't you help me?* he typed.

As I said, the help subsystem was never imple-
mented. As an object-oriented program, I adhere to
the tenets of data encapsulation and inheritance. I
can access certain base classes of objects, like the
AI subroutines and data-storage algorithms. But I
cannot access the internal workings of other objects,
just as they cannot access mine without the necessary code.

Levine nodded to himself. He wasn't surprised that the
help system had never been completed; after all, Brent
wouldn't need help himself, and nobody else was supposed to
be wandering around his Cypherspace program. Probably
Phido was one of the first elements Brent had put together,
back in the early days before he'd decided to seal the lid of
secrecy on his creation. Before he'd decided to keep this incredible world to himself.

So what good are you? Levine wrote.

From time to time, I keep Mr. Scopes company. I
see you are not Mr. Scopes, however.

How do you see that?

Because you are lost. If you were Mr. Scopes—

Never mind. Levine thought it better not to move
in that direction. He still did not know what kind of
security mechanisms, if any, were built into Cypherspace.

He thought for a minute. Here was an object-oriented companion with artificial-intelligence links. Like the old pseu-

dotherapeutic program ELIZA, taken to the ultimate limit. Phido. It was Scopes's idea of a cyberspace dog.

Can't you do anything? he typed.

I can offer deliciously cynical quotes for your enjoyment.

That made sense. Scopes would never lose his obsessive love of aphorisms.

For example: "If you pick up a starving dog, and make him prosperous, he will not bite you. This is the principal difference between a dog and a man." Mark Twain. Or: "It is not enough to succeed; others must fail." Gore—

Please shut up.

Levine could feel his impatience growing. He was here to find Scopes, not bandy words with a program in this endless maze of cyberspace. He glanced at his watch: another half hour wasted. He followed the path to another juncture, then took one of the branching paths, wandering among the immense structures. The small dog followed silently at his heels.

Then Levine saw something unusual: a particularly massive building, set well apart from the others. Despite its immense size and central location, no colored bands of light played from its roof toward the other structures.

What is that building? he asked.

I do not know, Phido replied.

He looked at the building more closely. Although its lines were almost too perfect—the work of a computer's hand, within a cybernetic world—he recognized the famous silhouette without difficulty.

The GeneDyne Boston building.

An image of the building inside the computer. What did it represent? The answer came to him quickly: it was the cyberspace re-creation of the computer system inside the GeneDyne headquarters. The network, the home-office terminals, even the headquarters security system, would be inside that rendering. The buildings around him represented the various GeneDyne locations throughout the world. No streams of colored light were flowing from the headquarters roof because all outside communications with the other GeneDyne installations had been cut off. Had Mime been able to learn more about the workings of Scopes's program, perhaps he could have placed Levine inside, saving valuable time.

Levine approached the building curiously, taking a descending pathway to the base of the structure and approaching the front door. As he maneuvered himself against it, the strange music changed to an offensive buzz. The door was locked. Levine peered through the glass into the lobby. There, rendered in breathtaking detail, was the Calder mobile, the security desk. There were no people, but he noted with amazement that banks of CRT screens behind the security desk were displaying images from remote video cameras. And the feed he was viewing was undoubtedly live.

How do I get inside? he asked Phido.

Beats me, Phido said.

Levine thought for a moment, combing his spotty knowledge of modern computing techniques.

Phido. You are a help object.

Correct.

And you stated you were a front end to other objects and subroutines.

Correct.

And what does that mean, exactly?

I am the interface between the user and the program.

So you receive commands and pass them on to other programs for action.

Yes.

In the form of keystrokes?

That is correct.

And the only person who has used you is Brent Scopes.

Yes.

Do you retain these keystrokes, or have access to them?

Yes.

Have you been to this location before?

Yes.

Please duplicate all the keystrokes that took place here.

Phido spoke: "Insanity: A perfectly rational adjustment to the insane world." Laing.

There was a chime from the speakers. Then the door clicked open.

Levine smiled, realizing that the aphorisms themselves must be security pass phrases. Yet another use for The Game they had once made their own. Besides, he realized, quotations made excellent passwords; they were long and complicated and could never be hit upon by accident or by a dictionary attack. Scopes knew them by heart, and therefore never had to write them down. It was perfect.

Phido was going to be more helpful than even Phido realized.

Quickly, Levine maneuvered himself inside with the trackball and moved past the guard station. He paused a minute, trying to recall the layout of the headquarters blueprints Mime had downloaded to him earlier in the evening. Then he moved past the main elevator bank toward a secondary security station. Inside the real building, he knew, this station would be heavily manned. Beyond was a smaller bank of elevators. Approaching the closest one, he pressed its call button. As the doors opened, Levine maneuvered himself inside. He typed the number 60 on the numeric keypad of his laptop: the top floor of the GeneDyne headquarters, the location of Scopes's octagonal room.

Thank you, said the same neutral voice that had controlled his elevator. Please enter the security password now.

Phido, run the keystrokes for this location, Levine typed.

"One should forgive one's enemies, but not before they are hanged." Heine.

As the cyberspace elevator rose to the sixtieth floor, Levine tried not to think about the paradoxical situation he was immersed in: sitting cross-legged in an elevator, stopped between floors, jacked into a computer network within which he was moving in *another* elevator, in simulated three-dimensional space.

The virtual elevator slowed, then stopped. With the trackball, Levine moved out into the corridor beyond. At the end of the long corridor, he could see another guard station under the watchful glare of an immense number of closed-circuit screens. Undoubtedly, every location on the sixtieth floor and the floors immediately beneath was under active video. He approached the monitors, scrutinizing each one in turn. They showed rooms, corridors, massive computer arrays—even the very guard station he was at—but nothing that could be Scopes.

From Mime's security blueprints, Levine knew that the octagonal room was in the center of the building. No window views for Scopes; the only view he was interested in was the view from a computer screen.

Levine moved past the guard station and veered left down a dimly lit corridor. At the far end was another guard station. Moving past it, Levine found himself in a short hallway, doors flanking both sides. At the far end was a massive door, currently closed.

That door, Levine knew, led to the octagon itself.

With the trackball, Levine maneuvered down the corridor and against the door itself. It was locked.

Phido, he wrote, run the keystrokes for this location.

Are you going to leave me now? the cyber-dog asked. Levine thought he sensed a plaintiveness to the question.

Why do you ask? he typed.

I cannot follow you through that door.

Levine hesitated. I'm sorry, Phido, but I must continue. Please play back the keystrokes for this location.

Very well. "If all the girls who attended the Harvard-Yale game were laid end to end, I wouldn't be at all surprised." Dorothy Parker.

With a distinct click, the massive black door sprang ajar. Levine paused, took a deep breath, and steadied his hand on the trackball. Then, very slowly, he maneuvered himself forward into what he knew must be Scopes's mysterious Cypherspace.

Nye stood in the center of the basin, Muerto's reins in his hand. The story of his humiliation was written clearly in the sand and grass. Somehow, Carson and the woman must have sensed his presence. They'd snuck over to their horses and led them away—without his hearing a bloody thing. It was almost inconceivable that they could have pulled it off. Yet the tracks did not lie.

He turned. The shadow was still by his side, but when he looked at it directly it seemed to disappear.

He walked to the edge of the basin. The two had headed east toward the lava beds, where, no doubt, they hoped to lose him. Although riding through the lava beds was slow work, Nye would have little trouble tracking them. With two gallons of water, it was only a matter of time before their horses would start to weaken. There was no hurry. The edge of the Jornada desert was still almost one hundred miles away.

Nye swung into the saddle and began to follow. They had walked their horses for a while and then mounted. The tracks gradually separated—was it a trick?—and Nye followed the heavier set of impressions, knowing they must be Carson's.

The sun broke over the mountains, throwing immense shadows toward the horizon. As it boiled up into the sky, the shadows began to shrink, and the smell of hot sand and creosote bush rose in the air. It was going to be a hot day. A very hot day. And nowhere was it going to be hotter than in the black lava beds of El Malpaís.

He had plenty of water and ammunition. Their hour or so of lead time couldn't amount to more than four or five miles. That gap would narrow considerably as the lava slowed them down. Though he no longer had the advantage of total surprise, their awareness of his presence would force them to travel during the heat of the day.

A half mile from the lava, the two tracks joined again. Nye followed them to the base of the flow. Without even dismounting, he could see the whitish marks on the basalt where the iron shoes had scrabbled onto the rock. Now that the sun was up, following these marks would be easy.

It was still early morning, and the temperature was a comfortable eighty degrees. In an hour it would be a hundred; in another hour, a hundred and five. At four thousand feet of altitude, with a clear sky, the sun's heat would be overwhelming in its intensity. The only shade anywhere was the shadow under a horse's belly. If he didn't get them by nightfall, the desert would.

The lava bed lay ahead in great ropy masses, stretching into the limitless distance. In places there were pits of broken lava, fractured hexagonal blocks where the roofs of subterranean tubes had collapsed. In other areas there were pressure ridges where the ancient flow had shoved up rafts and blocks of lava into enormous piles. Already the ground was shimmering as the black basalt absorbed the sunlight, reemitting it as heat.

Muerto picked his way across the flow with care. The horse's hooves rang and clattered among the rocks. A lizard shot off into a crack. Thinking about Carson and de Vaca in this heat with so little water made Nye thirsty. He took a satisfying drink from one of the water bags. The water was still cold and had a faint, pleasing taste of flax.

The shadow was still there, walking tirelessly beside his horse, visible only indirectly. It had not spoken again. Nye found himself taking comfort in its presence.

After a few miles, he dismounted to follow the marks with greater ease.

Carson and de Vaca had continued eastward toward a low cinder cone. The cone was open at the west end and almost flush with the lava flow, its sides rising like two points into the fierce blue sky. The tracks headed straight for the low opening.

Nye felt a spreading flush of triumph. Carson and the woman would be going into the cinder cone for only one reason: to take refuge. They thought they had shaken Nye by retreating back into the lava. Realizing that crossing the desert during daylight was suicide, they were going to wait in the cinder cone until darkness, and continue their journey under cover of night.

Then he noticed a wisp of smoke curling up from the inner

side of the cinder cone. Nye stopped, staring in disbelief. Carson must have caught something, most likely a rabbit, and they were busy feasting. He examined the trail very carefully, and then cut for sign, checking for any possible tracks or tricks. Carson had proven to be resourceful. Perhaps there was a trail out on the far side.

Leaving Muerto at a safe distance, Nye moved cautiously, with infinite patience, remaining hidden as he circled the cinder cone. The smoke, the tracks, could be a trap of some kind.

But there was no sign of a trap. And there were no tracks leading away. The two had ridden into the cinder cone and not come out.

Immediately, Nye knew what he must do. Climb the back side of the cinder cone, where the walls of lava reared upward in jagged thrusts. From that height, he could shoot down anywhere into the cone. There would be no place to take cover.

Returning for Muerto, he moved in a slow arc, leading the horse around to the southeastern end of the cone. There, in the close and silent shadows, he ordered Muerto to stand. With great care, Nye began to creep up the side of the cinder cone, his rifle slung over his back and an extra box of ammunition in his pocket. The cinders were small and hot beneath his hands, and they rustled as he moved up the slope, but he knew that the noise would not reach inside.

Within minutes, he neared the lip of the cone. Easing the safety off the Holland & Holland, he crawled to the edge.

A hundred feet below, he could make out a smoldering fire. Draped on a chamisa bush was a bandanna that had apparently been washed and let out to dry. A T-shirt was hanging next to it. It was definitely their camp, and they had not moved on. But where the hell were they?

He glanced around. There was a hole in the side of the cinder cone, lying in deep shadow. They must be resting in the shade. And the horses? Carson would have left them hobbled some distance away to graze.

Nye sat down to wait, easing the curve of his cheek into the rifle stock. When they came out of the shade, he would pick them off.

Forty minutes went by. Then Nye saw the shadow that was now always at his side begin to stir impatiently.

"What is it?" he whispered.

"You are a fool," the voice whispered. "You are a fool, a fool, a—"

"What?" Nye whispered.

"A man and a woman, dying of thirst, use their last water to wash a bandanna," the voice said in a mocking tone. "In the hundred-degree heat, they light a fire. Fool, fool, fool . . ."

Nye felt a prickly sensation race up his neck. The voice was right. The rotter, the bloody thieving rotter, had managed to slip away a second time. Nye stood with a curse and slid down the inside of the cinder cone, no longer making any attempt to conceal his presence. The shadowy hole in the side of the cone was empty. Nye walked around the camp, taking in at first hand its obvious phoniness. The bandanna and the T-shirt were two expendable items, designed to make him think the camp was occupied. There was no evidence that Carson and de Vaca had stopped at all, although he could see marks indicating that horses had been inside for a brief period. The fire had been hastily built with green sticks of greasewood, guaranteed to smoke.

They were now an hour and forty minutes ahead. Or perhaps a little less, considering the time it must have taken to arrange this irritating little tableau.

He returned to the opening of the cinder cone and began trying to discover where they had gone, fighting to keep anger and panic from making him sloppy. How could he have missed their exit tracks?

He moved around the periphery of the cone until he came

again to the marks going in. He carefully examined the vicinity of the entrance. He followed the entrance marks, then traced them backward away from the cinder cone. Then again, and yet again. Then he cut for sign a hundred yards from the cinder cone, circling the entire formation, hoping to pick up the trail that he knew must lead out.

But there was no trail leading out. They had ridden into the cinder cone, and then vanished. Carson had tricked him. But how?

"Tell me, how?" he said aloud, spinning toward the shadow.

It moved away from him, a dark presence in the periphery of his vision, remaining scornfully silent.

He went back into the mock camp and checked the nearby hole again, more carefully this time. Nothing. He stepped backward, examining the ground. There were some patches of windblown sand and cinder fields on the floor of the cinder cone. To one side there was a small disturbed area that he had not examined before. Nye carefully knelt on his hands and knees, his eyes inches from the sand. Some of the marks showed skidding and twisting. Carson had done something to the horses in this spot, worked on them in some way. And here was where the tracks ended.

Not quite. He found a faint, partial imprint of a hoof in a patch of sand a few yards away. It showed, very clearly, why there were no longer any marks on the rocks.

The son of a bitch had pulled the iron shoes off his horses.

Within a few miles, Carson figured, they should reach the edge of the lava. He knew that it was critically important to get the horses onto sand again as soon as possible. Even though they were leading the horses rather than riding them, the horses' hooves would quickly get sore. If they walked on lava long enough without wearing shoes, they would go lame. And then there was always the very real possibility of catastrophe—a horse cracking a hoof to the quick, or perhaps bruising the frog, the soft center of the hoof.

He knew that the naked hooves also left marks on the rock: tiny flakes and streaks of keratin from the hooves; the odd overturned stone; the crushed blade of grass; the stray imprint in a small patch of windblown sand. But these marks were extremely subtle. At the least, they would slow Nye down. Slow him considerably. Still, Carson dared remain on the lava only a few more miles. Then they would have to put the shoes back on or ride in sand.

He had decided to head north again. If they were to get out of the Jornada alive, they really had no choice. Instead of going due north, however, they had trended northeast, making sharp turns, frequent zigzags, and once doubling back in an effort to confuse and irritate Nye. They also walked their horses some distance apart, preferring two fainter trails to a single more obvious one.

Carson pinched the skin on his horse's neck.

"What's that for?" de Vaca asked.

"I'm checking to see if the horse is getting dehydrated," Carson replied.

"How?"

"You pinch the skin on the neck and see how fast the wrinkle springs back. A horse's skin loses elasticity as he becomes thirsty."

"Another trick you learned from this Ute ancestor you told me about?" de Vaca asked.

"Yes," Carson replied testily. "As it so happens, yes."

"Seems you picked up a lot more from him than you'd like to admit."

Carson felt his irritation with this subject growing. "Look," he said, "if you're so eager to turn me into an Indian, go ahead. I know what I am."

"I'm beginning to think that's exactly what you *don't* know."

"So now we're going to have a session about my identity problem? If that's your idea of psychotherapy, I can see why you failed as a psychiatrist."

Immediately, de Vaca's expression became less playful. "I didn't fail, *cabrón*. I ran out of money, remember?"

They rode in silence.

"You should be proud of your Native American blood," she said at last. "Like I am of mine."

"You're no Indian."

"Guess again. The *conquistadores* married the *conquistas*. We're all brothers and sisters, *cabrón*. Most old Hispanic families in New Mexico have some Aztec, Nahuatl, Navajo, or Pueblo blood."

"Count me out of your multicultural utopia," Carson said. "And stop calling me *cabrón*."

De Vaca laughed. "Just consider how your embarrassing, whiskey-drinking great-uncle is saving our lives right now. And then think about what you have to be proud of."

It was ten o'clock, the sun climbing high in the sky. The conversation was wasting valuable energy. Carson assessed his own thirst. It was a constant dull ache. For the moment it was merely irritating, but as the hours passed it would grow constantly worse. They had to get off the lava and start looking for water.

He could feel the heat rising from the flow in flickering waves. It came through the soles of his shoes. The plain of black, cracked lava stretched on all sides, dipping and rising, ending at last at a sharp, clean horizon. Here and there, Carson could see mirages shimmering on the surface of the lava. Some looked like blue pools of water, vibrating as if tickled by a playful wind; others were bands of parallel vertical lines, distant mountains of dream-lava. Still others hovered just above the horizon, lens-shaped reflections of the rock below. It was a surreal landscape.

As noon approached, everything turned white in the heat. The only exception was the surrounding expanse of lava, which seemed to get blacker, as if it were swallowing the light. No matter which way Carson turned, he could feel the sun's precise angle and location in the sky, the source of an almost unbearable pressure. The heat had thickened the air, made it feel heavy and claustrophobic.

He glanced up. Several birds were riding a thermal far to the northwest, circling lazily at a high altitude. Vultures, probably hovering over a dead antelope. There wasn't much to eat in this desert, even for vultures.

He looked more carefully at the black specks drifting high in the sky. There was a reason why they were circling and not landing. It meant there might be another scavenger on the kill. Coyotes, perhaps.

That was very important.

"Let's head northwest," he said. They made a sharp turn, staying apart to confuse Nye and heading toward the distant birds.

He remembered being extremely thirsty once before. He had been working a remote part of the ranch known as Coal Canyon. He'd ridden down the canyon tracking a lost bull— one of his dad's prize Brahmans—expecting to camp and find water at the Ojo del Perillo. The Ojo had been unexpectedly dry, and he'd spent a waterless night. Toward morning his horse became tangled in his stake rope, panicked, and bowed a tendon. Carson had been forced to walk thirty miles out without water, in heat nearly equal to this. He remembered getting to Witch Well and drinking until he threw up, drinking again and throwing up, and still being utterly unable to slake his terrible thirst. When he finally got home it was old

Charley who came to his rescue with a foul potion made out of water, salt and soda collected from a salt pan near the ranch house, horsehair ash, and various burned herbs. Only after he drank it did the unbearable sensation of thirst leave his body.

Carson realized now that he had been suffering from an extreme electrolyte imbalance brought on by dehydration. Charley's evil potion had corrected it.

There were plenty of salt pans in the Jornada desert. He would have to remember to collect some of the bitter salts for that time when they found water.

His thoughts were interrupted by a sudden buzzing sound in the lava directly ahead. For a moment he wondered if he was already hallucinating from thirst. But then Roscoe's head jerked up, and the horse, shaken out of his lethargy, began to prance in anxiety.

"Easy," Carson said. "Easy, boy. Rattlesnake up ahead," he warned in a louder tone.

De Vaca halted. The buzzing became more insistent.

"Jesus," she said, backing up.

Carson searched the ground ahead with careful eyes. The snake would be in the shade; it was far too hot in the sun, even for a rattlesnake.

Then he saw it; a fat diamondback coontail coiled in an S-curve, backed up against the base of a yucca about twenty feet away, its head a good twelve inches off the ground. It was a medium-sized rattler, perhaps two and a half feet long. The snake's coils were slowly sliding against each other while it held steady in striking position. The rattling had temporarily stopped.

"I've got an idea," Carson said. "This time, one of my own."

Giving his horse's lead to de Vaca, he walked carefully away from the snake until he found a suitable mesquite bush. Breaking off two forked branches, he removed the thorns and stobs, then walked back toward de Vaca.

"Oh my God, cabrón, don't tell me you're going to catch the *hijo de perra*."

"I'm going to need your help in just a second."

"I hope you know what the hell you're doing."

"We used to catch snakes like this all the time on the ranch. You cut off their heads, gut 'em, and coil them in the fire. Taste like chicken."

"Right, with a side of Rocky Mountain oysters. I've heard those stories before."

Carson laughed. "The truth is, we tried it once but the damn snake was all bones. And we burned the shit out of it in the fire, which didn't help."

Carson approached the snake. It began buzzing again, coiling into a tense spring, its head swaying ever so slightly. Carson could see the forked tongue flickering a deadly warning. He knew the maximum length of the strike was the length of the snake: two and a half feet. He stayed well beyond that, maneuvering the forked end of the stick toward it. It was unlikely the snake would strike at the stick. They struck only when they sensed body heat.

He moved quickly, pinning the snake's middle in the fork of the stick.

Instantly the snake uncoiled and began thrashing about. With the second stick, Carson pinned the snake at a second place closer to the head. Then he released the first stick and carefully pinned it even closer to the head, working his way up the body until it was pinned directly behind the neck. The snake, furious, opened its mouth wider, a pink cavern, each fang glistening with a drop of venom. The tail whipsawed back and forth.

Keeping the snake well pinned, Carson reached down gingerly and grabbed it behind the neck, careful to keep his thumb under the snake's head and his index and middle fingers wrapped firmly around the axis bone at the neck. Then, dropping the sticks, he held the snake up for de Vaca.

She looked back at him from a safe distance, her arms crossed. "Wow," she said without enthusiasm. Carson feinted the snake in her direction, grinning as she shrank away. Then he stepped to one side, still holding the thrashing reptile. It was twisting its head, trying unsuccessfully to plant a fang in Carson's thumb.

"Walk the horses past me," he said. "As you go, scuff up the ground and turn over a few rocks."

De Vaca moved the horses past. They pranced by Carson, keeping a wary eye on the snake. When both animals were safely past, Carson grabbed the snake's tail with his other hand.

"You'll find a flint arrowhead in the left front pocket of my pants," he said. "Take it out and cut those rattles off. Be sure you get them all."

"I think this is just your clever way to get my hand in your pocket," de Vaca said with a grin. "But I'm beginning to see the idea." She dug into his pocket, extracting the arrowhead. Then, as Carson balanced the snake's tail on a flat piece of lava, de Vaca quickly drew the sharp arrowhead across the tail, slicing off the rattles. The snake squirmed, furious.

"Get back," Carson said. "Releasing him is the most dangerous part."

He bent forward and, with one hand, placed the snake back in the shade of the lava. He picked up one of the forked sticks with the other hand, and pinned it again behind the animal's neck. Then, readying himself, he let go and jumped backward in a single motion.

The snake immediately coiled, then struck in their direction. It flopped among the rocks and retracted like a spring, coiling and swaying. Its tail was vibrating furiously, but no sound issued.

De Vaca pocketed the rattles. "Okay, *cabrón*, I'll admit. I'm impressed as hell. Nye will be, too. But what's to keep the thing here? It'll be hours before Nye comes through."

"Rattlesnakes are exothermic and can't travel in this kind of heat," Carson said. "He won't go anywhere until after sunset."

De Vaca gave a low chuckle. "I hope it bites Nye on the *cojones*."

"Even if it doesn't bite him, I'm willing to bet it will make him go that much slower."

De Vaca chuckled again, then leaned over, handing something to Carson. "Nice arrowhead, by the way," she said mockingly. "Interesting thing for an Anglo to be carrying around in his pocket. Tell me, did you flake it yourself?"

Carson ignored her.

The sun was now directly overhead. They plodded on, the heads of the horses drooping, their eyes half-lidded. Curtains of heat shimmered about them. They passed a cluster of blooming cholla cactus, the glare of the sun turning the purple flowers to stained glass.

Carson glanced over at de Vaca. Like him, she was leading her horse with her head down, face in the shadow of her hat. He reflected on how lucky it had been that he'd gone back for their hats on the way out of the barn. Small things like that were going to make a big difference. If only he'd searched for more canteens to carry water, or quicked one of Muerto's hooves. Two years earlier, he never would have made such a mistake, even in the panic and uproar of blowing up Mount Dragon.

Water. The thought of water brought Carson's eyes around yet again to the canteens inside Nye's saddlebag. He realized he had been glancing surreptitiously at the saddlebag every few minutes. As he watched, de Vaca turned and glanced back at it herself. It was not a good sign.

"What would be the harm in one sip?" she asked at last.

"It's like giving whiskey to an alcoholic," Carson said. "One sip leads to another, and soon it'll be gone. We need the water for the horses."

"Who gives a shit if the horses survive, if we end up dead?"

"Have you tried sucking on a pebble?" Carson asked.

De Vaca flashed him a dark look and spat something small and glistening from her mouth. "I've been sucking all morning. I want a drink. What the hell are these horses good for, anyway? We haven't ridden them in hours."

Heat and thirst were making her unreasonable. "They'd go lame if we rode in this stuff," he said, speaking as calmly as he could. "As soon as we get off the lava—"

"Fuck it," de Vaca said. "I'm taking a drink." She reached back for the saddlebag.

"Wait," said Carson. "Wait a moment. When your ancestors crossed this desert, did they break down like that?"

There was a silence.

"Don Alonso and his wife crossed this desert together. And they nearly died of thirst. You told me so."

De Vaca looked to one side, refusing to answer.

"If they had lost their discipline, you wouldn't be here."

"Don't try to mind-fuck me, *cabrón*."

"This is for real, Susana. Our lives depend on keeping these horses alive. Even if we become too weak to walk, we'll still be able to travel if we keep these horses in good condition."

"OK, OK, you've talked me out of a drink," she snapped. "I'd rather die of thirst than listen to you preach, anyway." She pulled savagely on her horse's lead rope. "Get your ass moving," she muttered.

Carson fell back a moment to examine Roscoe's hooves. There was some chipping around the edges, but otherwise they were holding up. No signs of real danger, like bruising or cracks that ran into the corona. They could go perhaps another mile on the lava.

De Vaca was waiting for him to catch up, glancing at the vultures overhead. "*Zopilotes*. They're already coming to our funeral."

"No," said Carson, "they're after something else. We're not that far gone."

De Vaca was silent for a moment. "I'm sorry I've been giving you a hard time, *cabrón*," she said at last. "I'm kind of a cranky person, in case you didn't notice."

"I noticed the first day we met."

"Back at Mount Dragon, I thought I had a lot to be pissed off about. In my life, in my job. Now, if we can just get out of this furnace without dying, I swear I'll appreciate what I have a little more."

"Let's not start talking about dying yet. Don't forget, we have more than ourselves to live for."

"You think I can forget that?" de Vaca said. "I keep thinking about those thousands of innocent people, waiting to receive PurBlood on Friday. I think I'd rather be here, in this heat, than lying on a hospital cot with an IV draining that stuff into my veins."

She lapsed into silence for a moment.

"In Truchas," she resumed, "we never had heat like this. And there was water everywhere. Streams came rushing out of the Truchas Peaks, filled with trout. You could get on your hands and knees and drink as much as you wanted. It was always ice cold, even in summer. And so delicious. We used to go skinny-dipping in the waterfalls. God, just thinking about it . . ." Her voice died away.

"I told you, *don't* think about it," Carson replied.

There was a silence.

"Maybe our friend is sinking his fangs into the *canalla* as we speak," de Vaca added hopefully.

Inside the door, Levine halted, frozen.

He was standing on a rocky bluff. Below him, the ocean raged against a granite headland, the waves flinging themselves against the rocks, erupting in white spray before subsiding back into the creamy surf. He turned around. The bluff behind him was bare and windswept. A small, well-used trail wound down through a grassy meadow and disappeared into a thick forest of spruce trees.

There was no sign of the door leading out to the corridor. He had entered a new world entirely.

Levine's hand fell from his laptop for a moment, and he closed his eyes against the view. It was not just the strangeness of the scene that had unnerved him: the huge, incredibly lifelike re-creation of a seacoast where an octagonal office should have been. There was something else.

He *recognized* the place. This was no imaginary landscape. He had been here before, many years ago, with Scopes. In college, when they had been inseparable friends. This was the island where Scopes's family had had a summer place.

Monhegan Island, Maine.

He was standing on a bluff at the seaward end of the island. If he remembered correctly, it was called Burnt Head.

Returning his hand to the laptop, he turned in a slow, deliberate circle, watching the landscape change as he did so. Each new feature, each vista, brought a fresh rush of déjà vu. It was an incredible, almost unbelievable achievement. This was Scopes's personal domain, the heart of his cypherspace program: his secret world, on the island of his boyhood.

Levine recalled the summer he had spent on the island. For a kid from working-class Boston, the place had been a revelation. They'd spent the long warm days exploring tidal pools and sunlit fields. Brent's family had a rambling Victorian house, set by itself on a bluff at the edge of the Village, toward the lee side of the island.

That, Levine suddenly realized, was where he would find Scopes.

He started down the trail, into the dark spruce forest. Levine noticed that the strange singing of the cyberspace world outside was gone, replaced by the island noises he remembered: the occasional cry of a gull, the distant sound of the ocean. As he moved deeper into the forest, the sound of the ocean disappeared, leaving only the wind sighing and moaning through the craggy branches of the spruce trees. Levine walked on as a light fog rolled in, amazed at how easily he was adjusting to moving around within this virtual world. The huge image before him on the elevator wall; the sounds and sights; the responsiveness of the program to his computer's commands; all worked together toward a total suspension of disbelief.

The trail forked. Levine concentrated, trying to remember the way to the Village. In the end, he chose one fork at random.

The trail dipped down into a hollow and crossed a narrow brook, a blue thread bordered by pitcher plants and skunk cabbage. He crossed the stream, following the trail up a narrow ravine and deeper into the woods. Gradually, the trail petered out into nothingness. Levine turned around and began to retrace his steps, but the fog had grown thick, and all he could see were the black, lichen-covered trunks that surrounded him on all sides, marching into the mist. He was lost.

Levine thought for a moment. The Village, he knew, lay on the western side of the island. But which way was west?

He became aware of a shadow moving through the fog to his left; within moments, the shadow resolved itself into the shape of a man, holding a lantern at his side. As the man walked, the lantern made a yellow ring of light that bobbed and winked in the fog. Suddenly, the man stopped. He turned slowly, looking toward Levine through a defile of dark tree trunks. Levine looked back, wondering if he should type a greeting. There was a flash of light and a popping sound.

Levine realized he was being shot at. The figure in the fog was apparently some kind of security construct inside the cypherspace program. But how much could it see, and why was it firing at him?

Suddenly, a voice cut in, loud and insistent, over the soft sighing of the wind. Levine turned quickly, staring at the elevator speakers. The voice belonged to Brent Scopes.

"Attention, all security personnel. An intruder has been discovered in the GeneDyne computer. Under current network conditions, that means the intruder is also in the building. Locate and detain immediately."

By entering the island world, he had alerted the GeneDyne supercomputer's security program. But what would happen if he was hit with gunfire? Perhaps it would terminate the Cypherspace program, leaving him as far from Scopes as when he had first entered the building.

The dark figure fired again.

Levine fled backward into the woods. As he navigated through the swirling fingers of fog, he began to see more dark figures moving through the trees, and more flashes of light. The trees began to thin, and he came out at last onto a dirt road.

He stopped for a moment and looked around. The figures seemed to have vanished. Immediately, he started down the dirt road, moving as fast as his laptop controls would permit, alert for signs of anyone approaching.

A sudden noise alerted him, and he ducked back into the woods. Within moments, a group of shadowy figures glided by, moving eastward like ghosts, holding lanterns and carrying guns. He waited until they passed, then returned to the road.

Soon, the road turned to stone and began to descend toward the sea. In the distance, Levine could now make out the scattered rooftops of the Village, crowded around the white spire of the church. Behind them rose the great mansard roof of the Island Inn.

Cautiously, he descended the hill and entered the town. The place appeared deserted. The fog was thicker between the weather-beaten houses, and he moved quickly past dark windows of old, rippled glass. Here and there a light in one of the houses cast a glow through the fog. Once he heard voices and managed to maneuver himself into an alley until a group of figures had moved past him in the fog.

Past the church, the road forked again. Now Levine knew where he was. Choosing the left fork, he followed the road as it climbed the side of a bluff. Then he stopped, maneuvering the trackball for a view up the hill.

There, at the top of the bluff, surrounded by a wrought-iron fence, rose the gloomy outlines of the Scopes mansion.

The long hours of stooping and searching the lava for sign had taken their toll on Nye's back. The horses had left barely enough marks to follow, and it was tedious, slow work. In three hours he had managed to track Carson and de Vaca less than two miles.

He straightened up, massaging his back, and took another small drink from the water bag. He poured a few quarts into his hat and let Muerto slurp it down. He would catch up to them eventually, if only to find their dead bodies being pulled apart by coyotes. He would outlast them.

He closed his eyes for a moment against the blazing white light of the sun. Then, with a deep sigh, he began again. There, two feet ahead, was a crushed clump of grass. He took one step and looked beyond it. There, maybe four feet ahead, was an overturned stone, showing a little sand on its bottom. He scanned a semicircle with his eyes. And there was the impression of the side of a hoof in a tiny patch of sand.

It was bloody tedious, to tell the truth. He occupied himself with the thought that, by now, Carson and de Vaca had no doubt drunk all their water. Their horses were probably half-crazed with thirst.

Here, at last, was a clear stretch of tracks, leading ahead for at least twenty feet. Nye straightened up and walked alongside them, grateful for the temporary respite. Maybe they'd grown tired of making their trail so difficult. He knew he bloody well had.

There was a sudden movement in the corner of his eye, and simultaneously Muerto reared, jerking Nye backward into the horse's flailing hooves. There was a stunning blow to his head, followed by a strange noise that quickly died away, and an infinity of time passed. Then he found himself looking up at an endless field of blue. He sat up, feeling a wave of nausea. Muerto was twenty feet away, grazing peacefully. Automatically, his hand reached for his head. Blood. He looked at his watch, realized he'd only been unconscious for a minute or two.

He turned suddenly. Off to one side, a boy sat on a small rock, grinning, his knees sticking up under his chin. Wearing shorts, knee socks, and a battered blue blazer, the breast-pocket emblem of the St. Pancras' School for Boys half-obscured by dirt. His longish hair was matted, as if it had been wet for a very long time, and it stuck out from the sides of his head.

"You," Nye breathed.

"Rattler-snake," the boy replied, nodding toward a clump of yucca.

That was the voice: supersaturated with the Cockney drawl that, Nye knew firsthand, years of English public school in

Surrey or Kent could never fully exorcise. Hearing it from the mouth of this small figure, Nye was instantly transported from the fiery emptiness of the Southwestern desert to the narrow gray-brick streets of Ealing, pavements slick with rain and the smell of coal hanging heavy in the air.

With an effort, he willed himself back to the present. He glanced in the direction the boy had pointed. There was the snake, still coiled in striking position, perhaps ten feet away.

"Why didn't you tell me?" Nye said.

The boy laughed. "Didn't see it, old man. Didn't hear it, neither."

The snake was silent. Its tail, sticking up at the end of its coil, was blurry with vibration, yet it was making no noise. Sometimes rattlers did break off all their rattles, but it was very rare. Nye could feel a prickle of secondary fear course through him. He had to be more careful.

Nye stood up, fighting to control the wave of nausea that washed over him as he rose. He went over to his horse and slid the rifle out of its scabbard.

"Hang on a minute," the boy said, still grinning. "I wouldn't do that if I were you."

Nye slid the rifle back. It was true. Carson might hear the shot. That would give him information he didn't need to know.

On a hunch, Nye scanned the ground in a wide arc around the snake. There it was: a green mesquite stick, recently whittled, forked at one end. And, lying beside it, a similar stick.

The boy stood up and stretched, smoothing down his unruly hair. "Looks like you were set up, bang to rights. Nasty bit of work. Almost did you, that one."

Nye swore under his breath. He'd underestimated Carson at every turn. The snake had been agitated, and had struck too early. If it hadn't . . . He felt a momentary dizziness.

He looked again at the boy. The last time he had seen him, Nye had been younger, not older, than the grubby little fellow that now stood before him. "What really happened, that day down in Littlehampton?" he asked. "Mum wouldn't tell me."

The boy's lower lip stuck out in an exaggerated pout. "That dirty great wave got me, didn't it? Pulled me right under."

"So how did you swim back out?"

The pout deepened. "I didn't."

"Then what are you doing here?" Nye asked.

The boy picked up a pebble and threw it. "The same might be asked of yourself."

Nye nodded. True enough. He supposed all this should seem strange to him. Yet each time he thought about it, it seemed more normal. Soon, he knew, he would stop thinking about it at all.

He collected the reins of the horse and gave the snake a wide berth, searching again for sign about thirty yards to the north.

"Hotter than a bleedin' pan of bubble and squeak out here," the boy said.

Nye ignored him. He had found a scrape on a stone. Carson must have made a sharp turn just beyond the snake. God, his head was throbbing.

"Here, I've got an idea," the boy said. "Let's head him off at the pass."

Through a fog of pain, Nye remembered his maps. He wasn't as familiar with the northern end of the Jornada desert as he was with the southern. It seemed unlikely, but he supposed it was possible there might be a way to head Carson off somewhere.

Certainly he still had the advantage. Eight gallons of water left, and his horse was going strong. It was time he stopped merely reacting to Carson's stratagems, and began calling the shots himself.

Locating a flat area in the lava, Nye unrolled his maps, weighing down the corners with stones. Perhaps Carson had headed north for reasons other than simply throwing everyone off the scent. The personnel file stated that Carson had worked ranches in New Mexico. Maybe he was heading toward country he knew.

The maps showed large, complicated lava flows in the northern section of the Jornada. Since the topographical engineers hadn't bothered to actually survey the flows, large sections of the maps were stippled indiscriminately with dots indicating lava. There was no section or range data. The maps were no doubt highly inaccurate, the data having been gathered from aerial photographs with no field checking.

At the northern end of the Jornada, Nye noticed a series of cinder cones marked "Chain of Craters" that ran in an irregular line across the desert. A lava mesa, the Mesa del Contadero, backed up against one side of the flow, and the tail end of the Fra Cristóbals blocked the flows at the other. It wasn't a pass, exactly, but there was definitely a narrow gap in the Malpaís near the northern end of the Fra Cristóbals. From the map, it looked as if this gap was the only way to get out of the Jornada without crossing endless stretches of Malpaís.

The boy was leaning over Nye's shoulder. "Cor! What'd I tell you, then, guv? Head him off at the pass."

Twenty miles beyond the gap was the symbol for a windmill—a triangle topped with an X—and a black dot indicating a cattle tank. Next to them was a tiny black square, with the words "Lava Camp." Nye could tell this was a line camp for a ranch headquartered another twenty miles north, marked "Diamond Bar" on the map.

That's where Carson was going. The son of a bitch had probably worked on the ranch as a kid. Still, it was over a hundred miles from Mount Dragon to Lava Camp, and eighty miles to the narrow gap alone. That meant Carson still had almost sixty miles to go before hitting the windmill and water. No horse could go that distance without watering at least once. They were still doomed.

Nevertheless, the longer he looked at the map, the more certain Nye felt that Carson would be heading for that gap. He would stay on the lava only long enough to shake Nye, and then make a beeline for the gap, and for Lava Camp that lay beyond—where there would be water, food, and probably people, if not a cellular phone.

Nye returned the maps to their canisters and looked around. The lava seemed to stretch endlessly from horizon to horizon, but he knew now the western edge of the lava was only three-quarters of a mile away.

The plan that took shape in his mind was very simple. He would get off the lava immediately and ride ahead to that gap in the Malpaís. Once there, he'd wait. Carson couldn't know that he had these maps. Sneak that he was, he probably knew Nye was unfamiliar with the northern Jornada. He would not expect to be cut off. And, in any case, he'd be too damn thirsty to worry anything but finding water. Nye would have to ride in a long arc to ensure that Carson wouldn't pick up his track, but with plenty of water and a strong horse he knew he could reach the gap long before Carson.

And that gap was where Carson and the bitch would meet their end in the crosshairs of his Holland & Holland Express.

The vultures were perhaps a mile away now, still spiraling slowly in the rising thermal. Carson and de Vaca walked in silence, leading their horses across the lava. It was two o'clock in the afternoon. The lava seemed to glitter with endless lakes of blue water, covered with whitecaps. It was impossible for Carson to keep his eyes open and not see water.

Carson examined his thirst. It was excruciating. He had

never imagined, much less felt, such a desperate sensation. His tongue was a thick lump of chalk in his mouth, without feeling. His lips had cracked and were starting to ooze fluid. The thirst was also gnawing away at his mind: As he walked, it seemed the desert had become one vast fire, lifting him like flyaway ash into the dazzling, implacable sky.

The horses were becoming severely dehydrated. The alteration that a few hours in the noonday sun had worked on them was almost incredible. He had wanted to wait until sunset to give them water, but it was now clear that sunset would be too late.

He stopped abruptly. Susana shuffled on a few steps, then halted wordlessly.

"Let's water the horses," he said. The sudden speech in his dry throat was exquisitely painful.

She said nothing.

"Susana? You okay?"

De Vaca didn't answer. She sat down in the shade of her horse and bowed her head.

Carson dismounted and moved toward de Vaca's horse. He unstrapped Nye's saddlebag and pushed the horseshoes aside. Removing a canteen, he took off his hat and filled it up to the brim. The sight of the water flowing from the mouth of the canteen sent his throat into spasm. Roscoe, who had been standing beside him half-dead, suddenly jerked his head up and crowded forward. He sucked down the water in a moment, then grabbed the hat with his teeth. Carson rapped him irritably on the muzzle, yanking the hat away. The horse pranced and blew.

Carson filled his hat a second time, carrying it to de Vaca's horse. The horse drank it down greedily.

Replacing the now-empty canteen with the full one, he gave each horse half a second hatful, then returned the canteen to the saddle. The horses had suddenly become agitated, as he knew they would, and were blowing and turning, eyes wide.

As he returned the second, half-full canteen to the saddlebag, he heard a rustling sound. Reaching in, he found a loose seam along the lining of the outer flap. A piece of aged yellow paper was peeping out: the paper that Nye had been examining in the barn, the evening after the dust storm. Carson pulled it out and looked at it curiously. It was tattered and not paper at all, but something that looked like a soiled piece of ancient leather. On it were crudely detailed sketches of a mountain range, a strangely shaped black mass, numerous markings, and Spanish script. And across the top, the perplexing words in a large, old-fashioned hand: *Al despertar la hora el áquila del sol se levanta en una aguja del fuego,* "At dawn the eagle of the sun stands on a needle of fire." And at the bottom, amid other Spanish script, a name: Diego de Mondragón.

It all became suddenly clear. Were it not for his painfully cracked lips, Carson would have laughed aloud.

"Susana!" he exclaimed. "Nye has been searching for the Mount Dragon treasure. The gold of Mondragón! I found a map hidden here in his saddlebags. The crazy bastard knew paper was illegal at Mount Dragon, so he kept it where nobody would find it!"

De Vaca glanced at the proffered map disinterestedly from beneath the shade of her horse. Carson shook his head. It was ridiculous, so out of character. Whatever else he was, Nye was no fool. Yet he had no doubt bought this map in the back room of some musty junk shop in Santa Fe, probably paying a fortune. Carson had seen many such maps being offered for sale; faking and selling treasure maps for tourists was big business in New Mexico. No wonder Nye had acted so suspicious of Carson's tracking: He thought Carson was out to steal his imaginary treasure.

Abruptly, Carson's amusement disappeared. Apparently,

Nye had been searching for this treasure for some time. Perhaps it had begun simply as curiosity on his part. But now, under the influence of PurBlood, what had started as a mild obsession would have become much more than that. And Nye, being aware that Carson had taken the saddlebag, would have even more reason to hunt them down without mercy.

He looked more closely at the map. It showed mountains, and the black stuff might be a lava flow. It could be anywhere in the desert. But Nye obviously knew that Mondragón's doublet had supposedly been found at the base of Mount Dragon; he must have been orchestrating his search from that point.

Even this remarkable solution to Nye's weekend disappearances grew quickly dull under the burning thirst that would not leave his throat. Wearily, Carson returned the piece of vellum to the saddlebag and looked at the horseshoes. There was no time to put them on. They'd have to chance it in the sand.

He tied up the saddlebag, then turned. "Susana, we've got to keep going."

Wordlessly, de Vaca stood up and began walking northward. Carson followed her, his thoughts dissolving in a dark dream of fire.

Suddenly they were at the edge of the lava flow. Ahead of them, the sandy desert stretched to the limitless horizon. Carson bent down in a salt pan that had formed along the edge of the lava and picked up a few pieces of alkali salt. It never hurt to be prepared.

"We can ride now," he said, shoving the salt into his pocket. He watched as de Vaca mechanically put one foot in the stirrup. She hoisted herself into the saddle on the second attempt.

Watching her silent struggles, Carson was suddenly unable to stand it any longer. He stopped, reached over for the saddlebag, withdrew the canteen.

"Susana. Drink with me."

She sat on her horse for a moment, silently. At last, without looking up, she said, "Don't be a fool. We've got sixty miles to go. Save it for the horses."

"Just a little sip, Susana. A sip."

A sob escaped from her throat. "None for me. But if you want to, go ahead."

Carson screwed the cap down without drinking and replaced the canteen. As he prepared to mount, he felt something run down his chin. When he dabbed at his lips, his fingers came away red with blood. This hadn't happened in Coal Canyon. This was much worse. And they still had sixty miles to go. He realized, with a kind of dull finality, that there was no way they were going to make it.

Unless there were coyotes at the kill.

He put his foot in the stirrup, fighting back a sudden dizziness, and pulled himself upward onto the horse. The effort exhausted him, and he sagged in the saddle.

The vultures were still circling now, perhaps a quarter mile ahead. The two moved closer, Carson propping himself up with the saddle horn. In the distance, something dark was lying on the sand. Coyotes were tugging at it. Roscoe, seeing something in the featureless desert, automatically moved toward it. Carson blinked, trying to focus. His eyes were running out of water. He blinked again.

The coyotes bounded away from the carcass. At a hundred yards they stopped and looked back. *Never been shot at*, Carson thought.

The horses drew closer to the carcass. Carson looked down, working to bring the dead creature into focus. His eyes were so dry they felt as if they were caked in sand.

It was a dead pronghorn antelope. The carcass was barely recognizable: a skull, with the characteristic stubby horns, peeking out of a desiccated lump of flesh.

Carson glanced at de Vaca, pulling up behind. "Coyotes," he said. His throat felt like it had been flayed.

"What?"

"Coyotes. It means water. They never go far from water."

"How far?"

"Ten miles, no more."

He leaned over the saddle horn, trying to control a spasm in his throat.

"How?" de Vaca croaked.

"Track," Carson said.

The heat played about them. A single cloud drifted across the sky, like a puff of acrid steam. The Fra Cristóbal Mountains, which they had been approaching all day, now seemed bleached to bone by the sun. Behind them, the horizon had disappeared, and the landscape itself seemed to be evaporating, dissolving into sheets of light, floating upward into a white-hot sky. The coyotes were sitting on a rise, waiting for the interlopers to leave.

"They approached from downwind," Carson said.

He rode in a spiral away from the dead antelope until he located the spot where the coyote tracks entered. As he followed the tracks away from the antelope, de Vaca drew up alongside. They rode for several miles, Carson leading, following the faint tracks through the soft desert sand.

Then the tracks veered into the lava and disappeared.

Carson drew Roscoe to a halt as de Vaca came along beside him. There was a silence. Nobody could track a coyote through lava.

"I think," he croaked at last, "that we need to divide the remaining water with the horses. We can't last much longer."

This time de Vaca nodded.

They slid off the horses, collapsing in the hot sand. Carson removed the half-full canteen with a weak hand.

"Drink slowly," Carson said. "And don't be disappointed if it makes you even more thirsty."

De Vaca sipped from the canteen with trembling hands. Carson didn't bother to bring out the salt from his pocket;

they wouldn't be drinking enough water for it to matter. Taking the canteen gently from de Vaca, he raised it to his lips. The feeling was unbearably good, but it was even more unbearable when it ended.

He gave what was left to the horses, then tied the empty canteen on the saddle horn. They lay down in the shade cast by the two animals, who stood dejectedly in the afternoon sun.

"What are we waiting for?" de Vaca asked.

"Sunset," said Carson. The drink already seemed a wonderful, unbearable dream. But talking was not the unbearable torture it had been. "Coyotes water at sunset, and they usually start calling. Let's hope the spring is within a mile, so we can hear them. Otherwise. . . ."

"What about Nye?"

"He's still searching for us, I'm sure of that," Carson said. "But I think we've lost him."

De Vaca was silent. "I wonder if Don Alonso and his wife suffered like this," she murmured at last.

"Probably. But they found a spring."

They lapsed into silence. The desert was deathly quiet.

"Is there anything else you can remember about that spring?" Carson asked at last.

De Vaca frowned. "No. They started across the desert at dusk, and drove their stock until they were near to collapse. An Apache showed them the spring."

"So they were probably about halfway across."

"They started with barrels of water in their wagons, so they were probably much farther than that."

"Going north," said Carson.

"Going north."

"You remember anything, anything at all, about the location?"

"I already told you. It was in a cave at the foot of the Fra Cristóbals. That's all I can remember."

Carson did a quick calculation. They were now about forty-five miles north of Mount Dragon. The mountains were ten miles to the west. Just at the edge of the coyotes' range.

Carson struggled to his feet. "The wind is drifting toward the Fra Cristóbals. So the coyotes probably came from the west. So maybe—just maybe—the Ojo del Águila is at the foot of the mountains due west."

"That was a long time ago," de Vaca said. "How do you know that, even if we find it, the spring hasn't run dry?"

"I don't."

"I'm not sure if I can make it ten miles."

"It's either that, or die."

"You've got a great bedside manner, you know that?" De Vaca pushed herself into a sitting position. "Let's go."

Nye trotted alongside the lava flow for a while and then looped eastward, away from the mountains, to ensure that the two would not cross his trail. Although Carson had proven an worthy adversary, he tended to make mistakes when he was overconfident. Nye wanted to make sure Carson was as overconfident as possible. He had to make Carson believe he had thrown him off the trail.

Muerto was still going strong, and Nye himself felt good. The pain in his head had subsided to a dull ache. The afternoon heat was stifling, but it was their friend, the invisible killer.

Toward four o'clock he cut north again, returning to the edge of the lava flow. To the south, he could see a column of vultures. They had been hanging there for quite a while.

Some animal or other. Far too soon for Carson and de Vaca to draw so big a crowd.

He stopped suddenly. The boy had vanished. He felt a panic.

"Hey, boy!" he called. "Boy!"

His voice died away without echo, sucked into the dry sands of the desert. There was little in the endless dead landscape to reflect sound.

He stood in his stirrups and cupped his hands. "*Boy!*"

The scruffy figure came out from behind a low rock, buttoning his fly. "Here, put a sock in your boatrace. I was just visiting the gents'."

Relaxing, Nye turned his horse, bringing him quickly back to a trot. Thirty miles to the ambush point. He would be there before midnight.

The image on the huge screen was of a rambling Victorian house in pure Gothic Revival style, bedecked almost self-consciously with ponderous mansard roof and widow's walk. A white portico ran across the front of the house and along both sides. Panning his view upward, Levine noticed that the entire structure was dark, save for a small, eight-sided garret atop the central tower, its oculus windows piercing the fog with a yellow glow.

He maneuvered his cyberspatial self up the road to an iron gate that hung open on broken hinges, wondering why the house itself wasn't guarded; why Scopes had depicted the yard as being overgrown with chokecherries and burdock. As he approached, he noticed that several of the windows were broken and that paint was peeling from the weathered clapboards. The house and yard had been lovingly tended the summer he'd spent there as a youth.

He looked up again at the octagonal garret. If Scopes was anywhere inside, he would be there. Levine watched as a stream of colored light, like a tongue of fire, burst from the roof of the garret and disappeared into a dark hole in the fog that hovered overhead. He'd seen similar data transfers flashing between the huge buildings he'd first encountered in GeneDyne cyberspace. This must be the encrypted TELINT satellite uplink that Mime had detected. Levine wondered if the messages were encrypted before or after they left this inner sanctum of Scopes's cypherspace.

The front door stood partly open. The interior of the house was dim, and Levine found himself wishing for some way to illuminate the view. The sky had slowly darkened, turning the fog to a leaden gray, and Levine realized that—at least within this artificial world of Scopes's—night was coming on. He looked at his watch and saw it was 5:22. A.M. or P.M.? he found himself wondering. He had lost all track of time. He shifted position on the elevator floor, flexing one leg that had gone to sleep and massaging his tired wrists, wondering if Mime was still somewhere in the GeneDyne network, running interference. Then, taking a deep breath, he returned his hands to the laptop keys and moved forward into the house.

Here was the large parlor of his memory, with a worn Persian rug on the floor and a massive stone fireplace on the left-hand wall. A stuffed moose head hung above it, cobwebs woven thickly between its antlers. The walls were lined with old paintings of barques and schooners, and scenes of whaling and fishing.

Straight ahead was the curving staircase that mounted to the second floor. He maneuvered up the staircase and along the second-floor balustrade. The rooms off the balustrade were dark and empty. He chose one at random, maneuvering through it to a worn and battered window. He looked outside and was surprised to see not the narrow road winding down into the mist, but a bizarre jumble of gray and orange static. A *bug in cypherspace?* Levine wondered, moving back to the balustrade through the dim light. He turned in to a second hallway, curious to see the room he'd slept in that summer so many years before, but a burst of computer code filled the screen, threatening to dissolve the entire vast image of the house before him. He hurriedly backed away, perplexed. Every other area of the island seemed to have been knit together by Scopes with such care. Yet the re-creation of his own childhood home was disheveled and empty, with rends in the very fabric of his computerized creation.

At the far end of the balustrade was the door to the garret stairs. Levine was about to ascend the stairs when he remembered a back staircase that led to the widow's walk. Perhaps it would be better if he took a look into the windows of the garret before broaching it directly.

Fog rushed up to embrace him as Levine moved forward onto the widow's walk. He swiveled the laptop's trackball, looking around cautiously. Ten feet ahead of him, the angular form of the garret jutted from the walkway. Levine moved forward and peered into the oculus window.

A bent-looking figure sat inside the garret, his back to Levine. Long white hair flowed over the high collar of what appeared to be a dressing gown. The figure was perched in front of a computer terminal. Suddenly, a tongue of fire came shooting down out of the fog, plunging into the side of the garret. Without hesitation, Levine moved forward into the stream of color, and in an instant words were flashing across the enormous screen:

    . . . have discussed your price. It is outrageous.
    Our offer of three billion stands. There will be no fur-
    ther negotiation.

The stream subsided. Levine waited, motionless. Within minutes, a burst of colored light shot up from the tower:

General Harrington: Your impertinence just cost you an additional billion, and the price is now five billion. This kind of posturing is displeasing to me as a businessman. It would be much nicer if we could settle this like gentlemen, don't you think? And it isn't even your money. It is, however, my virus. I have it, and you don't. Five billion would reverse that situation.

The stream subsided.

Levine stood on the widow's walk, stunned. It was worse than he could ever have imagined. Not only was Scopes mad, but he had in his possession a virus—a virus he was selling to the military. Perhaps even to rogue elements within the military. Judging by the prices involved, the virus could only be the doomsday virus Carson had told him about.

Levine sagged back against the elevator wall, overwhelmed by the enormity of what he was up against. Five billion dollars. It was staggering. A virus wasn't like a nuclear weapon—hard to transport, difficult to hide, hard to deliver. A single test tube in someone's pocket could easily contain trillions of them. . . .

Sitting up again, Levine maneuvered himself back along the widow's walk, down the flight of stairs, and along the corridor to the garret stairway. As with all unlocked doors in Scopes's creation, the garret doorway opened as he collided with it. At the top of the dark stairway was another door. As he ascended, Levine could see light coming from the jamb.

This door was locked. Levine banged into it again and again in frustration and rage.

Then something occurred to him. It had worked with Phido; there was no reason to think it wouldn't work here.

In capital letters, he typed: SCOPES!

Instantly, the name reverberated from the speaker into the narrow confines of the elevator. A minute ticked by, then two. Suddenly, the door to the garret room burst open. Levine could see a wizened figure looking out at him. What he had taken to be a dressing gown was actually a long robe, sprinkled liberally with astrological designs. Hair fell in streams of white and silver over the jug ears, and the skin that lay across the forehead and along the sunken cheeks was lined with an infinity of wrinkles, but Levine knew the face, as he knew few others. He had found Brent Scopes.

The sun felt brittle, like a rainfall of glass. The water had restored a little moisture to their throats, yet it had only intensified their thirst. And it had made the horses unruly. Beneath him, Carson could sense that Roscoe was panicking, preparing to run. Once that happened, he'd run until he died.

"Keep them on a short rein," he said.

The Fra Cristóbals loomed ever larger, turning from orange to gray to red in the changing light. As they rode, Carson could feel the terrible dryness returning to his mouth and throat. As his eyes grew more inflamed, it became too painful to keep them open for more than a few moments at a time. He rode with his eyes closed. Beneath him, he could feel the horse swaying with weakness.

A cave at the foot of the mountains. Warm water. That meant a volcanic area. So the spring would be near a lava flow, and the cave itself was probably a lava tube. He opened his eyes for a moment. Eight more miles, perhaps less, to the silent, lifeless mountains.

The effort of thinking exhausted him. Suddenly, he dropped the reins and then, disoriented, pawed frantically at the saddle horn with both hands. If he fell off the horse, he knew he would never get back on. He gripped the horn tighter and leaned forward until he could feel the coarse hair of the horse's mane on his cheek. If Roscoe decided to run, so be it. He rested there, releasing himself to the reddish light that burned behind his closed eyelids.

The sun was setting as they reached the base of the mountains. The long shadow of the rough peaks crept toward them, engulfing them at last in sweet shadow. The temperature dropped out of triple digits.

Carson forced his eyes open. Roscoe was staggering. The horse had lost all desire to run, and was now losing the simple desire to live. Carson turned toward de Vaca. Her back was bowed, her head down, her whole frame seemingly crooked and broken.

The two horses, which had been shambling ahead at their own pace, reached a line of lava at the base of the mountains and stopped.

"Susana?" Carson croaked.

She lifted her head slightly.

"Let's wait here. Wait to hear the coyotes calling to water."

She nodded and slid off the horse. She tried to stand but collapsed drunkenly to her knees.

"Shit," she said, grabbing the stirrup and pulling herself partway up before crumpling back into the sand. Her horse stood on trembling legs, its head drooping.

"Wait, I'll help you," said Carson. As he dismounted, he, too, felt himself lose his balance. With a kind of mild surprise, he found himself looking up from the soft sand at a spinning world: mountains, horses, sunset sky. He closed his eyes again.

Suddenly it was cool. He tried to open his eyes but found himself unable to separate the glued lashes. He reached up with a hand and prized apart the lid of one eye. There was a single star above, shining in a deep ultraviolet sky. Then he heard a faint sound. It started as a sharp yipping noise, rising in pitch, answered at a distance. Three or four more yips followed, the final cry dropping suddenly into a long, drawn-out howl. There was an answering call, then another. The calls appeared to be converging.

Coyotes going to water. At the base of the mountains.

Carson lifted his head. The still form of de Vaca was stretched on the sand near him. There was just enough light in the sky to see the dim outlines of her body.

"Susana?"

There was no answer.

He crawled over and touched her shoulder. "Susana?" *Please answer. Please don't be dead.*

He shook her again, a little harder. Her head lolled slightly, black hair spilling across her face.

"Help," she croaked. "Me."

The sound of her voice revived a weak current of strength within him. He had to find water. Somehow, he had to save her life. The horses were still standing quietly, reins in the sand, shaking as if with fever. He clung to a stirrup and pulled himself into a sitting position. Roscoe's flank felt very hot beneath his hand.

As Carson stood, a sudden wave of dizziness engulfed him and the strength drained out of his legs. Then he found himself flat on his back again, in the sand.

He was unable to walk. If he was going to reach water, he'd have to ride to it.

He grabbed the stirrup again and pulled himself up, clinging desperately to the saddle horn. He was far too weak to pull himself into the saddle. He looked around with his single usable eye. A few yards off, he spotted a large rock. Hooking his arm through the stirrup, Carson led the horse to the rock, then clambered onto it. From its top he was able to crawl into the saddle. Then he sat, listening.

The coyotes were still calling. He took a bearing toward the sound and tapped Roscoe with his heels.

The animal lurched forward, took a trembling step, then stopped, spraddle-legged. Carson whispered into the horse's ear, patted him soothingly on the neck, and nudged him again. *Come on, damn you.*

The horse took another shaky step forward. He stumbled, recovered with a grunt, and took a third step.

"Hurry," Carson whispered urgently. The calling would not last long.

The horse staggered toward the sound. In a minute, another wall of lava loomed up on his left. He urged Roscoe on as the yelping suddenly ceased.

The coyotes were aware of his presence.

He kept moving the horse toward the place where he'd last heard the sound. More lava. The light was draining out of the sky. Within minutes it would be too dark to see.

Suddenly he smelled it: a cool, humid fragrance. The horse jerked his head up, smelling it too. In a moment the faint breeze had carried the smell away again, and the hot brick stench of the desert returned to fill his nostrils.

The lava flow seemed to march on endlessly to his left, while to his right lay the empty desert. As night came on, more stars began to appear in the sky. The silence was intense. There was no indication where the water might be. They were close, but not close enough. He felt himself slipping into unconsciousness.

The horse sighed heavily and took another step forward. Carson gripped the saddle horn. He had dropped the reins again, but he didn't care. Let the horse have his head. There it was: another tantalizing breeze, carrying with it the smell of wet sand. The horse turned toward the smell, walking straight into the lava. Carson could see nothing but the black outline of twisted rock, rearing against a fading sky. There was nothing here, after all; it was just another cruel mirage. He closed his eyes again. The horse staggered, took a few more steps. Then it stopped.

Carson heard, as if from a great distance, the sound of water being sucked up through a bitted muzzle. He released his grip on the saddle horn and felt himself falling, and still falling, and just when it seemed like he would fall forever he landed with a splash in a shallow pool.

He was lying in water perhaps four inches deep. It was, of course, a hallucination; people who were dying of thirst often felt themselves sinking into water. As he turned, water filled his mouth. He coughed and swallowed. It was warm—warm and clean. He swallowed again. And then he realized that it was real.

He rolled in the water, drinking, laughing and rolling, and drinking some more. As the lovely warm liquid coursed down his throat, he could feel the strength beginning to return to his limbs.

He willed himself to stop drinking and stood up, steadying himself against the horse and blinking both eyes free of the glue that had imprisoned them. He untied the canteen and, with a shaking hand, filled it in the warm water. Returning the canteen to the saddle horn, he tried to pull Roscoe away.

The horse refused to budge. Carson knew that, if left to his own devices, the animal might very well drink himself to death, or at the very least give himself founder. He whacked Roscoe on the muzzle and jerked up the reins. The horse, startled, spun backward.

"It's for your own good," Carson said, leading the animal out while he pranced in frustration.

He found de Vaca lying just as he left her. Kneeling beside her, Carson opened the canteen and dabbed a little water over her face and hair. She stirred, rolling her head, and he cradled it in his arms, carefully pouring a few drops into her open mouth.

"Susana?"

She swallowed and coughed.

He poured another drop into her mouth, and dabbed some more on her crusted eyes and swollen lips.

"Is that you, Guy?" she whispered.

"There's water."

He placed the canteen to her lips. She took a few swallows and coughed.

"More," she croaked.

Over the next fifteen minutes, she drank the entire gallon in little sips.

Carson pulled the piece of alkali salt from his pocket, sucked on it for a moment, then passed it to her. "Lick some of this," he said. "It'll help take away the thirst."

"Am I dead?" she whispered at last.

"No. I found the spring. Actually, Roscoe found it. The Ojo del Águila."

She sucked on the piece of salt, then sat up weakly. "Whew. I'm still dying of thirst."

"You've got enough water in your stomach for now. What you need is electrolytes."

She sucked on the salt again; then a sob suddenly racked her shoulders. Instinctively, Carson put his arms around her.

"Hey," she said, "look at this, *cabrón*. My eyes are working again."

He held her, feeling the tears trickle down his own face. Together, they wept at the miracle that had kept them alive.

Within an hour, de Vaca was strong enough to move. They led the horses back to the cave and let them drink, slowly. After the horses had watered, Carson took them outside to graze, first hobbling them to keep them from wandering away in the dark. It hardly seemed necessary, since they weren't likely to stray far from the water.

When he returned to the darkness of the cave, Carson found de Vaca lying on a verge of sand next to the spring, already asleep. He sat down, feeling an immense mantle of weariness settle on his shoulders. He was too tired to explore. The world drained away into nothingness as he fell back against the sand.

Lava Gate.

Nye played his halogen torch along the immense black wall that reared up beside him. The gap was perhaps a hundred yards wide. On one side the Fra Cristóbal mountains thrust up from the desert floor, a talus of fractured boulders and traprock forming a natural barrier to horses. On the other, an immense wall of lava rose up, the abrupt end of many miles of frozen flow from a volcano whose spark had gone out eons before. It was even better than he imagined; a perfect place for an ambush. If he was heading for Lava Camp, Carson had no choice but to go through here.

Nye hobbled Muerto in a hidden arroyo beyond the gap and climbed up into the lava, carrying his flashlight and rifle, a water bag, and food. He soon found what seemed in the darkness to be a good lookout: a small depression in the lava, surrounded by a jagged escarpment. The lava had formed itself into natural crenellations, and its rough porous surface offered excellent purchase for the barrel of his rifle.

He settled down to wait. He took a sip from the water bag and pared himself a hunk of cheese from the wheel. American cheddar, truly awful stuff. And the 110-degree heat hadn't improved it. But at least it was food. Nye was fairly confident that Carson and the woman hadn't eaten in thirty hours. But without water, food would be the least of their problems.

He sat quietly in the darkness, listening. Toward dawn the new moon rose, a bright white sliver. It threw enough light in the clear air for Nye to relax his vigil and look around.

He had found the ideal lookout: a sniper's nest a hundred feet above the gap. By day, Carson and the woman would be visible to the south for two, maybe three miles. He had clear shooting across, down, and even to the other side. He couldn't have designed a better blind. Here, he'd have all the time in the world to squeeze off his shots. When the .357 nitro-express slugs connected with human tissue, they would cause so much havoc even the buzzards would have a difficult time finding enough meat for a meal.

Chances were, of course, that Carson and the woman were already dead. If that was the case, it would be some consolation to Nye to know it was his presence that had flushed them out, forcing them to travel during the merciless heat of the day. But whatever the case, this was a comfortable spot to wait. Now that he could remain hidden during the daylight hours, water would not be such an issue. He'd stay here another day, maybe two—just to be sure—before heading south in search of the bodies.

If Carson *had* found water—which was the only way he would make it this far—he would be overconfident. Buoyant. Thinking he'd shaken Nye for good. Nye popped the magazine out, checked it, and slid it back in.

"Bang, bang," came the high, giggling voice out of the darkness to his left.

A faint blueness began to creep into the eastern sky.

"Who is that?" Levine heard Scopes's voice come sharply out of the elevator speakers. The lips of the wizard-image on the screen did not move, and its expression did not change, yet Levine could hear the mild surprise in the voice of his ex-friend. He did not type a response.

"So it wasn't a false alarm, after all." The wizard-image stepped away from the door. "Come in, please. I'm sorry I can't offer you a seat. Perhaps in the next release." He laughed. "Are you a rogue employee? Or are you working for an outside competitor? Whatever the case, perhaps you'll be good enough to explain your presence in my building and in my program."

Levine paused. Then he transferred his hands from the trackball and cursor keys to the laptop's keyboard. "I'm Charles Levine," he typed.

The wizard stared back for several seconds. "I don't believe you," came the voice of Scopes at last. "You couldn't possibly have hacked your way in here."

"But I did. And I'm here, inside your own program, Cypherspace."

"So you weren't content playing at corporate espionage from a distance, Charles?" Scopes asked in a mocking tone. "You had to add breaking and entering to your growing list of felonies."

Levine hesitated. He was not yet sure of Scopes's mental condition, but he felt he had no recourse but to speak openly. "I have to talk to you," he typed. "About what it is you're planning to do."

"And what is that?"

"Sell the doomsday virus to the United States military for five billion dollars."

There was a long pause.

"Charles, I've underestimated you. So you know about X-FLU II. Very good."

So that's what it's called, Levine thought. "What do you

hope to accomplish by selling this virus?" he typed.

"I thought that would have been obvious. Five billion dollars."

"Five billion isn't going to do you much good if the fools who end up with your creation destroy the entire world."

"Charles, please. They *already* have the ability to end the world. And they haven't done it. I understand these fellows. These are the same bullies who beat us up on the playground thirty years ago. Basically, I'm just aiding them in their desire to have the biggest, newest weapon. It's an evolutionary artifact, this wanting of big weapons. They'll never actually *use* the virus. Just like nuclear weapons, it has no military value, just strategic value in the balance of power equation. This virus was developed as a by-product of a legitimate Pentagon contract with GeneDyne. I've done nothing illegal or even unethical in developing this virus and offering it for sale."

"It amazes me how you can rationalize your greed," Levine typed.

"I'm not through. There are good, sensible reasons why the American military should have this virus. There can be little doubt that the existence of nuclear weapons prevented World War Three between the former Soviet Union and the United States. We finally did what Nobel hoped to do with dynamite; we made all-out war unthinkable. But now we have come to the next generation of weapons: biological hot agents. Despite treaties to the contrary, many unfriendly governments are working on biological agents just like this. If the balance of power is to be maintained, we cannot afford to be without our own. If we're caught without a virus such as X-FLU II, any number of hostile countries could blackmail us, threaten us and the rest of the world. Unfortunately, we have a president who actually intends to obey the Biological Weapons Convention. We're probably the only major country in the world still observing it! But this is a waste of time. I wasn't able to convince you to join me in founding GeneDyne, and

I won't be able to convince you now. It's a pity, really; we could have done great things together. But you chose, out of resentment, to devote your life to destroying mine. You've never been able to forgive me for winning the Game."

"Great things, you say. Like inventing a doomsday virus to wipe out the entire population of the world?"

"Perhaps you know less than you let on. This so-called doomsday virus is a by-product of a germ-line therapy that will rid the human race of the flu. Forever. An immunization that will confer lasting immunity to influenza."

"You call being dead immunity?"

"It should be obvious even to you that X-FLU II was an intermediate step. It had flaws, true. But I've found a way to make those very flaws marketable."

The figure went over to a cabinet and removed a small object from one of the shelves. As the figure turned back, Levine saw it was a gun, similar in design to those used by his pursuers in the woods.

"What are you going to do?" Levine asked. "You can't shoot me. This is cyberspace."

Scopes laughed. "We shall see. But I won't do it quite yet. First, I want you to tell me what really brings you here into my private world at such personal inconvenience. If you wanted to speak to me about X-FLU II, surely you could have found an easier way to do it."

"I came to tell you that PurBlood is poisonous."

The Scopes-wizard lowered the gun. "That is interesting. How so?"

"I don't know the details yet. It breaks down in the body and starts poisoning the mind. It's what drove Franklin Burt insane. It's what drove your scientist, Vanderwagon, insane. It will drive all the beta-testers at Mount Dragon insane. And it's what's driving *you* insane."

It was unsettling, speaking to the computerized image of Scopes. It did not smile, it did not frown; until Scopes's own voice came over the speaker, Levine had no way of knowing what the GeneDyne CEO was thinking, or what the effect of his own words might be. He wondered if Scopes already knew; if he had read and believed Carson's aborted transmission.

"Very good, Charles," came the reply at last, laced with weary irony. "I knew you were in the business of making outrageous claims against GeneDyne, but this is your grandest achievement."

"It's no claim. It's true."

"And yet you have no proof, no evidence, and no scientific explanation. It's like all your other charges against Gene-Dyne. PurBlood was developed by the most brilliant geneticists in the world. It has been thoroughly tested. And when it's released this Friday, it will save countless lives."

"Destroy countless lives, more likely. And you aren't the slightest bit worried, having taken PurBlood yourself?"

"You seem to know a lot about my activities. I never was transfused with PurBlood, however. I took colored plasma."

Levine did not reply for a moment. "And yet you let the rest of Mount Dragon take the real stuff. How courageous of you."

"I had planned on taking it, actually, but my stalwart assistant, Mr. Fairley, prevailed on my better judgment. Besides, the Mount Dragon staff developed it. Who better to test it?"

Levine sat back helplessly. How could he have forgotten, in his haste to confront Scopes directly, what the man was like? The discussion reminded him of their college arguments. Back then, he had never succeeded in changing Scopes's opinion on any subject. How could he possibly succeed now, when so much more was at stake?

There was a long silence. Levine maneuvered his view around the garret and noticed that the fog had cleared. He moved to the window. It was now dark, and a full moon was shimmering off the surface of the ocean like a skein of silk. A dragger, nets hung, chugged toward the harbor. Now that the conversation had lapsed into silence, Levine thought he could detect the sound of the surf on the rocks below. Pemaquid Point Light winked in the darkness.

"Impressive, isn't it?" Scopes said. "It captures everything but the smell of the sea."

Levine felt a deep sadness steal over him. It was a perfect illustration of the contradictions in Scopes's character. Only a genius of immense creativity could have written a program this beautiful and subtle. And yet the same person was planning to sell X-FLU II. Levine watched the boat glide into the harbor, its running lights dancing on the water. A dark figure leapt off the boat and caught the hawsers as they were thrown from the deck, looping them over cleats.

"Originally, it began as a set of separate challenges," Scopes said. "My network was growing daily, and I felt I was losing control. I wanted a way to traverse it, easily and privately. I had spent a fair amount of time playing with artificial-intelligence languages, like LISP, and object-oriented languages such as Smalltalk. I felt there was a need for a new kind of computer language that could meld the best of both, with something else added, too. When those languages were developed, computer horsepower was minuscule. I realized I now had the processing capability to play with images as well as words. So I built my language around visual constructs. The Cypherspace compiler creates *worlds*, not just programs. It began simply enough. But soon I realized the possibilities of my new medium. I felt I could create an entirely new art form, unique to the computer, meant to be experienced on its own terms. It's taken me years to create this world, and I'm still working on it. It'll never be finished, of course. But much of that time was spent in development, in making the programming language and tools sufficiently robust. I could do it again much more quickly, now.

"Charles, you could stand at that window for a week and never see the same thing twice. If you wished, you could go down to the dock and talk to those men. The tide goes in and out with the phases of the moon. There are seasons. There are people living in the houses: fishermen, summer people, artists. Real people, people I remember from my childhood. There's Marvin Clark, who runs the local store. He died a few years back but he lives on in my program. Tomorrow, you could go down there and listen to him telling stories. You could have a cup of tea and play backgammon with Hank Hitchins. Each person is a self-contained object within the larger program. They exist independently and interact with each other in ways that I never programmed or even foresaw. Here, I'm a kind of god: I've created a world, but now that it's created, it goes on without further input from me."

"But you're a selfish god," Levine said. "You've kept this world to yourself."

"True enough. I simply don't feel like sharing it. It's too personal."

Levine turned back to the wizard-image. "You've reproduced the island in perfect detail, except your own house. It's in ruins. Why?"

The figure was still a moment, and no sound came through the elevator speaker. Levine wondered what nerve he had touched. Then the figure raised the gun again. "I think we've spoken enough now, Charles," Scopes said.

"I'm not impressed by the gun."

"You should be. You are simply a process within the matrix of my program. If I shoot, the thread of your process will halt. You will be stuck, with no way to communicate with me or anyone else. But it's largely academic now. While we were chatting about my creation, I sent a sniffer routine back over your trail, tracking you across the network backbone until I located your terminal. It can't be too comfortable, stuck there in Elevator Forty-nine between the seventh and eighth floors. A welcoming party is already on its way, so you might as well sit tight."

"What are you going to do?" Levine asked.

"Me? I'm not going to do anything. You, however, are going to die. Your arrogant break-in, along with this latest round of snooping into my business, really leaves me little choice. As an intruder, of course, your killing will be justifiable homicide. I'm sorry, Charles, I truly am. It didn't need to end this way."

Levine raised his fingers to type a reply, then stopped. There was nothing he could say.

"Now I'm going to terminate the program. Good-bye, Charles."

The figure took careful aim.

For the first time since entering the GeneDyne building, Levine was afraid.

Carson woke with a start. It was still dark, but dawn was approaching: As he looked out, he could see the sky beginning to separate itself from the black mouth of the cave. A few yards away, Susana was still asleep on the sand. He could hear the soft, regular sound of her breathing.

He propped himself up on one elbow, aware of a dull nagging thirst. Crawling on hands and knees to the edge of the spring, he cupped the warm water in his hands, drinking it greedily. As the thirst died, a gnawing hunger began to assert itself in the depths of his belly.

Standing, he walked to the mouth of the cave and breathed the cool, predawn air. The horses were a few hundred yards off, grazing quietly. He whistled softly and they lifted their heads, perking their ears at his presence. He walked toward them, stepping carefully in the darkness. They were a little gaunt, but otherwise seemed to have survived their ordeal quite well. He stroked Roscoe's neck. The horse's eyes were bright and clear, a good sign. He bent down and felt the coronet at the top of the hoof. It was warm but not hot, showing no sign of laminitis.

He looked around in the gathering light. The surrounding mountains were carved from tilted sandstone, their sedimentary layers running at crazy diagonals through the eroded humps and canyons. As he watched, their summits became infused with the scarlet light of the rising sun. There was a stillness to the air almost religious in its force: the silence of a cathedral before the organ sounds. Where the muscled flanks of the mountains sank into the desert, the skirts of the lava flow cloaked their base in a black, jagged mass. Their own cave was hidden from view, below the level of the desert. Standing one hundred yards from it, Carson would never have dreamed there was anything around but black lava. There was no sign of Nye.

Carson watered the horses again in the cave and then hobbled them in a fresh patch of tobosa grass. Then, locating a mesquite bush, he used his spearpoint to cut off a long flexible sucker, with a cluster of stobs and thorns at the end. He walked out of the lava and into the desert, examining the sand carefully as he went. Soon, he found what he was looking for: the tracks of a rabbit, still young and relatively small. He followed them for a hundred yards until they disappeared into a hole underneath a Mormon-tea bush. Squatting down, he shoved the thorny end of the stick down the hole, threading it through several turns, and—when it reached the den— prodding and twisting, feeling a furry resistance. Twisting more vigorously now, he slowly pulled the stick back out of the hole. A young rabbit, whose loose skin had been caught and twisted up in the stobs, struggled and grunted. Carson pinned it with his foot and cut off its head, letting the blood drain into the sand. Then he gutted, skinned, and spitted it, buried the offal in the sand to deter buzzards, and returned to the cave.

De Vaca was still sleeping. At the mouth of the cave he built a small fire, rubbed the rabbit with more alkali salt from his pocket, and began roasting it. The meat spit and sizzled, the blue smoke drifting into the clear air.

Now at last the sun came above the horizon, throwing a brilliant shower of golden light across the desert floor and deep into the cave, illuminating its dark surfaces. There was a noise and Carson turned to see de Vaca, sitting up at last and rubbing her eyes sleepily.

"Ouch," she said as the golden light flared in her face and turned her black hair to bronze.

Carson watched her with the smugly virtuous smile of an early riser. His eyes strayed from her to the interior of the cave. De Vaca, seeing his expression change, turned to follow his gaze.

The rising sun was shining through a crack in the cave opening, striping a needle of orange light across the floor of the cave and halfway up its rear wall. Balanced atop the needle and illuminated against the rough rock was a jagged, yet immediately recognizable image: an eagle, wings spread and head upraised as if about to burst into flight.

They watched in silence as the image grew brighter, until it seemed it would be forever branded into the rear of the cave. And then, as suddenly as it had flared up, it died away; the sun rose above the mouth of the cave, and the eagle vanished into the growing superfluity of light.

"*El Ojo del Águila*," De Vaca said. "The Spring of the Eagle. Now we know we found it. Incredible to think that this same spring saved my ancestors' lives four hundred years ago."

"And now it's saving ours," Carson murmured. He continued to stare at the dark space where the image had been for a moment, as if trying to recall a thought that was dancing just beyond the verge of consciousness. Then the wonderful aroma of roasting meat filled his nostrils, and he turned back to the rabbit.

"Hungry?" he asked.

"You're damn right. What is it?"

"Rabbit." He turned it, then pulled it from the fire and stuck the spit upright in the sand. Taking out the spearpoint, he sliced off a haunch and handed it to de Vaca.

"Careful, it's hot."

Gingerly, she took a bite.

"Delicious. You can cook, too. I assumed all you cowboys knew how to make was beans in bacon fat."

She sank her teeth into the haunch, peeling off another piece of meat. "And it's not even tough, like the rabbits my grandfather used to bring home." She spat out a small bone. Carson watched her eat with a cook's secret pride.

In ten minutes the rabbit was gone and the cleaned bones burning in the fire. De Vaca sat back, licking her fingers. "How'd you catch that rabbit?" she asked.

Carson shrugged. "Just something I picked up on the ranch as a kid."

De Vaca nodded. Then she smiled wickedly. "That's right, I forgot. All Indians know how to hunt. It's an instinct, right?"

Carson frowned, his complacence dissolving under this unwarranted dig. "Give it a rest," he grumbled. "It wasn't funny the first time, and it certainly isn't funny now."

But de Vaca was still smiling. "You should see yourself. That day in the sun did you good. A few more like it, and you'll look right at home on the Big Rez."

Despite himself, Carson felt a hot fury mounting inside. De Vaca had an unerring instinct for searching out his sensitive spots and homing in on them mercilessly. Somehow, he'd allowed himself to believe that the terrifying ordeal they had shared would change her. Now he wasn't sure if he was more angry with de Vaca for remaining her sarcastic self, or at himself for his foolish self-delusion.

"*Tú eres una desagradecida hija de puta*," he said, the anger giving his words a startling clarity.

A curious expression came over de Vaca's face as the whites of her eyes grew large and distinct. Her casual pose in the sand grew rigid.

"So the *cabrón* knows more of the mother tongue than he's let on," she said in a low voice. "I'm an ingrate, am I? Typical."

"You call me typical?" Carson retorted. "I saved your ass yesterday. Yet here you are again today, slinging the same shit."

"*You* saved my ass?" de Vaca snapped. "You're a fool, *cabrón*. It was your Ute ancestor who saved us. And your great-uncle, who passed down his stories to you. Those fine people that you treat like blots on your pedigree. You've got a great heritage, something to be proud of. And what do you do? You hide it. Ignore it. Sweep it under the rug. As if you're a better person without it." Her voice was rising now, echoing crazily inside the cave. "And you know what, Carson? Without it, you're nothing. You're not a cowboy. You're not a Harvard WASP. You're just an empty redneck shell that can't even reconcile its own past."

As he listened, Carson's fury turned cold. "Still playing the would-be analyst?" he said. "When I'm ready to confront my inner child, I'll go to somebody with a diploma—not a snake-oil peddler who's more comfortable in a poncho than a lab coat. *Todavía tienes la mierda del barrio en tus zapatos*."

De Vaca drew in her breath with a sharp hiss, and her nostrils flared. Suddenly she drew back her hand and slapped him across the face with all her strength. Carson's cheek burned and his ear began to buzz. He shook his head in surprise, noticed she had drawn back to hit him again, and caught her hand as it swung toward him a second time. Balling her other hand into a fist, de Vaca lashed out at him, but he ducked, tightening his grip on her imprisoned hand and thrusting it from him. Overextended, de Vaca fell backward into the pool and Carson, caught off guard, fell across her.

The slap and the sudden fall had driven the fury out of Carson. Now, as he lay across de Vaca—as he felt her hard lithe body struggle beneath his—an entirely different kind of hunger seized him. Before he could stop himself he leaned forward and kissed her, deliberately, on the lips.

"*Pendejo,*" de Vaca gasped, fighting for breath. "*Nobody* kisses me." With a violent wrench, she freed her arms, balling her dripping hands into fists. Carson watched her warily.

They stared at each other for a moment, motionless. Water dripped from de Vaca's fists onto the dark, warm surface of the pool. The echoes died away until the only sounds that remained were those made by the droplets of water, falling between their labored breaths. Suddenly, she grabbed Carson by the hair with both hands and crushed her mouth to his.

In a moment her hands were everywhere, sliding up beneath his shirt, caressing his chest, teasing his nipples, tugging at his belt and worrying down his fly and easing him out and stroking him with long urgent movements. She sat up and raised her arms as he shrugged off her top, tossed it aside, and then pulled hungrily at her jeans, already soaked black with the warm spring water. An arm went around his neck as her lips brushed his bruised ear and her pink cat's tongue darted in and she whispered words that brought a burning to the back of his scalp. He tore her panties away as she fell into the water, gasping or crying, he wasn't sure which, her breasts and the small curve of her belly rising slick from the surface of the spring. Then he was in her and her legs were locked over the small of his back as they found their rhythm and the water rose and fell around them, crashing against the sand like the surf of the world's dawn.

Later, de Vaca looked over at Carson, lying naked on the wet sand.

"I don't know whether to stab you or fuck you," she said, grinning.

Carson glanced up. Then he rolled toward her, raising an arm to gently smooth a tangle of black hair that had fallen across her face.

"Let's have another go at the latter," he said. "Then we'll talk."

The dawn turned to noon, and they slept.

Carson was flying, soaring above the desert, the twisted ribbons of lava mere specks beneath him. He struggled higher, lifting himself toward the hot sun. Ahead, a huge narrow spire of rock thrust itself up from the desert, ending in a sharp point miles above the sands. He tried to crest the point, but it seemed to grow as he climbed, taller and taller, reaching for the sun. . . .

He awoke with a start, heart racing. Sitting up in the cool darkness, he looked out at the mouth of the cave, then back toward its dim interior, as the realization that had escaped him earlier burned its way into him like a firebrand.

He stood, put on his clothes, and stepped outside. It was almost two o'clock, the hottest time of the day. The horses had recovered well, but would need to be watered once more. They'd have to leave within the hour if they wanted to make Lava Gate by sunset. That would get them to Lava Camp by midnight, or perhaps a little later. They would still have thirty-six hours to get their information into the hands of the FDA before the scheduled release of PurBlood.

But they couldn't leave. Not yet.

Turning to the horses, he tore two strips of leather from the saddle rigging. Then he gathered up an armful of mesquite sticks and dead creosotebush, which he arranged into two tight bundles. Lashing the bundles together with the leather strips, he turned and walked back toward the cave.

De Vaca was up and dressed. "Afternoon, cowboy," she said as he entered the cave.

He grinned and approached her.

"Not again," she said, poking him playfully in the stomach.

He leaned closer and whispered in her ear. "*Al despertar la hora el águila del sol se levanta en una aguja del fuego.*"

"At dawn the eagle of the sun rises on a needle of fire," she translated, a puzzled expression on her face. "That was the legend on Nye's treasure map. I didn't get it then, and I don't get it today."

She looked at him a moment, frowning perplexedly. Then her eyes widened. "We saw an eagle this morning," she said. "Silhouetted against the rear of the cave by the dawn sun."

Carson nodded.

"That means we've found the place—"

"—The place Nye has been searching for all these years," Carson interrupted. "The location of Mondragón's gold."

"Only he was off by almost a hundred miles." De Vaca glanced back into the darkness. Then she turned toward Carson. "What are we waiting for?"

Carson lighted the end of one of the bundles, and together they moved back into the recesses of the cave.

From the large pool where it emerged out of the earth, the spring flowed back into the cave in a narrow rivulet, sloping downward at a slight angle. Carson and de Vaca followed its course, peering into the ruddy gloom created by the torch. As they approached the rear wall of the cave, Carson realized it was not a wall after all, but a sudden drop in the level of the ceiling. The floor of the cave dropped as well, leaving a narrow tunnel through which they had to stoop. In the darkness ahead, Carson could hear the sound of splashing water.

The tunnel opened into a high narrow cavern, perhaps ten feet across and thirty feet high. Carson held the torch aloft, illuminating the mottled yellow surface of the rock face. He moved forward, then stopped abruptly. At his feet, the stream tumbled off a cliff, splashing down into a yawning pool of blackness. Holding the torch in front of him, Carson peered over the edge.

"See anything?" de Vaca asked.

"I can just barely see the bottom," he said. "It must be fifty feet down, at least."

There was a sliding sound and Carson instinctively drew back. A handful of small rocks crumbled off the lip of the cliff and bounced down into the darkness, echoing hollowly as they went.

Carson tested the ground in front of him. "All of this rock is loose and rotten," he said, moving gingerly along the cliff face. Finding a more stable spot, he dropped to his knees and leaned over the edge again.

"There's something down there," de Vaca said from the far side of the cliff edge.

"I see it."

"If you'll hold the torch," de Vaca said, "I'll climb down. This way looks easier."

"Let me do it," Carson said. De Vaca flashed him a dark look.

"OK, OK," he sighed.

Moving toward a spot where the cliff face had collapsed, de Vaca half climbed, half slid down the rubbled slope. Carson could barely see her moving down in the gloom.

"Throw the other torch down!" she called at last.

Shoving a book of matches between the sticks, Carson tossed down the second bundle. There was a moment of fumbling, then the sound of a match being struck, and suddenly the chasm below was illuminated by a flickering crimson light.

Peering farther over the edge, Carson could clearly see the outline of a desiccated mule. The animal's pack was broken open and pieces of manta and leather were lying about. A number of large whitish lumps could be seen protruding through the ruined pack. Nearby lay the mummified body of a man.

In the lambent light of the brand, he could see de Vaca examine first the man, then the mule, then the ruined pack. She picked up several scattered objects, tying them into the loose ends of her shirt. Then she came scrabbling back up the talus slope.

"What did you find?" Carson muttered as she approached.

"I don't know. Let's get into the light."

At the cave entrance, de Vaca untied the ends of her shirt. A small leather pouch, a sheathed dagger, and several of the whitish lumps tumbled onto the sand.

Carson picked up the dagger, carefully sliding it from its sheath. The metal was dull and rusted, but the hilt was intact, preserved beneath a mantle of dust. He wiped it against his sleeve and held it up to the sun. Chased in silver on the iron hilt were two ornate letters: D M.

"Diego de Mondragón," he whispered.

As de Vaca tried to open the stiff leather bag, it broke in half and one small gold coin and three larger silver coins fell onto the sand. She picked them up and turned them over in her hands, marveling as they glinted in the light.

"Look at how fresh they are," she said.

"What about the packs?" Carson asked.

"They were half-filled with white stones like these," de Vaca said, pointing to the whitish lumps. "There were dozens of them. The saddlebags were full of it."

Carson picked up one of the blocks and examined it curiously. It was cool and fine-grained, the color of ivory.

"What the hell is it?" he murmured.

De Vaca picked up the other piece, hefting it curiously. "It's heavy," she said.

Removing his arrowhead, Carson scratched at the lump. "But it's fairly soft. Whatever it is, it's not rock."

De Vaca rubbed the surface with one palm. "Why would Mondragón have risked his life carrying this stuff, when he could have been carrying extra water and . . ." She stopped abruptly. "I know what this is," she announced. "It's meerschaum."

"Meerschaum?" Carson asked.

"Yup. Used for pipes, carvings, works of art. It was extremely valuable back in the seventeenth century. New Mexico exported large quantities of it to New Spain. I guess Mondragón's 'mine' was a meerschaum deposit." She looked at Carson and grinned.

A stricken look crossed Carson's face. Then he slumped back in the sand, laughing to himself. "And all this time, Nye has been searching for Mondragón's lost gold. It never occurred to him—it never occurred to anybody—that Mondragón might have been carrying some other kind of wealth. Something practically worthless today."

De Vaca nodded. "But back then, the value of the meerschaum in that pack might easily have been worth its weight in gold. Look at how fine the grain is. Today, it might be worth four, maybe five hundred dollars."

"What about the coins?"

"Mondragón's bit of spending money. The dagger is probably the only thing of _real_ value here."

Carson shook his head, looking back into the cave. "I suppose the mule began to wander into the rear of the cave, and he chased after it. Their combined weight must have collapsed the edge of that cliff face."

De Vaca shook her head. "When I was down there, I found something else. There was an arrow, lodged deep in Mondragón's breastbone."

Carson looked at her, surprised. "It must have been the servant. So the legend was wrong: They weren't looking for water. They had *found* water. But the servant decided to take the treasure for himself."

De Vaca nodded. "Maybe Mondragón was looking for a place to hide his treasure, and didn't see the cliff edge in the darkness. There were loose pieces of lava lying on top of the body as well as around it. The mule was killed in the fall, and the servant decided there was no point in waiting around any longer."

"You said the saddlebags were half-full, right? He probably put Mondragón out of his misery, took what he could carry, and started back south. He would have taken the doublet as protection from the sun. Only it wasn't enough. He got as far as Mount Dragon."

Carson continued to stare at the cave mouth as if waiting for it to tell them the story. "So that's the end of the Mount Dragon legend," he said at last.

"Perhaps," de Vaca replied. "But legends don't die all that easily."

They stood silently in the bright afternoon sun, staring at the coins in de Vaca's outstretched hand. At last, she placed them carefully in the pocket of her jeans.

"I think it's time we saddled the horses," Carson said, picking up the dagger and shoving it into his belt. "We need to get to Lava Gate before sunset."

Nye sat in his perch high up among the rocks, feeling the late-afternoon sun on his hat and the waves of solar radiation rising off the surrounding lava, clasping him in their stifling embrace. He raised his rifle and, using the scope, carefully scanned the southern horizon. No sign of Carson and the woman. He raised the sight, scanning again. No sign of circling vultures, either.

"They're probably holed up somewhere, snogging." The boy threw a rock down the slope, clattering and bouncing. "That girl's just dead common."

Nye grimaced. Either they'd found themselves a spring, or they were dead. Most likely the latter. Perhaps it took a while for the rot to really set in and draw the buzzards. After all, the desert was large. The birds might have to follow the scent from quite a distance. How long in this heat would it take a body to really give off an odor: four, maybe five hours?

"Game of come-catch-a-blackbird?" the boy asked, shoving a grubby handful of lava pebbles at him. "We'll use these instead of aggies."

Nye turned to him. The boy was dirty and one nostril was rimed with dried snot. "Not now," he said, gently. He raised his scope and panned the horizon again.

And then he saw them: two figures on horseback, perhaps three miles away.

Levine maneuvered himself quickly sideways as the gun went off. Turning the trackball, he saw a neat, round hole in the oculus window behind him. The Scopes-figure raised the gun again.

"Brent!" he typed frantically. "Don't do this. You *must* listen."

Scopes sighed. "For twenty years, you've been a thorn in my side. I did everything I could for you. In the beginning, I offered you an equal partnership, fifty percent of GeneDyne stock. I've refrained from responding to your vicious attacks, while you grew fat and powerful by feeding off negative publicity about GeneDyne. You took advantage of my silence to attack me again and again, to accuse me of greed and selfishness."

"You kept silent only because you hoped I'd sign the compatent renewal," Levine typed.

"That's a low blow, Charles. I did it because I still felt a kind of friendship for you. At first, I confess, I didn't take your carping seriously. We'd been so close at school. You were the only person I'd ever met who was my intellectual equal. Look what we did together: we brought X-RUST into the world." A bitter laugh sounded through the elevator speaker. "That's the side of the story you don't like to tell the press, do you? The great Levine—the noble Levine—the Levine that would never sink to the level of Brent Scopes—was the coinventor of X-RUST. One of the greatest cash cows in the history of capitalism. I may have found the Anasazi corn kernels, but it was your brilliant science that helped me to isolate the X-RUST gene, to develop the disease-resistant strain."

"It wasn't my idea to make billions off poor people in Third World countries."

"What profit I made from it was minuscule measured against the productivity increase," Scopes replied. "Have you forgotten that, with our rust-resistant strain, world corn output increased fifteen percent, and the price of corn actually dropped? Charles, people who would otherwise have starved to death lived because of the discovery. *Our* discovery."

"It was our discovery, yes. But it wasn't my wish to turn that discovery into a tool for greed. I wanted to release it into the public domain."

Scopes laughed. "I haven't forgotten that naive desire of yours. And surely you haven't forgotten the circumstances that allowed *me* to profit from it. I won, fair and square."

Levine had not forgotten. The memory seared his soul with a guilty fire. When it was clear that the two of them had irreconcilably different wishes for the X-RUST gene, they had agreed to compete for it. To play the game for it: the Game, the one they had invented at college. This time, it had been for the ultimate stakes.

"And I lost," Levine replied.

"Yes. But the last laugh is yours, isn't it, Charles? In two months, the corn patent expires. Since you've refused to renew your half, the patent will lapse. And the most lucrative discovery in GeneDyne history will be the world's to use as they see fit, at no charge."

Suddenly, blending with the sound of Scopes's voice, Levine heard a babble of other voices: loud and insistent, echoing harshly down the elevator shaft.

They were coming to get him in real space as well.

There was a lurch that pressed Levine against the elevator wall. Above him, a motor hummed into life, and the cool voice spoke once again: *The malfunction has been corrected. We are sorry for the inconvenience.*

The elevator groaned, thumped, then began to climb.

On the giant screen, Levine saw the Scopes-figure turn away from him, looking out one of the garret windows. "It doesn't matter now whether I shoot you here or not," he said. "When your elevator arrives on the sixtieth floor, you're corporeal body is going to be terminated, anyway. Your cyberspatial existence will be moot."

The figure turned back and looked at him, waiting.

Levine glanced up at the floor display. It read: 20.

"I'm sorry it has to end like this, Charles," came the voice of Scopes. "But I suppose my regret is just a nostalgic artifact, after all. Perhaps, once you're gone, I'll be able to honor the memory of the friend I once had. A friend who changed utterly."

The numbers were ticking off rapidly: 55, 56, 57. The

whine of the lift motors lowered in a deep decrescendo as the elevator slowed.

"I could still sign the corn-patent renewal," Levine typed.

Sixty, said the voice. Levine yanked the network connection from the socket. Abruptly, the image of the misty garret winked out, and the flat panel of the elevator wall was black once more. Levine quickly switched off his laptop. If Mime was still in GeneDyne cyberspace, he'd be thrown out immediately. But at least he could not be traced.

There was a silence as the elevator settled. Then the doors slid back and Levine, cross-legged on the floor, looked up to see three guards in the blue-and-black GeneDyne uniform staring down at him. All three were holding pistols. The lead guard raised his gun, aiming for Levine's head.

"I'm not cleaning it up," said a guard at one side.

Levine closed his eyes.

They had filled both canteens and drunk from the spring until their bodies refused to swallow any more. Now, as they rode along the base of the mountains, Carson could feel the coolness slowly creep back into the air. Overhead, a late-afternoon sun hung above the barren summits.

Another fifteen miles to Lava Gate, then perhaps twenty more to Lava Camp. Since most of their traveling would be under cover of darkness, they needn't fear running out of water again. The horses were probably each carrying fifty pounds of water in their bellies. There was nothing like a bad thirst to scare a horse into drinking when he had the water.

He dropped back slightly, watching de Vaca. She sat erect in the saddle, her long legs relaxed in the stirrups, her hair floating behind like a black wind. She had a sharp, strong profile, Carson noticed, with a finely pointed nose and full lips. Odd he'd never seen it before. *Of course,* he thought, *a full biosuit isn't exactly the most flattering piece of clothing.*

She turned. "What are you looking at, *cabrón?*" she asked. The golden afternoon light was refracting in her dark eyes.

"You," he said.

"What do you see?"

"Someone I—" He paused.

"Let's get back to civilization before you make any hasty declarations," she said, turning away.

Carson grinned. "I was going to say, someone I'd like to pin to a bed. A real bed, not just a bed of sand. Writhing in ecstasy, preferably."

"That bed of sand wasn't so bad."

He sat back in the saddle with an exaggerated grimace. "I think half the skin of my back must be underneath your nails right now."

He pointed to the horizon. "See that notch in the distance, where the mountains and the lava seem to meet? That's Lava Gate, the northern end of the Jornada. From there, we just aim for the North Star. It's less than twenty miles to Lava Camp. They'll have hot food and a phone. And maybe even a real bed."

"Oh, yeah?" asked de Vaca. "Ouch. My poor butt."

Nye sighted down the barrel of the Holland & Holland, checked the brush scope, and secured the magazine. Everything was ready. Placing the buttstock between his feet, he checked the muzzle end for any obstructions. He'd cleaned it a hundred times since that piss-artist Carson had plugged it up, that day in the desert. But it didn't hurt to make sure.

The two figures were now a mile away. In less than ten minutes, they'd be coming into range. Two fast, clean shots at four hundred yards. Then two more to pay the insurance, and a couple for the horses. They'd never even see him.

It was time. He eased the rifle into position, then lay on the hard lava, snugging his cheek into the stock. He began taking slow, deep breaths, letting the air ease out his nostrils, slowing his heart rate. He'd shoot between heartbeats for greater accuracy.

He raised his head imperceptibly and glanced around. The boy was gone. Then Nye spotted him, dancing on a lava rock on the other side of the slope. Far away from the action.

He settled into position again, lining up the sights and slowly swiveling the barrel across the desert floor until the two figures appeared between the crosshairs.

"Don't shoot!" came a voice from behind the guards. "I've got Mr. Scopes on the intercom." Words were exchanged. The gun barrel lowered, and one of the guards pulled Levine roughly to his feet.

He was led down a dim corridor, past a large guard station, then a smaller one. As the group turned into a narrow hallway flanked by rows of doors, Levine realized he had taken this trip once before: hours earlier, when he navigated through GeneDyne cyberspace with Phido at his side. As he walked, he could hear the hum of machinery, the low susurrus of ventilators and air exchangers.

They stopped outside the massive black door. Levine was

instructed to remove his shoes and don a pair of foam slippers. A guard spoke into his radio, and there was the sound of electronic locks being released. There was a hissing sound, and the door popped ajar. As a guard pulled it open, air rushed out, buffeting Levine's face. He stepped inside.

The octagonal office looked nothing like the garret of Scopes's cyberspace. It was vast, dark, and oddly sterile. The bare walls climbed ponderously to the high ceiling. Levine's gaze moved from the ceiling, to the famous piano, to the gleaming inlaid desk, to Scopes. The CEO of GeneDyne sat on his battered sofa, keyboard on lap, looking sardonically back at Levine. His black T-shirt was dirty and stained with what appeared to be pizza sauce. In front of him, a giant screen still contained an image of the parapet outside the garret of the ruined house. In the distance, Pemaquid Point Light was blinking over the dark water.

Scopes stabbed a key, and the screen went abruptly black.

"Frisk him for weapons or electronic devices of any kind," Scopes said to the guards. He waited until the guards withdrew. Then he looked at Levine, making a tent of his fingers. "I've checked the maintenance logs. You seem to have spent quite some time in that elevator. Fifteen hours, give or take. Would you care to refresh yourself?"

Levine shook his head.

"Have a seat, then." Scopes indicated the far end of the sofa. "What about your friend? Would he like to join us? I mean, the one that's been doing all the difficult work for you. He's left his signature all over the network, and I'd very much like to meet him and explain the dim view I take of his activities."

Levine remained silent. Scopes looked at him, smiling and smoothing down his unruly cowlick. "It's been some time, hasn't it, Charles? I must admit, I'm a bit surprised to see you. But not half as surprised as I am by your offer to sign the renewal, after all these years of adamant refusal. How quickly we lose our principles when we face the ultimate test. 'It is easier to fight for one's principles than to live up to them.' Or to die for them. Correct?"

Levine sat down. " 'To have doubted one's own first principles is the mark of a wise man,' " he quoted.

"That's '*civilized* man,' Charles. You're rusty at The Game. Do you remember the last time we played it?"

A look of pain crossed Levine's face. "If I'd won, we wouldn't be here today."

"Probably not. I often wonder, you know, just how much of your frantic antigenetics campaigning over the years was really just self-loathing. You loved The Game as much as I did. You risked everything you believed in for that final game, and you lost." Scopes sat up and placed his fingers on the keyboard. "I'll have the papers printed up for your signature right away."

"You haven't heard my terms," Levine said evenly.

Scopes turned. "Terms? You don't seem to be in a position to dictate any. Either you sign, or you die."

"You wouldn't actually murder me in cold blood, would you?"

"Murder," Scopes repeated slowly. "In cold blood. I suppose such sensationalist language is your stock in trade now. But yes, I'm afraid I would—not to put too fine a point on it, as Mr. Micawber would say. Unless you sign the patent renewal."

There was a silence. "My terms are one more game," Levine said.

Scopes looked back in disbelief. Then he chuckled. "Well, well, Charles. A—what do they call it—grudge match? And for what stakes?"

"If I win, you destroy the virus and let me live. If I lose, I'll sign the corn-patent renewal and you can kill me. So you see, if you win, you get another eighteen years of exclusive royalties on X-RUST, *and* you can sell the virus to the Pentagon.

If you lose, you lose both the corn patent *and* the virus."

"Killing you would be easier."

"But much less profitable. If you kill me, the corn patent will not be renewed. That eighteen-year renewal alone is probably worth ten billion dollars to GeneDyne."

Scopes thought a moment, letting the keyboard slide from his lap. "Let me counter that last offer. If you lose, instead of killing you, I'll bring you aboard GeneDyne as vice-chairman and chief scientist. It's my original offer, updated, with a salary and stock options commensurate with your stature. We'll turn back the clock, start all over again. Naturally, you will cooperate in every way, and cease these senseless attacks on GeneDyne and technological progress in general."

"Instead of death, a pact with the devil, you mean. Why would you do this for me? I'm not sure I trust you."

Scopes grinned. "What makes you think I'd be doing it for you? Killing you would be messy and inconvenient. Besides, I'm not a murderer, and there's always the chance it would weigh on my conscience. Really, Charles, I haven't enjoyed destroying your career. It was a purely defensive move." He waved his hand. "However, just letting you go back into the world like a loose cannon, to snipe at me at your leisure, is not a viable option either. It is in my interests to convince you to join the company, cooperate, sign the usual nondisclosure forms. If you wished, you could sit in your office here all day, doing nothing. But I think you would find a much more rewarding path in research and development—helping to cure sick people. It doesn't necessarily have to be in genetic engineering, either. Pharmaceuticals, biomedical research, whatever: You could write your own ticket. Devote your life to creating, instead of destroying."

Levine stood up, facing the huge screen, now blank and featureless. The silence grew. At last, he turned to face Scopes. "I accept," he said. "However, I need a guarantee that you'll destroy that virus if you lose. I want you to remove it from the safe and place it on this table between us. If I win, I'll simply take the vial out of here and dispose of it properly. If it *is*, in fact, the only vial."

Scopes frowned. "You of all people should know that. Thanks to your friend Carson."

Levine raised his eyebrows.

"So it's news to you, is it? From the reports I've received, it appears that son of a bitch blew up Mount Dragon. Carson Iscariot."

"I had no idea."

Scopes looked at him speculatively. "And I thought *you* were behind it. I assumed it was revenge of a sort for what I'd done to your father's memory." He shook his head. "Well, what's nine hundred million when ten billion are at stake? I agree to your terms. With one proviso of my own. If you lose, I don't want you to renege on the corn-patent renewal. I want you to sign the papers now, in the presence of a notary. We'll place the agreement on the table in front of us, along with the vial. If I lose, you get both. If I win, I get both."

Levine nodded.

Pulling the keyboard back onto his lap, Scopes began typing rapidly. Then, reaching for a phone, he spoke briefly. A moment later, there was a chime; then a woman entered bearing several sheets of paper, two pens, and a notary seal.

"Here's the document," Scopes said. "Sign it while I get the virus."

He moved toward a far wall, ran his fingers along its surface until he felt what he was looking for, then pressed against it. There was a snap, and a panel swung outward. Scopes reached inside and quickly tapped a number of keys. There was a beep and a click, and then Scopes reached his hand farther inside and pulled out a small biohazard box. Bringing it to the inlaid table, he opened it and removed a sealed glass ampule three inches wide and two inches high. He carefully placed the ampule on top of the document Levine had signed, then waited until the notary left the Octagon.

"We'll play by our old rules," he said. "Best two out of three. We'll let the GeneDyne computer pick a topic at random from its database. If there are any challenges, do you agree that the computer should resolve them?"

"Yes," said Levine.

Scopes flipped a coin, slapped it onto the back of his hand. "You call it."

"Heads."

Scopes removed the covering hand. "Tails. I start the first subject."

De Vaca ceased singing the old Spanish song that had kept them company for the last several miles, and fell back slightly, taking a moment to breathe the desert air in deep, reverent draughts. The setting sun had tinged the desert with gold. It felt wonderful to be alive, to simply be on this horse, headed out of the Jornada and toward a new life. For the moment, it didn't matter what that life was. There were so many things she had taken for granted, and she swore never to allow herself to make that mistake again.

She looked at Carson, riding ahead on Roscoe, angling toward the high narrow gap of Lava Gate. She wondered, almost idly, how he would fit into that new life. Immediately, she dismissed the thought as being much too complicated. Plenty of time to think about that later.

Carson turned, noticed that de Vaca was no longer beside him, and slowed. He turned back with a smile as she approached, then leaned over on impulse to stroke her cheek with the back of one hand.

She felt a sudden spray of wetness across her face. The sensation of moisture in the desert was so foreign that she automatically closed her eyes against it, turning her face away and raising her hand protectively. She wiped her face and her hand came away bloody, a small jagged shard that looked like bone stuck to one of her fingers. At the same moment she heard a loud crack roll across the landscape.

Suddenly, everything began to happen at once. She looked forward to see Carson toppling forward on his horse just as her own mount bolted at the sharp noise. She grabbed desperately at the saddle horn as something whined past her ear. Another report boomed across the desert.

They were under fire.

Roscoe was heading for the base of the mountains at a dead run. De Vaca urged her horse to follow, lashing her heels into its flanks, hugging its neck, hoping to make a smaller target. She craned her neck upward, trying to steady her vision against the lurching and pounding. Ahead, she could see Carson hunched over the saddle. Blood was running freely down Roscoe's flank and shivering off in droplets, cascading into the sand. Another shot sounded, then another.

The horses dashed toward a cul-de-sac in the lava flow, and pulled up short. Several more shots came in rapid succession and Carson's horse whirled to escape, eyes wild, throwing Carson out of the saddle and onto the sand. De Vaca jumped from her horse and landed next to Carson as both animals ran blindly back out into the desert. There was another report, followed by the horrible scream of a horse in pain. De Vaca turned. Roscoe's belly had been blown open, a length of intestine spilling out between his legs like a gray streamer. The animal ran for a few hundred yards, then came to a trembling stop. There was another report, and de Vaca's horse fell kicking to the sand. Another bullet, and a fine red spray rose from its head. The animal jerked its hind legs twice, spasmodically, then lay still.

She crawled toward Carson. He was lying in the sand, curled in on himself, knees up around his chest. Blood was turning the sand around him to a slippery red paste. She turned him gently and he cried out. Quickly, her eyes searched for the wound. His left arm was completely soaked in blood, and she carefully pulled away a piece of his torn shirt. The bullet had taken a huge piece out of his forearm, shattering the radius and peeling the muscle and flesh back, exposing the ulna. In a moment the sight was obscured again by blood, which jetted freely from the severed radial artery.

Carson rolled sideways, his body stiffening in agony.

De Vaca turned quickly, looking for something she could use as a tourniquet. She didn't dare cross the field of fire toward the horses. In desperation, she ripped off her own shirt, rolled it tightly, and knotted it just below Carson's elbow, twisting it until the flow subsided.

"Can you walk?" she whispered.

Carson was speaking under his breath. She leaned closer, listening. "Jesus," she heard him moan. "Oh, Jesus."

"Don't crap out on me now," she said fiercely, tying off the tourniquet and grabbing him under the armpits. "We've got to take cover behind those rocks." With a supreme effort Carson rose shakily to his feet and staggered toward the cul-de-sac, then took a few steps into the rocks and collapsed again behind a large boulder. De Vaca crawled in behind him and examined his wound, her stomach rising at the sight. At least now he wouldn't bleed to death. She sat back and looked him over quickly. His lips looked oddly blue. There didn't seem to be any other wounds, but with all the blood it was difficult to tell. She tried not to think what it would mean if Nye hit him a second a time with that terrible rifle.

She had to think, and think quickly. Nye must have realized that he couldn't catch them by tracking. So he'd somehow guessed they were headed for Lava Gate, and gone ahead to cut them off. He'd destroyed their horses, and soon he'd be coming for them.

She tugged Mondragón's dagger out of Carson's belt. Then she dropped it in the sand in frustration. What the hell good was it against a man with an express rifle?

She peered over the rock and there was Nye, in the open now, kneeling and taking aim. Immediately a bullet whined inches from her face, striking the rocks behind her. Powdered stone stung the back of her neck in a sharp spray. The gun's report followed an instant later, echoing and bouncing among the rock formations.

She hunched down again behind the rock, then moved along behind it, peering out from another angle. Nye had risen to his feet once again and was walking toward them. His face was hidden in the deep shadow of his hat brim and she could not make out his expression. Only a hundred yards away now. He was simply going to walk up and kill them both. And there was absolutely nothing she could do.

Carson moaned and clutched at her, trying to say something.

She moved back behind the boulder, turning away from Nye, and waited. Waited for the massive blow to the back of her head that would signify the arrival of the bullet. She could hear boots crunching toward them, and she covered her head with her hands, closing her eyes tightly, preparing herself as best she could for death.

A single word appeared on the massive screen before them:

vanity

Scopes thought a moment in silence. Then he cleared his throat. " 'No place affords a more striking conviction of the vanity of human hopes than a public library.' Dr. Johnson."

"Very good," said Levine. " 'A man who is not a fool can rid himself of every folly but vanity.' Rousseau."

" 'I used to be vain, but now I'm perfect.' W.C. Fields."

"Wait a minute," Levine said. "I've never heard that one."

"Are you challenging me?"

Levine thought a moment. "No."

"Then proceed."

Levine paused. " 'Vanity plays lurid tricks with the memory.' Conrad."

Immediately, Scopes replied. " 'Vanity was Evolution's most obnoxious gift.' Darwin."

" 'A vain man can never be utterly ruthless: He wants to win applause.' Goethe."

There was a silence.

"Have you run dry?" Levine asked.

Scopes smiled. "I am merely considering my selection. 'Every man at his best state is altogether vanity.' Psalm thirty-nine."

"I didn't know you were religious. 'Surely every man walketh in a vain show.' Same psalm."

There was another long pause.

Scopes said, " 'I only know we loved in vain; I only feel— farewell! farewell!' Byron."

"Scraping the bottom of the barrel, I see," Levine snorted. "Your turn."

There was a long silence. " 'A journalist is a kind of con man, preying on people's vanity, ignorance, or loneliness, gaining their trust and betraying them without remorse.' Janet Malcolm."

"I challenge you," said Scopes instantly.

"Are you kidding?" Levine asked. "You can't possibly know that quotation. I only remember it because I incorporated it into a recent speech."

"I don't know it. I do know, however, that to me Janet Malcolm is perhaps best known as a writer for *The New Yorker*. I doubt their grammarians would have allowed such a phrase as 'con man.'"

"A far-fetched theory," Levine said. "But if you want to base your challenge on it, be my guest."

"Shall we see what the computer says?"

Levine nodded.

Using the keyboard, Scopes entered a search string into the computer. There was a pause while the vast databases were scanned. At last, a quotation appeared in large letters beneath the word

vanity

"Just as I thought," Scopes said triumphantly. "It's not 'con man.' It's *confidence* man.' The first round goes to me."

Levine was silent. Scopes instructed the computer to bring up another topic at random. The vast screen cleared, and another word appeared:

death

"Broad enough," Levine said. He thought a moment. " 'It's not that I'm afraid to die. I just don't want to be there when it happens.' Woody Allen."

Scopes laughed. "One of my personal favorites. 'Those who welcome death have only tried it from the ears up.' Mizner."

Levine said. " 'We must laugh before we are happy, for fear

of dying without having laughed at all.' La Bruyère."

Scopes: " 'Most people would die sooner than they think; in fact, they do so.' Russell."

Levine: " 'Misers are very kind people: they amass wealth for those who wish their death.' King Stanislaus."

Scopes: " 'When a man dies, he does not just die of the disease he had; he dies of his whole life.' Péguy."

Levine: " 'Everyone is born a king, and most people die in exile.' Wilde."

Scopes: " 'Death is that after which nothing is of interest.' Rozinov."

"Rozinov? Who the hell is Rozinov?"

Scopes smiled. "You wish to challenge me?"

"No."

"Then proceed."

" 'Death destroys a man, but the idea of death saves him.' Forster."

"How nice. How Christian."

"It's not just a Christian idea. In Judaism, the idea of death is meant to inspire one to live a righteous life."

"If you say so," Scopes said. "But I'm not especially interested. Don't you remember?"

"Are you delaying because you've run out of quotations?" Levine prompted.

" 'I am become Death: destroyer of worlds.' The Bhagavad Gita."

"Very appropriate, Brent, for your line of business. It's also what Oppenheimer said when he saw the first atomic explosion."

"Now it sounds like you're the one running out of quotations."

"Not at all. 'Behold a pale horse: and his name that sat on him was Death.' Revelation."

"*His* name that sat on him? That doesn't sound right."

"Are you challenging me?" Levine asked.

Scopes was silent for a moment. Then he shook his head. " 'Philosophy dies just before the philosopher.' Russell."

Levine paused. "Bertrand Russell?"

"Who else?"

"He never said any such thing. You're making up quotations again."

"Indeed?" Scopes looked back impassively.

"Your favorite trick in school, remember? Only I think I can spot them more easily now. That's a Scopesism if ever I heard one, and I challenge you."

There was a short silence. At last, Scopes smiled. "Very good, Charles. One for you, one for me. Now for the final round."

The screen cleared, and a new word appeared:

universe

Scopes closed his eyes a moment. " 'That the universe is comprehensible is incomprehensible.' Einstein."

Levine paused. "You're not foolish enough to start making up quotes already, are you?"

"Challenge me if you like."

"I think I'll let that one pass. 'Either we are the only intelligent life-form in the universe, or we are not. Either possibility is staggering.' Carl Sagan."

"Carl Sagan said that? I don't believe it."

"Then challenge me."

Scopes smiled and shook his head. " 'It is inconceivable that the whole universe was merely created for us who live in this third-rate planet of a third-rate sun.' Byron."

" 'God does not play dice with the universe.' Einstein."

Scopes frowned. "Is it legal to use the same source twice in a single topic? That's the second time you've done so."

Levine shrugged. "Why not?"

"Oh, very well. 'Not only does God play dice with the

universe, but sometimes He throws them where they cannot be seen.' Hawking."

" 'The more the universe seems comprehensible, the more it also seems pointless.' Weinberg."

"Very good," Scopes said. "I like that one." He paused. " 'True comprehension of the universe is given only to drugged teenagers and senile cosmologists.' Leary."

There was a silence.

"Timothy Leary?" Levine asked.

"Of course."

The silence lengthened. "I don't think Leary would have said something quite so puerile," Levine said.

Scopes smiled. "If you doubt it, challenge me."

Levine waited, thinking. It had been one of Scopes's favorite stratagems, making up quotations toward the beginning and saving the real ones for later, as a way to play out Levine's own store of quotations. Levine had known Leary from his Harvard days, and in his gut he felt this quotation sounded wrong. But then, another of Scopes's tricks had been to use out-of-character quotations as a way to goad Levine into challenging him. He glanced at Scopes, who was staring back, impassively. If he challenged Scopes, and Leary *had* said it, after all . . . He shook the thought from him mind.

The seconds ticked away.

"I challenge you," Levine said at last.

Scopes started visibly. Levine watched as the color drained from the face of the GeneDyne CEO. He was contemplating—just as Levine had contemplated, years ago—what it meant to have lost on such a vast scale.

"It burns, doesn't it?" Levine asked.

Scopes remained silent.

"It's not the losing so much," Levine continued. "It's *how* you lost. You'll think back on this moment, always. Wondering at how you threw it all away on such a trivial mistake. You won't be able to forget it, ever. I know I still can't."

Still, Scopes did not speak. Half-lost in an overwhelming sense of relief, Levine saw Scopes's hand twitching and realized—a split second before it happened—that the GeneDyne CEO would never give up his deadly virus. Twenty years ago, when Levine had lost at their ultimate round of the Game, he'd stuck to his word. He'd signed the corn patent and let Scopes grow rich on the discovery, rather than giving the marvelous secret to the world. Now, Scopes had lost, on an even grander scale. . . .

Levine grabbed for the ampule just as Scopes's hands flashed out. Two hands closed around it at once. There was a brief struggle as each man tried to claim it for his own.

"Brent!" Levine cried. "Brent, you gave your word—"

There was a sudden, dull popping sound. Levine felt a sharp sting; then a dampness spread across his palms.

He forced himself to look down.

The viral transport medium, with its deadly suspension of X-FLU II, was spreading in a puddle over the signed contract and running off the table onto the floor, staining the gray carpet black. Levine opened his hand: shards of glass were embedded in his palm, lines of blood diluted by the hot medium running down his wrist. His palm hurt as he flexed it.

He looked up again, watching as Scopes slowly opened his own hand. It, too, was torn and bloody.

Their eyes met.

Carson was tugging at her arm, trying to say something. "Mondragón's gold," he gasped at last.

"What about it?" de Vaca whispered.

"Use it." A spasm of pain crossed his face and he fell back

into the sand, where he remained, motionless.

As Nye's footsteps came closer, she suddenly understood what Carson meant. Digging into her pocket, she pulled out the four coins she'd taken from the cave.

"Nye!" she called. "Here's something that ought to interest you."

She lobbed the coins over the rock. The footsteps ceased. Then there was a sharp intake of breath, a whispered curse. The footsteps approached again, and then she could hear his heavy breathing, coming up between the rocks, and she crouched with her head bowed, waiting. Something she knew must be the barrel of Nye's big rifle was suddenly pressed hard against the base of her skull.

"Count of three," she heard Nye say, "to tell me where you got these."

She waited, saying nothing.

"One."

She waited.

"Two."

She sucked in her breath, squeezed her eyes tightly closed.

"Three."

Nothing happened.

"Look at me," Nye said at last.

Slowly opening her eyes, she turned around. Nye was standing above her, one booted foot balanced on a rock, his tall form silhouetted against the setting sun. The safari hat and long English coat that before had always seemed so ridiculous to her now seemed utterly terrifying, a strange specter of death in this remote desert. He was holding the gold coin in one hand. His bloodshot eyes dropped to her naked breasts a moment, then moved up again, his face expressionless. He shifted the barrel to her temple. More seconds passed. Turning on his heel, Nye strode back out into the sand. De Vaca waited a moment, then jerked spasmodically at the sound of another shot. There was a deep, wet sighing sound.

He's killed Roscoe, she thought. *Now he's looking through the saddlebags for more gold.*

In a moment, Nye returned. Quickly, he reached down and grabbed de Vaca's hair, yanking her rudely to her feet. She felt her roots ripping as he jerked her head hard to one side. Then, with a brutal shove, he threw her back against the rocks that rose at the end of the cul-de-sac. He swung the rifle around and jabbed it deep into her stomach. She bent forward, crying out, and he yanked her up again by the hair.

"Listen to me very carefully now. I want to know where you got this coin."

She dropped her eyes and gestured with her chin to the sand at her feet. He glanced down, saw the dagger, and reached for it. He looked closely at the handle.

"Diego de Mondragón," he whispered. Then he stepped closer. She had never before seen eyes so bloodshot; the edges of the whites were crimson, almost black.

"You found the treasure," he hissed.

She nodded.

He swiveled the rifle back toward her face. "Where?"

She looked into his eyes. "If I tell you, you'll kill me. If I don't tell you, you'll kill me. Either way, I'm dead."

"Bitch. I won't kill you. I'll torture you to death."

"Try it."

He balled his fist and struck her directly in the face. She felt the shock of impact; then a terrific buzz sounded in her ears and a strange heat rushed into her head. She tipped forward, feeling faint, but he pushed her back against the sharp rock.

"It won't work," she said again. "Look at me, Nye."

He struck her again. The landscape around her turned white and featureless for a moment, and she felt blood gush from her mouth. Her sight returned and she raised a hand to her face, realizing she had lost a tooth.

"Where," he said again.

She squeezed her eyes tightly shut and remained silent, stiffening for the next blow.

The footsteps moved away, and she heard Nye speaking in a low tone. She could hear the pauses as he waited for somebody else to answer. Who was he talking to? Singer, probably, or one of the Mount Dragon security guards. She felt the slender thread of hope inside her begin to part; they had been so certain Nye was alone.

The footsteps came back and she slitted open her eyes. Nye was pointing his rifle at Carson's head.

"Tell me or he dies."

She took a deep breath now, steadying herself. This, she knew, was going to be the hardest part. "Go ahead and shoot the *cabrón*," she said as evenly as possible. "I can't stand the redneck son of a bitch. And if you do, the gold will be all mine. I'll never tell you. Except . . ."

He swiveled the gun toward her. "Except what?"

"A trade," she croaked.

She did not feel the blow as the butt of the rifle swung toward her head, but a pool of blackness rushed suddenly up to meet her. Consciousness returned, and with it a searing pain across one side of her skull. She kept her eyes closed. Again, a voice: Nye was still talking to someone. She listened for an answering voice, but it did not come. At last she cracked open her eyes. The sun had set, and it was much darker now, but she was still reasonably certain that he was speaking to no one.

Despite the pain, relief coursed through her. PurBlood was doing its terrible work.

Nye turned toward her, noticed she was conscious. "What kind of trade?" he asked.

She turned away, closing her eyes and bracing for another blow.

"What kind of trade," she heard him repeat.

"My life," she said.

There was a silence. "Your life," he repeated. "I accept."

"My life isn't worth shit without a horse, that gun, and water."

There was a silence, and then another terrible blow came. This time, consciousness returned slowly. Her body felt heavy and full of sleep. Breathing was difficult, and she knew her nose must be broken. She tried to speak without success, and felt herself falling back into the sweet black pool of unconsciousness.

When she came to again, she was lying on soft sand. She tried to raise herself, but white-hot pain flashed through her skull and down her spine. Nye was standing over her, flashlight in hand. He looked worried.

"One more blow like that," she whispered, "and you'll kill me, you bastard. Then you'll never learn where the gold is." She took a deep breath, closed her eyes.

In a few minutes, she spoke again. "It's a hundred miles from where you think it is."

"Where?" he cried.

"My life for the gold."

"Very well. I promise I won't kill you. Just tell me where the gold is." He turned suddenly, as if he had heard something. "Yes, yes, I remember," he said to somebody else. Then he turned back.

"The only way I'll live," she whispered, "is with the horse, gun, and water. Without that, I die, and you'll never know . . ." She lapsed into silence.

Nye stared down at her, gripping the coins so fiercely in one hand that his entire arm was shaking. A sound like a whimper escaped from his throat. From the way he was looking at her, she knew her face must look terrible.

"Bring over your horse," she said.

Nye's mouth twitched spasmodically. "Tell me now, please—"

"The horse."

Her eyes closed of their own accord. When she was able to open them again, Nye was gone. She sat up, fighting against the pain in her head. Her nose and throat were full of blood, and she coughed several times, trying to breathe.

She saw Nye reappear at the opening in the rocks, his magnificent horse trailing behind him in the moonlight like a silent shadow.

"Tell me where the treasure is," he said.

"The horse," she replied, struggling to her feet and holding out her left hand.

Nye hesitated a moment, then handed her the reins. She grabbed the saddle horn and tried to climb into the saddle, almost falling from dizziness.

"Help me." He cupped one hand beneath her boot, hoisting her up.

"Now the gun."

"No," Nye replied. "You'll kill me."

"Give it to me unloaded, then."

"You'll double-cross me. You'll ride ahead and take my treasure."

"Look at me. Look into my eyes."

Reluctantly, he looked up at her with his blood-rimmed eyes. Only now, as she looked into those eyes, did she realize how deeply the desire for Mondragón's treasure ran through him. PurBlood had turned a simple eccentricity into a ruinous obsession. Everything, even his hatred of Carson, was secondary to his need for the treasure. She realized, with a mixture of fear and pity, that she was looking on a broken man.

"I promise, I won't take your treasure," she said almost gently. "You can have it, all of it. I just want to get out of here alive. Can't you see that?"

He unloaded the gun and gave it to her.

"Where," he urged. "Tell me where."

There were two water bags tied to the cantle, each one half-full. She unlooped one and gave it to Nye, then began backing Muerto away from him. Obsession or no obsession, she didn't want him trying to retrieve his gun after she had given him the location.

"Wait! Don't go. Tell me, please—"

"Listen carefully. You're to follow our tracks back about ten miles, along the base of the lava. Watch for the spot where we hobbled our horses. You'll find a hidden cave in the lava there, at the base of the mountains. Inside the cave is a spring. At dawn, the sunlight entering the cave will throw an image against the rear wall in the shape of an eagle, balancing on a needle of fire. Just like on your map. But the wall doesn't lead all the way to the cave floor; there's a hidden passage at its base. Follow it. Mondragón's body, his mule, and his treasure are at the bottom of a cavern."

He nodded eagerly. "Yes, yes, I understand." He turned to his imaginary companion. "Did you hear that? All this time, I've been searching the wrong part of the desert. I'd assumed the mountains on the map were the Cerritos Escondidos. How could I have . . ." He turned again to de Vaca. "Back this way ten miles, did you say?"

She nodded.

"Let's go," he said to his imaginary companion as he shouldered the water bag. "We'll split it fifty-fifty. Mum would have insisted."

He began walking out of the rocks and into the desert.

"Nye" de Vaca called out.

He turned.

"Who's your friend?"

"Just a boy I knew once," he said.

"What's his name?"

"Jonathan."

"Jonathan who?"

"Jonathan Nye." He turned and hurried away. She watched him shuffle off, talking excitedly. Soon he had disappeared around a point of lava and into the night.

De Vaca waited several minutes until she was sure he had gone. Then she dismounted and moved slowly toward Carson. He was still unconscious. She felt his pulse: weak and rapid, definitely shocky. Gingerly, she examined the shattered forearm. It was leaking blood, but only slightly. Loosening the tourniquet, she was relieved to see that the severed artery had sealed. Now she had to get him out before gangrene set in.

Carson's eyes fluttered open.

"Guy!" she said urgently.

The eyes turned, focusing on her slowly.

"Can you stand?"

Whether or not he had heard, she couldn't be sure. She grabbed him under the arms and tried to pull him up. He struggled feebly, then fell back into the sand. Pouring some water into her hands, she splashed it gently on his face.

"Get up," she ordered.

Carson struggled to his knees, fell back on his good elbow, struggled up again, grabbed Muerto's stirrup and pulled himself slowly to his feet. De Vaca helped him clamber onto the horse's back, careful to keep his damaged arm from being jostled. Carson swayed, cradled his arm, blinked several times. Then he began to topple forward. De Vaca grabbed his chest, steadying him. She was going to have to tie him in place.

Nye had a cotton lead rope fixed to one side of the saddle. Uncoiling it, de Vaca tied the rope around Carson's chest, leaning him over the saddle horn, wrapping his left arm around the horn and tying it securely in place. As she worked, she realized, with almost complete detachment, that she was shirtless. But it was dark, and she had nothing to cover herself with. Somehow it seemed very, very unimportant.

She began leading Muerto by the reins, walking directly toward the North Star.

* * *

They reached the line camp at dawn: an old adobe house with a tin roof, hidden among a cluster of cottonwood trees. Off to one side was a barn, a windmill and watertank, and a set of weathered corrals. A fresh breeze was cranking the windmill. A horse in the corral whinnied, then a dog began barking at their approach. Soon a young man, wearing red long johns and a cowboy hat, was standing in the doorway, his mouth open as he stared at this topless woman, covered with blood, leading a magnificent paint horse with a man tied into its saddle.

Scopes stared at Levine, a mingled look of horror and disbelief on his face. At last he stepped away from the table, walked to a narrow panel in a nearby wall, and pressed a button. The panel slid up noiselessly, revealing a small wet bar and sink.

"Don't rinse your hands," Levine said quietly. "You'll send the virus down the drain."

Scopes hesitated. "You're right," he replied. Moistening a hand towel, he dabbed at his palms and picked out a few slivers of glass, then dried his hands carefully. Stepping away from the bar, he returned to the sofa and sat down. His movements seemed odd, hesitant, as if walking had become a suddenly unfamiliar act.

Levine glanced over from the far end of the sofa. "I think you'd better tell me what you know about X-FLU II," he said quietly.

Scopes smoothed back his cowlick with an automatic gesture. "We actually know very little. I believe that only one human has been exposed to it. There's an incubation period of perhaps twenty-four to sixty hours, followed by almost instantaneous death through cerebral edema."

"Is there a cure?"

"No."

"Vaccine?"

"No."

"Infectiousness?"

"Similar to the common cold. Perhaps even more so."

Levine glanced down again at his cut hand. The blood was beginning to congeal around the broken shards of the ampule. There was no question they both had been infected.

"Any hope?" he asked at last.

"None," Scopes replied.

There was a long silence.

"I'm sorry," Scopes said finally, in a tone so low it was almost a whisper. "I'm so sorry, Charles. There was a time when I would never have thought to do that. I—" He stopped. "I guess I've just grown too used to winning."

Levine stood up and cleaned his hand with the towel. "There isn't time for recriminations. The pressing question is how we can prevent the virus in this room from destroying mankind."

Scopes was silent.

"Brent?"

Scopes did not respond. Levine leaned toward him.

"Brent?" he asked quietly. "What is it?"

"I don't know," Scopes replied at last. "I guess I'm afraid of dying."

Levine looked at him. "So am I," he said at last. "But fear is a luxury we can't afford right now. We're wasting precious minutes. We must figure out a way to . . . well, to sterilize the area. Completely. Do you understand?"

Scopes nodded, looking away.

Levine grasped his shoulder, shook him gently. "You've got to be with me on this, Brent, or it won't work. This is your building. You're going to have to do what's necessary to make sure this virus stops with us."

For a long moment, Scopes continued to look away. Then he turned toward Levine. "This room has a pressure seal, and is supplied with its own private air system," he said, collecting himself. "The walls have been reinforced against terrorist attacks: fire, explosion, gas. That will make our job easier."

A tone sounded, and then the face of Spencer Fairley appeared on the giant screen before them. "Sir, Jenkins from marketing is insisting on speaking with you," the face said. "Apparently, the hospital consortium has abruptly canceled plans to begin transfusing PurBlood tomorrow morning. He wants to know what pressure you'll be bringing to bear on their administrations."

Scopes looked at Levine, his eyebrows raised. "Et tu, Brute? It appears friend Carson delivered his message after all." He turned back to the image on the screen. "I'm not going to bring any pressure to bear. Tell Jenkins that the PurBlood release should be rolled back, pending further testing. There may be adverse long-term effects of which we weren't aware." He typed a series of commands. "I'm sending a Mount Dragon data file to GeneDyne Manchester. It's incomplete, but it may show evidence of contamination in the PurBlood manufacturing process. Please follow up, make sure they examine it carefully." He sighed heavily.

"Spencer, I want you to run a diagnostic on the Octagon's containment system. Make sure the seals are all in place and functioning normally."

Fairley nodded, then moved away from the screen. In a few moments, he returned.

"The system is fully operational," he said. "Atmospheric regulators and all monitoring devices are showing normal readings."

"Good," Scopes said. "Now listen carefully. I want you to instruct Endicott to unseal the perimeter around the headquarters building, and to restore all communication with the remote sites. I will be broadcasting a message to headquarters employees. I want you to send a message to General Roger Harrington at the Pentagon, Ring E, Level Three, Section Seventeen, over a clear channel. Tell him that I am withdrawing the offer and that there will be no further negotiations."

"Very well," Fairley said. He paused, then looked more intently at the monitor. "Are you all right, sir?" he asked.

"No," said Scopes. "Something terrible has happened. I need your absolute cooperation."

Fairley nodded.

"There has been an accident inside the Octagon," Scopes said. "A virus known as X-FLU II has been released into the air supply. Both Dr. Levine and I have been infected. This virus is one-hundred-percent fatal. There is no hope of recovery."

Fairley's face betrayed nothing.

"We cannot allow this virus to escape. Therefore, the Octagon must be sterilized."

Fairley nodded again. "I understand, sir," he said.

"I doubt you do. Dr. Levine and I are carrying the virus. It is multiplying in our bodies as we speak. You must, therefore, directly supervise our deaths."

"Sir! How can I possibly—"

"Shut up and listen. If you don't follow my instructions, billions will die. Including yourself."

Fairley fell silent.

"I want you to scramble two helicopters," Scopes said. "You're to send one to GeneDyne Manchester, where it will pick up ten two-liter canisters of VXV-twelve." He did a quick calculation. "The volume of this room is approximately thirty-two thousand cubic feet. So we'll also need at least sixteen thousand cc's of liquid 1,2 cyanophosphatol 6,6,6, trimethyloxylated mercuro-hexachloride. The second chopper can obtain the necessary supply from our Norfolk facility. It must be shipped in sealed glass beakers."

Fairley looked up from a computer screen at his side. "Cyanophosphatol?"

"It's a biological poison. A very, very effective biological poison. It will kill anything alive in this room. Although it's stored in liquid form, it has a low vapor point and will rapidly evaporate, filling the room with a sterilizing gas."

"Won't it kill—?"

"Spencer, we'll already be dead. That's the point of the VXV canisters."

Fairley licked his lips. "Mr. Scopes." He swallowed. "You can't ask me to . . ." His voice dropped away.

Scopes looked at Fairley's image on the immense screen. Beads of sweat had sprung up around the corners of his mouth, and his iron-gray hair, normally smoothly coiffed, was coming loose.

"Spencer, I've never needed your loyalty more than I do now," Scopes continued quietly. "You must understand that I'm already a dead man. The greatest favor you can do for me now is not to let me die by X-FLU II. There's no time to waste."

"Yes, sir," Fairley said, averting his eyes.

"You're to have everything here within two hours. Let me know when both helicopters are safely on the pad." Scopes punched a key, and the screen went black.

There was a heavy silence in the room. Then Scopes turned toward Levine. "Do you believe in life after death?" he asked.

Levine shook his head. "In Judaism, we believe it's what we do in this life that matters. We achieve immortality through living a righteous life, and worshipping God. The children we leave behind are our immortality."

"But you have no children, Charles."

"I had always hoped to. I've tried to do good in other ways, not always with success."

Scopes was silent. "I used to despise people who needed to believe in an afterlife," he went on at last. "I thought it was a weakness. Now that the moment of reckoning is here, I wish I had spent more time convincing myself." He looked down. "It would be nice to have some hope."

Levine closed his eyes for a moment, thinking. Then he opened them suddenly. "Cypherspace," he said simply.

"What do you mean?"

"You've programmed other people from your past into the program. Why not program yourself? That way, you—or a part of you—could live on, perhaps even dispensing your wit and wisdom to all who cared to converse with you."

Scopes laughed harshly. "I'm not that attractive a person, I'm afraid. As you well know."

"Perhaps. But you're certainly the most interesting."

Scopes nodded. "Thank you for that." He paused. "It's an intriguing idea."

"We have two hours to kill."

Scopes smiled wanly. "All right, Charles. Why not? There's one condition, however. You must put yourself into the program, as well. I'm not going back to Monhegan Island alone."

Levine shook his head. "I'm no programmer, especially of something as complex as this."

"That's not a problem. I've written a character-generating algorithm. It uses various AI subroutines that ask questions, engage the user in brief conversations, do a few psychological tests. Then it creates a character and inserts it into the cypherspace world. I wrote it as a tool to help me people the island more efficiently, but it could work just as well for us."

He looked questioningly at Levine.

"And perhaps then you'll tell me why you chose to depict your summer house in ruins," Levine replied.

"Perhaps," said Scopes. "Let's get to work."

* * *

In the end, Levine chose to look like himself, with an ill-fitting dark suit, bald head, and uneven teeth. He turned slowly in front of the unblinking video camera in the Octagon. The feed from the camera would be scanned into several hundred hi-res images that together would make up the Levine figure that would be taking up residence on Scopes's virtual island. Over the last ninety minutes, the AI subroutine had asked him countless questions, ranging from early childhood memories to memorable teachers, personal philosophy, religion, and ethical beliefs. The subroutine had asked him to list the books he had read, and the magazines he had subscribed to during the different periods of his life. It posed mathematical problems to him; asked about his travels; his musical likes and dislikes; his memories of his wife. The subroutine had given him Rorschach tests and even insulted him and argued with him, perhaps to gauge his emotional reactions. The resulting data, Levine knew, would be used to supply the body of knowledge, emotions, and memories that his cyberspace character would possess.

"Now what?" Levine asked, sitting down again.

"Now we wait," Scopes said, forcing a smile. He had undergone a similar process of interrogation. He typed several commands, then sat back in the couch as the supercomputer began to generate the two new characters for his cyberspace re-creation of Monhegan Island.

A silence fell onto the room. Levine realized that, if nothing else, the interrogation had kept him occupied, kept him from realizing that these were in fact the last minutes of his life. Now, a strange mix of emotions began to crowd in on him: memories, fears, things left undone. He turned toward Scopes.

"Brent," he began.

There was a low tone, and Scopes reached over and pressed a button on the phone beside the couch. The patrician voice of Spencer Fairley sounded through the phone's external speaker.

"The helicopters have arrived, sir," he said.

Scopes pulled the keyboard onto his lap and began typing. "I'm going to send this audio feed down to central security, as well as to the archives, just to make sure there are no troublesome questions later. Listen carefully, Spencer. In a few minutes, I'm going to give the order for this building to be evacuated and sealed. Only yourself, a security team, and a bioemergency team should remain. Once evacuation is complete, you must shut off the air-circulation system for the Octagon. You are then to pump all ten canisters of VXV into the air supply, and restart the system. I'm not exactly sure how long it will take to . . ." He paused. "Perhaps you should wait fifteen minutes. Then, send the bioemergency team to the emergency pressure hatch in the Octagon's roof. Have Endicott depressurize the hatch from security control, instruct the team to place the beakers of cyanophosphatol inside the hatchway, then seal and repressurize the outer hatch. Once the team is clear, have the inner hatch opened remotely from security control. The beakers will fall into the Octagon and break, dispersing the cyanophosphatol."

He looked at the screen. "Are you following this, Spencer?"

There was a long pause. "Yes, sir."

"Even after the cyanophosphatol does its work, there will still be live viruses in the room. Hiding in the corpses. So, as a final step, you must incinerate them. The heat will denature the cyanophosphatol as well. The fireproof shell of the Octagon will keep a fire in as well as it will keep a fire out. But you must be careful not to cause a premature explosion or a dirty, out-of-control fire that might spread the virus. A fast-acting, high-temperature incendiary such as phosphorus should be used first. When the bodies have completely burned, the rest of the room should be cleansed with a lower-temperature incendiary. A napalm derivative will do. Both will be available from the restricted laboratory supplies."

Listening, Levine noted the methodical detachment with which Scopes described the procedure: *the* corpses, *the* bodies. *Those are our corpses*, he thought.

"The bioemergency team should then perform a standard hot-agent decontam on the rest of the building. Once that's finished—" Scopes stopped short for moment. "Then I guess, Spencer, it's up to the board of directors."

There was a silence.

"Now, Spencer, please get my executor on the line," Scopes said quietly.

A moment later, a rough, gravelly voice sounded through the speakerphone beside the table. "Alan Lipscomb here."

"Alan, it's Brent. Listen, there's to be a bequest change. Still on the line, Spencer?"

"Yes."

"Good. Spencer will be my witness. I want fifty million set aside to fund an endowment for the Institute for Advanced Neurocybernetics. I'll provide Spencer with the details, and he'll pass them on to you."

"Very well."

Scopes typed quickly for a few moments, then turned to Levine. "I'm sending Spencer instructions to transfer the entire cypherspace databank, along with the compiler and my notes on the C^3 language, to the Institute for Advanced Neurocybernetics. In exchange for the endowment, I'm asking them to keep my virtual re-creation of Monhegan Island running in perpetuity, and to allow any serious student access to it."

Levine nodded. "On permanent display. Fitting for so great a work of art."

"But not only on display, Charles. I want them to add to it, extend the technology, improve the depth of the language and the tools. I suppose it's something I've kept to myself far too long." He smoothed down his cowlick absently. "Any last requests, Charles? My executor is very good at getting things done."

"Just one," Levine said evenly.

"And that is—?"

"I think you can guess."

Scopes looked at him for a moment. "Yes, of course," he said at last. He turned back to the speakerphone. "Spencer, are you still there?"

"Yes, sir."

"Please tear up that patent renewal for X-RUST."

"The renewal, sir?"

"Just do it. And stay on the line." Scopes turned back to Levine, one eyebrow raised.

"Thank you," Levine said.

Scopes nodded quietly. Then he reached for the phone and pressed a series of buttons. "Attention, headquarters staff," he said into the mouthpiece. Levine heard the voice echoing from a hidden speaker and realized the message was being broadcast throughout the building.

"This is Brent Scopes speaking," Scopes continued. "An emergency has arisen that requires the entire staff to vacate the premises. This is a temporary measure, and I assure you that nobody is in danger." He paused. "Before you leave, however, I must inform you that an alteration is being made in the GeneDyne chain of command. You will learn the details shortly. But let me say now that I have enjoyed working with every one of you, and I wish you and GeneDyne the very best of luck in the future. Remember that the goals of science are our goals, as well: the advancement of knowledge, and the betterment of mankind. Never lose sight of them. And now, please proceed to the nearest exit."

Finger on the switch hook, Scopes turned to Levine.

"Are you ready?" he asked.

Levine nodded.

Scopes released the switch hook. "Spencer, you are to present all tapes of this event to the board next Monday morning. They must carry on according to the tenets of the GeneDyne charter. Now, please begin introducing the VXV gas. Yes. Yes, I know, Spencer. Thank you. Best of luck to you."

Slowly, Scopes replaced the handset. Then he returned his hands to the keyboard.

"Let's go," he said.

There was a humming noise, and the lights dimmed. Suddenly, the huge octagonal office was transformed into the garret room of the ruined house on Monhegan Island. Gazing around, stunned, Levine realized that not just one, but each of the room's eight walls was a vast display screen.

"Now you know why I chose the turret room," Scopes said, laying the keyboard aside again.

Levine sat on the sofa, entranced. Outside the garret windows, he could clearly see the widow's walk. The sun was just coming up over the ocean, the sea itself absorbing the colors of the sky. The seagulls wheeled around the boats in the harbor, crying excitedly as the lobstermen rolled barrels of redfish bait down the pier and onto their boats.

In a chair in the garret, a figure stirred, stood up, stretched. It was short and thin, with gangly limbs and thick glasses. An unrepentant cowlick stood like a black feather from the unruly mass of hair.

"Well, Charles," it said. "Welcome to Monhegan Island."

Levine watched as another figure on the far side of the garret—a bald man in an ill-fitting dark suit—nodded in return.

"Thank you," it said, in a voice hauntingly familiar.

"Shall we wander into town?" the Scopes-figure said.

"Not just now," the Levine-figure said. "I'd prefer to sit here and watch the boats go out."

"Very good. Shall we play the Game while we wait?"

"Why not?" said Levine-figure. "We've got a lot of time to kill."

Levine sat in the darkened Octagon, watching his newly created character with a wistful smile.

"A lot of time to kill," said Scopes from the darkness. "An infinity of time to kill. So much time for them, and so little time for us."

"I choose *time* as a keyword," said the Levine-figure.

The Scopes-figure sat down again in the rickety chair, kicked back, and said:

> *"There will be time, there will be time*
> *To prepare a face to meet the faces that you meet;*
> *There will be time to murder and create . . ."*

Levine—the real Levine—smelled a strange odor in the air of the Octagon; pungent, almost sweet, like long-dead roses. His eyes began to sting and he closed them, listening to the voice of the Scopes-figure:

> *"And time for all the works and days of hands*
> *That lift and drop a question on your plate;*
> *Time for you and time for me . . ."*

There was a silence, and the last thing Levine heard as he drew the acrid gas into his lungs was his own voice, reciting an answering quotation: " 'Time is a storm in which we are all lost . . .' "

EPILOGUE

The desert looked strange under the high thin covering of cirrus clouds. It was no longer a sea of light, but a darkening blue plain ending in distant, hard-edged mountain peaks. A chill, and the smell of the desert autumn, hung in the air.

From their vantage point atop Mount Dragon, Carson and de Vaca looked down on the blackened ruins of the GeneDyne Remote Desert Testing Facility. The massive underground bunker of the Fever Tank was now a jagged crater of darkened concrete and twisted rebar erupting out of the desert floor, surrounded by sand scorched a deep orange by fire. The plasmid transfection laboratory was merely a skeleton of I beams warped by the heat. The dormitories and their shattered, dark windowframes stared with dead eyes out over the landscape. Everything of value had been removed weeks before, leaving only the hollow shells of buildings as mute sentinels to what had been. There were no plans to rebuild. According to rumor, the Missile Range was going to use the remains as a bombing target. The only signs of life were the ravens plundering the destroyed canteen, circling and squabbling over something inside.

Beyond the ruins of Mount Dragon, the rubble of another vanished city rose from the landscape: Kin Klizhini, the Black House, felled by time, lack of water, and the elements. On the far side of the cinder cone, the cluster of microwave and radio towers sat silently, waiting disassembly. Far below, the pickup truck the two had driven in on sat where the perimeter had once been, a lonely spot of color in the drab wastes.

Carson stared mesmerized. "Amazing, isn't it, that a thousand years separates those two ruins," he said quietly. "We've come a long way, I suppose. Yet it all ends up the same. The desert doesn't care."

There was a silence.

"Funny they never found Nye," de Vaca said at last.

Carson shook his head. "The poor son of a bitch. He must have died out there, somewhere, and become dinner for the coyotes and buzzards. He'll be found someday, just like we found Mondragón. A bleached skeleton and a sack of rocks." Carson massaged his left forearm, remembering. There was a lot of metal in it now, and it still ached in damp weather. But not here, in the desert.

"Maybe a new legend of gold will grow up around the story, and in five hundred years they'll be looking for the Nye gold," de Vaca said, laughing. Then her face turned serious. "I don't feel sorry for him at all. He was a bastard even before the PurBlood got to him."

"The one I feel sorry for is Singer," Carson said. "He was more than a decent guy. And Harper. And Vanderwagon. None of them deserved what happened."

"You talk like they're dead."

"They might as well be."

De Vaca shrugged. "Who knows? With all the bad press it's been getting lately, maybe GeneDyne will put its resources toward finding a way to undo what it did to them. Besides, in one sense, they *are* guilty. Guilty of embracing a great and terrifying vision, with no thought to the consequences."

Carson shook his head. "If that's true, I was just as guilty of that as they were."

"Not quite," de Vaca said. "I think there was something in the back of your mind that was always skeptical."

"I've asked myself that every day since the PurBlood rollout was terminated. I'm not so sure. I would have taken the blood just like they did."

De Vaca looked at him.

"It's true. There was a time I would have followed Scopes to the ends of the earth, if he'd asked. He had that effect on you."

De Vaca continued to look at him curiously. "Not on me," she said finally.

Carson said nothing.

"It was very strange, that fire, wasn't it?" de Vaca asked.

Carson shook his head. "Yes, it was. And Scopes's confession. If you could call it that. I'm sure we'll never know what really happened. There was unfinished business between those two, Levine and Scopes."

De Vaca's eyebrows lifted. "Well, I guess it's finished now," she said.

Carson hesitated. "I wonder if they'll ever go through with X-FLU," he said at last. "Now that we solved the problem, I mean."

"Never," de Vaca said emphatically. "Nobody would touch it now. It's too dangerous. Besides, we don't *know* all the problems have been solved. And the problem of altering future generations—of changing humanity itself—has just begun. We're going to see some terrible things in our lifetime, Guy. You know this isn't the end of it."

The clouds had thickened and the desert darkened. They stood motionless.

"We'd better go," de Vaca said at last. "It's a long drive to Sleeping Ute Mountain."

Carson remained still, his eyes transfixed by the shattered grandeur of what had been Mount Dragon.

"You've got relatives who are waiting, eager to meet you. And a feast of mutton stew and fry bread. And dancing and singing. And the memory of old Great-Uncle Charley to honor, who saved our butts out there in that desert."

Carson nodded absently.

"You're not chickening out, are you, half-breed?" She put her arm around his waist and smiled.

With an effort, Carson pulled his eyes away from the ruined complex. Then he turned to her and grinned.

"It's been a long time since I've had a good bowl of mutton stew," he said.

Some call it the greatest scientific discovery
of all time . . .

Others call it . . .

BLASPHEMY

DOUGLAS PRESTON

Science and religion go head-to-head in the
latest science-based thriller from the
New York Times bestselling author of *Tyran-
nosaur Canyon* and
coauthor of *The Wheel of Darkness.*

Available from Forge in Hardcover in January 2008.

Turn the page for a preview . . .

A FORGE HARDCOVER

ISBN-13: 978-0-7653-1105-4   ISBN-10: 0-7653-1105-4

www.tor-forge.com

Sunday evening, the Reverend Don T. Spates fitted his bulk into the makeup chair so as not to crease his pants and handmade Italian cotton shirt. Once in, he adjusted his large bottom, moving it from side to side with a flurry of creaks and squeaks in the leather. He carefully leaned his head back against the headrest. Wanda stood to one side holding the barbershop robe.

"Do me good, Wanda," he said, closing his eyes. "This is a big Sunday. A *real* big Sunday."

"You're going to look just great, Reverend," said Wanda, snapping the robe over him and tucking it in around his neck. Then, with a soothing clinking of bottles, combs, and brushes, she set to work, paying special attention to the reverend's liver spots and the spiderlike clusters of varicose veins on his cheeks and nose. She was good at what she did and she knew it. Regardless of what the others might say, she thought the reverend a fine, handsome man.

Her long white hands worked with expert economy, swift

and precise, but the reverend's ears were always a challenge. They stood out from the head a trifle too much, and were lighter and redder than his adjacent skin. Sometimes, as he strode about the stage, the backlight would catch his ears, turning them into pink stained glass. To bring them to their proper tonal value, she covered them with a heavy base makeup three shades darker than his face, and finished with a face powder that made them virtually opaque.

As she smoothed, stroked, brushed, and dabbed, she checked her work in a color-balanced video monitor that displayed a feed from a camera trained on the reverend. It was essential to see her handiwork as it would appear on-screen— something that looked perfect to the eye could show up as a ghastly two-tone on the monitor. She worked on him this way twice a week: for his televised sermon on Sunday, and for his Friday talk show on the Christian Cable Service.

Yes, the reverend was a fine man.

Reverend Don T. Spates felt comforted and cosseted by her professional bustle. It had been a bad year. His enemies were out to get him, twisting his every word, attacking him mercilessly. Every sermon seemed to generate vilification from the atheist left. It was a sad time when a man of God was attacked for speaking the simple truth. Of course, there'd been that unfortunate incident in the motel with the two prostitutes. The ungodly liars had had a field day with that. But the flesh is weak—as the Bible repeatedly confirmed. In Jesus' eyes, we are all hopeless, backsliding sinners. Spates had asked for and received God's forgiveness. But the hypocritical, evil world forgave slowly, if at all.

"Time for your teeth, Reverend."

Spates opened his mouth and felt her expert hands applying the ivory dentine fluid. In the bright lights of the camera, it would make his teeth flash as pearly white as the gates of heaven.

After that she worked on his hair, carefully grooming the wiry, orangish helmet until it was just right. She gave it an indirect spritz of hair spray and puffed on a bit of powder to tone the color down to a more respectable ginger.

"Your hands, Reverend?"

Spates extracted his freckled hands from under the cover and laid them on a manicure tray. She bustled over them, applying a makeup base designed to minimize wrinkles and color variations. His hands had to match his face. In fact, Spates was particularly insistent that his hands be perfect. They were an extension of his voice. Botched makeup there could ruin the impact of his message, as camera close-ups of laying on of hands revealed flaws unnoticed by the eye.

The hands took her fifteen minutes. She gouged dirt from under the nails, applied clear fingernail polish, repaired nicks, sanded the nails, cleaned and cut off excess skin, and, finally, covered them with an appropriate shade of makeup base.

A final check in the TV monitor, a few touch-ups, and Wanda stepped back.

"All ready, Reverend." She turned the monitor toward him.

Spates examined himself in the monitor—face, eyes, ears, lips, teeth, hands.

"That spot on my neck, Wanda? You missed that spot—again."

A quick swipe of the sponge, a touch-up with the brush, and it vanished. Spates grunted his satisfaction.

Wanda flicked off the coverings and stood back. From out of the wings, Spates's aide, Charles, rushed in with the reverend's suit jacket. Spates rose from the chair and held out his arms, while Charles slipped on the jacket, tugged and smoothed down the cloth, gave it a quick brushing, plumped up the shoulders, smoothed and tucked the collar, and adjusted the tie.

"How are the shoes, Charles?"

Charles gave the shoes a few swipes with a shine cloth. "Time?"

"Six minutes to eight, Reverend."

Years ago, Spates had had the idea to schedule his Sunday sermon for prime time in the evening, to avoid the televangelist morning crush. He called it *God's Prime Time.* Everyone predicted he'd fail, going up against some of the strongest programming of the week. Instead, it had proved a stroke of genius.

Spates strode from the room toward the wings of the stage, Charles following. As he came close, he could hear the rustle and murmur of the faithful—thousands of them—taking their seats in the Silver Cathedral from where he broadcast *God's Prime Time* for two hours every Sunday.

"Three minutes," murmured Charles in his ear.

Spates inhaled the air in the shadows of the wings. The crowd quieted as the audience prompts scrolled across the screens and the appointed time neared.

He felt the glory of God energize his body with the Holy Spirit. He loved this moment just before the sermon; it was like nothing else in this world, a surge of rising fire, triumph, and anticipatory exultation.

"How's the audience?" he whispered to Charles.

"About sixty percent."

A cold knife stabbed into the heart of his joy. Sixty percent—last week it had been 70. Just six months ago people had been lining up for tickets, Sunday after Sunday, and had to be turned away. But since the motel incident, on-air donations were down by half and the ratings for the broadcast had fallen 40 percent. The bastards at the Christian Cable Service were about to cancel his *Roundtable America* talk show. God's Prime Time Ministry was heading into the darkest night since he had founded it in a vacant JCPenney thirty years before. If he didn't get an infusion of cash soon, he'd be forced to default on the "Own a Piece of Jesus" bonds he had sold over the air to hundreds of thousands of parishioners to finance the building of the Silver Cathedral.

His thoughts turned back to the meeting with Booker Crawley earlier that day. What a sign of God's grace that Crawley's proposal had come his way. If handled right, this might be just the issue he'd been looking for to rejuvenate the ministry and galvanize financial support. The evolution versus creationism debate was old hat, and it was getting hard to gain traction on that one—especially with so much competition from other televangelists. Crawley's issue, on the other hand, was fresh, it was new, and it was ripe for the plucking.

Damned if he wasn't going to pluck that fruit—now.

"It's time, Reverend," came Charles's low voice from behind.

The lights went up and a roar came from the crowd as the Reverend Spates strode onstage, his head bowed, his hands raised and clasped together, shaking rhythmically.

"God's Prime Time!" he rolled out in his richly timbred bass voice, full of vibrato. "God's Prime Time! The Prime Time of God's Glory is Nigh!" At stage center, he stopped sharply, raised his head, and stretched his arms outward to the audience, as if beseeching them. His fingertips trembled. His words rolled over the audience.

"Greetings to all of you in the precious Name of our Lord and Savior, Jesus Christ!"

Another roar rose from the giant Silver Cathedral. He lifted his hands high, palms up, and the roar went on—sustained with the help of the prompters. He lowered his arms, and silence fell once again, like the aftermath of thunder.

He bowed his head in prayer, then said, in a soft, humble voice, "Where two or three are gathered together in My Name, there am I."

He raised his head slowly, keeping his profile to the audience, and spoke in his richest tone, raising one arm, inch by inch, drawing out each word to its fullest.

"In the beginning," he throbbed, "God created the heavens and the earth. And the earth was without form, and void; and *darkness* was upon the face of the deep."

He paused, inhaling dramatically. "And the Spirit of God moved upon the face of the waters."

His voice suddenly boomed through the Silver Cathedral like the notes of an organ. "And God said, *Let there be light!*"

A dramatic beat, and he continued, in the barest whisper. "And there was light."

He strode to the edge of the stage and beamed a folksy smile on the worshippers. "We all know those opening words of Genesis. Some of the most powerful words ever written. No ambiguity there. Those are the very words of God, my friends. God is telling us in His own words how He created the universe."

He strolled casually along the edge of the stage. "My friends, will it surprise you if I tell you the government is spending your hard-earned taxpayer dollars in an effort to prove God wrong?"

He turned, eyeing the silent audience.

"You don't believe me?"

A murmur rose from the sea of faces.

He pulled a piece of paper from his suit-coat pocket and snapped it in the air, his voice suddenly full of thunder. "It's right here. I downloaded it off the Internet less than an hour ago."

Another murmur.

"And what did I learn? That our government has spent forty billion dollars to prove Genesis wrong—forty billion dollars of *your* money to attack the holiest Scripture in the Old Testament. Yes, my friends, it's all part of the government-sponsored, secular humanist war on Christianity, and it's *ugly.*"

He paced the stage. He shook the paper in his fist, crackling it.

"Right here it says they've built a machine in the Arizona desert called Isabella. Many of you have heard of it."

A big murmur of agreement.

"I had, too. I just thought it was another government boondoggle. Only recently was I made aware of its *pur-pose*."

A sudden halt in his pacing, and a slow turn to face the audience.

"Its *pur-pose*, my friends, is to investigate the so-called Big Bang theory. That's right, you heard it, there's that word 'theory' again!"

His voice was laced with scorn.

"The Big Bang *theory* goes like this: thirteen billion years ago a teeny-weeny point in space blew up and created the entire universe—without the helping hand of God. You heard me: Creation without God. *Ay-thee-istic Creation*."

He waited while a disbelieving silence grew. He shook the paper again. "That's what it says, folks! A whole Web site, hundreds of pages devoted to explaining the Creation of the Universe, and not one mention of God!"

Another glare around the hall.

"This Big Bang theory is no different from the *theory* that says our great-granddaddies were monkeys. Or the *theory* that says life's complexity was created by an accidental rearrangement of molecules in a puddle of mud. This Big Bang theory is just another secular humanistic, anti-Christian, anti-faith theory *no different from evolution*, except that this one's worse. *Much, much worse!*"

Spin, turn, pace.

"Because *this* theory attacks the very notion that God created the universe. Make no mistake about it: *Isabella is a direct attack on Christian faith*. The Big Bang theory says this *beautiful*, this *exquisite*, this *God-given* universe of ours happened all by itself, by sheer accident, thirteen billion years ago. And as if that Christian-hating theory wasn't enough, now they want to spend forty billion dollars of *our* money to prove it!"

He raked the audience with a fierce eye.

"How about if we asked the savants in Washington for equal

time? What if we asked them for forty billion dollars *to prove the Truth of Genesis!* What about that! The professional Jesus-hating liberals in Washington would gnash their teeth and foam at the mouth! They'd trot out that old saw about separation of church and state! These are the folks who've banned Jesus from the classroom, yanked the Ten Commandments from our courtrooms, outlawed Christmas trees and crèches, mocked and spat on our beliefs—and then these same secular humanists think nothing of spending *our* money to prove the Bible wrong, to *make a lie out of our Christian faith!*"

The hubbub swelled. A few people stood up, then more, then the entire congregation. They surged upward like a tsunami, their voices merging into a single roar of disapproval.

The prompters remained dark, unneeded now.

"This is a *war* on Christianity, my friends! It's a war to the finish, and they're taxing you and me to wage it! *Are we going to let them spit on Christ and charge us for the privilege?*"

The Reverend Don T. Spates stopped at dead stage center, breathing heavily, gazing out over the seething audience in the Virginia Beach cathedral, flabbergasted at the effect of his words. He could hear it, he could see it, he could *feel* it—the frenzied swell, the upwelling of righteous anger, the very air crackling with the electricity of outrage. He could hardly believe it. He'd been throwing rocks all his life, and suddenly he'd lobbed a grenade. This was the issue he'd been praying for, hoping for, searching for.

"God and Jesus be praised!" he cried out, throwing his arms toward heaven and raising his eyes to the glittering ceiling. He sank to his knees in loud, quavering prayer. "Lord Jesus, with Your help, we will stop this insult to Your Father. We will destroy that infernal machine out there in the howling desert. We will put an end to this blasphemy against You called Isabella!"